HANNIBAL FOGG *and*

THE SUPREME SECRET OF MAN

Hannibal Fogg *and*
the Supreme Secret of Man

Tahir Shah

Secretum Mundi Publishing
MMXVIII

Deus Ex Machina
God from the Machine
Horace's *The Art of Poetry*

This book is dedicated to my dearest friend,
Hugh Carless, the most impeccable gentleman
I have ever had the good fortune to know.

HANNIBAL G. FOGG

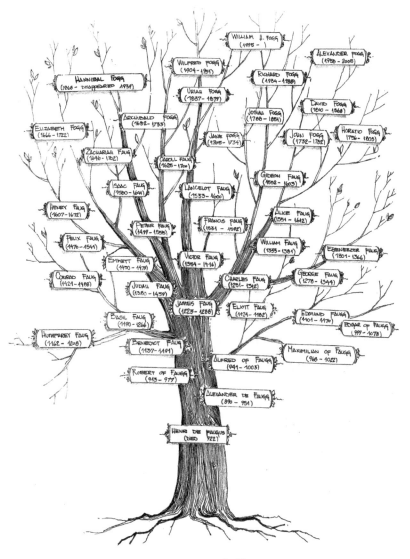

The House of Fogg

Secretum Mundi Publishing Ltd.

PO Box 5299

Bath BA1 0WS

United Kingdom

www.secretum-mundi.com

info@secretum-mundi.com

First published by Secretum Mundi Publishing Ltd., 2018

HANNIBAL FOGG AND THE SUPREME SECRET OF MAN

© TAHIR SHAH

Tahir Shah asserts the right to be identified as the Author of the Work in accordance with the Copyright, Designs and Patents Act 1988. A CIP catalogue record for this title is available from the British Library.

Visit the author's website at: www.tahirshah.com

ISBN 978-0-9572429-7-5

Hannibal's Timeline

1868	Born at Loch Lomond
1881	Attends Wellington School
1886	Goes up to Balliol College, Oxford
1888	Discovery at Antikythera Island
	Sent down from Oxford
1889	Presented with Dar Jnoun by Morocco's Sultan Abdelhafid
	Visits Sir Richard Burton in Damascus
	The Mountains of the Moon Expedition
1890	The Sakhalin Expedition
	The Ngorongoro Expedition
1891	Undertakes secret mission for King Rama V of Siam
	Presented to Madame Blavatsky in Calcutta
	The Great Australian Expedition
1892	Passage from Southampton to New York on SS Manitoba
	The Antarctic Expedition
	The Desert of Death Expedition
1893	Conceived The CODEX-434 while in Vienna
	The Alaskan Expedition
	The Aral Sea Expedition
1894	Engaged as a tutor to Tsar Alexander III's children
	The Eastern Himalayan Expedition
1895	The Gobi Desert Expedition
1896	The Mariana Expedition
1897	The Sahara Expedition
	The White Nile Expedition
1901	In Peking during the Boxer Rebellion
	The Bamiyan Expedition

1902	Buys Alina Pasternak at auction while on the Volga
1903	Gains access to the Vatican Archives
1904	In the Amazon on the quest for the Golden Tumi
	Becomes a father to Wilfred
	The Tierra del Fuego Expedition
1905	The South Atlantic Expedition
	The Great Siberian Expedition
1906	Quest in West Africa in search of the Orisha Stone
	The Blue Nile Expedition
1907	Passage aboard RMS Campania
1919	Presented with the blue diamond of Australia
	The Oceana Expedition
1923	The Caspian Sea Expedition
	Alina Fogg dies from poisoning
1924	Leaves London on the Orient Express
1925	Crosses Afghanistan and reaches Rangoon
	Becomes ruler of the Garuda Tribe, Indonesia
1928	The Bhutan Expedition
	Arrested, charged with treason, and imprisoned
	Great Foggian Purge
1929	Exiled to Morocco
	The Timbuctoo Expedition
	The Equator Expedition
1930	The Egyptian Expedition
	The Turkana Expedition
1931	The Arctic Expedition
1932	The Great Andean Expedition
1933	The Kalahari Expedition
	The Karakorum Expedition
	The Xanadu Expedition

Hannibal's Publications

Lost Years (*1890*)

The Pain of Silence (*1891*)

Twixt Hell and Marshland (*1892*)

Ballads of Hope and Anguish (*1894*)

Advanced Techniques in Swordsmanship (*1896*)

Experiments in Metallurgy (*1897*)

A Poem of Love (*1898*)

Considerations on the Subject of Desert Fauna (*1899*)

Short-blade Weaponry (*1899*)

Warfare in the Tribal Context (*1899*)

Elementary Mechanics (*1900*)

Electro-Mechanics Made Easy (*1901*)

Variants of Shaolin Kung Fu (*1901*)

An Evaluation of the Nile and Its Sources (*1902*)

Joy on the Volga (*1903*)

Flight in Ancient Times (*1904*)

Lichen Growth and Its Unique Specification (*1912*)

Destinations Unknown (*1913*)

Methods and Mysteries of Shrinking Heads (*1913*)

Siamese Bronzes (*1913*)

Philatelic Irregularities (*1914*)

Sexual Dysfunction Among the Hema Tribe of the Belgian
    Congo (*1914*)

Letters to Satan (*1914*)

Why?! (*1915*)

Philately of Empire (*1915*)

A New Approach to Mechanics (*1916*)

In Search of Hidden Animals (*1916*)

The Orisha Stone and Its Role in Cultural Ethnography with Reference to the Human Leopard Society of Sierra Leone (*1916*)

Perfidious Albion (*1917*)

Advanced Maori Etymology (*1918*)

Accelerated Learning Techniques (*1919*)

Penis Sheaths of Oceania (*1920*)

Common Misconceptions in the Study of Oriental Folklore (*1920*)

Forty Truths Regarding Advanced Palaeontology (*1921*)

Cartographic Conundrums (*1922*)

Manx Birdlife (*1923*)

Horror of War (*1923*)

Ancient Egyptian Necromancy (*1925*)

Encoded Mnemonics (*1925*)

Further Ancient Egyptian Necromancy (*1926*)

Cyclonic Ciphers (*1926*)

A Short Treatise on the Study of Mechanical Instrumentation (*1927*)

Unexpected Phobias (*1927*)

Collected Poetry (*1928*)

Mathematic Brevity (*1928*)

Finite Infinity (*1929*)

Studies in Assyrian Masonry (*1930*)

Eleven Poems (*1931*)

A Bibliographic Appraisal of the Dark Arts (*1931*)

Travels in Disguise (*1931*)

An Eye to the Future (*1932*)

An Investigation into the Practices of Three-toed Sloths (*1933*)

Palaeontology for Beginners (*1934*)

Berber Love Magic (*1934*)
Spells of the African Hinterland (*1934*)
Myths and Legends of Central Africa (*1934*)
Ceremonies in Black Magic (*1935*)
Advanced Philatelic Considerations (*1936*)
Carpology and Its Uses (*1936*)
Astronomy and Related Cartography (*1937*)
Social Rethinking (*1938*)
Forced Ineptitude (*1938*)

Reference Sources Relating to Hannibal Fogg

THE HANNIBAL FOGG SOCIETY
http://hannibalfoggsociety.org

BIOGRAPHICAL ENTRY
http://wikisearch-hannibalfogg.org

PLAN OF DAR JNOUN

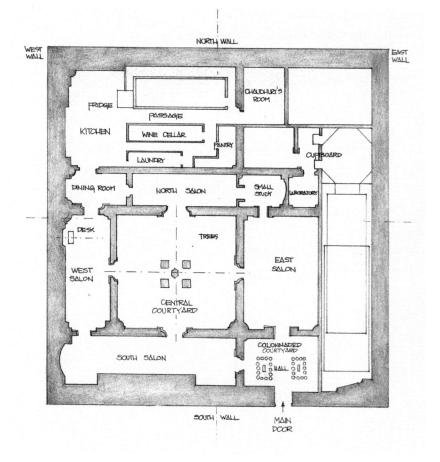

Part I

THE WORLD OF HANNIBAL FOGG

One

30TH MARCH 327 BC

FROM THE SNOW-LADEN CRAGS of the Hindu Kush, the vast army of Alexander, King of the Macedonians and subjugator of the known world, seemed to move in total silence.

The battle cortège comprised more than a hundred thousand men, marching eastwards toward the Khyber Pass, gateway to India.

The cavalry led the way.

Among them was Alexander himself, his burnished bronze armour glinting in the early spring light.

Behind the horsemen followed snaking lines of archers and miles of infantry, camp followers and equipment, animals and supplies.

The men had endured the bitter winter months of Bactria, the crossroads of Central Asia, by rubbing sesame oil into their frozen skin. Battle-hardened and exhausted, they were far from home.

Alexander's campaign had lasted more than a decade — a conquest in which he had taken the Balkans and Asia Minor, sacked the mighty Persian Empire of Darius, and finally brought his men to the gentle waters of the Indus.

Few had ever imagined their great leader would triumph for so long, and without a single defeat.

It seemed like a miracle.

But the young Macedonian king had a secret.

A secret had rendered his army invincible and allowed him to cleave a path from West to East in what was the greatest military campaign in human history.

Far behind the lines of cavalry, the archers and endless legions of foot soldiers, the camel corps booming like thunder with their giant timpani, was a huge canvas tent perched on a wooden platform. Like everything and everyone, it too was moving forward. A cohort of battle elephants was dragging it, their riders armed with lances tipped with blades of tempered steel.

Filling the tent was an object so precious that it was guarded day and night by soldiers hailing from Alexander's own elite Macedonian brigade. So great was the level of secrecy surrounding it that none of them had ever been permitted to see inside.

Had they done so and pushed through the six concentric curtains of sewn canvas, they would have set eyes on a truly astonishing sight: a mechanical machine of magnificent proportions, fashioned from silver, brass and gold. Pendulums and cantilevers swung on their axes, gears clattering as they engaged row upon row of interlinking cogs.

There were flywheels blurred by frantic spinning, pistons mounted on diamond bearings racing back and forth, and dials — hundreds and hundreds of dials. A system of conduits united the individual parts, running with liquid mercury like an infernal flow of supernatural blood.

Once across the Indus, Alexander spent an evening alone in the canvas tent. Those who saw him exit in the light of the full moon said he was trembling, his eyes touched with fear.

The next morning, he doubled the guard on the secret machine. Then, having rallied his weary legions one last time, Alexander led them into the mother of all battles against Porus, the Indian giant-king.

Although exhausted, his legions engaged the foe with a ferocity, brilliance and ease that have amazed scholars ever since.

Despite the overwhelming odds facing Alexander's army, the victory was his...

...Yet again.

Two

ARRANGED ACROSS THE SURFACE of the workbench was an assortment of machinery and equipment, laid out neatly in order of size and complexity.

There were laptops stripped of their casings, multi-core motherboards, processor cooling systems and optical drives, home-made modems, and half a dozen disassembled smartphones.

On the right of the workbench, behind a perfectly

squared pile of *Wired* sorted in order of date, stood a dual channel oscilloscope. Between it and a desktop computer, was a shoebox packed with electrical components.

Above the bench hung a bookshelf, arranged alphabetically by subject: Algorithms, Chess, Cryptovirology, Postage Stamps and Spyware.

Adjacent to the bench, reclining on a single bed, was William Fogg.

In his hands was a textbook on quantum mechanics. As thick as a brick, it was bound in royal blue cloth. Laying the volume on his chest, Will rubbed his eyes with his thumbs, and sighed heavily. The mid-term exam was twelve hours away and he felt unprepared. He always felt unprepared, despite the fact that he never failed to triumph in the end.

Pushing himself up against the wall, he found himself gazing over at his roommate's portion of the room. It was strewn with empty beer cans, overflowing ashtrays, and dirty clothes. The bed was lost in an abyss of abandoned coursework on the history of printing, and what looked like the rear fender of a pickup truck.

Will had given up hope of ever achieving his ambition — a dorm room of his own. But students on full scholarship at San Francisco State had to share, and that was that. His line of sight moving back to the book, he squinted, his eyes focusing on the miniature text once again.

Suddenly, the door was thrust open wide.

A burly young man stormed in. Tanned and buffed, he had the physique of a heavyweight boxer. On his arm was a frizzy-haired blonde with a big toothy grin.

'But Todd... your roommate's here!' the girl blurted.

'He'll cover his eyes, babe... won't you Will?!'

Glancing up from his book, Will grunted as Todd corralled his latest conquest towards his end of the room and turned off the light. The fender was hurled to the floor, followed by the mass of stinking clothes and papers.

Will put on his iPhone's light and pressed his face into the textbook. Turning the page, he read a paragraph on particle physics, and read it again.

Just then, there was a knock at the door.

Will stumbled over, opened it and stuck his head out.

Standing in the corridor was a gorgeous brunette. Her hair was long and straight, brushed to one side, her lips glowing with raspberry gloss. As she smiled engagingly, Will tightened his knees so that he didn't collapse.

'Todd's kind of tied up,' he explained awkwardly.

'*Todd*? No, no... I haven't come for him.'

'Oh?'

'You the guy who fixes electronics?'

'Huh?'

The girl held up a phone.

'It stopped working.'

'Did you drop it?'

'No… well, not really.' The brunette grinned. 'You see, it fell in the toilet.'

'That wouldn't do the circuitry any good.'

'Can you fix it?'

Will was about to reply when Todd's blonde let out a muffled wail of passion in the darkness behind him.

'Oh, sorry, you're not alone,' said the girl, her face warming in a blush.

'Leave it with me and I'll give it a going over.'

'Thank you *so* much. I'm Britney by the way. Britney from upstairs. Room C21.'

Three

1888

AT 5.22 A.M., THE TALL, slim silhouette of a young man glanced at his pocket chronometer, observing the second hand sweeping silently past the Roman numeral twelve.

He had arranged for the sponge divers to collect him from the shore at five o'clock sharp. Nothing riled him more than tardiness. The man motioned to an Indian figure standing beside him, his manservant. Using the extra time to their advantage, they checked the equipment, stowing it in a special rubberised kit bag, stencilled with a curious monogram.

The night before, the servant had done as his master instructed — opening and cleaning the valves, double-

6

checking the pressure gauges for accuracy, and sealing the copper diving helmet with aged buffalo grease.

The tall figure touched his tongue to his upper lip and gazed out at the sea. It was as calm as he could have hoped, the surface lightly rippled by the hint of rain on the breeze.

At 5.37, the boat appeared.

Low in the water, it was little more than a skiff, the stern weighed down by half a dozen mariners. Their leader, a rough old dog of a sailor named Constantinos, waved a hand toward the quay and shouted a greeting. The tall man lifted his equipment aboard and replied in faultless Greek. Although a stranger, he had a knack for language, believing it polite when possible to address others in their native tongue.

Fifteen minutes after leaving the shore of Antikythera Island, the sailors stowed the oars. Constantinos kissed a crucifix to his puckered lips. Pulling off their shirts, he and the other men began breathing deeply, inhaling and exhaling in a rhythm their forefathers had perfected over generations.

The foreigner unlaced his rubberised kit bag and carefully removed a copper canister the size and shape of a fire extinguisher. Turning it on its end, he attached a curved copper tube, screwing it into the canister's supply valve. The other end of the tube he attached with wing-nuts to an odd-looking diving helmet, concave at the top.

Still breathing hard to oxygenate their blood, the

sponge divers watched as the foreigner readied his equipment.

A few years before, Constantinos and the others had themselves experimented with standard diving suits. They had been able to dive down to seventy yards, their sealed helmets supplied by air hoses rising up like serpents to the surface.

The newfangled technology had allowed them to reach the kind of sponges they had always dreamed of harvesting. They had spotted fish and coral never seen before, and had discovered wrecked ships. To their delight, the sponges sold for a high price on the island — everyone had wanted them.

But then, some of the divers had been pulled to the surface mysteriously paralysed, as though poisoned. Soon, the expensive diving suits were abandoned, and the prized sponges forgotten.

The divers in Constantinos's team went back to tried and tested methods. They returned to the ways their ancestors had used for centuries — diving naked while clinging to a stone so that they descended faster.

None of the sponge divers in Constantinos's group had ever seen a diving canister before.

Of course they hadn't.

For the contrivance was one of a kind, designed by the foreigner himself.

Christening it a 'Pressurised Respiration Apparatus', he was the only man alive to have ever tested it at depth.

Once their blood was oxygenated, the divers stripped off their clothing, rubbed each other with olive oil, and leapt into the water.

As they did so, the stranger swung the copper diving canister onto his back, fastened the leather straps around his chest, and buckled a weight belt to his waist. Then, clipping the helmet over his head, he eased on the flow of air.

Before he knew it, he was breathing below the surface.

The early morning sun was a distorted ball of pale yellow above him, the sea dark below.

Swimming down, he sensed the water cool by gradual degrees until it numbed his limbs. All the while he controlled his breathing, urging himself to stay focused and not to give in to panic.

To his right, Constantinos and his men were cutting sponges from a ledge, working in a frenzy of activity before their single lungful of air ran out. As it did so, they ascended, the morning's harvest gathered in the net bags.

The foreigner kept descending until the sponge divers were specks silhouetted in the distant blur of the sun. He might have wondered whether it was the right spot, or worried that his own air supply might run out. But in childhood, he had learned to minimise anxiety through a meticulous and perfect preparation.

In any case, the old fisherman on Kos had described the place exactly and had even flashed a coin he claimed had come from the wreck. At once, the foreigner had recognised it as a silver tetradrachm bearing Alexander's profile.

Twenty yards lower, the water was so cold that his muscles were overwhelmed with lactic acid. Twisting the supply valve eight and a third degrees clockwise, he took an extra deep breath, and scoured the darkness.

Absolute black.

Gradually, as his eyes adjusted, he saw something.

There it was again.

A vertical object standing proud behind a school of mackerel.

Pulling a home-made flare from his weight belt, he broke it in half. The calcium phosphide erupted into an explosion of light.

Darkness dissolved — replaced by fantasy.

Ten yards from the flare lay the stern of a ship, the remnants of a massive trireme war galley lying on the port side, the bow sheered clean away.

In the flare's riotous light, the stranger made out the precious cargo — great bronze sculptures of towering warriors, marble busts and Corinthian capitals, enormous amphora encrusted in barnacles, and a row of lead caskets. Prising off the lid of one with his knife, he found it brimming with gold coins from the time of Alexander.

But it wasn't treasure he was after.

Guided by the flare's light, the foreigner swam fast in and out of the wreck, urgently searching.

High above, the sponge divers were going down for a second harvest. The flare's light was waning. When it died, the one and only chance to locate the device would be at an end. Next day the foreigner would be bound home for England, and for the tedious routine of an Oxford undergraduate once again.

Terribly fatigued, his muscles felt as if knives were stabbing into them. Enduring the pain, he swam to and fro, scanning the wreck, running his fingers through the fine silt.

It was no good.

Despite a characteristic run of good fortune, the object of his quest had eluded him.

The flare died, the calcium phosphide crystals spent.

One last glance.

A last poke with the tip of his razor-sharp diving knife.

No hope.

His head reeling back in the helmet, his chest swelled, as carbon dioxide poisoning took hold.

Jabbing urgently, he dropped the knife and began scooping with his hands.

There… in the silt!

Shoving away a fistful of gold coins, as brilliant as the day they were minted, he caught his first blurred glimpse of it.

The device.

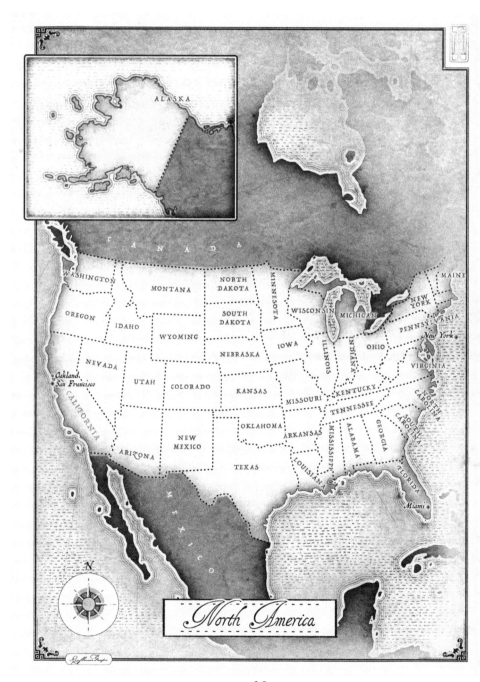

North America

Four

ON THE MORNING OF 30th April, Will clambered out of bed a little after seven and made his way sleepily to the dorm's foul toilet at the end of the corridor.

As a small child, his father had taught him to follow the Inuit tradition of drinking masses of water before turning in. The more you drink, he had said, the earlier you rise, and the better the catch you'll get down at the ice holes.

On the other side of the room, Todd was lying in a heap on the floor, still drunk. Glancing down at him disapprovingly, Will rolled his eyes, and hurried out into the bright spring sunlight.

By a quarter to nine, he was down on Market Street, striding briskly into the long shadows. He was in fine spirits, as though misfortune might never visit him again.

There was every reason to be happy — it was a very special day after all.

Will got a flash of the accident on his ninth birthday — the day his parents had died. Too painful to think about properly, the memory tinged his tongue with bile, and forced the optimism from his step.

The sudden sound of footsteps shook him back to the present.

Leather shoes.

A man's leather shoes.

Will's ears caught the sound of the steel-tipped heels

snapping down squarely on the paving stones. A hefty bulk balanced over extra-wide feet.

The footsteps were getting faster.

And closer.

Will turned, almost losing balance as he did so.

Looked left and right.

But no one was there.

Taking a deep breath, he quickened his step. The bank was only three or four blocks away now. With any luck, he would be the first person in through the door.

He crossed Van Ness and was blinded for a moment by a shaft of sunlight streaming between the buildings. A few feet away, he spotted a figure in a shabby overcoat, a silhouette.

The man made a quick movement.

Lunging, arms outstretched, he attacked a woman passing in the opposite direction. Grabbing her by the collar, he bawled a salvo of expletives.

The woman fumbled and shook as her body folded down onto the ground.

'Help me! Help me!' she whimpered in a shrill voice. 'Get him!'

The appeal was directed at Will and to him alone — he was the only person for fifty feet.

For a fraction of a second they caught eye contact.

Will felt himself buckling with fear, as though ingesting the woman's own fear as it spilled out.

Scanning right, then left, he looked quickly down at the woman.

Then, in the fight or flight response of his ancestors on the savannah, he ran.

Charging down Market Street. Left on Sutter. Panting, chest tight, eyes welling with terror, his blood was bathed in adrenalin and his mind in shame.

What seemed like only moments later, he was standing in the entrance of the Union Bank of California.

Silence and decorum.

Except for the jingle of a child's nickel collection, the coins tumbling through the teller's counting machine.

The bank promised to process new credit card applications in fifteen minutes or less.

Filling out the form, Will passed it to the clerk sitting primly at the customer service desk. A little brass plaque advertised her name — Rosario Gonzalez.

She smiled infectiously, her hair still damp from the shower, a mug of thin black coffee to the right of her hand.

Studiously, she reviewed the form.

'Happy birthday,' she gushed, the desk planner catching the corner of her eye.

'Thank you.'

'Twenty-one today?'

'That's right, yes.'

Will returned Rosario's smile. Unlike hers, his was automatic and feigned.

15

All he could think of was the woman being mugged minutes before, and the fact that he had been too chicken to help.

'Who's Edith Fogg?' Rosario asked.

'Huh?'

The question was repeated.

'Oh, my great-aunt. I was raised by her. By my two great-aunts actually.' Will paused, then added: 'When my parents died.'

'I'm so sorry,' Rosario said, touching a finger to her hoop earring. 'We'll get this processed right away. Why don't you go over there and take a seat?'

After five minutes of watching the ebb and flow of early customers washing in and out, Will was called to the service desk.

Rosario glanced at the form, confused.

'Something wrong?'

'Well, it seems as though your application's been turned down.'

Will forced a last begrudging smile.

'Can you please tell me the reason?'

The clerk shrugged.

'Just says, "REJECTED". See the stamp down here, the one in big red letters?'

'I don't know why,' Will moaned after a pause. 'It's always the same. Anything I've ever applied for has been refused, or "lost in the system". It's as if there's a conspiracy against me.'

Rosario appeared genuinely sorrowful.

'Have a wonderful birthday, sweetheart,' she said.

Thanking her, Will turned and headed for the door.

As he did so, a hand raised the receiver of the red phone on the duty manager's desk, and dialled a number fast.

'It's Fogg. He's come and gone. Yes, sir... as instructed his application was refused.'

Five

A HIT BY IMAGINE Dragons pounded over speakers hidden in the ceiling at The Milk Bar on Haight.

The moment he got there, Will found himself wishing he hadn't allowed Todd to choose the setting for his first legal drink.

Pressed up fearfully near the back wall were his three college friends — Bill, Mike and Phil. They were straining to look cool, even though they were regarded by everyone — and even by each other — as geeks of the first order.

Along with Will, they had been grouped together as freshmen, ostracised by the *in*-crowd, left to befriend one another.

Mike was the only one with a gift, although mildly embarrassed by it.

'You shouldn't have,' Will said, tearing away the

reused Christmas wrapping.

'It's nothing.'

Will tapped an assortment of paper shapes onto his palm.

'Postage stamps?' said Phil.

'They're from Brazil,' Mike mumbled apologetically.

'Thank you.'

'Really, they're nothing. Not valuable, just kind of nice.'

The four friends paused for a moment, staring at the stamps, while Will tried to think of something to say. The unease was broken by Todd, who drifted over, the sea of people parting for him.

'Happy Birthday!'

'Thanks.'

'What, no first legal drink?'

'Huh? Um, no. Haven't managed to get served yet.'

Todd whistled at the bartender. Thirty seconds later, all five of them were clinking the necks of Coronas. Will slid out his iPhone and captured the moment for posterity.

Todd was soon making out with a girl he had met while going to the loo. Will and the others made excuses and sloped away. There were plenty of girls to dance with, but the geeks were all too shy to ask. In any case, none of them ever stayed out late on a school night.

Back on campus, as Will's fingers turned the handle of his door, his iPhone vibrated. Glancing at the number, he put the phone to his ear.

'Aunt Helen! Thank you! Yeah, had a great one.

Couldn't get through? Oh, I was in a bar. That's right…
a bar! I'm back now. Tomorrow? Sure. I promise. What
time? Eleven? OK. See you then.'

Kicking off his shoes, Will thought of the Inuit,
glugged down a couple of mugs of water, put out the
garbage, and slumped on his bed.

Time to check if he was loved by anyone else.

Half a dozen automatic emails from online firms who
knew his birth date, and a handful of Facebook messages.
One was from a girl he had had a crush on since he was
twelve. She had stayed friends more out of pity than
anything else. In the message, she made a joke about his
all time favourite book, *Jonathan Livingston Seagull*.

Touched that she had remembered, the corner of
Will's mouth eased up in a smile.

Just before turning off the light, he went back to his
email folder and checked the spam box. His life was
characterised by spam on a grand scale, just as it was by
bad luck. No one else he knew got so much junk mail.

As expected, there were dozens of unwanted
messages. Those that didn't promise the world seethed
with threats and abuse.

Somewhere near the top was a different sort of
message.

The subject heading read:

The Inheritance of William Fogg.

Will sighed, groaned.

And, without opening it, he hit 'delete'.

19

Six

T<small>HE LURE OF THE</small> Inuit ice holes had Will up early as usual, a little after seven.

Lumbering out into the corridor, he tripped over his garbage sack, which had been ripped open and its contents strewn about.

As he stooped down to clean it up, he noticed something odd.

All the crumpled balls of paper had been straightened out — as though someone had gone through it, searching for something.

Back in his room, Will opened up Britney's phone. Clipping it under a magnifying glass, he tested the circuits, and found the power amplifier had blown. Removing it, he soldered in a replacement sourced from his shoebox of spare parts. Once booted up, the display came alive with a picture of Britney's dog.

Will pressed down his hair with his hand, looked in the mirror, and sighed.

A minute later, he was standing outside Britney's room, his mouth dry. It wasn't yet eight, but he was too fearful to have cared.

He knocked hard.

A drowsy voice called out and, after a long pause, the door clicked open. Britney was standing in its frame, wearing a short nightdress, hair pinned up on her head.

Confused, she frowned.

'Can I help you?'

'Your iPhone… I've fixed it.' Will held up the phone. 'It was the power amplifier.'

'The what?'

'Um… er… water damage.'

'Thank you so much! What do I owe you?'

Will looked down at the floor bashfully.

'Nothing,' he said. 'It was my pleasure.'

Britney's lips parted slowly.

'You're so sweet.'

Will's eyes didn't move.

'I'd better go.'

Britney reached out, touching his shoulder as he turned.

'Listen… I'm going to my uncle's gallery opening this afternoon,' she said tenderly. 'Wanna come?'

Will breathed deep.

'Oh, wow, yeah, I'd love to… but…'

'*But…?*'

'I promised my great-aunts I'd go see them. They'd kill me if I bailed.'

Britney smiled again.

'Well, another time then.'

'Sure, another time.'

Seven

1888

HIDDEN AWAY IN HIS study at Balliol, Hannibal Fogg cleared the oak desk of books, placing a heavy iron retort at one end.

The journey back from the Greek Islands had been painfully slow, and had filled him with anxiety, as though an ancient way of life was about to collide headlong with a grand new order.

During days and nights at sea he had found himself imagining what breakthroughs the future might hold, and how they might shape the life of his descendants.

One day, he felt sure that man would travel the open skies in powered gliders, travelling faster than the speed of sound. He conceived a time in which people would communicate through miniature contrivances, sending messages anywhere in the blink of an eye. A time in which electrical machinery would usher in an age of unimagined possibility. A glorious future inspired by the genius of the ancients. The same genius that had created the device from Antikythera Island.

Hannibal's study was cramped, with a single window high on the east wall. At least a third of the space was packed with boxes of equipment, with discarded scientific experiments, anatomical samples, and note-books tied up with coarse brown string.

In one corner, a home-made cooling system had been rigged up — coiled tubes, conical flasks, and jars half-filled with ammonia.

At eleven minutes past nine, Hannibal placed his silver pocket chronometer on the bench, heaved the salvaged device onto the retort, and began the examination. Beside his left hand were fifty sheets of fine white foolscap paper and half a dozen sharpened pencils.

By lunchtime, twenty sheets had been filled with mathematical calculations, equations, sketches, scribbled details, and pages and pages of notes.

Hannibal linked the device up to a series of coloured wires leading to a home-made electrical generating machine. Taking off his jacket, he rolled up his shirt-sleeves, his thoughts lost in concentration.

There was a knock at the door.

'Fogg, are you there?'

Before he could reply, a slender figure with aristocratic Arab features swept in.

'Good news my dear friend! I've received the funds for the new prototype. My father must be in a good mood! He was unusually generous this time. Shall we call it Prototype-B? If we get moving, we'll have it built by the solstice.'

Hannibal was so engrossed in the gears that he didn't look up.

'Fogg...?'

The visitor clapped his hands.

'Did you hear me, Fogg?'

'Hmm? Oh, Osman, hello… How are you? Look at this!'

'What is it?'

'The very most extraordinary object in existence!'

'What?'

'Proof of the genius of the ancients!'

'It looks like a clock.'

'It is! It is! But it's so much more than that!'

Osman stepped closer and his shadow fell over the device. As best friend and confidant, he was permitted rare and privileged access into Hannibal's world.

'Is that a gear?' he asked, taking in the concentric rings.

'Yes, but not just one gear. There are dozens of them!'

Straightening his necktie, Hannibal took in his friend, his cheeks flushed with anticipation.

'It's an elliptical gear transfer system, created a thousand years before the great Arab inventors!'

Osman shrugged.

'Did you ever doubt the expertise of my people?'

'Of course not.'

'So what is it for?'

Hannibal caressed a hand over the device.

'Once we have discovered its secret,' he said, 'the world will never be the same again!'

Eight

THAT AFTERNOON, AS HE strolled down to the mail room, all Will could think of was Britney, and how stupid he must have sounded to her. Kicking himself, he made a plan to ask Todd for girl advice.

The clerk handed over a letter, a heavy envelope bearing English postage stamps. Will recognised the profile of Queen Elizabeth right away, as he did the lack of a country name. Every philatelist knows that British stamps are not required to feature a nationality — reward for inventing prepaid postage in the first place.

The envelope was filthy, as if it had passed through dozens of hands and destinations.

Tearing it open, Will took out the letter.

Inside was a single sheet of cream writing paper crowned with an ornate embossed letterhead. Beneath a few lines of impeccable manual type was a flamboyant signature in maroon-coloured ink.

The letter was apparently from a British legal firm, Messrs Penshaw, Willis, Smink & Company, founded in 1678.

Will's eyes scanned the typed text:

MESSRS. PENSHAW, WILLIS, SMINK & CO.
187 Fleet Street, London EC4P 4DQ
Established in 1678

16th January 2017

Dear Mr Fogg,

We write to you as Executors acting for the Estate
of your great-great-grandfather, Hannibal
Garrett Fogg.

On 30th April of this year, having reached
maturity, you will be confirmed as sole inheritor
to the Fogg Estate. Upon the precise orders of
Hannibal Fogg himself, the full complement of the
Estate shall pass to you, and to you alone.

In order for our firm to administer to you the
inheritance which is due, we require that you be
present for the formal reading of the Will, at
16.00 hours precisely on Tuesday 2nd May 2017 at
our offices here in London.

We are, sir, your obedient servants,

Basil Penshaw
Partner
Messrs. Penshaw, Willis, Smink & Co.

When Will had finished reading the letter, he let out a groan, and took a closer look at the postage stamps. Junk mail might be rarer than it was, but the quality was certainly improving… improvements no doubt a result of the data gathering centres Will had read about in the Far East. After all, how could anyone have known he had an ancestor named Hannibal?

He had only heard the name once himself — even then it had been uttered in anger. Great-aunt Edith had provided it as sole reason for the family's dire financial state.

Slipping the letter back in its envelope, Will stuffed it in his pocket, and ambled back to his dorm.

Inside, Todd was lying on his bed, hung-over and bleary.

'Where is she?' he mumbled, confused.

'Who?'

'That little blonde. The one who came over last night.'

'Guess she had classes.'

'No chance of that.'

'Why not?'

'Cos I picked her up at the diner.'

Will unlaced his Converse All Stars, took them off, and slid them neatly under his bed.

'You're not the only one who got lucky,' he said.

'Huh? You telling me you got some action?'

'Yeah, well, almost. I'll be getting some soon.'

'Who's the lucky lady?'

'An angel up in C21.'

'Slick!'

Will grinned.

'What if I was fabulously rich... and English?'

'*English?*'

'Yeah.'

'Oh sure. That'd help. Chicas love an accent.'

Reaching for his pocket, Will pulled out the letter.

'Have a look at that.'

Todd strained on the lines of type.

'An inheritance?'

'Yeah, well, kinda. Would be if it wasn't junk.'

Holding the letter to the light, Todd rubbed the paper between his fingers.

'Watermarked full bond,' he said. 'And the heading's been die-stamped. We're talking hand printed on a Heidelberg, or something with real punch. And look at that signature. Hand-signed in Indian ink. This isn't junk, Will.'

'Then what is it?'

'It's a frigging work of art!'

Nine

1888

AN IMPENETRABLE GREEN SMOG had swept silently down the Thames and laid siege to the genteel district of Bloomsbury.

One by one, the residents in the town houses set around magnificent squares shut their windows and turned up their gas lamps.

The faint aroma of roasting chestnuts hung on the breeze along with muffled strains of music.

Beyond the front gates of the British Museum an organ grinder was standing at his usual pitch, his right hand wheeling a crank handle slow and hard.

On the right side of the organ, lost in smog, lay the grinder's cap, as invisible as it was empty.

From time to time, the wail of a policeman's whistle cut through the fog, urging anyone left outside to quicken their step, for fear of thievery.

A minute before one, the outline of a gentleman hurried past the organ grinder from the direction of Great Russell Street. Navigating through the pea-souper effortlessly, as if by echo-location, he bounded up the museum's steps. He took them two at a time, the soles of his hand-made Lobbs hardly touched the stone.

The figure raced into the grand circular Reading Room, a twill gabardine overcoat thrown over his arm. Without wasting a moment, he made a beeline for the rows of green index files, poised in the middle of the room.

Finding the author catalogue labelled TWI–UTA, he opened it, drawing a fingertip down tight columns of titles.

Soon his shadow was roaming the bookshelves, his

feet running furiously over the parquet, as the hunt began.

Scanning the uppermost row of leather-bound books, then down at ankle height, he lurched left and right.

Tossing his overcoat to the floor, he stopped in his tracks.

There it was…

A slim volume bound in cherry-red morocco, gold embossed lettering down the spine.

The Secret Life of Alexander the Great.

Slumping in a reader's chair, Hannibal opened the book, thumbing his way quickly towards the back. His face streaming with perspiration, he flicked forwards, and back.

Then, turning a page, he breathed in sharply like a man in fear of drowning.

'My God!' he exclaimed. 'I cannot believe it!'

Placing the volume on one of the desk's turquoise leather surfaces, Hannibal swept out from the Reading Room.

His pace gathered speed again.

By the time he was in the museum foyer, he was running full tilt.

Down the long stone corridor.

Through the Assyrian Gallery, past the massive winged lions of Mesopotamia.

Around a corner.

Towards the spiral stairs.

Down, down, down into the belly of Bloomsbury, beneath the great treasure house itself.

More corridors, far narrower than those on the surface.

A series of doors, each dustier and more forgotten than the one before.

As he reached the last, Room 64B, Hannibal caught a flash of his childhood.

A memory of cool lemonade on a winter afternoon, a field freckled in buttercups, a meandering river pungent with wild garlic.

Knocking, the joint of his middle finger stung from the force.

'Open up at once!' he cried. 'I know it... I know it! The Secret! The Supreme Secret of Man!'

Ten

GREAT-AUNTS HELEN AND EDITH were reclining on a pair of matching red velvet chairs set at right angles to one another in the living-room of their modest Oakland home.

They were so old they could remember a time when people were proud to live in the apartment block, back in an age when the walls had been white — free from gang graffiti and grime.

On a good day, their balcony was a pleasant place to

sit and soak up the sun. Strain one's nostrils and you could just smell the honeysuckle growing in flowerpots on a balcony opposite.

On a not-so-good day, one had to cover the mouth and nose from the stench of rotting garbage festering in the unemptied bins down below.

Aunt Helen had made cherry flan, a family recipe her mother had passed on two-thirds of a lifetime before. She had placed it on the low coffee table to cool. Next to it were three Wedgwood side plates rimmed in royal blue. Next to them, silver cake forks lined up, hallmarks on the handles.

Great-aunts Edith and Helen had always lived together. Neither had ever married, although Edith had once fallen in love with a Latvian sailor who had eventually run off with her best friend. Never well off, they had always struggled to make ends meet.

Both harboured dreams of winning the lottery, which they played in secret each week. Neither ever told the other — not even when they won.

Part of the reason was the sense of shame.

Over the years the winnings had gone from scarce to almost non-existent. Indeed, they rarely even won the small-fry ten or twenty bucks that kept diehard players hooked.

Dead centre in the middle of the table was a gift.

Wrapped in Little Bo Peep paper, it was tied up with yellow string.

'I hope he won't be late,' said aunt Edith testily.

'Hush. He's got a long way to come,' replied her sister. 'We should feel fortunate he bothers with us at all.'

'The flan will get cold.'

'The cherries are better at room temperature in any case.'

'I thought gooseberry is what he likes.'

Aunt Helen looked up.

'No, no,' she said firmly. 'Everyone knows, cherry is William's favourite.'

Edith pretended not to listen. She looked out of the window, her nose catching the scent of honeysuckle.

Footsteps.

The doorbell.

A familiar voice.

Before he had even made it through the hall, Will was crushed to great-aunt Helen's abundant chest.

'Thank you for coming, darling,' she said, tears welling in her eyes.

'Of course I came.'

'She's made a flan,' said aunt Edith, plopping her knitting down on the chair.

'I'll cut you a piece.'

While aunt Helen reached for the knife, her sister pointed to Little Bo Peep.

'Aren't you going to open it, William?'

'Can't wait to.'

Will slipped off the string and the paper fell away, as

if the gift were unwrapping itself. He stared at a tattered old album, bound between beige canvas boards. On the cover the name of a previous owner had been crossed out in magic marker.

Flicking through the pages, Will's gaze took in the rows of unusual and colourful postage stamps.

'I absolutely love it. Thank you!'

'We are so pleased,' said aunt Helen, speaking for them both.

'Where did you get it?'

'At a thrift store,' aunt Edith said icily.

The cherry flan was cut and served.

Moist in the middle as it was supposed to be, its pastry crumbled at the touch of silver prongs.

Silence followed.

A silence in which the pair of great-aunts waited for their grandnephew to praise the flan.

'More delicious than ever,' he said, dusting crumbs from his shirt.

Aunt Helen smiled wickedly.

'I'll pass on the recipe to your wife one day.'

'That'll be no time soon.'

'What, a handsome boy like you still without a girl?'

Will felt awkward discussing dating, especially with his great-aunts. Struggling to change the conversation, he exclaimed:

'Guess what? I got a letter from a lawyer in London. Apparently I'm the inheritor of an Estate.'

'An Estate?'

'What Estate?'

'The Estate of Hannibal Fogg.'

The great-aunts looked up, their cake forks hitting the bone china at the exact same moment.

'They want me to go to London to claim what they say is mine.'

'*Hannibal?*' gasped great-aunt Helen.

'Curse that man! Curse his memory!' great-aunt Edith spat caustically. Pressing a hand to the mother-of-pearl cameo pinned neatly over the top button of her blouse, she seemed short of breath.

Will took the letter out from his pocket and unfolded it with care.

As soon as the cream bond paper was in the light, aunt Edith's birdlike talons snatched it and ripped it into shreds.

'Hannibal Fogg was evil personified!' she growled. 'He was a traitor to the English Crown! He was a spy in the employ of the Nazis — shamed and discredited by one and all!'

Aunt Helen placed her plate on the coffee table, her customary smile gone.

'He disowned his only son, Wilfred — our father,' she said. 'And our dear brother died of shame.'

'Shame of what?' Will asked.

'At bearing the Fogg name.'

'May Hannibal rot in hell,' aunt Edith grunted.

'He was the black sheep of the family — the reason our darling father emigrated to America.'

'Why?'

'To avoid the shame!'

'When was that?'

'In the '30s... After the Purge.'

'What Purge?'

Great-aunt Helen let out a pained sigh, but did not look up. Her eyes were locked into the pattern of the faux Persian rug.

'All the books he'd written were gathered up from libraries and bookshops and were destroyed. Anyone found owning one of Hannibal Fogg's works was fined, or threatened with imprisonment. A special commission was established by the English government. It hunted down all memory of the man... and burned it all.'

Standing, Will stepped over to the window and looked out at the honeysuckle on the balcony opposite.

'Who exactly was Hannibal Fogg?' he asked.

'I've told you, William,' snapped aunt Edith, 'he was a spy!'

'He was a soldier,' aunt Helen corrected, 'an explorer, a genius in his own peculiar way.'

Great-aunt Edith regarded her sister with a poisonous glance.

'He was no genius!' she countered. 'He's the reason we've lived in poverty our entire lives. If I were you, I would forget you ever heard his name.'

'What became of him?'

'He fled to North Africa,' said aunt Helen.

'Did he die there?'

Aunt Helen looked up, and found herself staring into her grandnephew's eyes.

'He disappeared,' she said. 'No one really knows what happened. He was last seen in Manchuria.'

'When?'

'On Christmas Day, 1939.'

Eleven

THE STAIRWELL OF THE great-aunts' building was so festooned in gang graffiti that there was no easy way of telling the original colour of the walls.

Descending the central staircase slowly, Will's thoughts were on the awkward conversation at tea. Through the years of his childhood, neither of his great-aunts had ever expressed a strong opinion of any kind, and never anger. Their conversation was always prim and prudish, and rarely featured condemnations — least of all of a relative.

Will was just about to cross the litter-strewn patch of dirt that had once been grass, when he heard the sound of feet shuffling behind.

The shuffling was accompanied by wheezing.

He turned.

Great-aunt Helen was reeling towards him, clutching

a rattling old biscuit tin in her arthritic fingers.

'Dearest!' she cried, fighting to catch her breath. 'You must listen to me! Edith will skin me alive, but I must tell you!'

'Tell me what?'

'Hannibal was a black sheep indeed,' great-aunt Helen wheezed. 'But that's only part of the story.'

'What story?'

'Hannibal's story! You see, he was a man whose life was a tapestry of secrets.'

'Secrets?'

'Yes, secrets! Secrets which have never been explained. Since Hannibal's public disgrace there's been a curse on us all.'

'What curse?'

'It may sound far-fetched, and perhaps it is, but we've all been blocked by the system — locked out in the cold. It's as though there's a conspiracy against all Foggs.'

'What kind of conspiracy?'

'One that has prevented us from succeeding at anything at all.'

Great-aunt Helen took half a step forward. She was so close that Will could see the cataracts clouding her eyes.

'Listen carefully to me, William,' she said. 'The stamp album didn't come from a thrift store. It belonged to Hannibal Fogg… It's the only possession any of us have of his. Before he died, our father asked that it be given to you when you came of age.'

Will opened his daypack and brushed a hand over the album's canvas cover.

'I'll treasure it,' he said.

Aunt Helen's expression darkened like an approaching storm cloud.

'We *must* break the cycle!' she screeched. 'Not for me and Edith, but for your generation, and for the children you will one day have. Let the curse go on, and you'll be resigned to failure, like the rest of us.'

'But how do I break the cycle?'

'Go to London. Meet the legal firm and listen to what they say.'

'But the letter…'

Aunt Helen pulled the shreds of cream writing paper from her apron pocket.

'Here it is.'

Will sorted through the scraps of paper.

'The meeting's tomorrow. I'll never make it.'

'Yes you will! Get on a plane tonight!'

'But I can't afford lunch, let alone a flight all the way to Europe.'

Great-aunt Helen shoved the biscuit tin into Will's chest.

'Take this,' she said. 'It should be enough to get you started.'

Will shrugged.

'Started on what?'

'Started on an adventure of course!'

Twelve

1888

AN ELDERLY GENTLEMAN WAS sitting at a long refectory table in Room 64B. His complexion was oyster grey, much of his face obscured by a grand white beard reaching down as far as his solar plexus.

The wall behind the table was taken up by rows of numbered mahogany drawers — hundreds of them, each one containing a fossilised treasure.

Sir William Calcraft-Ross had spent a lifetime classifying and labelling the contents of the drawers, most of which were filled with species of ammonite. They ranged from almost microscopic to very large, with every size in between.

The aged scholar was regarded by most of the British Museum's other staff as a crackpot of the highest order. They frowned on his theories, and on the constant stream of inventions he claimed would shape the future.

Calcraft-Ross had worked at the Museum longer than anyone else, so the other staff tended to leave him alone. None of them ever visited his study, down in the bowels of the basement.

The only visitor to venture there was Hannibal Fogg.

He considered Calcraft-Ross a mentor, and the one man alive with sufficient moral fibre to stand up to the establishment.

'I've found it!' cried Hannibal as he entered.

'Found it, found *what*?'

Fogg tossed his gabardine coat onto the table and, with considerable care, unbuckled the leather straps of the canvas satchel slung over his right shoulder. From it, he withdrew something, about the size and shape of a shoebox.

Calcraft-Ross turned up the oil lamp's wick and observed the object.

'Where did you come by it?'

'From a Roman vessel, wrecked off Antikythera Island, thirty fathoms down.'

'How did you ever manage to get down that deep… in a diving bell?'

'I have developed a method of breathing underwater,' Hannibal replied. 'A Pressurised Respiration Apparatus.'

Easing up the lamp's wick, Sir William Calcraft-Ross slid an oversized magnifying lens between him and the object.

'Tell me what you know,' he said.

'Undoubtedly from ancient Greece. I'm certain of it, for the treasure aboard was all Hellenistic. I had heard from fishermen that intricate sections of a mechanism had been washed up in their nets. This tallied with the observations made by Pliny the Elder.'

'Observations?'

'That a mechanical apparatus created more than three centuries before the birth of Christ was used by Alexander on his campaigns.'

'Used to what end?'

Dabbing the perspiration from his brow, Hannibal stepped into the pool of light flowing over the side of the desk.

'To give him an advantage over his enemies,' he said.

'And how did this "Alexander Mechanism" work?'

'I don't know yet,' Hannibal said. 'But I intend to find out!'

Thirteen

IN THE TWELVE YEARS since his parents' death, Will had never once been on an aeroplane.

Four years before, his great-aunts planned to take him to Paris. They had applied for their passports, and even chosen hotels and flights — but funds required for the journey had never quite materialised. So, the French trip never happened. Like so much in his life, it was a milestone of childhood disappointment.

On the evening of his visit to Oakland, Will picked his way through an in-flight meal on the direct Virgin Atlantic service to London. Cruising at 37,000 feet, he had amazed himself — buying a last-minute ticket was the single most spontaneous act of his life.

Once the trays were cleared, Will watched *Die Hard* on the screen set into the seat-back inches from his face.

As always, he felt irritated that Hollywood dared to pass such implausible high drama off as reality.

The thought of drama led him to Hannibal Fogg, and the question of what his own secretive legacy might have been. The idea that he was descended from such a mysterious character, expunged from existence, was almost too much to believe. As Will pondered it, the trip to Europe was worth it, if only to put to rest the riddle of Hannibal Fogg.

At Heathrow Terminal 3, Will took the Piccadilly Line into London. He was worn out from doing nothing, his body clock catapulted forward in time.

Before the tube train slipped into the tunnels, he stared out of the window, taking in the tight rows of matchbox homes, and the grey anonymous sky.

The flight had been an hour late. Even so, Will calculated there should be enough time to get to the lawyer's office.

He glanced at his watch.

It was 2.10 p.m.

The underground train ground to a halt between stations and the lights went out. To his surprise, the other passengers stayed calm. When the lights eventually came back to life, a Cockney woman snapped:

'Bleeding tube. It 'appens all the time.'

Holding the shreds of paper together to read the address, Will tried his iPhone, but there was no signal.

'Where you trying to go, love?' the woman asked.

'Fleet Street.'

'Get off at South Ken,' she said, 'take the Circle Line to Temple. You can walk from there.'

Will glanced at his watch again.

'Got a meeting, dear?'

'Yeah… at four.'

The Cockney woman looked at her own watch, a pink Casio.

'Better get a move on,' she said. 'It's gone three fifteen.'

Will cursed. He had got the time difference wrong.

At South Kensington, the woman pointed to the door.

'Change here, love.'

Fifteen minutes later he sprinted out of Temple Station, and launched Google Maps. But his iPhone wasn't working — he had forgotten to set up roaming.

3.51… nine minutes to go.

Running like a maniac, he yelled out the address.

A man in a suit cocked his head in the direction of a narrow street.

Before he knew it, Will was in a maze of alleys. He swore he heard the sound of feet following fast behind him.

He turned once, then again.

Nothing.

Was it an echo?

Or the tortuous obsession of being followed again?

More running, more asking.

Then a sign: Fleet Street.

Counting down the numbers, he found himself standing in an open doorway.

3.58.

Hurrying inside, he waved the shredded letter.

'I've made it!' he hollered at the porter, dressed in a bow tie and wool morning coat. 'Is this Penshaw...?' Will checked the letter heading, 'Penshaw, Willis, Smink & Company.'

'Indeed it is, sir.'

'I've come about the inheritance, the Estate of Hannibal Fogg.'

Solemnly, the porter motioned to a waiting room.

'I shall inform the partners of your arrival, sir.'

'Thank you.'

Will strode across creaking boards overlaid by an Afghan rug. He sat down on a grand antique chesterfield, antimacassars on the back. A selection of sporting magazines were laid out on a side table. Oil portraits of stiff-looking men in legal robes stared down from oak-panelled walls. All had beards and some had pipes.

As he sat there alone, Will had the distinct feeling he was being watched, as he so often did. He checked the eyes of the portraits, half-expecting them to move.

A moon-face grandfather clock struck the hour in the corner of the waiting room.

On the fourth chime the sound of feet was heard out in the corridor. A second porter appeared and led Will into the partners' meeting room.

A third attendant entered, carrying a pewter salver at chest height. Upon it was a crystal glass filled with dark cherry-coloured liquid.

'A glass of port, sir?' he asked gravely.

Unsure of the correct etiquette, Will took the glass and sipped.

One of the senior partners entered.

He was servile and meek, his hands freckled in liver spots. His head was crowned by a horseshoe of oyster-grey hair, his nose was noticeably elongated as though stretched in childhood.

'Basil Penshaw at your service, sir,' he said. 'May I presume you are Mr William Fogg?'

'That's right.'

Penshaw let out a chuckle.

'We had a devil of a time tracking you down. Did you not receive our emails? Had them sent out specially. You see, electrical technology is not our strong point at Penshaw, Willis, Smink.'

'I assumed they were junk,' Will explained, taking a second sip of port.

Penshaw wasn't listening.

'Before we begin, I shall need to see something by way of identification.'

'Of course.'

Fumbling, Will pulled out his passport. He held it open at the photo page. The lawyer glanced at it vacantly.

'Very good,' he said. 'Now we can begin.'

'Begin?'

'With the inheritance.'

Sitting down, Will perched anxiously at the front of the chair.

Penshaw considered a yellowed sheet of paper on the table.

'May I ask what you know about Mr Fogg?' he enquired.

'You mean…'

'Mr Hannibal Fogg.'

'That he was my great-great-grandfather, and that he was an explorer who was disgraced for…'

'For being a spy?'

'That's what I heard.'

'Do you know anything else about him?'

'Not really, no… Except that we shared a love of postage stamps.'

Penshaw pinched the tip of his elongated nose.

'Hannibal Garrett Fogg was born at the family's castle near Loch Lomond in 1868,' he said.

'*Castle?* He was born in a castle?'

Penshaw pinched his nose again.

'Indeed, he was. Although he was raised mostly at the family's country estate in Somerset. But that wasn't the extent of the Foggs' wealth. You see, the family owned a large portion of Mayfair here in London as well, and property stretching from Marble Arch to the River Thames.'

Will sank back into his chair, his mouth bone dry from the idea of instant and unimaginable wealth.

'Before his disappearance in China in 1939, Mr Fogg left this document.' Pausing, Penshaw sniffed, his brow furrowing. 'The peculiar thing is, sir, that Mr Fogg named you as the sole successor of his Estate... decades before you were actually born.'

'I get it all?'

'Technically speaking, it would seem so, sir.'

Will leaned forwards, his fingertips moistening.

'Could you tell me exactly what I get? The castle... do I get the castle?'

Penshaw sighed.

'This firm has provided legal counsel to Foggs for eleven generations,' he said, his back straightening. 'And in that time, we at Penshaw, Willis, Smink have had the privilege to attend to the family's fortunes, as well as to their not inconsiderable difficulties.'

'Difficulties?'

Basil Penshaw slipped a pair of pince-nez bifocals from a hard lizard-skin case, and put them on. They made his nose seem a little less extreme.

'In 1928, Mr Hannibal Fogg was accused of espionage, spying for the German state. He was arrested, imprisoned in the Tower of London and, in the months that followed, a Purge took place.

'Anything and everything connected with his life was systematically gathered up and destroyed. It was as if he had never lived at all. His ancestral titles, possessions and property were appropriated by the Crown, confiscated and distributed to others.'

'What about Hannibal himself... how long did he spend locked up?'

'A few months. No more than that. By chance he was released during an impromptu state visit by the Sultan Abdelhafid of Morocco. Permitted to live in exile, he travelled there — forbidden from ever returning to the land of his birth. As I understand it, he disappeared shortly afterwards during an expedition to Manchuria.'

Will downed the last drops of port.

'Was there nothing left? Nothing that wasn't seized or destroyed?'

Penshaw adjusted the pince-nez.

'No,' he said. 'Well. Not really.'

Opening a green box file on the table, he took out a key and slipped it across the table's polished surface. As large as a man's hand, it was made from solid silver.

'Nothing except for this.'

'What does this open?'

'One cannot be certain.'

'Can't you give me a clue?'

'There is an address.'

'Where?'

Penshaw scribbled down a few lines in maroon ink.

'In Marrakesh,' he said.

Fourteen

1888

SNOW HAD FALLEN SOFTLY through the night, laying siege to the rooftops, the buttresses and the crenellated battlements of Oxford's revered Balliol College.

Hannibal slept with the window open, a practice he had begun at prep school, and one he found impossible to change. He believed that nature expected humankind to live according to the temperature it prescribed, even in the coldest winter months.

For this reason, Hannibal shunned heating. He found the cold filled him with a raw and intense vigour which allowed him to think.

Peering through the open window, he took in the pristine blanket of white. The snow was still perfectly virgin, touched by neither feet nor wheels.

Hannibal had an idea.

Quickly, he wrestled with his dressing gown, knotted the belt cord tight, and hurtled down the stairs.

'Osman! Osman!' he cried, pounding at the second door on the right.

Inside, a commotion was followed by the sound of Hannibal's friend swearing in Arabic.

The door was opened by Osman, who was rubbing his foot.

'It's been snowing,' reported Hannibal cheerily.

'As if your country were not cold enough already!'

'It has to be today!' Hannibal snapped immediately. 'We must fly the Prototype-B today… this morning!'

Osman rubbed his hands to his face. Until three minutes before, he had been peacefully asleep, dreaming of warmth and home.

'Let's wait until the snow melts,' he said. 'Please!'

Hannibal Fogg shook his head.

'Quite impossible,' he replied. 'I've done the calculations, and the snow will last for weeks. At least until the end of the Michaelmas term.' Hannibal paused. 'I'll give you half an hour. Then I'm flying whether you're ready or not.'

WITH THE WIND STEADY at fifteen knots, the pair of undergrads hoisted the Prototype-B in sections up onto the roof of the Balliol Tower. Osman was in charge of its assembly. After all he had been responsible for the engineering, working to plans drawn up by his great friend and co-pilot.

The glider was built in such a way that the wings folded outwards from stowage points along the fuselage. The tail section and the fixed landing gear were bolted on, then tested for strength.

Once ready, the Prototype-B was aimed in the direction of Trinity College. The plan was to land on its snow-covered expanse. Fearing the landing gear to be the glider's weakest point, Hannibal regarded the snow as a godsend. Even the hardest of landings would be cushioned.

While Hannibal ratcheted up the propelling mechanism, Osman took the rear seat.

The system of pulleys, springs and cantilevers was wound tight with the aid of a crank handle.

'Hurry, Fogg!' called Osman, glancing back at the sky. 'Looks like the blizzard's almost here!'

'Just another couple of turns.'

Hannibal wiped his brow, jerked out the crank, and took his place in the front seat.

'Goggles?'

'Check.'

'Ailerons?'

'Thirty degrees.'

'Wind?'

Licking the tip of a finger, Hannibal held it above his head.

'North-north-east. I'd say eleven knots.'

'Five, four, three, two, one... *release!*'

The two passengers held still, bracing themselves.

Nothing happened.

Silence, but for the sound of the wind, and a dog barking out on Broad Street.

'Release!' cried Osman a second time.

'I did! I did release!'

Again, Hannibal whacked a fist to the release plate.

The propelling mechanism recoiled.

A second later the Prototype-B was moving fast in the direction of the great snowy expanse.

Had they time to breathe in, Hannibal and Osman might have whooped. Rigid like wax figures, they braced themselves for the inevitable impact.

As the distance between the glider and the snow decreased, a freak gust of wind swept in.

It was as forceful as it was unexpected.

The Prototype-B changed course.

Gliding low over St Giles, it reeled ahead in absolute silence.

Hannibal struggled with the controls.

Lower and lower the glider descended, the nose lining up with the Ashmolean's casement windows.

Impact!

The next thing Hannibal could remember was dragging his Moroccan friend from the flames. Having disintegrated on impact, the aircraft's wings were torn off, while the fuselage was propelled far into the Ashmolean Museum.

Ruptured in the carnage, a pipe carrying coal gas was ignited by a spark.

Next day, battered and bandaged, Hannibal and Osman were called to the Master's study. Having been castigated and addressed with every imaginable expletive, they were sent down.

Returning to the family home in Somerset, Hannibal withdrew to his bedroom.

He remained inside for eleven months.

From dawn until dusk, he worked on his designs. Some of them featured mechanical instruments to aid modern living. Others featured equipment for expeditions, or to be used by the military on distant campaigns.

Immersing himself in the business of invention, Hannibal turned his hand to solving all kinds of technical problems. He even took up furniture design — inventing a new system of demountable furniture using tapered bayonet fittings.

When he was not designing, Hannibal focused on his linguistic skills. He taught himself Swahili, Hausa and Mandarin, and perfected his own advanced method of language learning, which he termed '*Linguamatics*'.

In November the snow began falling once again.

Taking out an extra large sheet of draughtsman's paper, Hannibal began work on a new glider. Designed from the ground up, he called it the Prototype-C.

When it was finished, he wrote to Osman, who had returned to Morocco in disgrace.

Months passed.

Hannibal presumed the letter had never reached his friend. But one spring morning a reply arrived by uniformed messenger.

The letter explained that Osman's father wanted to thank him personally for pulling his eldest son from the Ashmolean's flames.

Three weeks later, Hannibal arrived in Tangier, having reached Morocco by packet boat from Marseilles.

Waiting for him on the quayside was the Sharifian guard. Raising an eyebrow, Hannibal wondered who exactly Osman's father could be.

All became apparent when the royal guard had escorted him into the hinterland, to the ancient city of Fez. A cavalcade of soldiers processed out to accompany the carriage inside the great palace walls.

Once there, Hannibal was reunited with Osman. They laughed together, thanked providence for saving them from death, and feasted on platters of couscous and lamb.

The next afternoon, Sultan Abdelhafid, Osman's father, received Hannibal in the throne room. Dressed in ceremonial robes, he was flanked by his prime minister, his generals, leading courtiers and by the ever-present Sharifian Guard.

'I understand that you have been the truest friend to my son,' he said in a voice that commanded authority. 'And, as his truest friend, you, too, are my son.'

An equerry approached the sultan, a silver tray in his hands. Upon it was an emerald green presentation box.

'A small token of thanks,' he said, presenting the box to his guest.

Kissing the back of the sultan's hand, Hannibal gave thanks, and received the gift. With appropriate care, he opened the presentation box.

Inside was a large silver key.

Fifteen

AFTER THE MEETING AT Penshaw, Willis, Smink & Co., Will sauntered west along the Embankment overlooking the Thames.

Each pace was a struggle.

Staring down at the green-grey water, all soupy and wretched, he wondered why he had ever allowed great-aunt Helen to part with her savings, or how he could have clung to a dream of instant wealth — a dream doomed from the start.

His gaze moved listlessly from the river onto the pavement, taking in the grain of each individual flagstone. As he walked, his mind took hold of itself, playing over and over the first verse of the rhyme his aunts had whispered at night, coaxing him to sleep. It always helped in times of melancholy:

> *There was a man named Ernest Pie*
> *Who loved to laugh and grin and lie,*
> *He lived on mash and fish and moss*
> *Wandering much but never lost.*

Will strolled down The Mall towards Buckingham Palace. Through his childhood, he had longed to visit London — to see where the Queen of England lived, and to get a first-hand look at the Changing of the Guard.

But now he was there, he hardly cared.

The grandeur and the pomp didn't impress him — the Grenadiers' blood-red coats, the blazing brass buttons, or the clatter of hobnailed boots.

All he could think of was the overwhelming sense of self-pity.

Sitting on a bench in Green Park, he stared at the plane trees, cursing Hannibal Fogg for having blustered into his life.

How could a man spy for such a truly terrible enemy, or abandon his own son?

Will fished a hand through his daypack, his knuckles rubbing over the key's silver shaft.

Cursing Hannibal again, he sighed.

Then he remembered the birthday gift — the stamp album. He had brought it along, planning to go through its contents carefully on the flight. Digging it out, he pulled open the canvas cover and looked through the sheets of orderly stamps.

Sorted by country, they had been arranged in neat rows by a meticulous collector. Most of the names were unfamiliar to current geography — Tanganyika, Ceylon, Rhodesia, Siam. But Will knew them all the same, through his love of postage stamps.

As he progressed through the folios, Will noticed that the album's back cover was coming away. Where the hinges were detaching, he spotted a fragment of paper printed with a black and white pattern.

With care, he peeled the canvas away, and found himself taking in the plan of a city or, rather, part of a city.

Studying it for a minute or two, he turned the map into the light, and read the street names. Although in Roman script, they were adorned with accents and were certainly not English.

Half-wondering if it were simply binder's padding, Will looked closer. Something caught his eye — something on the top right corner of the city plan.

A red pencil line circling a cross and a square — the standard symbol for a church.

Photographing the map, he ran the image through an urban layout app. The plan was soon identified as the medieval heart of the Romanian capital, Bucharest.

Will may have been cursing his ancestor but, at the same time, he was intrigued. Hannibal Fogg may have been a traitor, and a wretched father, but there was something utterly alluring about him.

THE NEXT MORNING, AFTER a night in a gloomy hostel in Paddington, Will took the underground back to Heathrow. Making his way through the crowded terminal, he searched for the check-in counter for his flight to San Francisco. The information screens directed him to the far end of the hall.

The check-in desk for his flight wasn't yet open, but the one beside it was.

The counter was not only decorated with balloons, but featured a troupe of jugglers and acrobats — hyping a new budget airline's give-away prices on the next flight to Marrakesh.

Marrakesh?

Will couldn't take his eyes off the name.

'Don't be stupid!' he said aloud. 'Forget about Hannibal Fogg and his damned inheritance.'

As Will stood there, the acrobats tumbling about, a clutch of American college girls swanned up to the counter and checked in. Giggly and glowing, they were about Will's age.

Taking her boarding card, one of them caught his eye with hers and blushed.

Mischievous and seductive, she had the face of a siren.

She winked.

Will sunk his teeth into his upper lip.

The girl winked again, quizzically this time.

Wide-eyed and nodding, Will stepped up, and bought a ticket to Marrakesh.

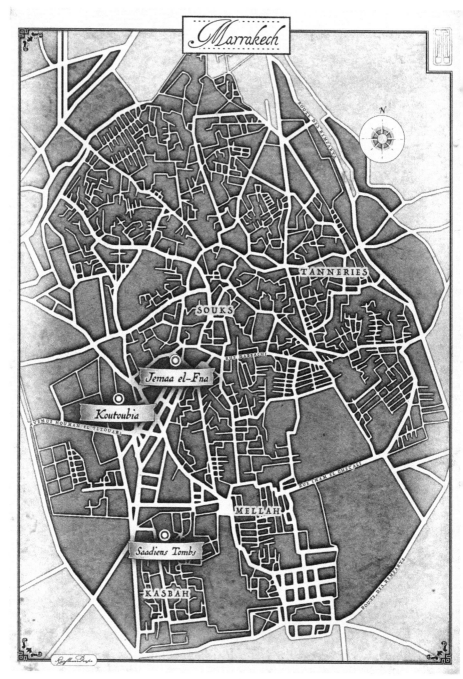

Sixteen

1889

A GROUP OF BOYS were playing marbles in the lane, tossing them in the shade of a heavy wooden door. They had chosen the spot as no one ever hurried past or demanded they leave.

People tended to stay well away from the narrow street altogether. Some said the building that lay behind the great wooden door was haunted. For this reason, it had become known locally as Dar Jnoun, 'The House of Jinns'.

What most of those living in the medina, the old city, of Marrakesh did not realise was that the house had been constructed almost six centuries earlier by a Berber necromancer. So as to be left alone, he spread a rumour that the lane itself was possessed.

With no one watching over him, he set about constructing a mansion unlike any other in existence. Designing it on a grid inspired by mathematical divination, he mixed into the foundations sand from seven deserts and water from seven seas.

Each section was aligned with a necromantic force, corresponding to a specific constellation. Surrounded by a thick outer wall, the building was laid out in such a way as to harness occult energy.

For decades, the sorcerer lived in seclusion at Dar Jnoun, toiling away at the greatest work of divination ever written. Entitled *The Supreme Book of Necromancy*, the work was regarded as so powerful that reading a single page would cause the uninitiated to drop dead.

Only three copies were ever produced.

The first two were burned on the sultan's orders — destroyed on a bonfire, with the magician himself.

The third copy survived.

Having seen his fate during a necromantic séance, the sorcerer built an altar in a secret vestibule, beneath the house. Upon it, in a box crafted from narwhal tusk, he placed his masterwork.

Following the magician's fiery end, Dar Jnoun was appropriated by the sultan, and presented to his grand vizier. Over the centuries, it was made available to a long roster of ministers, emissaries and visiting diplomats.

By chance, on the morning of Hannibal's arrival in Fez, the occupant of Dar Jnoun, a Prussian attaché, was found murdered as he slept.

The news was reported at once to the sultan who was holding court at the royal palace. Receiving Hannibal Fogg the next day, he decided to bestow the home as a gift — in gratitude for saving the life of his favourite son, Prince Osman.

As soon as the Prussian diplomat's body and effects had been removed, the house was cleaned, exorcised, sprinkled with rose water, and made ready for its new owner.

Six days after his audience with the sultan, Hannibal

arrived at the house. Officers from the Sharifian guard cleared the lane of marble-playing boys, and ordered for a magnificent carpet to be unfurled up to the door. Blowing trumpets and beating drums, the officers welcomed the Englishman to his new home.

Hannibal inserted the silver key — presented to him by Sultan Abdelhafid himself — into the lock and turned it. Pushing the door open, he felt a sharp blast of ice-cool air rinse his face.

Having stepped across the marble threshold for the first time, he stood stock still in the vaulted entrance. He sensed an inexplicable energy — as though past, present and future were somehow conjured into one.

Although he did not realise it, thirty feet below the very spot on which he was standing lay the magician's secret vestibule.

Rooted to the spot, the silver key in his hand, Hannibal knew his life would never be quite the same again.

Seventeen

At Marrakesh airport, the siren fell into the arms of a suave-looking man, kissed him passionately, and hurried away with him into the blinding desert light.

Will watched her go, touched by a sense of loneliness. He took a taxi into the main square and entered the labyrinth of passages that made up the old city, the medina. The commotion was like nothing he had experienced before.

There were butchers' shops with camels' heads on spikes.

Fleshy white tripe nestled on beds of fragrant mint.

Cages packed with live chickens, carried on porters' heads.

Barrels of virgin olive oil.

Blocks of beeswax.

Dentists hunched over bowls of second-hand teeth.

Magicians, fortune tellers and acrobats.

Fishing out the address Mr Penshaw had written down, Will showed it to a man selling dried damask roses.

Instantly, a crowd gathered, hands pointing north, west, east and south.

A boy of about eight tugged at Will's shirt.

'I show you,' he said.

'D'you know it?'

The boy nodded.

'Near to my home.'

Weaving in and out of alleyways, they passed pack-mules laden with crates of Coca-Cola, clambered up steps and down slopes, until they were standing at a monumental wooden door. Crafted from cedar, a Hand of Fatima emblem was nailed clumsily to the front.

A plaque to the left of the door read 'Dar Jnoun'.

Will rewarded the boy with a coin.

Taking the silver key out of his bag, he licked his lips.

The moment of truth.

Easing the key into the lock, he turned it.

Click.

Pushing open the door, Will felt a blast of cool air on his face.

A single footstep, and he was inside.

Eighteen

1890

OVER THE YEARS, HANNIBAL returned time and again to Morocco. He would travel up to Fez to visit his great friend, Prince Osman. Together they would plan grand expeditions, sketch out the designs of new aircraft, and laugh at the memories of Oxford. Then, Hannibal would journey south through the desert to Marrakesh, to time in seclusion at Dar Jnoun.

Secrecy was his preeminent concern. It surrounded every aspect of his association with the house. Always visiting it alone, he refused to allow anyone inside. The only exception were the craftsmen who, following his precise plans, remodelled the interior. Hired in the Spanish enclave of Ceuta, they were brought blind-folded to Dar Jnoun, and kept there as virtual prisoners before being escorted home.

In March, Hannibal reached Marrakesh in time to

see the last winter snow on the Atlas Mountains — his favourite sight in all the world. Standing on the terrace, he would gaze at the dazzling white peaks with the longing of unrequited love.

On that occasion he was up on the terrace, staring out, sipping a cup of medicinal tea, when he heard a rap at the front door. Never inviting anyone, he assumed it was a marble-playing boy on a prank.

The rapping came again, louder. This time it was accompanied by a high-pitched voice.

Descending, Hannibal walked briskly through the entrance and opened the front door.

To his surprise, a midget was standing in the lane.

 Dishevelled, he was dressed in little more than rags, and was missing both ears. They appeared to have been hacked off with a blunt knife. Despite the loss, the midget could apparently hear.

Before Hannibal had a chance to enquire what he wanted, the little man held out a fist.

The fist opened, revealing a ring.

On the lapis lazuli face, a simple motif was inscribed.

Mumbling something in Darija, the local dialect, the midget bowed. Still a novice at the language, Hannibal motioned him to repeat what he had said.

'The magician's ring,' said the midget. 'Entrusted to his servant before he was burned to death. For centuries we have guarded it, and now pass it on to you.'

Hannibal glanced down at the diminutive visitor.

66

'How do you know to give it to me?' he asked.

'Because it is written.'

'*Where?* Where is it written?'

The midget didn't answer.

Turning, he shuffled away down the lane.

Nineteen

NO PREPARATION COULD HAVE readied Will for what he found inside Dar Jnoun.

The entrance way delivered him into a great courtyard filled with orange trees, twisting wisteria vines and with birdsong. Constructed around a central garden, known as a *riad*, the house had an unsettling ambience, as though it concealed a treasure trove of secrets.

The floors were laid with glazed terracotta tiles, the walls layered in Venetian plaster — prepared from lime, marble dust and eggs. An elaborate mosaic fountain issued forth cool water, the sunlight reflecting on its central pool.

Four expansive reception rooms led off the central courtyard. Roaming through them, Will took in the furnishings and the details: sprawling divan sofas upholstered in indigo, brightly coloured kelim rugs, exquisite mahogany planters' chairs, and antique French fauteuils inlaid with beads of ivory.

The east salon was a little darker than the other

reception rooms. Almost every inch of wall space was hung with oils from another age.

Pictures of country houses in summer and in frost.

Red-coated huntsmen chasing down the fox.

Meadow flowers.

A boy with curls on a rocking horse.

A dead grouse in a gundog's mouth.

Scanning the pictures, Will found himself drawn in by each one. But it was the last that captivated his attention the most.

Five foot by three, it observed a suave figure face on, wearing military uniform, arms crossed defiantly, an expansive set of medals adorned his chest. The sitter was glaring, lips tight shut, as though tired of the world, or of the artist.

Will couldn't take his eyes off the face, for it bore an astonishing likeness to himself.

'It's you, isn't it, Hannibal?' he whispered, as a shiver shot down his spine.

Until that moment he hadn't quite joined the dots.

This was Hannibal's home — a man so foreign to him, yet, at the same time, so connected.

Strolling through the rooms a second time, Will paid more attention than before. Wherever he looked, he noticed hints of his great-great-grandfather's character — his apparent obsessions, his likes and loathings.

Will observed the way every seat had a notepad and an inkwell beside it, and how the curtains could be fastened together ensuring absolute darkness.

But the thing Will noticed most of all was the smell.

The pungent sweet scent of jasmine.

In the east salon stood a single bookcase crafted from aged oak. Opposite was a display case filled with medals and assorted military decorations. The glass door had a miniature keyhole, an African amulet hanging from it.

Beside the cabinet, suspended from a weighty brass chain, was a ship's bell, engraved 'SS Great Eastern'. To the left of it, a hermetically sealed water clock from the workshops of Jaeger LeCoultre. Will looked at his watch, which he had made sure to set correctly on landing at Marrakesh.

The clock was keeping perfect time.

Slowly, Will swivelled round.

Until then he hadn't realised it, but the home was in perfect order — bizarre considering Hannibal had disappeared so many decades before.

The potted plants were watered and well cared for. The vines in the courtyard were clipped and tied back. The floors, walls and furniture were impeccable, as though cleaned that very morning.

Will felt a pang of unease.

What if the house was owned by someone else?

But, then, how could it explain the endless odds and ends so apparently associated with an English gentleman?

Will had an idea.

If he could find a utility bill or a sheet of letter paper he would have the answer at once. In one of the salons he had noticed a grand roll-top writing bureau.

Rushing through, he tried to push back the curved rosewood cover.

No luck. It was fastened shut.

Strange, Will thought, because there was no lock.

Running his fingers along the desk's bottom edge, he was searching for a catch when he heard the sound of footsteps.

His head jolted up in fear.

He turned.

A young Indian man was standing in the doorway. A little older than Will, his dark complexion had paled from surprise. He was dressed in a tweed tailcoat and knee-length riding boots — curious costume given the heat.

'My God,' he said slowly in an aristocratic voice. 'I hardly believe it!'

'Excuse me,' Will gasped, leaping to his feet.

The young man took three paces forward.

Pressing his palms together in greeting, he dipped his head respectfully in a bow.

'Forgive me for disturbing you, Mr Fogg,' he said.

Twenty

AT THAT VERY MOMENT came the lyrical call of the
muezzin from a nearby minaret, summoning the faithful
to the mid-afternoon prayer.

Without thinking, the Indian plugged his ears with
his fingertips until there was silence once again.

'The mosque is close, sir,' he said, apologetically.

Confused, Will just stood there, looking at the man
in tweeds, waiting for everything to be explained.

'How do you know who I am?' he asked at length.

The Indian figure cleared his throat, bowed again,
and smiled.

'I am assuming you are Mr William, sir… Mr William
Fogg.'

'Yes, I am. But how do *you* know that?'

'Because of the letter, sir.'

'The letter?'

'Indeed.'

'Which letter?'

'The one written by Mr Fogg to my great-grandfather,
sir.'

'And who are you?'

'I am Chaudhury, sir.'

Will wiped a hand down over his mouth.

'That's not quite what I meant.'

Chaudhury raised an eyebrow.

'I am your manservant, sir,' he said.

'Man…?'

'…servant, sir.'

'How? Why?'

'My family have served Foggs for generations, sir.'

'Generations?'

'Yes, sir.'

'How many generations?'

Chaudhury counted on his fingers.

'*Eight* to be precise.'

Will shook his head.

'But that's ridiculous.'

'How so, sir?'

'Well, I don't have the money to pay you, for a start.'

The manservant held out a hand, as if to placate Will's concern.

'My salary is defrayed directly from the funds that were left, sir.'

'Left by who?'

Chaudhury glanced at the floor.

'Left by Mr Hannibal Fogg, sir.'

'But I still don't understand,' Will replied. 'How d'you know I existed, let alone that I'd turn up here in Marrakesh?'

'The letter… it was most specific, sir.'

Will frowned and, as he did so, Chaudhury removed a yellowed sheet of writing paper from the inside pocket of his jacket. Having been folded and refolded so many times, it almost looked like cloth.

Chaudhury had read it so often over the years, he knew the text by heart:

25th September 1939

My dear Chaudhury,

I shall keep this message brief because as you know I am about to depart on a Manchurian expedition — a journey I must undertake alone. I cannot reveal why I am writing this now, nor other information which makes the contents of this letter possible to pass on.

But you must know that with time your son will continue service and, after him, your grandson and your great-grandson. Fear not, provisions have been made to cover your salaries. There shall be a period of considerable tranquillity in which I expect the house and effects to be kept in perfect order.

Everything must be ready for William's arrival.

He shall be with you on Wednesday, 3rd May 2017.

Ever faithfully yours,
Hannibal Fogg

73

Chaudhury, the son of Chaudhury, grandson and great-grandson of Chaudhury, dipped his head.

'I have waited for you my entire life,' he whispered.

A mantel clock struck the hour.

'Until a week ago I had only ever heard the name Hannibal Fogg once,' said Will, 'and even then, it had been spoken in anger.'

'Well, sir, now that you have arrived, I shall do all I can to serve you in the years ahead.'

Will glowered.

'But I've got to get back to San Francisco!'

Chaudhury's expression seemed glaze over.

'I see, sir,' he said tautly. 'If you say so.'

'There's no way I'm going to spend my life in Marrakesh!'

The manservant sniffed.

'Shall I show you to your quarters?'

'Er, um. OK,' said Will.

A cream silk baldaquin trimmed in gold hung above the antique rosewood bed. The linen sheets had been pressed by Chaudhury that morning, with the heavy coal-iron Hannibal had bought ninety years before.

Located on the upper floor, the bedroom was lit by windows on three sides, decorated with objects from all corners of the earth.

Among them was a rawhide saddle from eastern Tibet, and a *kriss* dagger with a watered steel blade, once the property of a Malay magician. Beside it, a bowl sculpted from a huge calabash was filled with blown ostrich eggs.

Chaudhury led the way, Will's daypack in his hand.

'This was Mr Fogg's bedroom,' he said in a low voice.

'It's like a museum.'

'I believe the items in here were among Mr Fogg's favourites, sir,' said Chaudhury, placing the daypack on the satinwood dresser.

'He certainly had an eye for the unusual.'

The servant seemed anxious.

'I hope it is to your liking, sir. I have prepared it in accordance with what I understand to be your preferences.'

'My preferences?'

'In line with your liking, sir.'

Bowing once again, Chaudhury walked backwards to the door, and left.

Wondering what he had meant, Will looked around.

The bedroom had been prepared with touches according to his own taste.

At a basin, behind a carved damascene screen, was a fresh bar of glycerine soap — the brand his great-aunts had brought him up to use. On the mantel he found a bowl of his favourite mints. And, placed squarely on the pillow, was a hardback first edition of *Jonathan Livingston Seagull*.

Sitting down on the bed, Will opened the book, and read the first paragraph. His eyes lifted from the page and moved gradually to the floor.

For some reason, he found himself drawn to the carpet — a tribal rug from Afghanistan — bearing the *fil poy*, an elephant's foot motif.

But it wasn't the rug that kept his attention.

Something was poking out from one corner — a brass handle.

Stepping forward, Will tugged back the carpet.

Beneath it was a trapdoor.

Twenty-one

AS THE LIGHT BEGAN to fade, Will sat in the garden courtyard listening to the evening call to prayer from the minaret nearby. The orange trees were rustling, as the songbirds settled into their nests for the night.

Will felt ill at ease, as though he had stumbled into someone else's dream. At the same time, he was touched by a sense of perfect tranquillity. Hannibal's home may have been sinister but was welcoming and warm as well.

A few minutes before eight o'clock, Chaudhury appeared.

'Dinner is served, sir,' he said.

At the far end of the long dining table, a single place-setting had been laid, tapered candles throwing shadows over the starched linen cloth. The cutlery was sterling silver, embossed with an HF monogram, and a silk place mat was equidistant between knife and fork.

The manservant waited for his master to be seated.

Wearing spotless white gloves, he carried in a plate ceremoniously. Over it was a solid silver cloche. Setting the plate down on the mat, Chaudhury cleared his throat, as his father had instructed him to do.

'Toad in the hole,' he exclaimed, raising the dome.

'Toad in the *what*?'

'In the hole, sir. Sausages in batter. An English specialty.'

Will looked at the plate and sensed his stomach churn.

'Are you English?' he asked softly.

'No, sir. I am Indian by birth. From Cooch Behar… one of the former Princely States.'

'Then why are we eating an English specialty?'

'For the sake of tradition, sir. A legacy of the Raj.'

Will grinned, nudging a fork into the batter.

'What's for dessert? Snake in the grass?'

The manservant took a step backwards, away from the table.

'For pudding, I have prepared a cherry flan, sir,' he said.

Will's head jolted up fast.

'How do you know that?' he thundered, pushing his chair back from the table. 'How do you know any of this stuff?'

'Know what, sir?'

'Know that I love cherry flan, or that I've always used glycerine soap, or that my favourite book's *Jonathan Livingston Seagull*?'

Chaudhury laid the silver cloche on the sideboard.

'The information was passed down to me, sir,' he explained. 'Mr Fogg had informed my grandfather, who informed my father, and my father advised me.'

'But I don't understand. How could Hannibal have known anything about me? What soap I use, what dessert I like... what day I'd arrive. Hell, I don't get how he even knew I'd ever exist!'

The manservant didn't reply. Instead, he retreated to the kitchen to warm up the flan.

After picking his way through the toad in the hole, and eating two slices of the very good dessert, Will decided to go out for a stroll. He hadn't been in the house long, but it felt as if the walls were closing in.

The day's heat had waned, the shadows dark and long.

Will zigzagged through the maze of narrow streets, turning left, right, left, eventually spilling out into Jma al Fna. The great central square of Marrakesh, its name translated as 'Assembly of the Dead'.

Circled by clusters of eager listeners, fortune-tellers were conjuring tales from the *Arabian Nights*. Itinerant healers were drifting through the crowds, flasks of home-made potions dangling from their belts. There were jugglers too, musicians, and old crones begging — their hands outstretched.

Each evening, as dusk fell, the square transformed itself. Dozens of impromptu stalls were wheeled out, serving sheep-head soup, camel-meat kebabs, and other delicacies from the desert.

Plumes of oily smoke billowed up from the stalls, drifting into the night sky.

At the edge of the square, Will took a seat in a crowded café — illuminated by a myriad of paraffin lamps — marvelling at the scene.

Taking out his iPhone, he panned it slowly left to right, filming the sea of humanity. As he did so, he got a flash of his dorm room back in San Francisco. This is the *real* world, he thought to himself.

For the first time in his life he had broken free.

As he sat there, taking in the atmosphere, he heard a voice behind him speaking English. A woman's voice. Silky and soft, it was the kind of voice that advertisers use to sell you expensive perfume, chocolate, or glycerine soap.

The voice was describing the history of Marrakesh.

Will listened.

'The great mosque of Koutoubia dates to the twelfth century, and was completed in the reign of Caliph Yaqub al-Mansur, although there's a legend it was actually built by Jinns.'

The voice broke off to take a question — a question posed by a tourist from Kyoto. It answered in faultless Japanese, before taking a second question in Dutch.

79

As discreetly as he could manage, Will shuffled around in his chair, and strained to the left to see the face from which the voice had come.

Straining to focus between the tables, chairs and customers, he saw her.

He didn't move. He couldn't.

She was gorgeous — way out of his league.

Mid-twenties, cropped blonde hair, dark eyes, high cheek bones, and a fresh young smile that must have melted a thousand hearts.

Sipping her glass of mint tea, she made a joke in Spanish, and broke into a laugh.

A moment after that she was on her feet, gliding through the crowd towards the door.

Will sat stock still like a stone statue as she passed.

As she did so, the hem of her floral print dress touched his knee. He breathed in through his nose, taking in the delicate scent of perfume.

Closing his eyes, he held it in his chest.

Twenty-two

1891

AT SEVENTEEN CATHERINE STREET, a stone's throw from Aldwych, were located the workshops of Messrs Morgan and Sanders, cabinet makers to both royalty and the military for almost a hundred years.

The street was famed from Malaya to the Zambezi for the quality and ingenuity of the furniture it turned out.

Having worked with other firms, Hannibal had found Morgan and Sanders to be the most reliable, even though they were more expensive than the rest.

When in London, he always made a point of calling upon them. There was usually a canvas satchel slung over his shoulder, stuffed with sketches of work he planned to commission.

As far as Hannibal was concerned, the construction of furniture — like all equipment — was not a subject to be taken lightly. On no account did he ever leave decisions to the craftsmen themselves. As he saw it, the job of craftsmen was to craft, rather than to invent.

Although a favoured client, Hannibal tended to push those who worked for him to breaking point — and Morgan and Sanders was no exception. His exacting standards, not to mention bizarre requests, frequently left the firm's carpenters and the management at a loss for words.

But, fearing they might lose his much-valued business, the company's manager, Uriah Rawlins, laid on an especially fulsome welcome whenever the celebrated explorer arrived.

'Always a pleasure to see you, Mr Fogg,' he declared obsequiously, once Hannibal's hat and gloves had been taken by one of the junior staff.

'Send in Briggs right away, and be quick about it! No

time to waste!'

'Certainly, Mr Fogg.'

'I have the plans here for an entire suite of camp furniture.'

'Very good, sir.'

A moment slipped by, in which Hannibal rid his nose of the smell of sawdust with a pinch of Macouba snuff. A hunched figure with unkempt sideburns limped through the door, his head dipped in respect.

'Morning, Mr Fogg, sir.'

'Hello Briggs. Going to be leaving for Siam in two weeks. Have to help the King with something, so there's an avalanche of work. Tell your men to roll up their sleeves, they're going to be toiling round the clock.'

Briggs's head dipped again.

'Right you are, sir, Mr Fogg.'

In a single movement, Hannibal unbuckled his satchel and plucked out a sheaf of designs. He thrust them into the carpenter's chest.

'There, now that's dealt with, I am yearning to see the campaign desk. The oak roll-top,' he paused. 'I hope it's ready, Mr Briggs.'

The chief carpenter's head dipped a third time.

'Indeed it is Mr Fogg, sir. I shall have it brought through.'

An apprentice was sent into the workshop behind. Ten seconds later, the sound of steel wheels grinding against the floorboards filled the shop. An impressive piece of furniture, partly covered by a voluminous cotton sheet, was hauled in by three men.

Briggs pulled the veil away, revealing an exquisite pedestal writing bureau.

'Oh, Mr Briggs!' declared Hannibal at the top of his lungs. 'You have surpassed yourself!'

The carpenter stepped forward. His head bowed again.

'As per your instructions, the locking mechanism is concealed. And the entire desk is demountable as you specified.'

'Bayonet fittings?'

'Indeed, sir. According to your own patent.'

'Excellent!' Hannibal boomed. 'Get it packed up. I'll take it with me now. And, Briggs?'

'Yes sir, Mr Fogg?'

'Make another. The same, only larger. It'll do as a gift for the King of Siam.'

Twenty-three

AT SIX NEXT MORNING Will woke with a start, and immediately wondered where on earth he was. Gradually, he remembered the sequence of events which had led him to be lying in a grand bedstead, in a palatial mansion, somewhere in the old city of Marrakesh.

Getting out of bed, he crept downstairs, his bare feet pacing over the rough terracotta tiles. After strolling into

TAHIR SHAH

the courtyard, he backtracked into the east salon.

Just then, Chaudhury floated through from the kitchen, a tea tray held rigid between outstretched hands.

'Good morning to you, sir,' the manservant pronounced sombrely. 'I was not certain if you preferred English breakfast or Lapsang Souchong, and so I took the liberty of preparing a pot of each.'

'Tell me something, Chau...'

'*Chaudhury*, sir.'

'Tell me something, Chaudhury... how exactly did your family come to be in the service of mine?'

The retainer aligned the fingertips of his white gloves together pensively.

'Rather like toad in the hole, it is a legacy of the Raj, sir.'

'The Raj?'

'The British colonial rule of India. As I understand it, your ancestor Sir Archibald Fogg saved my own antecedent from being mauled by a tiger on the Sunderbans.'

'What are they?'

'The mangrove swamps of Bengal, sir. In gratitude, my ancestor ruled that his youngest son was to serve Sir Archibald as manservant, a tradition that can't be broken until a white tiger is born at our ancestral palace in Cooch Behar.'

'Your family lives in a palace?' asked Will, confused.

Chaudhury poured a cup of Lapsang Souchong, steam rising from the tip of the spout. He placed it on a small table beside Will's right hand. Then, in silence, he picked up the tea tray, and left.

Following a breakfast of poached kippers, eggs and toast, Will stepped across the threshold and out into the street. Dar Jnoun was by no means small, but it was curiously claustrophobic, being packed as it was with possessions and memories.

The tapered lanes of Marrakesh were jammed with life, cascading currents of people, animals, and an abundance of wares. Everything Will caught sight of gripped his attention — from the shopkeepers sprinkling water on the steps of their stores to keep down the dust, to the trays of freshly baked bread balanced on heads, to the cages of live poultry awaiting the chop.

Following the flow of pack mules and pilgrims, street hawkers and school children, Will once again found himself washed into the main square — Jma al Fna. Breaking out into the vast open space was like surfacing from beneath the waves. Will felt dazed, as if he was the only person there left out of a great secret.

Strolling in a diagonal line across the square, he took in the blur of storytellers, healers and snake charmers.

A man approached, eager to sell him a fistful of crumpled postcards. Then another offered him a necklace crafted from dried lizard skulls. Swishing them away with his hands, he sped up, pacing fast towards the shade.

A stream of Chinese tourists passed, each immaculate in designer safari gear, their cameras clicking like castanets. They were followed by a throng of French boy scouts. Hot on their heels was a posse of Englishmen, their frail skin charred by the ferocious African sun.

But Will's thoughts weren't on the rich human stew.

Rather, he was thinking about Dar Jnoun and Hannibal Fogg. Part of him wished he had never left his comfort zone.

After all, ignorance is bliss.

Turning it over in his mind, he pondered the unlikely situation — in an effort to fathom quite how or why Hannibal had lived in such a remote Moroccan home, with an Indian prince as a servant.

At that moment, he heard a commotion in a nearby lane.

Turning, Will strained to get a view of it.

A thickset hulk of a man was attacking someone far smaller, crouching on the ground. Despite the swarms of people all around, it was as if no one cared, or that they hadn't noticed the fracas.

Keeping his distance, Will crossed the lane to get a better view of what was going on. The man was frantically wresting an object — a purple backpack with bright yellow shoulder straps. His face was masked by a crazed expression, teeth clenched, cheek muscles taut like sprung elastic.

As the man moved into the light, Will noticed his

left eye was missing, the ocular cavity hollow, the skin around it crudely stretched over bone. The little finger on his right hand was missing as well.

Desperately grasping onto one of the yellow shoulder straps — as though her life depended on it — was a young woman. Screaming, her heels were dug into the dust.

Right away Will recognised the dress — its hem had brushed against his knee only hours before.

The young woman from the café.

Unsure of what to do, he thrust his arms up and yelled as loudly as he could.

The wall of sound that shot from his mouth broke over everything: over the clatter of the pack mules and the cries of the beggars, over the healers, the hawkers, and the acrobats performing out on the square.

Startled by the battle cry, the woman relaxed her grip and tumbled backwards in what seemed like slow motion.

As soon as she let go, the thief grabbed the daypack and sped off full tilt.

Lunging forward, Will leant down and helped the woman to her feet. She was shocked, bewildered, urgently trying to make sense of the encounter.

'He attacked me! Just like that…!'

'I saw it all.'

'My notes! He's taken my notes! My thesis…'

Threading her hands back through her hair, the woman began sobbing. Will leaned in close. He could smell her scent, the same delicious fragrance as from the evening before.

'Did he get anything else?' he asked gently.

'My clothes... my cash... my ticket home... *Everything*.' She dug a hand down the front of her dress, fishing out a blue passport from her bra. 'Well, at least he left me this.'

The woman took a deep breath. She looked up, her eyes locking onto Will's. He stuck out a hand.

'*Will*... William Fogg.'

The woman began sobbing again.

'Emma,' she sniffed.

'Pleased to meet you.'

'What am I gonna do?'

'You'll have to report it...'

'Who to? *The police?*'

Will nodded.

'Think I saw a police station back that way.'

Emma smiled, a twinkle of amusement in the dire situation.

'D'you just get to Morocco?'

'Is it that obvious?'

'I'd say it is.'

Will grinned, the wide-eyed grin of the newly arrived.

'Wanna grab a coffee?' he said.

Emma caught his eye, and Will felt his knees weaken.

'Love to,' she said. 'But I'm warning you, you're gonna have to treat me.'

Twenty-four

OVER CAFÉ NOIR THICK like crude oil, Emma told how she had come to Morocco to study the city's ancient Saadian tombs.

Will had sat with his back to the window, so that he could see the light playing over her face. He listened to her, mesmerised by the evenness of her voice and by the breadth of her knowledge.

She was an expert in First Kingdom Egyptology, in Renaissance murals and in Japanese haiku. She had studied yoga under a Tibetan master in Nepal, and said she had published a novel in French and another in Spanish. But, despite her all-encompassing know-how, she was modest beyond belief.

It felt to Will that he had known her his entire life.

'When I was five years old, I dreamed of stepping into *The Arabian Nights*,' Emma said with a smile. 'By coming to Morocco, I've succeeded in doing just that. This is the most magical land in the world.' Her enthusiasm seemed to evaporate, replaced by a look of fear. 'God knows what I'm going to do now.'

'Listen,' said Will, swallowing anxiously, 'I might be an axe-murderer for all you know, but you're welcome to come over to my house.'

'You've got a house here in Marrakesh?'

'Yeah…'

'Thought you said you'd just arrived.'

'That's true as well.'

'Huh?'

Grinning broadly, Will pushed a hand back through his hair.

'It's a long story.'

On the way to Dar Jnoun, he explained what he knew about the mysterious Hannibal Fogg. Recounting it to someone else for the first time, he realised how implausible it sounded. Emma insisted it wasn't crazy at all, but perfectly magical. She had let out a beautifully delicate laugh, looked him in the eye as they walked, and blushed.

Stepping inside the house itself, she could hardly believe it.

'This is a dream,' she whispered. 'A mirror of my own dream.'

Chaudhury found them in the courtyard. He served Pimm's, the glasses trimmed with orange wedges. Will introduced Emma and asked that one of the guest rooms be prepared.

'Very good, sir,' said the manservant solemnly. 'Luncheon will be served at one.'

'What are we having, Chaudhury?'

'Roast lamb, sir, followed by spotted dick.'

'Spotted *what*?' asked Emma with a giggle.

'*Dick*, miss. Spotted dick.'

After lunch, Chaudhury cleared the plates, and padded away towards the kitchen.

'I can't believe you have a butler!' said Emma when he was gone.

'Nor can I. And the weirdest thing is he's an Indian prince.'

'What?!'

'Yes… I'm telling you… this place is a Moroccan Twilight Zone.'

Emma's smile faded, her eyes having lost their sparkle.

'I'm so grateful,' she said earnestly. 'You found me at the worst moment imaginable. I just can't believe it. My friends left this morning, and now I'm here without anyone.'

'Hey, I'm happy to help,' Will said.

'I don't know how to thank you.'

Will smiled.

'So don't.'

Just then, Chaudhury came back into the dining-room and coughed discreetly into his fist.

'I shall show Miss Emma to her room,' he said. 'If you would follow me.'

He led the way up a second staircase, on the far side of the courtyard, ascending stairs inlaid with fragments of coloured mosaic. At the top of the last step was a painted wooden door.

Chaudhury turned the brass handle and pushed it open.

Inside stood an exquisite solid silver bed. Hannibal Fogg had been presented with it by the Maharajah of Wankaner in Gujarat in lieu of services rendered. As with Will's bedroom, objects from all corners of the world were strewn about.

Beside the bed, standing against the wall, was the polished wooden propeller from a de Havilland DH.82 Tiger Moth. Across from it was a pair of giant brass binoculars on a stand — once used by Japanese whalers off the coast of Sakhalin. And, near the window, there lay an unusual Etruscan sarcophagus made from terracotta.

The manservant enquired about the guest's luggage.

'I have none,' Emma responded. 'I was robbed this morning.'

'My goodness,' said Chaudhury, straightening his necktie. 'If you would permit me, I will send for a seamstress.'

'A what?'

'A seamstress to prepare some new clothing.'

Emma's face lit up.

'How wonderful,' she said.

Twenty-five

WILL DREAMT OF THE orange trees in the courtyard, of Hannibal's portrait and of Chaudhury's cherry flan. In the middle of the night, he stirred into lighter sleep, woke up and opened an eye.

The bedroom was quite still.

A stray beam of moonlight had broken through the gap in the padded silk curtains and was streaming across the bed. There was an ethereal quality about it, mixed with a sense of terrible danger.

As he focused on the moonlight, Will felt somehow as though Hannibal were right there in the room. Sitting up, he flicked on the bedside light.

On the corner of the bed a Siamese cat was watching him. He shooed it away, and saw it dart to the door.

At nine the next morning, Will went downstairs. He found a cup of hot coffee on the desk in the west salon, presumably placed there for him by Chaudhury. Thinking of Emma, he picked it up and went through to the second staircase. He climbed up, knocked lightly on the painted wooden door and said her name.

No reply.

He knocked again.

Still nothing.

Slowly, he rotated the brass handle, sensing the metal warm to his touch.

Stepping inside the bedroom, he approached the bedstead. The blankets were all ruffled up, hindering his view. It looked like no one was there. Strange, Will thought, as he hadn't heard Emma downstairs.

Another step and he was right up at the edge of the bed, a little unsure quite why he was so interested.

Screaming, Will sprang backwards, the coffee cup smashing on the floor.

Furled up in the mess of blankets, was Chaudhury.

He was stone cold dead.

His throat appeared to have been slashed, the bed soaked through in blood.

Will panicked.

He charged through the room, running out of the door in a frenzy of fear.

'Emma! Emma!' he shrieked at the top of his voice.

But there was silence.

Not a sound.

Careening down the stairs, into the north salon and into the courtyard, Will caught the chirping in the trees and the scent of orange blossom.

But the birds were the last thing on his mind.

Sponging a hand over his face, he began to retch. He couldn't stop. He coughed out a mouthful of bile. It felt as if his eyes were going to explode.

He strained to think straight.

Could there be a logical explanation to all this? Will's mind was racing, piecing together fragments of detail.

A dead Indian manservant.

A girl he had just met who had vanished.

A bizarre home in Marrakesh.

An ancestor he had only recently heard about.

Was it some sort of conspiracy? Was there something he had missed?

Will forced himself to go back up to the bedroom.

He yanked open the curtains, drenching the room in a cascade of morning light.

In a *Midnight Express* moment, he got a flash of raw fear. Banged up in some stinking Moroccan jail.

Racing back into his own bedroom, he dug both hands into his sports bag.

His passport was missing.

'Oh my God!'

At that moment the silence was broken by a fist thumping on the front door of the house. Could it be Emma?

Will hurried down. Taking a deep breath, he wrenched back the door.

A gendarme was standing on the other side. On his belt was a white leather holster, its button unfastened.

Alarmed, he barked something in Arabic, then French.

'I speak English,' Will said anxiously.

The police officer drew his weapon.

'The neighbour heard screaming,' he said in English laden heavily with an accent. 'A man screaming.'

Will got another flash of *Midnight Express*: steel cell doors slamming shut.

'Don't know what you mean,' he stammered.

A radio crackled in the policeman's hand. Without thinking, he wound down the volume.

'Come with me.'

'Where to?'

'To the Sûreté Nationale.'

'Why?'

'We have questions to ask you.'

Will inhaled sharply.

'I'm an American,' he said.

The officer beamed a smile of dirt-brown teeth. He reached out and pulled Will roughly by the arm, yanking him into the street.

The door to Dar Jnoun slammed shut.

'You will come with me,' the policeman growled, his patience wearing thin. 'The house will be… how do you say? It will be sealed, by my men.'

Will swivelled round and checked the policeman's shoulder for a sign of his rank.

Three stripes… an inspector.

His arm locked back in a half-nelson, he moved forward slowly, half a pace ahead of the policeman. Exhausted, he was shaking, the initial kick of adrenalin wearing off, his breathing shallow.

The alley wound around to the right, then to the left, up mule steps and down a steep gradient. Turning left again, they found themselves on the medina's main thoroughfare, either side of it shops touting tourist kitsch. The light was much dimmer there, the street roofed with wooden slats.

One of the stall-keepers called out to the officer, stepping up to greet him.

Seizing the moment, Will jerked himself free,

pirouetting around so that his arm didn't break from the force.

He ran.

His chest was swollen with air, his bloodstream injected with another surge of adrenalin. Behind him was the sound of the gendarme whistling the alarm, and enraged voices ordering him to halt.

But they soon died away. Either that, or Will filtered them out as he struggled to think.

What to do? Go to the American Consulate and explain? Call his great-aunts and ask for their help? No, no, no. They would drop dead from confusion and anyway it was the middle of the night in Oakland.

Running till he had a cramp, he turned into an empty lane, stood in a doorway there and retched.

Todd. He was the one person who would know what to do. He always had an answer for everything, and knew how to keep his cool in any situation. Will roamed the shadows until he found a public phone.

His hand trembling, he dialled the operator.

'Hello… yes, *oui*, *bonjour*, I need to make a collect call. Un call, collect to San Francisco. America.'

'*Oui, Etats-Unis?*'

The line went dead, then crackled back to life. A woman's voice came on… an American voice.

'Hello, yes, sir, how can I help you?'

'I'd like to make a collect call. Yes. 415 555 2338.'

Another pause.

A click.

The muffled sound of the operator was replaced by a gruff voice.

'*Todd*? That you?'

'Hey Will,' said a sleepy voice. 'How's London?'

'I'm not in London.'

'You back? What time is it?'

'It's the middle of the frigging night, Todd... and I'm not in London 'cos I'm in Marrakesh.'

'Marrakesh? Wow. Cool.'

'No, not cool! Todd... I need your help.'

Will ran through the sequence of events.

'You're on the run, is that right?'

'Yeah, I'm on the frigging run!'

'Stay calm. That's the first thing. Get all psyched up and you're not going to think right. Now, it's clear what to do.'

'What, Todd? What do I do?'

Will sensed his legs shaking. He felt he might collapse. Stiffening his shoulder-blades, he tried to breathe deep.

'You got to go back to the house.'

'They're going to seal it though.'

'Then climb up the damn roof. You have to get back into that bedroom. Scope it out.'

'That the best you can come up with?'

'Will, this could be heavy. There's Interpol and all that stuff over there. Haven't you seen *Midnight Express*?!'

The line went dead.

'Hello? Hello? Todd, you there?!'

Will slammed the receiver back on its hook.

Go back to the bedroom? It was a crazy idea. Finding the house would be a challenge in itself. The old city was a labyrinth of interwoven streets. They all looked exactly the same.

Wiping his T-shirt up over his face, Will swore again. Todd's plan sucked, but he hadn't come up with anything better.

After an hour and a half of twists and turns, dodging shadows and people, he tracked down the house.

Circling around, he made his way to the street parallel to Dar Jnoun. Not daring to look if it was actually sealed, the door guarded by police, he used the last of his strength to climb up onto the back wall. In the honeycomb of Marrakesh one building formed part of the next.

Edging his way along, Will clambered across the roof terrace of an intermediate building. Then, clambering over a low rusted fence, he got access to Dar Jnoun.

Down below he could make out the sound of voices in the street. At the mosque opposite, the imam blew sharply on his microphone to test it, before launching into the call to prayer.

Having crawled in through an open window, Will found himself in a guest bedroom, Emma's room.

Apprehensively, he neared the bed.

But the manservant's body was missing.

The blood on the sheets had oxidised, darkening, having seeped through the linen's weave.

Will stared incredulously at the uneven oval patch of blood. Little by little, he heard a voice in his mind.

'You have to think! Come on! Really think about this! Work out what happened!'

A flash of vivid memory.

He was sitting on his father's lap. They were at the beach and had been making sandcastles. Will's father drew his hands over his son's eyes.

'Always remember that you've got five senses,' he said in a tender voice. 'Never rely on your eyes. They tend to blinker you to what's real. Don't trust them.' Will felt the warmth of his father's fingers draw down over his face.

'Let your senses speak to me.'

Will wriggled and giggled.

'I can smell the ocean, Daddy,' he said. 'On my tongue I can taste the salt on the wind.'

'And what do you hear?'

'The gulls, I hear the gulls, Daddy.'

Scanning the bedroom, Will took in the Tiger Moth's propeller. Even from a distance, he could smell its wax polish. He ran a hand over the dresser, felt the dust on his fingertips.

He turned towards the bed again.

Just then, there was the sound of footsteps coming up the tiled stairs. They were moving slowly, as if framed in caution.

Grabbing a lead paperweight, Will hid behind the door next to the campaign desk. Holding it high, he braced himself, like a caveman about to strike a foe.

A shadow entered, followed by the form of a man.

Will couldn't see him yet, but he could smell him.

The scent of sandalwood.

His fingers tensing around the weapon, he clenched his teeth.

Calmly, the figure shut the door, exposing him in his hiding place.

It was Chaudhury.

Although drenched in blood, he was quite alive.

The manservant burst out laughing.

Will jabbed the paperweight towards Chaudhury's face.

'Tell me, you frigging weirdo! Tell me what's going on!'

Chaudhury was laughing so hard he couldn't speak.

'A little game,' he said, wiping away tears.

'A game? A frigging game?!'

'Indeed, sir.'

Twenty-six

'MR FOGG WAS MOST explicit,' said Chaudhury when they were downstairs. 'After your arrival, you were to be welcomed with an "Event".'

'*An Event?*'

'Yes sir, an Event.'

Will looked at Emma, who had just returned from the bakery with a clutch of hot round loaves paid for with money lent by Chaudhury.

'Did you know about this?'

She shook her head, confused why the Indian manservant was drenched in blood.

Exiting the salon, Chaudhury returned with an envelope and a miniature brass box.

'Following the Event, Mr Fogg left instructions for you to be given these.'

In the box Will found a ring with a lapis lazuli face. Across the stone's dark blue surface was cut a symbol — a rectangle bisected by a line. On the underside was a monogram comprising the letters 'HF'. Will remembered seeing it on the cutlery.

Emma jabbed a thumb at the ring's upper surface.

'Egyptian,' she said with certainty. 'That hieroglyph means "house".'

Will was impressed.

'You read hieroglyphs, too?'

'A few of them. I'm more fluent in hieratic.'

Will slipped the ring on. A perfect fit.

Emma cocked her head at Chaudhury's hand.

'Aren't you going to open the envelope? Maybe there's an explanation.'

Will looked at the front, where the address is normally

written. In green cursive script was his name, the 'W'
larger and more flamboyant than the other letters.

He ripped it open.

Inside there was no letter.

There was nothing at all, except for a postage stamp.

A pleasing shade of light blue, it bore the aged profile
of Benjamin Franklin.

Tapping it out on the palm of his hand, he examined
it hard.

'Oh my God!' he bellowed once and then again.

'What? What is it?' asked Emma.

'It's a Z-Grill.'

'A *what*?'

'The Holy Grail of postage stamps.'

Twenty-seven

1891

THE SCREAM OF PEACOCKS echoed through the grounds
of the Grand Palace, Bangkok, and was especially ear-
splitting in the East Wing, in which Hannibal had been
accommodated.

Finding the Siamese taste rather florid, he preferred
the solid robust lines of English-cut wood. For this
reason, he had asked the household chamberlain to allow
him to decorate the apartment with his own campaign
furniture, which had accompanied him on the expedition.

The journey had, by any standards, been hard going. Fifty men had perished from malaria, and half as many again from typhoid. One night a barque had overturned in a storm, drowning eleven more.

Hannibal himself had succumbed to sickness. Despite his formidable stamina, he had gone down with dengue fever and, at times, was close to death. He only recovered after downing an experimental tonic prepared from an extract of sacred lotus seeds.

Although there had been considerable loss of life, the mission was regarded as a resounding success, and King Rama V was beside himself with delight.

The idea of engaging a young and fearless Englishman to spy on the French had been one inspired by genius — a ruse for which the monarch took full credit. As he saw it, who better to understand the ways of Gallic chicanery than their own historical foe?

King Rama had heard a great deal about a young Englishman seemingly perfect for the undertaking — Hannibal Fogg.

The explorer was writing up his journals when the small muscular hand of an equerry rapped at the door.

'Come in.'

The servant entered, bowed, then saluted.

'His Majesty will receive you in the throne room, sir.'

Ten minutes later, Hannibal was standing alone with the King.

The monarch had ordered his advisers and the

retinue of military staff, courtiers and hangers on, to leave and not return until he called for them directly.

'My dear Mr Fogg,' said King Rama warmly when the last of the sycophants had exited. 'Nothing gives me greater pleasure than to receive you after such a triumphant success!'

Hannibal bowed deep and long. His head still dipped in subservience, he cleared his throat.

'And nothing gives me such delight, Your Majesty, as to be in your kingdom,' he said. 'Thank God the mission was successful.'

King Rama V grinned.

'My government and all my people are in your debt,' he replied. Glancing down at the floor, he sighed, before returning his gaze to Hannibal's face. 'These are trying times,' he remarked slowly. 'There's far too much talk of democracy, and Europe's rattling its sabres in — as you say — our neck of the woods.'

'At your service, Your Majesty.'

The monarch pressed a fingertip to the slim moustache tracing the curve of his upper lip.

'You are most kind,' he said. 'And it is me who has forgotten my manners. I did not thank you for the exquisite desk, which I have had placed in the library. One day I hope to learn the secret of opening it!'

Both men laughed.

King Rama stepped over to an antique writing table, walnut veneer with ormolu fittings. He picked a presentation box from its polished surface.

'In Siamese culture we have a tradition,' he said, 'When someone has faced hardship, they are rewarded with two precious gifts. One for the body and the other for the mind. So, I have a pair of small presentations for you.'

Standing tall, Hannibal straightened his back.

'The first,' said the King, opening the box, 'is awarded on behalf of my kingdom, and it is for you to wear — *The Most Exalted Order of the White Elephant*.' King Rama pinned the medal to Hannibal's chest. 'As for the second gift — it is a personal one from me.'

The monarch took an envelope from the walnut veneer and passed it to Hannibal Fogg. It was addressed simply:

His Majesty King Rama V, Siam

'It is a letter which I believe will interest and amuse you, written to me by my childhood governess,' said King Rama. 'An Englishwoman, named Anna. I received it in the weeks after my father's death. It reached me by way of America — a long and intriguing journey in itself.'

Hannibal Fogg looked at the envelope, his eyes feasting on the copperplate script. In the top right corner, glued in a line, were three postage stamps.

Two were cochineal red.

The third, light blue, bore the profile of an aged Benjamin Franklin.

Twenty-eight

THERE WAS NO NEED for Will to Google it. Every stamp collector on the face of the earth knew the legend of the Z-Grill.

'It was issued in 1868,' he explained as Emma listened in the courtyard's shade. 'There are only two known examples. Even though its face value is just one cent, the Z-Grill's worth a fortune.'

'How much?'

'The last one traded was exchanged for four stamps valued at about three million.'

'Three million bucks, for that tiny speck of paper?!'

'I know. It's incredible. But I don't understand how Hannibal would have known.'

'How he'd have known *what*?'

'That giving me a Z-Grill is like giving a Ferrari to anyone else. It's the coolest thing.'

Emma smoothed a hand back over her hair.

'So what are you going to do now?'

'Huh?'

'Well, now you've got the house and the stamp, what are you gonna do?'

'Cash in,' said Will. 'I'm going to cash in.'

AT FIVE THAT AFTERNOON, Chaudhury was in the kitchen polishing the brass. He was wearing a butler's apron, his shirt sleeves rolled up. There was a knock at the front door. The manservant bustled through to the entryway. But Will had already received the visitor — a shabby local man with a clipboard, bad breath, and fingers stained yellow with nicotine.

'I'll show you around,' he said purposefully.

The visitor walked slowly with a limp, taking in the rooms, one at a time.

'With the furniture?' he asked.

'Yes, the paintings, too. As I told you — the house and all its contents — *everything*.'

The estate agent cleared his throat.

'I can certainly assist you,' he said, trying to mask his greed.

'How much for it all?'

'Alas, sir, prices are not what they were,' the agent mumbled.

'So make me an offer I can't refuse,' Will replied.

A nicotine-stained fingertip touched the chin in thought.

'A hundred thousand dollars, give or take.'

'I'll think about it,' said Will.

At that moment Chaudhury emerged into the courtyard where they were standing. Clutching an orange polishing cloth, he seemed rattled, as though a catastrophe were about to take place.

Caustically, he enquired whether tea ought to be served.

Will shook his head. The agent handed over a grubby

business card and limped away.

'I'm going to sell this house next week,' said Will firmly when Chaudhury and he were alone.

The servant's face was taut, like a balloon stretched to full capacity. It seemed as though he might be about to weep.

'Very good, sir,' he said stiffly, inhaling through his nose.

Will touched the palms of his hands together awkwardly.

'As I'm selling the house, I no longer have any use for a butler, or any ancestral stuff, or staff.' He swallowed hard. 'What I am saying is that you're free to leave… to go back to your palace in India.'

In silence, Chaudhury tugged a perfectly pressed handkerchief from his pocket and dabbed a nostril. Without a word, he strode away in the direction of the kitchen.

Out in the lane there came the clamour of two dogs brawling, and the cries of a man selling river fish from a bucket. Will went into the salon and slumped into an old club chair. He was waiting for Emma to come back. She had gone to collect funds wired from her bank back home.

The morning's Event had left Will washed over with a sense of dread and fear, as if he were not safe. There had been highs and lows of emotion: the terror of the Event, followed by the elation of the Z-Grill.

Casting an eye across the sitting room, he wondered whether it was right to get rid of Hannibal's stuff. Of course it was. Look at it, he thought, it's a load of old junk. In any case, there was no way he could lug it all back to the States. Most of it was too big for a dorm room, and not the kind of stuff anyone needed.

Take the roll-top desk — it could sink a ship. Besides, it didn't even open.

Huffing with curiosity, Will got to his feet and strode over to the desk. There had to be a catch somewhere. He ran a hand over the sill, as he had done before. Nothing there. Did the same on the sides and on the top. Still nothing. Then, stooping down, he observed the grain. It was uniform, well polished, a masterpiece of joinery.

But wait a minute.

On the left side a square inch of wood had a different grain. Unlike the rest of the desk, which was oak, it was crafted from rosewood.

Using his knuckle, Will jabbed out the peg.

It fell onto the floor, leaving a tubular hole. Picking it up, he noticed a series of deep grooves on the peg's lower edge, like notches in a key.

That was it.

Instinctively, Will turned the peg round and inserted it back into the hole.

He pushed hard.

Click.

The desk's slatted cover flipped open, and rolled

back automatically, powered by a system of gears and lead weights.

Inside, revealed for the first time in many decades, was Hannibal's writing desk, cluttered with papers, notes and a dozen fountain pens.

Written on a card in Hannibal's hand, and pinned in a prominent place, was a phrase in Latin:

A caecus vir per videlicet os.

A coincidence, Will thought, as the maxim had been the motto of his school, the only high school he knew with a Latin proverb — 'A blind man sees with the sharpest sight'. But then, Will was unaware that coincidence didn't exist in the world of Hannibal Fogg.

He shuffled through the papers, a few of the envelopes, and examined the pens. All the nibs were narrow — except for one which was extra-wide. They were iridium-tipped gold, designed by Hannibal himself along the lines of the Romanian inventor Petrache Poenaru.

Unlike the other possessions at Dar Jnoun, the desk was shadowed by a sense of the ordinary. Yet, it was while seated there that Hannibal had conjured the extraordinary.

On the left-hand side of the blotter was a row of tiny drawers, with a locking system of their own. Will worked out how it worked, pleased he was learning to think like his ancestor.

In the middle drawer, no bigger than a pack of playing

cards, he came across a rectangular brass strip. Turning it into the light, it seemed to resemble a primitive credit card. In one corner, a motif was hammered into it, along with an uneven circular hole.

The motif caught Will's attention: the same symbol as on the lapis lazuli ring, the hieroglyph for the word 'house'.

His mind racing, Will came up with various connections, dismissing them each in turn, before hurrying up the stairs, the brass strip in his hand. Once in Hannibal's bedroom, he strode over to the rug, tugged back the corner and looked at the trapdoor.

There it was, the reverse curve of the ring's bezel... and, beside it, a slot.

Without being sure how he knew to do it, Will slipped off the ring and eased the bezel into the hole, aligning them. Almost as an afterthought, he urged the brass strip into the slot.

Nothing happened.

Will imagined Hannibal looking down at him, disappointed.

He went back downstairs and sat in the courtyard, the sequence of events turning over in his mind. There seemed no doubt that the ring and the brass strip were the solution — or at least part of it.

The hours passed, and Will sat there, the scent of orange blossom heavy in the air. All he could think of was how Hannibal would have devised the lock to work.

What was certain was that, however elaborate, it relied on a mechanical system.

Chaudhury swanned through from time to time, offering refreshments and single lines of polished wit. As the sun dipped down below the medina, he cursed his cheap digital watch.

Will looked up.

'I've noticed my iPhone loses time here, too,' he said. 'It doesn't make sense.'

The manservant leaned down to Will's ear.

'I blame the magnetic field, sir,' he whispered conspiratorially.

'What field?'

'The one in the walls, sir.'

'Don't think I understand.'

When Chaudhury had gone through to the kitchen, Will found himself thinking of magnetism, electricity and locks. Taking out his iPhone he toyed with it, his mind proposing solutions and dismissing them one by one.

Something struck him — an idea.

Opening the App Store, he found a magnetometer, downloaded it and went back upstairs to Hannibal's bedroom.

Placing the iPhone beside the trap door, he watched as the app registered an immense force, the digital needle burying itself in the red.

The app featured a magnetic reduction setting.

Giving it a go, Will pressed the button and watched the needle retreat, as the magnetic field reduced.

There was a loud twanging sound.

Propelled by clockwork, a brass gear mechanism spun out from the trapdoor.

Before he could react, the device snatched Will's wrist.

'What the hell?!'

He struggled to get free, but the more he struggled, the more the clamp took hold, ratcheting itself tight.

'Chaudhury! Chaudhury!' he yelled. 'Get in here! Help me, quick!'

But the manservant didn't come.

What looked like a steel proboscis fitted with an oversized hypodermic, shot from the mechanism. Will watched in horror as the needle approached. His face streaming with sweat, he wrestled to get free.

The needle pricked a vein on the back of his hand, then retracted. Will struggled all the more. He was ready to leave the house, Chaudhury and Hannibal Fogg right then.

Uncertain of exactly what was going on, it seemed to him as though the mechanism had taken a sample of his blood. The dull sound of a clockwork escapement turning over was accompanied by the stench of ammonia.

A flap slid back on the upper surface of the trapdoor.

Exposing a display panel, it revealed a string of numbers, like an old-fashioned slot machine. Spinning

114

one at a time, the rotors spat out a numerical string:
1-4-7-3-8-9-2-3.

A grinding noise came and went, then the smell of
crushed garlic.

A bell chimed three times.

The mechanism released Will's wrist.

The bell chimed again, then the trapdoor flew back.

Stupefied, Will craned forward.

There were steps leading down.

Twenty-nine

ON NIGHTS WHEN HE couldn't sleep, Will would go to
the window of his dorm room and stare out at the dark.
A group of local kids had smashed the street lamps years
before. Every time they were fixed, they were instantly
smashed again. In the end, the city didn't bother with
repairs. Someone with a pencil behind his ear in City
Hall figured he would wait for the kids to grow up
and move on to other things. He didn't count on one
generation of wayward boys replacing the last.

Suffering from insomnia brought on by the worry
of midterms, Will would stare out at the dark. At the
beginning, it terrified him. He would stand there, his
face an inch from the glass pane, his eyes shielded with a
hand. But, as the months passed, he learned to control a
fear of what he didn't know or understand.

One night in his senior year, he clambered from the bed, pulled back the curtain and gazed out at the black.

It didn't scare him any longer.

Fumbling for his iPhone, Will checked the time.

It was a little after four.

Slipping on his bathrobe, he went out into the dorm's corridor, and forced down the bar on the escape door.

One push and he was outside, alone at night — and for the first time he was comfortable with it.

From that moment, Will understood that fear was something he could control. The secret was confronting it face on.

The dorm room and the smashed street lights were a million miles from Marrakesh. But the conquest of fear was something unconnected to place or time. It was hardwired into his psyche.

Peering down into the black, Will sensed a stream of cool air spilling out from the hole.

Gritting his teeth, he lowered his right foot onto the first tread, and climbed down.

The steps had been finished in concrete rather than glazed tiles as elsewhere at Dar Jnoun. They ended in an expanse of black.

Will's eyes slowly adjusted to the lack of light. As they did so, the black melted into grey.

Squinting, Will edged forward.

His hand brushed against something, a cord with a frayed tassel at the end. He tugged it.

A row of ceiling lights flashed on, bathing the secret room with wonder.

Elongated, rectangular and windowless, it was lined with rows of magnificent glass-fronted cabinets each one fashioned from teak. But it wasn't the wood or craftsmanship that caught Will's attention.

Rather, it was their contents.

On either side, the cabinets ran down the length of the room. In the space between them was a long refectory table. Hanging above it, suspended by cord, hung a birch-bark canoe, the bow adorned with Hannibal's monogram.

Glancing back at the stairs, Will checked the trapdoor was still open. Then, wiping the dust from his eyes, he stepped forward to examine the first glass-fronted cabinet.

It was filled with tribal skulls, arranged in order of size. There must have been eighty of them at least. Some were trepanned; others were missing their lower jaws or upper teeth.

Will couldn't take his eyes off them.

He noticed that each skull had been labelled with a miniature tag, a date and the name of a location. With care, he opened the cabinet's glass door, and examined one of the labels. On the reverse, he found a reference number, in faded green fountain pen ink. One of the skulls stood out as particularly fine. None of the teeth were missing and it appeared to have been lacquered.

The label bore the words *Ceylon 1907*, and a number — *0371*.

The second cabinet was taller than the first. Displayed inside was an arrangement of tribal masks. Some were ornate, fashioned from iron overlaid with silver or gold. Others had haunting features, and were sculpted from ebony and walnut wood.

A third cabinet contained Hannibal's collection of penis sheaths. A decade before the Great War he had acquired them on an expedition through the highlands of New Guinea. Prizing the collection almost beyond anything else, he had cornered the local market in an ornamental variety, known to scholars as 'phallocrypts'. Such was Hannibal's interest in the tradition that in 1920 he had published a concise monograph entitled *Penis Sheaths of Oceania*. A copy was displayed in the cabinet along with the collection, bound in lizard-green leather.

Beyond it there were six more cabinets filled with fossils, many of them ammonites. On the other side of the chamber was a very large cabinet. Extremely wide, it was illuminated by a series of electric lamps set into the back. Contained inside were rows of glass bell jars — each one home to medical samples preserved in clear liquid. Some of the jars contained internal organs, segments of human brain, and a variety of growths excised during surgery.

On the adjacent wall, arranged on a set of plain shelves,

was a collection of brass astrolabes, laid out in rows of nine. Below them was an assortment of magical Arab amulets, and a series of bizarre talismanic undershirts — worn beneath Saracen armour during the Crusades.

Will paced the length of the room, taking in the artifacts one by one. As he progressed from cabinet to cabinet, he found himself mesmerised by the idea of Hannibal Fogg. The cabinets of curiosity revealed far more about his ancestor than the house itself had done.

Gradually Will's attention moved from the cabinets, down onto the table. Unlike the order of the collections, it was haphazard, as though abandoned in haste.

The surface was strewn with notebooks, with scientific apparatus, mineral samples, all sorts of curious equipment, and with piles of neatly squared reference books. Casting an eye over it all, Will got a sense that great breakthroughs in science had been made right there.

As with everything else in the room, the table was entombed in decades of dust. Will ran a fingertip through it and, without thinking, he drew the HF monogram.

He was about to turn round towards the steps, when something caught his eye.

An ordinary desk calendar, the kind that's set each day — day of the week, month and year. The strange thing was that the date was set at Saturday 6th May 2017.

Will let out a groan.

'Chaudhury!'

Pivoting round on his heel, he ran up the stairs and

down to the kitchen, where the manservant was cleaning the fanlight.

'Why didn't you tell me?' Will asked accusingly.

'Excuse me, sir?'

'Why didn't you tell me about the trapdoor... about the museum?'

Lowering the cloth, Chaudhury brushed a knuckle over his nose.

'I must inform you most respectfully that I have no idea about what you are speaking, sir.'

'The room upstairs... the one filled with all that weird tribal stuff?'

The manservant climbed down from the chair on which he had been standing.

'Would you show me?' he said.

Will led the way up into the bedroom, and down through the trapdoor.

'My God,' Chaudhury said in a whisper, as he descended the steps. 'I have spent half of my life in this house, and I never knew this was here.'

'But why was it opened for me?'

'Because you are the bloodline of Mr Fogg,' said the servant. 'The price of entry is the knowledge to know.'

'To know what?'

'To know how.'

Chaudhury untied his butler's apron, allowing the straps to flop down to the sides.

As he did so, Will closed his eyes, thought for a

moment, and slowly opened them again.

'Tell me something.'

'Yes, sir?'

'Do you think there's other wacky stuff in this house waiting to be found?'

'*Wacky*, sir?'

'You know, other secret rooms filled with crazy old junk?'

Chaudhury's back stiffened.

'Nothing in the least would surprise me, sir,' he replied. 'After all, this was the home of Hannibal Fogg.'

Thirty

1877

THE WINDOWS WERE OPEN to the garden, where a pair of little girls were running the length of the herbaceous border trailing home-made kites.

Hannibal's sisters, Victoria and Laetitia, were dressed in identical cotton dresses, the hems skimming over the newly mown grass.

At a makeshift workbench up in his bedroom, Hannibal was attending to far more pressing matters than kite flying. He was half way through dissecting a pregnant female rat. The gardener had brought her in from the stables, having whopped her over the head with a spade.

Standing before him, shiny and black, was a child's microscope with interchangeable lenses. A gift from his father, it had been presented the week before, on Hannibal's ninth birthday. Painted in capital letters on the viewing stem were the letters, H. F.

A few inches away, spattered in rat blood, lay a notebook. It was open at a partial yet neat diagram of the creature's abdomen.

With the tip of his scalpel Hannibal removed the rat's right kidney, sliced a fine segment and transferred it onto the glass slide. Peering down the tube, he eased the wheel until the segment was in sharp focus.

All afternoon he worked away at a detailed illustration of what he had seen under the lens, labelling the various parts using their Latin names.

Outside, the sound of his sisters was getting louder. They would soon be in for tea, or to beg their beloved older brother to amaze them with one of his inventions.

Grimacing at the thought of being distracted, Hannibal peered once again into the viewing tube.

As he turned the focus wheel, a bee flew in and stung him on the face.

Without flinching, he drew out the sting with his fingernails and placed it on a glass slide. Then, turning to a fresh page in his notebook, he applied his left eye to the viewing tube again.

Thirty-one

EMMA RETURNED TO DAR Jnoun a little later, her expression sullen.

'I've spent the last three hours trying to get the cash that was supposedly wired from my account in the States,' she said. 'But for some mysterious reason my account's been frozen.'

'Why?'

'Don't know.' Emma touched a hand to her nose, blinked, and a lone tear rolled straight down her cheek. 'Not going crawling to my parents,' she said. 'Can't stand the thought of yet another "I-told-you-so" lecture.'

Will stepped up close.

'Stay here for as long as you like,' he said. 'It'll all work out — it always does.'

'I don't deserve your kindness, really I don't.'

Will clapped his hands.

'You've got to see something!'

'What?'

'The last thing you'd ever expect.'

He led Emma down through the trapdoor, into Hannibal's secret study.

Together, they explored the room, pointing out individual objects to one another.

'Look at this feather mask,' said Will, squinting to make out the label. '*Peruvian Amazon, 1904*. How cool is that?'

'Not as cool as this!' Emma's finger pointed at something in the next cabinet.

'What?'

'*That!*'

Inside, suspended on invisible fishing twine were five shrunken human heads. Tiny miniaturised faces, each one set against a backdrop of long black hair.

'I've heard about these,' Will said.

'They're called *tsantsas*,' replied Emma knowledgeably, 'the work of the Shuar tribe of the Upper Amazon. They shrank the heads of their enemies as a way of placating the avenging soul. Although they never regarded the heads as specially important, they became something of a curiosity when brought to the outside world.'

Will looked at Emma dubiously.

'How d'you know all that?'

'Wikipedia,' she said. 'It's an addiction.'

Will moved over to the opposite wall.

Standing on a varnished plinth between two of the display cabinets was a child's microscope. Will stepped round the table to get to it.

'Look…' he said. 'Those are Hannibal's initials on the front.'

Emma said something. She was at the far end of the room. Will didn't hear or, if he did, he didn't reply.

'There's something going on here,' he said absently.

'Huh?'

'I said, there's something going on. I don't know what. But it's about me being here, in his home.'

Emma shrugged.

'How do you mean?'

'It's as if everything's been carefully prearranged and primed.' Will's expression froze. He swallowed hard. 'This sounds nuts but I'm getting a sense that Hannibal's trying to communicate something to me.'

'*Like?*'

'Like something he couldn't just have written down and left in a letter on the mantel.'

Taking the envelope from his pocket, Will tapped the Z-Grill onto his palm. He scrutinised it with care.

Then, taking the microscope down from the plinth, he slipped the stamp onto the slide, angled the mirror up towards the light.

'It's perfect,' he said.

'What is?'

'The grill's intact.'

'What does that mean?'

'That I'm a zillionaire.'

Shuddering, Will pulled his eye away from the viewing tube.

'But it isn't about that,' he said.

'About what?'

'About money.'

Emma didn't follow.

'It's about something else.'

Turning, Will scanned the cabinets. His eyes moved fast over canopic jars from ancient Egypt, porcelain figurines, and onto an arrangement of life-size marble busts.

'Who are they?'

Emma read out the plaques beneath each one.

'Faraday, da Vinci, Michelangelo and Franklin.'

'*Franklin*… as on the Z-Grill.'

Rushing over, Will grabbed the last bust by the neck, flipping it upside down.

Chiselled into the bottom was an inscription.

'*Fatigue is the best pillow.*'

'What d'you think that means?'

'That you sleep better when you're tired?'

Will looked around the room.

To the left of the stairs, he spied a small square water-colour. Hung in a plain frame, it featured a shepherd resting in the meadow, circled by his flock. The shepherd's head was lying on a pillow — a pillow made of thorns.

Lifting the picture from its hook, he paced back into the light, turning it over.

Nothing unusual.

Nothing except that a strand of scarlet thread was dangling from the lining.

A sharp tug and the frame came away, revealing an envelope, the wax seal stamped with Hannibal's monogram.

His fingertips moist with anticipation, Will broke the seal and removed a sheet of folded paper.

He opened it out.

'It's a letter,' he said. 'A letter from Hannibal.'

Flabbergasted, Emma threw up her arms.

'Gonna try and tell me you just worked all that out?'

Will scratched his head.

'He thinks just like I do,' he said.

Thirty-two

26th September 1939

My dear William,

I cannot imagine what you think of me behaving in such a cloak and dagger fashion.

Yet if you are reading this message, I hope that I may assume correctly you have followed the stepping stones I have laid for you.

Forgive me, but it is not possible to be as transparent as I should like. You must understand that we are connected together not only by blood but by a thread of danger. Time is short, and so I shall do my best to illuminate the situation. It is my earnest hope that you will come to comprehend the dilemma that faces us both.

During my life, I have become involved in a certain project — one that is of extreme importance not to myself alone, but to all humanity. Due to various intractable circumstances, it is not possible for me to complete the duty to which I have devoted a lifetime as have other members of our family before me.

The resulting situation will lead to the discrediting of my life's work, and the confiscation of the Fogg family fortunes. I can only imagine how your father, your grandfather, and my own son, will suffer. But by the time you read this, the present will be the distant past. They will have endured terrible anguish, each of them believing me to be a traitor and a failure, at least in their eyes.

Unfortunately, there was no way for me to defend myself or our possessions at the time, so great was the fear of infernal calamity.

But, now the window of opportunity has almost approached. I promise you, my dear William, that if you can muster the courage to trust me, I shall not let you down. I am here to assist you in restoring our ancestral fortunes and, by doing so, to clear my own name.

I ask that you take your time and regard the illumination of my home with clarity, allowing the mission I have left for you to emerge.

With my affection always,
Hannibal G. Fogg

Thirty-three

WILL FOLLOWED CHAUDHURY THROUGH Dar Jnoun, urging him to remember anything of importance.

'You've lived here for years,' he said, an undertone of annoyance in his voice. 'So you must know what Hannibal was talking about.'

The manservant didn't reply. Instead, he went about his chores, raising an eyebrow testily once his back was turned.

Emma read the letter again.

'Like he says — it's cloak and dagger.'

'You mean theatrical innuendo?'

'Look at this... it's got to be the key line... "Take your time and regard the illumination of my home".'

'*Illumination of my home?*'

'Kind of a weird way to put it, right?'

'You think he meant the lights?'

'That'd be too easy.'

Will climbed on a chair, checked the chandeliers in each of the salons, and shrugged.

'What if he's referring to another meaning of "illumination".'

'As in the religious sense?'

'A divine presence...'

'Maybe.'

'But in what context?'

'An object?'

'This is ridiculous,' said Will. 'We could spend the rest of our lives trawling through this place. For God's sake, there's less stuff in the Smithsonian!'

Emma grinned.

'C'mon, let's at least have a look.'

Together they scoured the salons, unsure what exactly they were searching for. Will picked up a model lighthouse, examined it and shook his head. Then Emma found the porcelain figurine of an angel, a serial number etched into the base.

'It's kind of divine.'

'Too obvious.'

Will remembered something. A detail.

'When I was a kid,' he said, 'my great-aunts Edith and Helen used to take me to church on Sundays. It was a musty old place in Oakland. In that ragtag church, there was a Bible — the most beautiful thing I'd ever seen. I can still see it so clearly. The pages were all gilded and shiny.'

'*Illuminated*?'

Will nodded.

'An illuminated manuscript containing the word of God.'

'A Bible?'

Emma had already found one, lying on the coffee table. Two inches thick, it was bound in what looked like tanned lizard skin, with elaborate brass corners and a silver clasp.

Undoing the catch, she flipped back the cover.

'Who's Uriah Fogg?'

'Must be Hannibal's father.'

'This belonged to him.'

'The name's written in green ink.'

'So?'

'Hannibal's letter was in green, the same green.'

'So? Maybe they both liked green.'

Will wasn't listening.

'Uriah,' he said. 'He was in Samuel, wasn't he?'

Emma slipped him a smile.

'Never went to Sunday school.'

Will's fingers moved fast through the Old Testament, arriving at the Second Book of Samuel.

'Here it is…. Chapter Eleven, Verse Six: "So David sent this word to Joab: Send me Uriah the Hittite".'

'*And?*'

'Dunno. Unless…'

'Unless what?'

Will carried the Bible out into the courtyard, sneezed once and then again.

'It's covered in dust,' said Emma.

'That's what I'm looking at.'

'Huh?'

Will had noticed that where the dust had come into contact with the paper, it had been distributed unevenly. Something occurred to him. What if there was a message written over the text?

'You've got to excuse me for being a geek,' he said.

131

'I like your geekiness.'

'I really mean it. You have to forgive me, especially if this works, 'cos it's proof I'm a geek cum laude.'

Emma leant forward and touched his wrist with her hand. 'I forgive you for being a geek,' she whispered.

Will hurried up to Hannibal's bedroom. He had remembered the scent of ammonia on the trapdoor's mechanism. On further examination, he found the reason: a bottle of the strong-smelling liquid had been connected to the lock by a copper capillary pipe.

Unfastening the bottle, he hurried back downstairs and asked Emma to hold the Bible upside down. Then, having warmed the liquid in the bright sunlight, he held the bottle under the Second Book of Samuel, and released the stopper.

A minute slipped by.

Will nodded to Emma, prompting her to turn the Bible upright. She did so.

'My God,' she said. 'Without doubt, it's geek cum laude!'

Written over the passage about David and Uriah was a second text. It was in Hannibal's distinct hand, in faint green ink.

'Can you read it?'

'I'll have a go,' said Will, straining not only because of the script, but because at least a third of the words were unclear.

'It's talking about an octagonal motif,' he said,

'and explains that a whole comprises a mosaic of components. And here…'

'What?'

'This bit… It's saying something about a machine… a mechanism, "*The Alexander Mechanism*".'

Thirty-four

IT WAS EMMA WHO first sowed the seeds of doubt about Chaudhury.

'You know so little about him,' she said.

'But his family have served the Foggs for decades,' Will replied.

'How do you know that?'

'Because he told me.'

'And you believe it?'

'Yes, well, I guess so.'

'Why don't you do a little investigating?'

'Huh?'

'Have a look through his room.'

Waiting until Chaudhury went out to the vegetable market, Will strode through the kitchen and down the narrow corridor where he assumed the manservant's quarters to be.

At the far end, he found a pair of doors.

On the right was a small storeroom packed floor to ceiling with clutter and cleaning supplies. The other, much larger, was a bedroom.

Slipping inside, Will closed the door behind him.

Against the back wall stood a single bedstead crafted from brass. At the head was an elaborate crest, bearing a pair of tigers, crossed swords, and the words 'Cooch Behar'. The same motif was embroidered into the bedspread, which flowed down to touch the exquisite Persian carpet on the floor.

The walls were hung with oil portraits of Indian maharajas and with sepia prints of other Indian royalty. Tinged with the scent of mothballs, the bedroom was quite different from the other rooms, as though distinctly out of place.

Uncertain quite what he was searching for, Will went over to the desk, adjacent to the bed. Heaped with dismantled computers, programming manuals, hard drives and cables, it reminded Will of his own desk back at the dorm.

At one end, away from the equipment, he found a stack of leather-bound journals. Each one was packed with scribbled notes, diagrams and what looked like codes.

To the left of the desk stood a low table on which were arranged a dozen photographs, each in a solid silver frame bearing the same crest as the bed.

Will considered them one by one.

At least half were sepia, exhibiting yet more portraits of Indian royalty, replete with turbans, swords and medals. A few of the photos were far more recent —

colour shots of Chaudhury with his family. In one he was posing in the back of a convertible Bentley, a vast red brick palace looming up behind.

Against one wall was a tea crate, the royal crest of Cooch Behar stencilled onto the side. Lifting the lid cautiously, Will found it full of Indian foods and spices, along with a letter written in an unfamiliar script.

Perplexed at how a prince could have been pressed into working as a manservant in a distant land, Will stood there in confusion.

Emma's voice snatched him from his thoughts.

'He's coming!' she cried.

Opening the door, Will dived into the corridor and darted back to the kitchen. Panting, he pretended to be making tea for himself.

'I shall do it for you at once,' said Chaudhury politely, taking a silver teapot down from the shelf.

'Thank you,' said Will.

'You are very welcome, sir.'

Turning on his heel, Will was about to pace back through into the salon, when he stopped.

'Tell me about your home,' he said.

Chaudhury glanced in the direction of his bedroom.

'This is my home, sir,' he replied.

'No, your real home... the one in India.'

The manservant's expression eased into a smile.

'The Princely State of Cooch Behar,' he responded, a lump forming in his throat. 'It is a fragment of paradise.'

'Will you tell me about it?'

Chaudhury's eyes focussed vacantly on the teapot, but in his mind he saw Cooch Behar.

'I grew up in the Victor Jubilee Palace,' he said. 'A large home constructed by my ancestors. I've heard it said that it was based on Buckingham Palace. To some it may seem a little ostentatious, for there are hundreds of rooms — salons and studies, durbars, bed chambers, kitchens, games rooms, treasure vaults, stables...'

Will's eyes were wide.

'Don't you miss it?' he asked.

The manservant put the teapot on the counter and brushed a hand down the side of his nose.

'I have my ancestral obligation to fulfil, sir,' he said resolutely.

'But you must miss being there with your family.'

Chaudhury turned to face Will, his eyes glazed with tears.

'Nothing gives me more pleasure than discharging the duties expected of me here, sir,' he said.

Thirty-five

THE AFTERNOON MELTED INTO evening and the lane outside Dar Jnoun was filled with music: piercing Berber oboes, tambours, and great iron castanets, the kind favoured by the Gnaoua brotherhood of the Sahara.

'A wedding, sir,' said Chaudhury tersely, 'and that means we shall have no peace tonight.'

Emma and Will reclined in the courtyard, waiting for Chaudhury to announce another culinary delight from the days of the British Raj.

'I've got to work out what Hannibal meant,' said Will.

'Why?'

'Why what?'

'*Why* do you have to, to work it out?'

Will touched the side of a hand to his chin.

'For my great-aunts,' he said. 'I was raised by them, and for them there's nothing in life as important as clearing the family name.'

'Would I be wrong to say you're more drawn to regaining Hannibal's lost fortune than cleansing the blackened family name?'

Will frowned.

'That's a little harsh.'

'So what's the answer?'

'I suppose it's both... the money and the family name. A little more of one and a little less of the other.'

The drumming grew louder, until the clamour was so strident that Emma led Will up onto the top terrace, so they might glimpse the procession as it washed through the streets.

'There it is!' she called. '*Look*! There's the bride!'

They looked down just in time to see the bride borne forward at shoulder height, resplendent on a silver dais.

Whooping at the top of her lungs, Emma's voice hardly broke over the pandemonium below.

Edging along the terrace, they managed to keep the procession in sight until it slipped away down the lane.

'There's nothing like the smile on a bride's face!' Emma shrieked.

'That's strange…'

'A bride's smile?'

'No, the wall,' said Will, pointing downwards.

'Don't get what you mean.'

'Look down there. That's the wall of Dar Jnoun. Can't you see how it curves round to the right?'

'Yeah.'

'Well, that's the curve of the salon you're looking at. But see how the wall extends, way further, out to the left.'

Will paused.

'You don't get it, do you?'

'Not exactly, no.'

'We've missed something…'

Racing downstairs, Will tore through the reception rooms and out into the small vestibule at the back of the house. Set against the far wall was a grand teak armoire, the kind found in French chateaux.

'Give me a hand,' said Will, forcing his shoulder against it.

Together they heaved, moving the vast piece of furniture away, just far enough to peer behind.

Where the armoire had stood for decades was a

doorway.

'Oh my God,' said Emma.

Chaudhury appeared, summoned by the commotion. He seemed as surprised as them at the discovery of yet another secret room.

Will was about to grasp the handle, when he remembered what happened with the trapdoor.

'I'll do it,' said Emma firmly.

Anxiously, Will looked her in the eye.

'*No*! It's got to be me,' he said.

Reaching out, his fingers touched the brass handle, their skin sensing the chill of the metal. This time, there was no sound of a mechanism, nor was there a needle.

The door wasn't even locked. Opening easily, it creaked back on its hinges, swinging out in an arc.

Will went first, followed by Emma and then Chaudhury.

Inside they found a second marvel from the world of Hannibal Fogg:

A magnificent galleried library, cedarwood shelves rising floor to ceiling — each shelf packed tight with books.

Bound uniformly in lizard-green leather, the volumes were arranged by subject and classified according to Hannibal's own system. There were sections devoted to topography and history, to mathematics, technology, languages, miscellaneous matters, and the occult.

The room must have been thirty feet high, the ceiling

shrouded in a coarse billowing fabric, giving the effect of a Bedouin tent.

As with Hannibal's study, the library was thick with dust, having presumably been left untouched since before the explorer disappeared in Manchuria back in '39.

'Look how the walls are angled,' said Emma. 'It's an octagon.'

Will swivelled a full three-sixty.

'You're right,' he said.

'You hardly notice it because of the shelves.'

'The octagonal motif mentioned in the Bible?' Will mumbled. 'Could it be this?'

Emma shrugged.

'It doesn't follow.'

'Why not?'

'If Hannibal had expected you to discover the library, surely he'd have thrown you something a little more obvious. After all, there's no way of knowing it's an octagon from the outside.'

Will crossed the room, pausing at the shelves devoted to the occult. At chest height, he found a series of books by the Satanist Aleister Crowley. The leather spines were a little darker than the rest.

Almost without thinking, he pulled out the volume with the most discolouration along the spine — *The Stratagem and Other Stories*.

Slipping a hand in the space where the book had lain undisturbed for so long, he tugged at something —

a cross between a lever and a switch.

The library's parquet floor opened up, like the aperture of a camera's lens, the hole widening.

Will and Emma looked in.

A steep flight of stone stairs led down.

'How the hell did you know that was there?' asked Emma in amazement.

Will breathed in hard.

'You'd never believe me if I told you.'

'Try me.'

He shook his head.

'Some secrets are better kept as secrets,' he said.

One at a time the three of them stepped down the steps.

Below the library they found a huge armoury.

There were two-handed Crusader swords, slender sabres and rapiers, boxed duelling pistols and crossbows, lances, bayonets, and even a rack of blunderbusses. As well as arms, there was armour: Gladiator breastplates and helmets adorned with plumage, Persian chain-mail, and Gothic silver plate.

'You could outfit an army with all this,' said Will uneasily. 'Look at the blade on this knife. Sharp as a cutthroat razor.'

'Watered steel,' said Emma, 'it holds an edge like nothing else.'

'Sounds like you know your knives.'

Pursing her lips, Emma swallowed.

'I've got brothers,' she said, 'brothers who aren't geeks.'

Thirty-six

1889

HASHIM, THE SON OF Abdul-Azim, was snoring on a chaise longue upholstered in threadbare calico, in a patch of syrupy winter sunlight at the front of his shop.

Lids drawn heavily over his eyes, the cheeks below them a spider's web of creases. Like every other shopkeeper in Damascus, he was sleeping off a fatty mutton lunch, dreaming of the day when he could retire.

On his lap was nestled a tabby kitten the colour of river sand and, on his feet, were a pair of shabby cavalry boots. They had been left to him by his brother on the day he was hanged.

Sprawling out behind the shopkeeper was a treasury gained from forty years of bartering, theft and mendacity. As far as Hashim was concerned, devious methods were merely the dark side of an honourable trade.

The shop was cavernous by any standards, every inch of it packed tight with a jamboree of loot: crusader battle standards blackened by fire, tortoiseshell jewel boxes, Qur'an stands carved from solid blocks of ebony, golden epaulettes and chamber pots, Andalusian fountainheads in bronze, silver bedsteads, medieval astrolabes, fabulous Mamluk mosque lamps in glass, and row upon row of bull elephant tusks.

The cool shadow of a customer inched over Hashim's face. Opening an eye, the shopkeeper jerked upright, the kitten tumbling to the floor.

'Oh great Sharif!' he crooned. 'What a great pleasure to have my humble emporium graced by your illustrious presence!'

Dressed in Arab robes, the customer was in actual fact an Englishman — the renowned soldier, linguist and traveller, Sir Richard Francis Burton.

He regarded the shopkeeper with disdain, his upper lip furled back as if he were about to spit out a rebuke.

'Your message reached my ears,' he said, drawing a hand down over the scar below his eye. 'If you are wasting my time, I shall have you taken out and thrashed.'

Hashim, the son of Abdul-Azim, clambered off the chaise longue, the soles of his riding boots kicking up the dust.

'Believe me, O Magnificence,' he fawned, squirming to conjure an appropriate compliment, 'I would never dare to be so discourteous as to waste a single fragment of your time.'

Making fists of his hands, Burton snarled.

'Show it to me, without delay!'

The shopkeeper shooed the kitten away from his heels.

Stepping over to the steel safe, he opened it and removed an object wrapped in a turquoise cloth.

Touching it to his lips, he held it out at arm's length.

'Here it is, Sidi,' he whispered, his head lowering.

Captain Burton unwrapped the cloth and caressed

the small marble tablet. Turning it towards the doorway, he inspected the inscription.

'It was found at Palmyra,' Hashim crowed, 'by the widower of an English lady.'

'Was it Lady Digby by any chance?'

'I believe so, O wise and benevolent Sharif.'

Burton sighed.

'We were well acquainted,' he said in a mumble, tilting the tablet into the light. 'My wife and I often dined in her home.'

'Was her salon not octagonal?' the shopkeeper asked.

'Indeed it was. Most celebrated and extraordinary.'

Lost in memory, Burton stared into the bric-a-brac for a moment. Grunting aggressively, he shook the tablet.

'How much do you want for it?'

Hashim fawned even more obsequiously than usual.

'A hundred guineas.'

'Hah!'

Trade hadn't been good of late, of which both shopkeeper and customer were well aware.

'I'll give you twenty,' said Burton. 'And if you ask for any more, I shall halve it to ten.'

THE FOLLOWING AFTERNOON A young man arrived at the Burtons' home. In his hand was a soiled envelope, bearing a letter of introduction.

Received by a manservant, a Copt from Alexandria, he was asked to wait until the document had been presented to the master of the house.

After fifteen minutes of staring down at the inter-locking weave of a hand-knotted Persian rug, he heard a gruff voice growling an order.

The servant hurried back to the antechamber.

'Sir Richard will see you now, Mr Fogg.'

Hannibal followed the attendant through a slender corridor lined with aspidistra plants on terracotta stands, into a salon. His father, Uriah Fogg, had known Burton since childhood. Hannibal himself had always longed to meet the man he regarded as a hero.

Striding briskly through the central reception room, his pulse quickening with anticipation, he took in the treasure trove of oddities.

He was soon out on the terrace.

Burton was reclining in a planter's chair, his left hand cupped round the silver knob of a malacca. The great explorer was just as Hannibal had imagined him — a lion, albeit one whose roar had been tempered by age.

'Sit here beside me.'

Hannibal pulled up a chair.

'I have read everything you have ever written, Sir Richard,' he said.

Uninterested, Burton stared out at the azaleas and, in his own time, took a pinch of snuff.

'What brings you to Damascus?' he asked at length.

'An interest in ancient script, sir.'

'Heard you were sent down from Oxford.'

'Indeed I was. An awkward episode with a glider.'

Burton's gruff old face broke into a smile.

'Did you learn from it?'

'Yes, sir,' said Hannibal, 'I learned never to depend on the wind, and that technology is only as proficient as the man who has designed it.'

'Valuable lessons indeed.'

'I like to think so.'

Hannibal was about to make a witty remark, when an object on the table caught his eye. A marble tablet, the surface etched with an ancient script.

'Cuneiform?' he asked, motioning to the stone.

'Indeed. I've been sitting here struggling with a translation.'

'Might I be so bold as to pour some water over the stone?'

Burton called for the servant.

A jug was brought, droplets of condensation on the side.

Hannibal poured carefully, so as to cover all the symbols.

His brow furrowed, he cleared his throat.

'In the time of Alexander the Great fear prevailed,' he said in a low voice. 'A time of enduring fear deriving from Macedonian invincibility...'

Sir Richard thrust up his hands in delight.

'My word! You read it well!' he cried.

Hannibal went on:

'...And an invincibility in turn deriving from a device. The Mechanism is made from silver, gold and mercury, thus replacing a forerunner crafted from humble bronze...'

The great traveller seemed concerned as to why his guest had fallen silent.

'It was not the Mechanism,' intoned Hannibal, bewildered. 'As the tablet says, the one from Antikythera was a forerunner — a prototype.'

'What are you talking about?' asked Sir Richard.

'My God! What tremendous news this is!'

'I have lost you, Mr Fogg.'

Hannibal laid the marble tablet down.

'Not long ago,' he began, 'following information provided by a Greek sponge diver, I dived down to a wrecked vessel off the coast of Antikythera Island, and recovered several fragments of an extraordinary device. The sponge divers know of a remarkable wreck there, but it will be years before they manage to reach it.'

'Device?' said Sir Richard. 'What manner of device?'

'A kind of mechanical mechanism.'

'And how was it... this mechanism?'

'Brilliantly crafted... centuries ahead of its time.'

'Was it functional?'

'Alas not... rendered useless on account of corrosion. I feared all was lost — that I might never understand whether the legend is true.'

'What legend?'

147

Hannibal got to his feet.

'The legend which explains how Alexander was never once vanquished in battle.'

'Superior fighting strength?' Burton prompted.

'Perhaps. Or perhaps not. You see, sir, there is a legend in Asia Minor, describing how Alexander had captured a mechanism that could somehow augment his chances on the battlefield.'

'How did you come by the legend, Mr Fogg?'

'From my father, sir. He spoke of it often, just as his father imparted the tale to him.'

'How interesting,' Burton growled. 'It may interest you to know that in my journeys through Arabia Felix all those decades ago, I too heard a tale.'

'Did it tell of Alexander?'

'No, it did not. But it did tell of a vast machine, a machine buried beneath the desert sands.'

'Where?'

Burton took a deep breath, his chest tightening.

'In Rub' al-Khali,' he said, 'the "Empty Quarter".'

Thirty-seven

THE DAY AFTER DISCOVERING the secret rooms, Will found a folded copy of the London *Times* stuffed into the back of a large picture frame.

It was dated 9th September 1901.

As with so much at Dar Jnoun, he wasn't sure whether the newspaper had been placed there deliberately — part of a treasure trail of clues left by Hannibal Fogg.

'Perhaps the painting's got something to do with it,' Emma suggested.

Will turned the frame over.

'Three fishermen in a storm.'

'They look terrified.'

'I would be with waves like that!' said Will.

'That one's holding something…'

'Looks like a bucket of vomit.'

Emma observed the brushstrokes.

'It's not a bucket,' she said. 'I think it's a weight.'

Opening out the newspaper, Will scanned the columns.

The front page was dominated by the shooting of President McKinley in Buffalo, New York.

'D'you think it's got something to do with McKinley?'

Emma read the lead story in the blink of an eye.

'Can't see anything about fishermen, or buckets of vomit. What about that… on the second page?'

'"Boxer Rebellion Ends".'

'Hannibal had definitely been in China,' said Emma, peering over her shoulder at a museum-quality Ming vase.

'I'm not getting the right feeling,' Will added.

'What feeling?'

'That it's a lead.'

149

Flipping the pages, Will weaved his way down through the usual assortment of suicides, bankruptcies and thefts.

'Look, there…' said Emma, pointing to a three-inch piece at the bottom of page five.

'It's a story about fishermen.'

'They're not fishermen. They're divers.'

'*Divers*? I thought Scuba was only invented after the War.'

'But people were diving before that, only not to any great depths. They held onto stone weights.'

'Weight theory trumps vomit theory,' said Will.

Emma read aloud:

'"A group of sponge divers working off the Greek island of Antikythera have located a number of precious objects from a wrecked Roman ship. The treasures are believed to date to ancient Greece, possibly to the time of Alexander the Great. They include many extraordinary bronze and marble sculptures."'

Will motioned to the final column.

'Listen to this: "The divers found a circular piece of machinery which has confounded locals and experts alike."'

'Machinery?'

'As in a Mechanism? The Alexander Mechanism.'

'The very same Hannibal talked about.'

'Wait, I know about this…' said Will, staring out at the courtyard.

'Know about what?'

'About the Mechanism, the Greek Mechanism found by sponge divers, in…' Will double-checked the newspaper's date. 'In 1901.'

'What d'you know about it?'

'There was a Greek national postage stamp printed to commemorate the find.'

'When?'

'Um, about a decade ago. I've got an example back home,' he said. 'They call it the "Antikythera Mechanism".'

'Same as the Alexander Mechanism?'

'Guess so.'

'But how does this link in with Hannibal's unfinished mission?'

Emma touched a hand to Will's arm.

'We've got one thing Hannibal would have killed for.'

'What's that?'

'Google,' she said.

Thirty-eight

AFTER FORTY MINUTES OF trawling online, Will felt a great deal wiser.

He had found an article about the so-called Antikythera Mechanism, and learned that the leading expert was an Englishman at the British Museum.

A man named Professor Henry Fotheringale-Smythe.

He supplemented his meagre academic wages by getting part-time work on film sets, where his expertise on ancient Greece was in high demand. A recent run of so-called 'Sword and Sandal' epics had seen him earn enough to buy a Dutch barge — a dream since childhood.

On emailing Fotheringale-Smythe, an automatic reply bounced back: 'In Ouarzazate at Atlas Studios filming *Apollo.*'

Will wondered out loud where Ouarzazate could be. Chaudhury, who was polishing the brass within ear's reach, offered an answer.

'In the Draa Valley, sir, south-east of Marrakesh.'

'It's in Morocco?'

'Indeed it is, sir.'

'What's the chance of that?'

'Gets rather cold at night in the desert,' the manservant said, as if through first-hand experience.

Will grimaced.

'Didn't bring any warm clothes.'

'I shall look through Mr Fogg's wardrobes, sir, and find you something appropriate.'

An hour later, Emma and Will were on the open road in a ramshackle communal taxi half as old as time. They were squished up with a dozen chickens, baskets laden with fruit, and with a pair of farmers' wives heading for the market.

The bald tyres zigzagged their way down to the

town of Ouarzazate.

Will endured the discomfort by humming the '*Rhyme of Ernest Pie*', as he tended to do when trying to separate himself from an unpleasant reality.

As the decrepit vehicle neared the desert town, it passed Jerusalem, then Mecca and, after it, the Egyptian temple at Karnak. They were constructed out on the desert plain.

'All world come to Ouarzazate!' the driver announced with a cackle. 'Ouarzazate very very good!'

Against all odds, the dead-end desert town had become fêted by Hollywood as the perfect blend of space, sunshine and cheap labour.

As the sun slipped down below the baked horizon, the worn-out Mercedes sashayed up to Atlas Studios.

Their heads spinning from the switchbacks, Will and Emma stumbled out, and the communal taxi sped away.

Ten minutes later, the pair were sitting under canvas on director's chairs, sipping mint tea. Beside them, quite unfazed that they had turned up, was Henry Fotheringale-Smythe. Dressed in a tweed suit and pink bow tie, he had dazzling opal green eyes and cheeks flushed from a fondness for drink.

Rather like Chaudhury, the professor was a throwback to another age — one in which women wore arm-length gloves and men smoothed down their hair with brilliantine.

'I shall tell you something,' Fotheringale-Smythe

remarked once Will and Emma had introduced themselves. 'There's no such thing as honour any more.'

Unsure how to respond, Will changed the subject.

'I am interested in the Alexander Mechanism.'

Moving in slow motion, the professor raised the glass of mint tea to his nose, breathing in the steam.

'Ahh,' he said. 'Tell me, why should such a sentence slip from your young lips?'

'I have an interest in it.'

'Do you now?'

'Yes. Well, it's a kind of family obsession.'

Professor Henry Fotheringale-Smythe looked up slowly.

'Then it seems as though we are reflections of one another.'

'What do you mean?'

'My father and grandfather were both preoccupied with the Mechanism. They were certain it was the reason why Alexander was never beaten in battle. Got the idea before the War from an eccentric English explorer.'

'Maybe Alexander had a better army,' Emma offered.

Fotheringale-Smythe poured more tea. Raising the spout high above the glass, he allowed the steam to billow outwards.

'His forces were well-armed and disciplined, but everyone gets beaten sooner or later. Haven't you ever had a winning streak in cricket?'

'No,' said Will. 'I haven't.'

The professor grinned.

'Pity,' he said.

Emma sensed the professor's attention was waning.

'How could a chunk of machinery like the Alexander Mechanism explain invincibility on the battlefield?' she asked.

Fotheringale-Smythe glanced out of the tent, his piercing green eyes taking in the droves of ancient Greeks heading for home.

'I haven't all the answers, but I can tell you that Pliny the Elder wrote a treatise on the subject. He said that Alexander's might derived from some kind of contrivance.'

'A weapon?'

'Unlikely. Rather, a device that seems to have been used to provide accurate information. Of course it would be utterly simplistic by our standards. But whatever it was, it gave Alexander an edge. Imagine it: a colossal mechanical machine, hauled in total secrecy through deserts, over rivers and mountain ranges.'

'But who would have made it?'

'The Order of Zoroaster.'

'The Order...?'

'Of Zoroaster — a brotherhood dedicated to maintaining harmony on earth.'

'Where were they?'

The professor drained his tea.

'Babylon,' he said. 'From what Pliny writes, it seems

that Alexander captured the Mechanism and used it for world domination.'

Emma balked.

'Does that explain why he was murdered, at just thirty-three?'

'Perhaps.'

'Who killed him?' Will asked.

'I suppose the Order did,' said Fotheringale-Smythe. 'Poisoned in the Palace of Nebuchadnezzar. And in the mayhem that followed they got their Mechanism back.'

'Did they destroy it?'

Fotheringale-Smythe hunched his shoulders.

'My grandfather was quite sure it was merely disabled and sequestered away somewhere. He used to say the Order were biding their time.'

'Until when?'

'Until the world was without a great conqueror.'

'An era of peace?'

'Precisely. One in which the Mechanism could be used towards the good of mankind.'

Will seemed confused.

'But if it wasn't destroyed, where could the Mechanism be — stuck away somewhere in a museum?'

Henry Fotheringale-Smythe shook his head.

'No chance of that. The Order would have concealed it.'

'Where?'

'Judging by what we know about them, they would

have made sure it was impossible to find, until the right moment.'

'But when would that be?'

Professor Fotheringale-Smythe glanced at his pocket watch.

'When a wise man is ready to take up the quest,' he said.

Tiring of the conversation, he was in need of a gin and tonic. A half-empty bottle of Bombay Sapphire was calling to him from his hotel room.

Will shuddered, as though frozen to the bone.

'I trust such talk isn't unsettling you.'

'Just feeling the cold.'

'The desert night can be perfidious.'

Will remembered the sweater Chaudhury had taken from Hannibal's dressing room. Rust-brown, it was curiously speckled in black. Unzipping his bag, he fished it out and slipped it on.

Fotheringale-Smythe blew his nose on an oversized polka-dot square of silk.

'I can assure you the Order took great care in making sure the Mechanism is ready for the right time,' he said. 'Who knows when that will be? Tomorrow... next month... or a thousand years from now.'

Jabbing a hand down the back of his neck, Will scratched. Hannibal's sweater was itchy beyond belief.

'Do you have a hunch... where it could be hidden?'

The professor smiled wryly. Even if he did, he was

the kind of man who kept his cards close to his chest.

'I'm afraid that I can't be much help,' he said. 'You see I have a rendezvous with a lady with sapphire eyes.'

As he stood up, a pang of gout shot down his right leg.

'Always remember the first rule of discovery,' he muttered in parting.

'What is it?'

'That the answer to a great mystery tends to be a reflection of simplicity.'

Part II

THE COMPONENTS

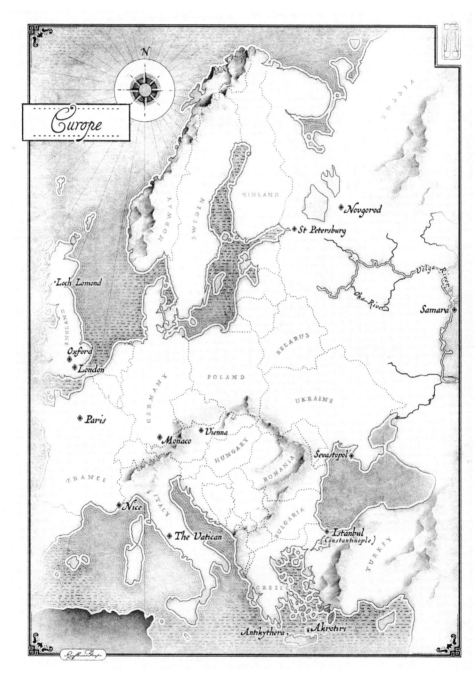

Thirty-nine

SIXTEEN FIGURES WERE CONVENED at a location known only to them and their immediate subordinates, somewhere in the vicinity of Sevastopol, on the Crimean Peninsula.

As the Order of Zoroaster's Supreme Council they represented established religion, and were bound by a sacred oath to maintain an obedience to God.

They were dressed in identical charcoal cassocks, braided hoods drooping down low over their brows. On the middle finger of the left hand, each of them wore an identical emerald ring. Together, they represented a cross-section of human culture — African, Caucasian, Latin and Oriental.

Seated in silence on exquisite golden thrones arranged in a horseshoe, they stared at their laps, waiting.

A clock struck midnight.

As the twelfth chime fell silent, the third figure in the arc dipped his head reverently, and introduced himself.

'I am the Proctor,' he said. 'As such, I welcome one and all to the Supreme Council of Divine Worship.'

His fellow members listened, but none spoke. After an extended pause, the Proctor continued with his address.

'This is the first conclave of our Order since the spring of 1917. In the limited lifespan of our race, we shall in all likelihood not meet again in this world. The next assembly shall convene on Friday 14th May 2117.'

An attendant entered the hall, moving fretfully, his felt slippers tramping fast over polished parquet. Having listened to a message whispered urgently in his left ear, the Proctor went on:

'As you are all aware, the Council meets once each century to make certain humanity is guided by the framework of our communal faiths. It is of course our shared belief that Man requires a reverent hierarchy to administer the Word of the Lord. We fulfil this role in different ways, naturally, but do so nonetheless. For without our divine guidance, humanity would perish in the abyss between good and evil.'

For ten full hours, the Supreme Council debated matters relating to established religion existing in all corners of the world. They discussed atheism, the falling numbers of worshippers, the question of false prophets, and the rise of destructive extremism — cloaked beneath the guise of religious fanaticism.

With the morning light pouring in through the latticed windows of the sacred hall, the Proctor concluded the assembly's business with a short prayer. Preparing to stand, he paused.

'It seems as if I have omitted one matter,' he intoned gravely. 'A matter recorded in the minutes of every session since far antiquity.'

The members of the Supreme Council looked up, their attention piqued.

'The matter of the so-called "Alexander Mechanism".'

The Proctor flicked through a weighty ledger of vellum sheets.

'The ancestral informants indicate there is no news — nothing to report. But they are ready and waiting, should the Bloodchild ever surface.'

With that, the Proctor rose to his feet, the folds of the charcoal gown tumbling away.

'I wish you all long and convivial lives,' he said. 'With God's will, our descendants shall reconvene on these hallowed thrones exactly a century forward from this day.'

Forty

THE MORE WILL THOUGHT about it, the more he felt certain Hannibal must have concealed a briefing within easy reach.

Once back in Marrakesh, he and Emma retraced their steps through the reception rooms, the library, and then the secret study, observing each object in a new way. Emma removed the shrunken heads from their suspension strings, peering into the hollow necks, uncertain quite what she was looking for — a slip of paper perhaps, or a key. Will opened the canopic jars and rooted through their dusty contents.

Every so often he begged Chaudhury to come clean, to reveal all he knew. But whenever he did so, the servant would hurry away to cook a meal, or would declare there was a pressing errand waiting to be done.

The temperature plunged, a cold breeze gusting down from the Atlas. Everyone was talking about it, and even the foreign newspapers carried stories about the freak weather in Marrakesh. Lured by the prospect of guaranteed heat, package tourists were up in arms at the freeze. Some were even demanding their money back.

Will was so frozen he was forced to wear Hannibal's speckled sweater, as the riad had no heating of any kind. As the days passed, he found himself growing used to the itchy wool.

A full week after returning from Ouarzazate, he woke in the middle of the night, pulled on the sweater and went down into the garden. Breathing in the scent of orange blossom, he sat on a wrought iron chair.

Out in the distance was the crazed furore of a donkey braying, and, on the terrace above, the rustling of citrus leaves in the wind.

'Where have you left the message, Hannibal?' Will said gruffly, the question swept instantly away on the breeze. 'I know it's here. But where?'

As he sat there growing numb from cold, Will pondered how, although cryptic, the clues he had found had been relatively easy to work out.

It was as if he was prepared for them or, rather, that circumstances had been prepared for him.

After all, what were the chances of him linking the

postage stamp to the watercolour of the shepherd — a deduction that had allowed him to locate the concealed letter? Or what real hope had there been for deciphering the script written invisibly on the Book of Samuel? Or the likelihood that Professor Fotheringale-Smythe would be just down the road in Ouarzazate?

It all seemed improbable in the extreme.

As for the reason which had prompted him to reach for Crowley's *The Stratagem and Other Stories*, Will could only marvel that his ancestor could have known it.

The wind whipped up even more.

Clutching his shoulders for warmth, Will's fingertips pressed into the coarse wool. So absorbed was he with the riddle, that the cold seemed to melt away.

Considering the pieces of the puzzle, he went through what he knew about Hannibal Fogg. Two things were for certain — that he had been meticulous in every conceivable way, and magnificently ahead of his time.

Somehow he had known that Will would be born, that he would discover the location of the study, the armoury and the library.

As another gust of freezing air shot through the court-yard, Will frowned hard.

It was as if Hannibal had glimpsed into the future.

The wind died down and Will caught the scent of oranges in the trees. The burst of citrus helped him to think.

Until this moment, Hannibal has laid out the clues

in order, presenting them when needed, knowing that I'd easily make sense of them. They're tailor-made for me, ready, staring me in the face.

So where could the next clue be?

Will crept through the salons and slipped down into the study. The shrunken heads and other ghoulish objects looked just as fearful as before, but he wasn't frightened any longer. The initial sense of horror had been replaced by intrigue.

Returning to the iron chair in the courtyard, he ran through what he knew again. The idea of getting back to bed tugged away at him.

But something had occurred to him.

If Hannibal was following a plan and a pattern, acquired from knowledge of the future, he would surely have taken specific circumstances into account.

Just as he had known Will would recognise the Z-Grill, or that he would make sense of the lapis lazuli ring.

Will shivered again.

The temperature was dropping.

Clenching his knees to stand, his mind lost in thought, he took a step away from the chair. As he did so, the sweater's hem caught on an iron curlicue. A thread was pulled out and, despite Will's attempt to stop it, a long strand of wool was unwound.

Again, he frowned.

This time, not because he didn't understand — but because he did.

Holding the thread between his fingertips, he hurried into the salon. With narrowed eyes, he held it into the light. It looked as though the speckling had been penned in by hand.

In disbelief, Will heaved out an arm's length of yarn.

'Oh my God!' he yelled. 'They're dots and dashes. It's Morse Code!'

Forty-one

FOR THE REMAINDER OF the night, Will worked on deciphering the encoded message.

Beginning at the neck, he progressed down the sweater's torso and along the left arm. As the Morse Code was decoded inch by inch, he got a recurring flash of himself racing through the Ham Radio exam. While the others had found it hard going, Will had completed it at lightning speed and had passed with flying colours.

By the time Chaudhury came down to prepare breakfast, just after seven, two-thirds of the Morse was decrypted. Stepping through to the kitchen, he did so in silence. His father had taught him never to pry into the business of others.

At the salon's writing bureau, Will was hunched over, a foolscap notepad beside his left hand and a giant ball of yarn next to his right. A third of the sweater was perched on his lap.

'Found it!' he said when Chaudhury appeared with a tea tray.

'Very good, sir.'

'Are you telling me you didn't know about this?'

The manservant raised an eyebrow.

'There appear to be so many mysteries, sir,' he said absently, padding back in the direction of the kitchen.

An hour later, Emma came down, wearing Hannibal's monogrammed bathrobe. Her hair was wet from the shower. Catching her scent, Will was reminded of the first moment he had heard her voice.

'You look like crap,' she said with a giggle.

'This is incredible!'

'Hannibal's knitting?'

Slipping onto a chesterfield, Emma pulled both knees up under her chin. She could sense that Will had made a breakthrough.

'Hannibal had known it would be freezing in Marrakesh — in the middle of summer!' he yelled.

'How?'

'Let's just call it the "Riddle of Hannibal Fogg". The weird thing is that he knew I'd need this information right now. God knows how he did it, but he worked out the perfect way of delivering it.'

'What am I missing?' Emma replied.

'The sweater.'

'What about it?'

'I started unravelling it, and the next thing I know

I've got six hundred yards of Morse.'

'Morse Code?'

'Yeah. Morse. In my teens I had this thing about Ham Radio. You need Morse to get the licence. Got pretty good at it.'

'You never cease to amaze me,' Emma said.

Will tapped a pen to the notepad.

'It's not me who's amazing,' he replied fast. 'It's Hannibal! Listen to this:

'"The Alexander Mechanism was designed through genius far more elevated than anything humanity had ever known. The Order of Zoroaster conceived it, then protected it, acting as its guardians. That is, until Alexander plundered it from the Temple of Zoroaster in Babylon. They only succeeded in retrieving it once again by poisoning him."'

'Just as the professor said?'

'Yes! Yes!... but listen to this: "The leaders of the Order feared so greatly that the Mechanism would be stolen once again, that they agreed to destroy it. Meeting at a grand assembly, they debated the matter. Just before the decision was passed to destroy the Mechanism, the wisest of the brethren spoke up. He suggested removing a key component and hiding it. The hope was that with time an inspired saviour would understand where the component was hidden, and fit it back in place. That saviour would, it was hoped, use the machine for the good of all mankind."'

169

'You mean like removing a spark plug from a car, so it can't be stolen.'

'I guess so.'

Will flicked through his notes.

'But the incredible thing was the way in which the component was hidden.'

'How?'

'It was hidden within religion,' he said.

Forty-two

1892

A COPY OF JULES Verne's *La Maison à Vapeur* was face down at page 122, beside a tall glass of gin and tonic, a stone's throw from the handrail of SS *Manitoba*.

Hannibal Fogg had stepped away from his seat to assist a lady whose bonnet had been blown off her head. She had swooned at the vision of such a gentleman in a pristine linen suit racing down the promenade deck on her behalf. Presenting her with the retrieved bonnet, he had introduced himself and bowed.

Since arriving home from Damascus, Hannibal had been fatigued by England, finding it dull however hard he tried. Having heard that the SS *Manitoba* was soon to embark on her maiden voyage to New York, he sent Chaudhury to buy a pair of first class tickets. One for the manservant and one for himself.

Hannibal believed that a gentleman ought, when possible, to take in the sea air — as it, and movement, helped one to think clearly.

A week later, he, Chaudhury and endless steamer trunks arrived at the Southampton quayside, where the *Manitoba* was moored, as the last of the supplies were being loaded.

Six of Hannibal's trunks were filled with books, bound by a firm in Clerkenwell in lizard-green leather. A further four contained clothing, ranging from casual to formal military attire. The others were packed with a variety of equipment and specialised paraphernalia.

Unlike his master, Chaudhury believed in travelling light. His own luggage was fitted into a suitcase the size and shape of a hatbox.

Hannibal regarded equipment as a necessity second only to education. Having been born into wealth, he was considered by his peers as the ultimate man of leisure.

As he saw it, with financial security there came grave duty — duty which involved pushing the boundaries of knowledge. For this reason he planned each day meticulously, in a desperate effort to waste not even a moment of time.

During his few hours of sleep, he slept with a metronome beside his right ear, and had done so since childhood. The ticking was, he believed, a way of bringing order to the dream world.

Each morning, long before dawn, he exercised

for forty minutes: a blend of callisthenic movements and martial arts, taken mostly from karate and wing chun. After that, he devoted four hours to the study of linguistics.

A further four hours followed in reading newly published academic papers.

When at sea, Hannibal would conduct experiments in his stateroom through half the afternoon. The same amount of time was spent working on the text of his latest book or monograph.

At dusk, he would sleep sitting upright for precisely forty-four minutes. Chaudhury would take care to wind the metronome and to place it in position beside the chair in which he snoozed.

In the evening Hannibal would dine alone or, in exceptional circumstances, at the captain's table. It was rare for him ever to accept the invitation of another passenger. Although he didn't feel superior, it was true to say that he regarded a great many people as a waste of time.

Three days out from Southampton, Chaudhury bore a polished salver through to the makeshift laboratory. His master was performing an experiment with an array of test tubes, to establish colloidal growth.

'An invitation, sir,' the servant remarked, solemnly.

'Oh?'

Hannibal opened the letter.

'It's from Baroness Longvic. I noticed her name on

the passenger list. She is inviting me to dine at her table tonight.'

'Ought I to make the customary excuse, sir?'

Hannibal Fogg touched the corner of the letter paper to his nose.

'*Brassavola nodosa*, Lady of the Night,' he intoned pensively. 'How very interesting. I thought the Baroness was dead.'

'Apparently not, sir.'

Fogg grunted in agreement.

'Think I shall make an exception. Have my white tie prepared — the one from Gieves & Hawkes.'

Chaudhury dipped his head in a bow.

'Very good, sir,' he said.

Forty-three

WITH THE COLD SNAP over, Will dozed through the heat of the afternoon, his dreams punctuated with dots and dashes. At around four he woke to the clamour of dogs brawling out in the street.

Down in the salon, he leafed through the decoded notes once again.

'There's everything I need to know,' he said to Emma. 'Except what I'm supposed to be looking for.'

'The component?'

Will nodded.

'Got the feeling I've missed something.'

'But we've scoured the house.'

'It doesn't work like that. Don't you see how it's arranged?'

'Guess not.'

'He's laying it out piecemeal, a little at a time. It's the only way of safeguarding the secrets.'

'Like a kind of firewall?'

'Exactly.'

'Shall we go through the rooms again?'

Will combed a hand back through his hair.

'Not sure it'll do any good, not until we know what we're searching for.'

He scanned the handwritten notes.

'Listen to this part: "William, I cannot reveal the entire picture due to the danger. The great fear is that precious information will fall into the hands of our enemies. For this reason I shall reveal to you what is necessary when necessary, or when you are ready to understand. Rest assured that you shall be protected — just as your father, grandfather and great-grandfather were in the years which spanned my lifetime and your own. But danger is everywhere. Any number of cults, sects, clandestine orders, and governments yearn to obtain the Mechanism. The only ones to fear are...'

'Are who?'

Will flipped through the notes.

'The Magi.'

'*Magi?*'

Emma broke into a smile.

'It sounds… kinda magical.'

'I'd laugh,' said Will. 'If I hadn't decoded this sentence: "The Magi will be your shadow. You'll never know they are there but they are — of that you can be certain. When ready, they will end your life in the most grotesque of ways. You will ultimately prevail by severing customary ways of thought. The information you need to continue may be found in the clockwork elephant."'

'Clockwork…?'

'…elephant.'

Emma cast an eye around the room.

'I've seen a lot of crazy stuff in this house but no clockwork elephant.'

'Nor have I.'

Chaudhury entered with a plate of hot buttered muffins. He had baked them himself, using a recipe brought to India in the 1861 edition of Mrs Beeton's *Book of Household Management*.

'Do you know where the clockwork elephant is?'

'I regret to say I do not, sir.'

'Are you sure?'

Will narrowed his eyes suspiciously.

'Perfectly so, sir.'

Chaudhury slipped out to the kitchen.

'Can't believe anyone could have lived here for so long without being aware of the secrets we've found,'

Will said.

Together, he and Emma began searching the house again, starting up in Hannibal's bedroom.

'There's no hope in this,' Will grumbled. 'We're thinking too literally, I can feel it. Don't you remember what he said?'

'Huh?'

'"You will only prevail by severing customary ways of thought."'

'What d'you think he means by that?'

'That we mustn't think logically.'

'So you think clockwork elephant's an anagram?'

'Maybe it is, or something quite different altogether.'

Will led the way to the library, where he strode over to the reference section.

Forty minutes later, he had found an elaborate description in a twelfth century Arab manuscript entitled *The Book of Knowledge of Ingenious Mechanical Devices*. The passage described a fanciful automaton designed by al-Jaziri, featuring not only a mechanical elephant but a dragon as well.

'Not sure I get how this ties in,' said Emma.

'And I'm not sure that it does.'

'What do you mean?'

'Well, when I was a kid,' Will said, 'great-aunt Edith used to go on and on about a story she had been told in her youth. In the tale there was a house in India. It was pulled by an amazing machine — a machine in the shape of an elephant.'

'Where was the story from?'

'Not sure.'

'Did you ever see it written down... in a book?'

'Don't think so.'

Pressing the heel of his palm down hard on his brow, he tried to remember.

'Yes, there was a book. I'm sure of it. I can see the illustration. A lithograph print of an elephant hauling this big old house.'

'Can you remember the title?'

'No.'

Will whipped out his iPhone. He tapped 'clockwork elephant pulling house' into Google. The answer flashed up instantly.

Jules Verne's La Maison à Vapeur.

'Of course!' Emma replied. 'The guy who wrote *Journey to the Centre of the Earth.*'

Will paced fast across the library, to shelves devoted to Victorian adventure. Running a fingertip over the identical green spines, he worked his way through Verne's titles, hampered by the fact they were in French.

His finger paused.

'This is it,' he said, '*La Maison à Vapeur, The Steam House.*'

He caught a memory of his great-aunt Edith snapping the book shut at bedtime, before clicking off the light.

Slipping it from the shelf, Will flicked to the title page.

'Published Paris, 1880.'

'Is that a clue?'

'Could be,' he said, turning to Chapter One. 'But this is definitely one...'

Emma craned forward.

A slim line of paper had been cut out from each page. Forced inside the recess was a curled strand of copper, verdigris shadowing one side.

Letters and shapes were etched into the surface, almost like notches on the edge of a key.

Will eased the copper from the book. Squinting, he read:

'"Ladder of Mithras".'

Emma went over to a dusty set of *Encyclopaedia Britannica*. Like everything else, it was bound in lizard-green leather.

Rolling his eyes, Will fished out his iPhone.

Almost instantly he was reading from the miniature screen.

'*Mithras, the Mithraic Mysteries...* um, here: "The initiation into the Mithraic cult was performed through ascending seven steps on a ritualistic ladder".'

'*A ladder?*'

'Yeah, a ladder,' said Will. 'A ladder hidden in religion.'

Forty-four

1892

BARONESS LONGVIC HAD SEATED Hannibal Fogg to her left and Captain Griffiths to her right. There were six other guests, three gentlemen and three ladies, arranged around a circular table, the centre of which was strewn with orchids, Lady of the Night.

The Baroness was a tall woman with strong Gallic features and a fondness for vintage Taittinger champagne. She had ordered seven bottles to be chilled for the dinner, together with half a dozen bottles of the 1864 Hospices de Beaune.

Ever the attentive hostess, the Baroness had heard it said that Mr Fogg favoured that vintage of burgundy. A little research by her staff had informed her the young explorer had purchased eleven cases of it, at Berry Brothers & Rudd, on St James's Street. Like everyone else present, she had heard a great deal of his singular genius and his wealth.

As the army of waiters served turtle soup, Hannibal engaged in trivial conversation, a pastime he deplored. He listened to the captain drone on about the might of the *Manitoba*'s engines and of his ambition of claiming the Blue Riband.

When the soup dishes had been cleared, the Baroness turned to Hannibal.

'Might I enquire, Mr Fogg, whether you followed the

fortunes of Mr Darwin?'

As soon as the scientist's name was mentioned, the entire table fell silent.

'Indeed I did, Baroness.'

'Did you give credence to his hypotheses?'

Hannibal Fogg pinched his chin in taut concentration.

'It seems to me, Baroness,' he said slowly, 'that Mr Darwin confused two distinct criteria. The evolvement of the species, and the existence of an Ultimate Being. It is my humble belief that Evolution, as it has been termed, is fact rather than theory. Evolution has surely taken place, but it does not preclude the existence of God.'

The remark elicited an outburst of ire from an elderly soldier seated opposite. In full dress uniform, the breast adorned with medals, he struck the end of his cane on the floor.

'How dare you give credence to such a preposterous notion, sir?! It is no more than poppycock!'

'My dear General,' Hannibal riposted, 'as far as I am concerned, the point of interest is not of supposed Evolution, but the question of religion itself.'

The Baroness motioned to the sommelier, requesting he serve yet more Taittinger.

'How so, sir?' she asked.

Narrowing his eyes, Hannibal Fogg considered his answer.

'Baroness, I would say there is God above, and

Mankind below,' he replied. 'And that is how the arrangement was intended to be. But, between one and the other lies an abhorrent layer of filth.'

'*Filth*, sir? What is this "abhorrent layer of filth" of which you speak?'

Hannibal took a long satisfying sip of champagne.

'By filth I refer to the bad apples within our Church,' he said.

Forty-five

AFTER DINNER, WILL PICKED up the curled sliver of copper and held it between forefinger and thumb.

'Wonder what this could be.'

Chaudhury raised an eyebrow.

'It appears to be copper, sir… if the corrosion is anything to go by.'

'Does the Ladder of Mithras ring any bells?'

'I regret to reply in the negative, sir.'

Will motioned to the strip.

'What do you think it is?'

'A key, perhaps?'

'If it's a key, where's the lock?'

'The only place I have seen copper like this is in the kitchen, sir.'

'Would you show me?'

The manservant took Will through and pointed at the

colossal wooden refrigerator. At the time when Hannibal had commissioned it back in 1904, the appliance had been at the cutting edge of modern convenience. He had specified that it be sufficiently large to accommodate a pair of cow carcasses, and had devised the cooling mechanism himself.

Will carefully examined the front and sides of the machine, taking in the nickel-plated hinges, the sprung handles and the bands of copper decoration.

'I think you're right,' he said after some time. 'It looks as if one of the bands is missing, do you see?'

Before Chaudhury had time to answer, Will stepped forward. He inserted the end of the curl into a niche on the upper right edge of the refrigerator. It fitted perfectly, the recessed lettering and symbols clicking into place like notches on a key.

A grinding sound came and went, followed by what appeared to be gears moving.

'Something's going on, and it doesn't sound like refrigeration,' said Will.

At that moment, Emma appeared.

'What's happening?'

There was a loud click, almost a bang, and the heavy wooden doors sprang open.

'Now, that's what I call a refrigerator!' she exclaimed.

Pulling both doors open wide, Will checked inside.

The shelves had vanished, along with the back of the machine. What looked like a tunnel stretched out, illuminated by low-watt bulbs.

'What on earth do you think's down there, sir?' asked Chaudhury.

Propping open the doors, Will stepped through.

'There's one way to find out,' he said.

The walls were panelled in cedar wood, the low ceiling hanging with bats.

Emma followed Will, and Chaudhury followed her down a flight of stone steps and along a passageway.

'Where are we?' asked Emma.

'We must be under the streets of Marrakesh, Madam,' the manservant replied. 'I once heard there was a tunnel running to the palace. This must be it.'

'Don't tell me Hannibal had it built,' Emma said.

'I think not, miss,' Chaudhury responded, his face warming in a blush. 'They say that six hundred years ago the first owner of Dar Jnoun was indulging in the sultan's harem.'

The passage turned sharply to the right, leading to a reinforced steel door. There was no handle or apparent lock — nothing except for a series of wheels lined with numbers.

'Looks like a calendar to me,' said Emma.

'Or a lock,' Will added.

'Perhaps it's both,' offered Chaudhury.

'But what date do we put in?'

'If Hannibal had seen the future,' said Will, 'he must have known that I would reach this point at this precise moment…'

'So?'

'So, this must be the time and date to punch in.'

Emma glanced at her watch — unlike Will's it didn't seem to lose time in Dar Jnoun.

'It's twelve twenty-two on 15th May 2017. So that would be 05-15-2017-12-22.'

One at a time Will rotated the numerical wheels until the date was displayed.

The door remained shut.

'Was worth a try,' said Emma with a sigh.

'We must be doing something wrong.'

'Maybe your watch is out.'

Chaudhury stepped forward.

'If you would permit me, sir,' he said. 'I believe I may have the answer. Being an Englishman, Mr Fogg would have arranged the date with the day before the month.'

'The opposite of what we do in the States.'

Will exchanged the 15 with the 05.

The armoured steel door unlocked and inched open.

As they stepped across the threshold, a deafening hissing sound prevailed, as though there was a gas leak. A series of dazzling electric lights blasted into life, illuminating the chamber.

Shielding their eyes, Will, Emma and Chaudhury stepped forward, in time for the steel security door to slam behind them.

Their eyes growing accustomed to the brightness,

they began to appreciate the scope and scale of the vault.

A hundred yards square and twenty feet high, its walls and floor were laid in reinforced steel. Packed with expedition equipment, the chamber appeared to have been designed so it could be destroyed in the event of attack. A series of high explosives had been fitted to the walls on steel housings.

As for the equipment, it was divided according to the climatic regions for which it was designed, arranged in racks.

The first contained leather protection suits and matching headwear, snow boots, shoes, ice picks, greased skis and skates, crampons, and tinted Alpine glasses.

The second unit held jungle equipment — machetes and gators, crates packed with hammocks, tents, backpacks, strapping, weaponry, and plenty of canned pemmican.

One entire section of the room was devoted to desert survival packs. Beside them were general mess kits and, beyond them, endless crates filled with campaign furniture.

Most of the equipment had been designed by Hannibal himself — even the primitive night-vision goggles. They were cutting-edge high tech in their day.

All the gear bore the HF monogram.

The sheer quantity of equipment and its pristine condition struck Will, along with the fact there was no dust.

'It's been hermetically sealed,' he said, turning three-sixty.

'Unbelievable,' whispered Emma, her mouth open wide. 'But what's it all for?'

Will held up both hands.

'Hannibal wouldn't have revealed it if there wasn't a reason.'

'Think he expects you to get kitted up?'

'Guess so. But where to begin?'

'A sturdy pair of boots, perhaps?' Chaudhury suggested.

Striding over to a display of footwear, he selected a pair of leather walking boots with rubberised soles.

'Try these on for size.'

Perching on a stool, Will eased the shoes on.

'Don't believe it,' he said, 'they're a perfect fit.'

'I'm getting the feeling it's not coincidence,' Emma smiled.

'Got the same feeling, as though it's all planned out.'

'All this expedition gear, but for an expedition to where?'

Will didn't reply.

Something at the far end of the chamber had caught his eye.

Mounted on the back wall, below a glass panel packed with high explosives, was a glass box. Inside was what looked like a mechanical device. Hanging below it was a dossier pouch crafted in mottled green ostrich-leather.

Together, the three of them approached.

'What d'you think it is?' Emma asked.

'The answer,' said Will.

'But to what question, sir?' uttered Chaudhury hesitantly.

Leaning forward until his face was inches from the box, Will cracked the glass seal and took out the object. As soon as it was in his hands, he felt its weight and knew full well that it was not only the answer but the key.

The size and shape of an old-fashioned carriage clock, the device was mounted in a hand-sewn leather case.

Along one edge was die-stamped 'CODEX-434'.

Unfastening the case, Will found a steel and brass machine housed inside. There were numerous dials and display windows, lenses, knobs, switches, and a miniature QWERTY keyboard made from Bakelite.

'I get the feeling this is more important than anything else in here,' he said.

Tilting the CODEX into the light, he examined the controls. They were arranged over five of the sides. On the sixth side was a glass window, measuring two inches by five. Behind it was a primitive split-flap alpha-numeric display — a giant form of which is used the world over at airports.

To the left of the display was what looked like a power switch.

Nudging back the guard, Will turned the device on. Nothing happened.

'The battery must be dead,' said Emma.

Will grunted. Unfastening a side panel, he scrutinised the internal workings — a miniaturised mass of cogs, gears and cloth-covered wires.

'Extraordinary,' he whispered. 'I've never seen anything like it.'

Once the display panel had been clipped back into place the CODEX began vibrating. Gradually, the vibration turned to whirring.

'It's waking up,' said Will.

A minute after that, a pair of green lights mounted on the front illuminated.

The central display flashed up a word: 'S-T-E-E-R'. Inside the device, the gears moved, and the word readjusted to read:

'R-E-S-E-T'.

Emma pointed to the ostrich-leather pouch.

'Think that has anything to do with it?'

'Have a look.'

Reaching up, she grasped it, broke the seal and removed the contents — a typed instruction booklet two hundred pages thick, along with an old-fashioned map backed on canvas.

'Says here that it's got to be calibrated,' she said.

'How?'

Emma leafed through the instructions.

'It's got to be configured for you.'

'Must be for security, sir,' said Chaudhury.

Emma held up the instructions, opened at page 9.

'I'll read out what to do.'

'Go ahead.'

'Number one: "Enter your father's birthday".'

'Fifteenth August,' Will replied at once. His fingers began typing the date. He paused. 'No, wait, was it the sixteenth? I always get it wrong.'

Emma choked.

'The note at the bottom might interest you,' she said softly.

'What note?'

'The one which says, "Any errors shall detonate the TNT built into the walls".'

'Damn it Hannibal!' railed Will. 'OK. OK. Let me think.' Closing his eyes he scrolled fast through a thousand fragments of memory. 'It was neither,' he said.

'Huh?'

'The fourteenth. It was August 14th.'

Chaudhury and Emma looked fearful.

'Are you sure?' they asked in unison.

'Think so,' answered Will, tapping in the date.

A bell began chiming. The device warmed until it was so hot Will could hardly hold it. The green indicator lamps flashed.

'Looks like you got it right,' said Emma.

'Thank God.'

'Next question: "In which year were postal ZIP codes introduced?"'

'Easy,' said Will. '1963.'

He tapped in the date and the CODEX chimed again.

'One more to go.'

'What is it?'

Emma looked Will in the eye.

'What's the face value of the most valuable postage stamp of all?'

'Um…'

'The Z-Grill?'

'No, no, it's valuable but not the *most* valuable.'

'Then?'

'I read about it somewhere… it was British Guiana. There was something about a kid finding it…' Will fought to focus on the newspaper article in his mind. 'His name was Vernon. Think he was from Scotland.'

'What about the stamp?'

'Black print on magenta paper. The face value was one cent.'

'Let's just Google it,' said Emma.

Will took out his iPhone and peered at the screen.

'No signal.'

'I could go out to the kitchen, sir,' said Chaudhury.

'Think you'll find we're locked in,' Emma interjected.

Will groaned.

'Sometimes in life you have to go it alone,' he said.

Tapping in the numeral '1', he took a deep breath.

Just before pressing the return symbol he stopped and frowned.

'That's not right,' he said.

'The Magenta one cent was trumped.'

'Trumped by what?'

'By the Treskilling Yellow.'

'What was it worth?'

'Three skillings.'

'*Skillings?*'

'Yup.'

Tapping 3, Will hit 'return'.

Warming again, the CODEX chimed three times. A pair of lamps flashed, as the rotor wheels inside span fast.

'Think it's calibrating,' said Will.

Little by little, the noise subsided, and the heat died away.

The central display window reset itself to a line of zeros.

'It's ready.'

'Ready for what?'

Will was about to say something, when the mechanism inside the CODEX started shaking. One at a time a set of numerals clicked into place on the main display:

9°00'59.76'N 38°45'27.94'E.

'What the hell's that?'

'You mean *where* is it?'

'What?'

'It's a grid reference,' said Will.

Chaudhury unfurled the map. Mounted on starched canvas, it had been printed by Sifton Praed & Co. of St James's back in 1937.

'I believe it is in Abyssinia, sir,' he said after a long pause.

'You mean Ethiopia?'

'Indeed.'

'Sounds like a wild goose chase if ever there was one,' said Will. 'How will I even pay for a ticket?'

While posing the question, he glanced down at the floor.

Right under where he was standing was a glass inspection window. He had been so preoccupied with the CODEX and the equipment that until that moment he hadn't noticed it.

'That looks like the answer,' Emma grinned.

Together, they crouched down on their knees and looked through the window.

In a recess under the floor were six orderly stacks of currency.

$50 bills, printed in the 1930s – $300,000 in all.

Beside the money was a note in Hannibal's hand.

It read simply:

'*All expenses will be covered in full.*'

Forty-six

NEXT EVENING, BEFORE WILL was due to leave for Ethiopia on the trail of the Ladder of Mithras, he and Emma sat on the rooftop terrace listening to the *muezzin* call out over the honeycomb of Marrakesh's old city.

'Can't believe this is happening,' he said softly.

'What?'

'All of this — the house, Chaudhury, Hannibal, Marrakesh, you...'

Leaning forward, Will smiled at Emma. Had he been twice as brave he might have kissed her. He was dying to.

'There's a great adventure ahead of you,' said Emma, her gaze tumbling to the cushions on which they were sitting. 'It's daunting.'

'It's terrifying. Don't know how I'll manage — how I'll find the Ladder, or find anything for that matter.'

'Hannibal Fogg will be with you.'

Will pushed himself up on the cushion.

'It's utterly crazy, but somehow I believe it too,' he said. 'When I first stepped into this house all I could think of was how much I'd be able to get for it. But as time's passed I've realised Hannibal needs me. He's counting on me. Why else would he have gone to such great lengths to prepare all this?'

'He was a very special man,' said Emma.

Their attention was distracted by a commotion

193

on the ground floor. It was followed by the sound of Chaudhury running fast up the stairs. By the time he reached the terrace he was panting.

'What's the matter?' asked Will urgently.

'The police are coming!'

'Where?'

'Here!'

'When?'

'Now!'

'What are you talking about?'

'Must leave right away, sir!'

Will sat up.

'What are you talking about?!'

In one hand the Indian manservant held up Will's passport and in the other a satchel stuffed with money.

'Have taken the liberty of packing a little equipment, and have booked your ticket.'

'Chaudhury, why are the police coming?'

'Cannot tell you, sir.'

'Cannot or will not?'

'Must insist you leave instantly!'

Emma looked into Will's eyes.

'Do as he says and go!'

'This is ridiculous!'

'Flight takes off in an hour and a half, sir.'

'Flight to where?'

'Addis Ababa. Connection in Frankfurt.'

'Can't I get a later one?'

Chaudhury's head blurred as it shook left, right, left.

'Sleep here another night and you'll be dead by morning, sir!'

Will snarled.

'Promise me this isn't another Hannibal "Event"!'

'Promise!' the manservant gasped.

Will hurried downstairs to find a pair of steamer trunks waiting in the back passage. Plastered with luggage stamps from distant destinations, they were both monogrammed with Hannibal's initials.

Chaudhury rounded up a posse of kids to haul the gear out to the main street. He didn't seem his usual calm and collected self.

'This is your last chance to tell me what's happening!'

'Cannot say, sir,' the servant declared again.

In a rush he led Will and Emma out of the back door and through the narrow lanes toward Bab Agnaou, one of the largest of the ancient city gates.

A taxi swerved up.

While Chaudhury piled the luggage on the roof, Emma hugged Will, her sadness mirroring his own.

'Take care,' she said tenderly.

'Come with me!'

'What?! I can't… I…'

'You can! *Please*! I have enough cash to cover us both. We'll share the adventure together!'

'But I can't take your money… *Hannibal's* money!'

Will thought fast.

'Then don't. I'll employ you,' he said, 'as my translator... my personal assistant....'

Emma laughed, and at that moment Will knew he could not leave without her.

'You sure?'

'Just tell me your passport's still stuffed down there.'

Emma reached a hand into her blouse, pulled out a dark blue American passport.

'I'd never keep it anywhere else,' she said.

Forty-seven

1893

A WAITER CROSSED THE café, a tray balanced on the upturned fingertips of his left hand. Having reached the table in the window, he served a cup of coffee and a glass of sparkling water. Hidden behind a copy of the morning's *Wiener Zeitung*, the customer mumbled thanks.

The newspaper did not move, not for another minute. Then, slowly, it folded back on itself like the wings of a giant black and white butterfly.

Laying it down beside him, Hannibal Fogg took a sip from the cup. Viennese *Kleiner Brauner* — his favourite.

As he sat there, staring out at the street, the explorer's thoughts progressed from the article he had been reading on Carl Benz's celebrated 1885 patent No. 37435, for the Patent-Motorwagen — to a journey he had made the year before through the jungles of Sumatra.

The expedition had sought to locate the rarest coffee on earth. Its beans were pre-digested and fermented in the stomach of *Paradoxurus hermaphroditis*, the palm civet cat.

The blast of a motor vehicle backfiring distracted Hannibal momentarily. Glancing out of the window again, he watched as a crowd gathered. Such was the force of the explosion that the automobile had collapsed, its driver lying injured nearby.

Hannibal took in the jumbled wreckage.

'The internal combustion engine is a curse to humanity,' he snarled, touching the cup's rim to his lips.

He was about to return to his newspaper when something occurred to him. What if an automobile's gearing system were employed for something far more useful... as in part of an elliptical cipher machine?

Withdrawing an iridium-tipped fountain pen from his jacket pocket, Hannibal sketched a series of wheels and rotors on the paper tablecloth. Around them, he drew a system of interlinking cogged teeth, labelling some with numbers and others with letters.

If there were 6 rotors, each with 26 teeth, then there would be 26 to the power 6. By further mounting the rotors in such a way that their order may be adjusted, one would increase the complexity many millions of times.

Ripping the diagram from the table, Hannibal pressed

down a coin and ran from the café. Hardly noticing the carnage outside, he pushed through the crowd and was soon at his apartment in Josefstadt.

Once there, he bolted the door and swept an arm over the workbench to clear the experiments and the books.

Placing the crude diagram on the middle of the desk, he began.

For days Hannibal stayed inside, working away at his calculations. The only time he went out was for supplies of emerald green Indian ink, and paper. He didn't change his clothing, shave, or wash, but spent every waking hour planning the mechanism of a machine. As for food, he lived entirely on canned pemmican, prepared months before by a butcher in Mile End.

Eleven days later, the prototype was ready.

The casing was made from a Georgian carriage clock, and the internal rotors were inspired by Pascal's calculator from 1642, and the workings of an ordinary mangle.

The time to test the device had come.

Hannibal set the display windows to Zero. He thought for a moment. What word to encode first? With a grin he typed in his own name:

H-A-N-N-I-B-A-L.

Pressing the encryption button, he heard the sound of cogs moving, and the encrypted text appeared:

C-O-D-E-X-4-3-4.

Forty-eight

VISAS WERE ISSUED ON entry at Addis Ababa's Bole Airport in half the usual time.

The clerk appeared surprised that any visitors were arriving at all. Most people were on the other side of the barrier, desperate to flee the Ethiopian capital, rather than enter it.

The government's redistribution of land along tribal lines had not been well received. All but the ruling Tigrayan tribe found themselves out in the cold.

The result: mass protests, strikes and civil unrest, the kind not seen in Addis Ababa since the fall of the Marxist Derg back in '91.

From the airport Will and Emma took a taxi towards the city centre, unsure quite what to do next. Back in Marrakesh the idea of searching for the Ladder of Mithras had been appealing. But now Will was on the ground, and in a country that appeared on the brink of collapse, he kicked himself for being so stupid — this was the opposite of a simple quest.

'Let's dump the gear and regroup,' he said as the taxi rumbled towards the city.

The sentence was interrupted by the clatter of small arms fire in the distance. Emma jerked round. Theirs was the only vehicle heading in the direction of town. Everyone else was racing at breakneck speed in the opposite direction.

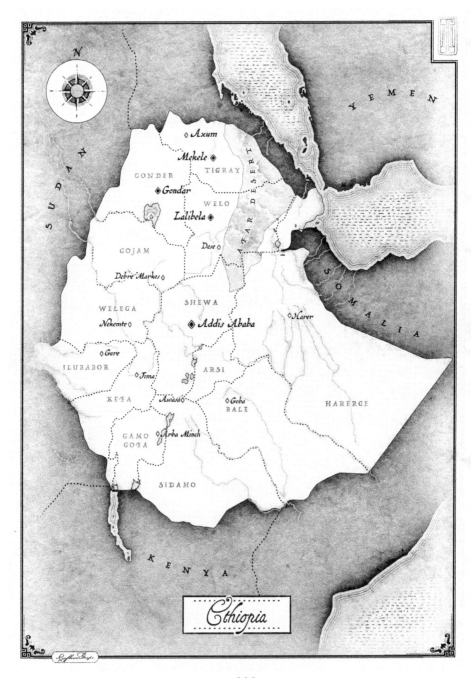

SUDAN

YEMEN

N

Axum

Mekele

GONDER   TIGRAY

Gondar

WELO

Lalibela

AFAR DESERT

GOJAM   Dese

SOMALIA

Debre Markos

SHEWA

WELEGA

Harer

Nekemte   Addis Ababa

Gore

ARSI

ILUBABOR

Jima

KEFA   Awasa   Goba
                              BALE   HARERGE

GAMO   Arba Minch
GOFA

SIDAMO

KENYA

Ethiopia

At Hotel Ghion, they unloaded the trunks, took a pair of adjoining rooms, and showered.

Down in the lobby, Will took out the CODEX and turned it on.

'Read me the coordinates,' Emma said, opening up Google Maps.

Making sure to get it right, Will read out the sequence, while Emma typed it into her phone.

'You're going to love this,' she said sarcastically.

'Love what?'

'Hope you brought a suit.'

'Why?'

'Looks like Hannibal's sending us to the Presidential Palace.'

'Double-check it.'

Emma looked up.

'I have. Twice. See for yourself. It's right there on Asmere Street.'

TEN MINUTES LATER THEY were in a bullet-riddled Lada approaching the palace. As the ramshackle taxi pushed through the lines of protestors, Will burst out laughing.

'So what's the opening line going to be, then: "Hello folks, we've just dropped in to pick up the Ladder of Mithras!"'

Emma shushed him.

'Don't smile, the protestors are eyeballing us, and they don't look exactly overjoyed.'

'This is totally screwed. Let's get out.'

Gingerly, Will and Emma got out of the Lada.

Will handed fifty birr through the open window. As soon as the driver's fingers touched the money, he threw the vehicle in reverse and sped away.

Pushing through the lines of protestors, Will and Emma strode up to the palace gates, where the Presidential guard were on duty.

'What do we say?' Emma asked.

'That we've come to discuss a matter relating to...'

'*To?*'

'To antiquities.'

Will shouted the explanation, his words drowned out by the protestors. To his surprise, the soldier nodded and snatched the cream-coloured telephone on the wall of the sentry post.

A minute later the gates opened. Will and Emma were ushered in.

A side door opened a crack.

A squat man with horn-rimmed glasses and a pained expression ran out.

'Quickly! Come with me!' he cried.

They followed and, before they knew it, were in the President's private study. The room was very large, the décor a mixture of Louis XIV and '70s kitsch.

'What's going on?' Emma whispered.

Will touched her arm reassuringly.

'Let's run with it.'

The man with horn-rimmed glasses disappeared. There were shouts from a back room, followed by the frenzied crack of an automatic rifle recoiling.

Another figure strode in.

Balding and confident, he was dressed in a dark suit — unquestionably the work of Savile Row. A photo of the same man hung on the study's wall. Under it ran a long and elaborate name, preceded by a title: 'His Excellency, the Head of State'.

'At last,' he said, his cheeks wincing into an uncomfortable smile. 'I expected you much earlier.'

'Expected us?'

'Indeed. Now, given the circumstances, I would ask you to begin immediately.'

Will looked at Emma.

'Um, yes, er.'

'I shall have my private secretary take you down to the vault. Time is of the essence. There's less than an hour before the helicopters arrive.'

Forty-nine

1894

THE MUSIC ROOM OF the sprawling green and white Winter Palace in St Petersburg was filled with the melody of Haydn's harpsichord sonata No. 37 in D major.

Tsar Alexander III had stepped out for a private

meeting with his Minister of War. Abandoning his daughter Grand Duchess Xenia Alexandrovna, who was playing his favourite piece, he left a glass of Cristal champagne and hurried out.

As it streamed in across the River Neva, the evening winter sunlight played over the lovely silk-covered walls.

'Much improved my dear,' declared an anaemic woman with an alabaster complexion, once the piece was at an end.

'Thank you, Governess. Ought I to play another? Perhaps a prelude by Mozart?'

The governess nodded. Staring into the fireplace, where a great log of elm was burning for atmosphere rather than for heat, she appeared distracted.

The music began again, a prelude by Mozart in C major.

As the duchess's slender young fingers caressed the harpsichord's ivory keys, the immense doors opened and a gentleman entered. Impeccably attired in white tie and tails, he moved swiftly, his steps precise, his back ramrod straight.

Looking up from the fire, the governess followed him as he drifted forwards in the direction of the musical instrument. She appeared out of breath, as though struggling to maintain her composure.

'Good evening, Governess.'

'Good evening to you, Mr Fogg.'

Hannibal paused at the curve of the instrument.

Listening intently, his mind lost in the music, he reached out for a glass of champagne — the one he could only imagine had been poured for him. The gilded rim touched his lips and, for the first time, he tasted Cristal Roederer.

When the duchess had reached the last bars of the prelude, he clapped softly, white gloves muffling the applause.

'Perhaps the tutor would reward his student for playing so perfectly,' the duchess mumbled with a grin.

Hannibal Fogg sipped the champagne.

'How so, Duchess Xenia?'

'By cancelling tomorrow's algebra examination, perhaps?'

The governess concealed her smile with the edge of her fan.

'I am sure Mr Fogg will take mercy upon you, my dear,' she said, 'especially as he has been so bold as to indulge in your father's glass of champagne.'

THAT NIGHT, WHEN THE Imperial household was asleep, and the palace silent but for the thud of the guards' hobnail boots out on the cobbles, Hannibal Fogg hurried from his bedroom. He was wearing a light cotton twill dressing gown and a pair of calfskin slippers.

In his left hand was clasped a leather-bound note-book, and in the right, a silver candelabra. Moving swiftly through the shadows, he made his way to the tsar's private library, located on the floor directly below his room.

Pushing open the teak doors, as he had done every night for almost a month, he made ready to continue the search.

Through almost an hour he criss-crossed the room, in a frantic search for the book.

Just as he was about to curse his uncharacteristically bad luck, he spotted a spider lowering itself on a strand of silk.

Intrigued by the arachnid, a species he had not observed before, he held the candelabra close so as to get a better view.

Hannibal's focus pulled from the eight legs to the spine of a thick volume on the shelf behind.

Blowing the spider away, he snatched the book and held it into the candlelight.

'At last!' he crooned, elated beyond belief.

Striding over to the central desk, Hannibal prised open the covers, and began reading the curious lettering — an early form of Ge'ez, the ancient language of Ethiopia.

'I can't believe it,' he said, baffled. 'It doesn't make any sense.'

As Hannibal scrutinised the text, the doors opened a crack.

A willowy figure gushed in.

The governess.

She was dressed in a flimsy silk nightgown, her hair

tied up on the back of her head.

'Mr Fogg, my dearest, dearest love!' she swooned, crossing the library as fast as her bare feet could manage. 'I have missed you, my darling!'

Hannibal inhaled sharply, his expression sour.

'As I have told you before, Miss Dupont, there is grave danger in your approaches. The Imperial chamberlain is sensible to your affection for me.'

'But my darling, I cannot contain my adoration a moment longer!'

Lunging forwards, the governess coiled her arms around Hannibal's neck. Unsure of what to do, he repelled her forcefully.

An instant later, the governess was lying on the library parquet.

Filled with horror at being scorned, she allowed her back to stiffen.

Her lungs filling with air, she screamed.

With the force of a hurricane, the terrible sound ripped through the Winter Palace, waking every soul.

An instant later the library's towering doors were thrust open.

The Imperial guard charged in.

Seizing Hannibal Fogg, they dragged him away.

Fifty

THE PRESIDENT'S PRIVATE SECRETARY corralled Emma and Will down into the Palace basement. Agitated, his face was dripping with perspiration.

'We are relying on you to instruct us which treasures are most valuable,' he said. 'You will find a lot of second rate items, most of them gifts to the late Emperor from other African leaders.'

The private secretary broke off at what sounded like an infantry charge outside. Tugging off his horn-rimmed glasses, he wiped them fitfully with a damp handkerchief.

'The protestors are gaining ground!' he exclaimed, his voice trembling. 'We will hold them off. But I must implore you to work with speed. Do you understand?'

Will signalled that they did.

The private secretary unlocked the reinforced steel door to the vault, and stepped back.

'I will leave you to your work,' he said. 'The President's guard shall be down in a few minutes to pack up the most valuable pieces. The helicopters are due very soon. One already left this morning with a dozen crates.' The private secretary paused again, as his ears caught the clamour of protestors nearby. 'The people of Ethiopia thank you,' he said solemnly.

Inside the treasure vault, Will and Emma found rows of shelving, packed with artifacts amassed through eight centuries of Imperial rule.

A central display housed the crowns of the emperors. Crafted from fine gold, they were laden with precious gems. There were solid silver tureens as well, and dinner sets bearing the Imperial seal of the Lion of Judah; and racks of ornate weaponry, orbs and sceptres, ornamental clocks, caskets brimming with ancient coins, rock crystal vases, and coronation robes.

'This is outrageous!' Will yelled.

'I've never seen anything like it.'

'Start looking for the Ladder.'

'Got any idea — size, shape, anything?'

Will shook his head.

'Just look for something that could have come from ancient Greece.'

They spread out, combing the stacks for the Ladder of Mithras.

Emma pointed to a robe in a glass case — black wool embroidered intricately with gold.

'I've seen that in old photos,' she said, impressed. 'It was worn by Haile Selassie, last emperor of Ethiopia, at his coronation.'

'How come they have emperors rather than kings like everyone else?' Will asked.

'Because they claim descent from King Solomon.'

'Solomon and who?'

'Solomon and the Queen of Sheba. To the Rastafarians he's God incarnate.'

'*Rastas*, you mean like Bob Marley?'

'Yup. They're named after him — *Ras Tafari*.'

'So what happened to the last emperor?' asked Will.

'Bustled away during a coup d'état in a Volkswagen Bug, smothered with a pillow and buried under President Mengistu's toilet.'

There was a clatter of automatic fire outside. Short bursts, louder and more frequent.

'We don't have much time,' shouted Will. 'I've got a feeling this is the wrong place to be right now!'

Emma was only half-listening. She had spotted something in a carved teak box — a silver and gold helmet, adorned with what looked like a ladder motif.

'Could this be it?'

Will rushed over.

'I'd love to say it was, but…'

Will's sentence was cut short by an explosion. He and Emma were flung to the ground, as the palace shook on its foundations.

At the far end of the vault, the shelving collapsed, choking them in clouds of dust.

Will grabbed Emma's hand.

'You OK?'

'Yeah, you?'

'Just about.'

Another blast ripped through. It was followed by cries of anger and pain, more gunfire, and by the dull thud of helicopter rotor blades in the distance.

'Sounds like they're gonna try and land out there.'

'It'll be suicide.'

Emma turned to the door.

'Ladder or no Ladder, we have to get out of here!'

Will thrust out a hand.

'*Wait!*'

'There's no time!'

Will didn't react. He was standing in front of a display case, its glass front smashed by the blast. Inside, covered in dust, was a mannequin decked out in Imperial robes. Skewed on the head was a solid gold crown ornamented with polished gems.

Snatching the crown, Will tossed it onto the floor. Then, with care, he reached in and pulled a silver pendant from the mannequin.

With Emma watching, he put it around his neck.

Just then a third explosion hit.

A Russian-made RPG fired at close range.

Deafened, enveloped in smoke and dust, Will and Emma spotted blue sky through the ceiling of the vault.

Choking, Emma led the way.

'Follow me!' she cried, clawing her way up over the sea of rubble. As she scrambled up, Will made out a line of rioters in blurred silhouette heading straight for her.

'Look out!'

Will tripped, his ankle trapped between two blocks of masonry. Emma reached back and yanked him free.

Inexplicably, the rioters were gone.

'Where are they?'

'Must have been shot,' yelled Emma, her blouse drenched in blood.

'They get you?'

'No, it's not mine.'

Will took Emma's hand. Together, they clambered through clouds of dust, up over the bodies and out into the daylight.

Protestors were streaming towards the palace from all directions, as the clamour of a Super Puma deafened them.

Against the odds, the pilot managed to perch it on the roof, the massive rotors sweeping invisibly round.

Will choked out a lungful of dust.

'Looks like the President's making his grand escape.'

'What do we do now?'

'How about getting out of here fast.'

'Where to?'

'The US Embassy. It's our only bet,' said Will.

Way in the distance Emma spotted a taxi approaching. A battered red Lada, its windscreen a spider's web of cracks. As it neared them, she flagged it down, surprised when the driver stopped.

They leapt into the back.

'To the American Embassy!'

The taxi driver spun round. He was about to say something, when a towering figure wearing military fatigues shattered the passenger window with the butt of a .44 revolver.

Without the faintest hint of emotion, he emptied three chambers into the driver's head.

Her face spattered in blood, Emma was screaming.

'What the…?!' cried Will.

The man in fatigues motioned to the passengers.

'Get out! Get out now!' his voice boomed over the clatter of gunfire in the palace behind.

Hands above their heads, they got out of the car.

'Put your hands down,' ordered the man, stuffing away his weapon. 'I've just saved your lives.'

Reaching through the shattered passenger window, he seized a 9 mm pistol from the driver's right hand.

'He was about to finish you off.'

Will felt faint. The man grabbed his shoulder, steadying him.

'Come with me! We'll go to where it's safe.'

'Who are you?'

'Solomon.'

Will touched Emma's hand.

'Can we trust him?' he whispered.

Jerking back as though he had overheard, Solomon's face lit up in a grin.

'Yes, you can trust me!'

'Why?'

'Because I have been sent for you.'

'Who by?'

Solomon sponged a hand over his face, wiping away the sweat.

'By Mr Hannibal Fogg,' he said.

Fifty-one

SLALOMING THROUGH THE LINES of rioters, Solomon steered the Lada away from the centre of town at breakneck speed. Without giving the killing a second thought, he had thrown the driver's body out onto the ground unceremoniously.

Behind them came the intermittent clatter of Kalashnikov gunfire, followed by an almighty explosion. It was accompanied by a plume of black smoke, mushrooming up into the heavens above the Ethiopian capital.

'Must be the palace arms dump going up,' said Solomon, spinning the wheel fast through his hands.

Will didn't hear him.

'Don't understand,' he stammered, his mind reeling. 'How could Hannibal have sent you?'

'It's a long story,' Solomon replied. 'And I'm not the man to tell it.'

'Then who is?'

'My grandfather.'

Craning her neck to the right, Emma caught her reflection in the driver's mirror. She broke down in tears.

'Look at me! I'm covered in blood!'

'Relax,' said Solomon calmly, aiming the vehicle at a double line of protestors. 'We'll be at the safe house in a minute.'

Will clapped his hands.

'No! We want the American Embassy!'

Solomon launched into a crazed laugh, blinding white teeth stretched between his ears.

'The Embassy got hit this morning,' he said.

THE SAFE HOUSE WAS guarded by a pair of figures with the same sinewy build as Solomon. They were both clutching cut-down AK-47s, their double magazines bound together with silver duct tape.

'My brothers Jonah and Yohannes,' Solomon said by way of introduction.

Will and Emma were taken inside, where they found themselves in a fortified room. The windows were blacked out, and the walls and floor made of concrete. A cluster of rickety old school chairs and an upturned packing crate did for furniture.

Solomon flicked a switch, and the room was bathed in neon light.

'I'm surprised we've still got electricity,' he said. 'It won't last for long.'

Will was shaking.

'Never been under fire before?'

'Take a wild guess.'

'The adrenalin's used up all your blood sugar. Eat some of these.'

Solomon ripped open a packet of wholemeal biscuits and passed them to Will. Chewing one, he strained to swallow. His throat was too dry to eat.

In reflex, he thumped a hand to his chest, his fist striking something hard. In all the excitement he had forgotten about the pendant. Digging it out from under his shirt, he took it off and nudged Emma.

'Look at this.'

'It's the monogram.'

'Yeah, but that's not all... it's a key as well.'

Just then, one of the guards outside wolf-whistled twice. The sound was followed by the silhouette of a man at the door. Unlike Solomon and his brothers, he was weak. Hunched low over a cane, he was presented as Tewodros.

'How do you do?' he enquired politely. 'I am very pleased to make your acquaintance, Mr William Fogg.'

Will scanned the man's wrinkled face, taking in his cataract-clouded eyes.

'How do you know who I am?'

Tewodros laughed.

'I knew your grandfather, Mr Hannibal Fogg.'

'He was my great-great-grandfather.'

The ancient took in the floor vacantly. 'I suppose that is right,' he said. 'After all, it was a very long while ago.'

Emma balked.

216

'You knew Hannibal?'

'Yes, indeed. When I was a young man, I was his assistant on one of his Abyssinian expeditions. He used to come here often and loved our country, although it almost stole his manhood on one occasion.'

The comment was lost on Will. He was still thinking about the bloodbath back at the palace, and about the pendant clutched in his hand.

'I don't understand,' he said again. 'How do you know who I am?'

Tewodros drew a long fingernail down his nose. He didn't reply. Will was about to repeat the question for a third time, when the old man spoke.

'Because Mr Fogg left instructions,' he said. 'He made me promise to commit this day to memory. He said that nothing was so important as today... 18th May 2017. Back then I did a calculation on my fingers, I remember it clearly. "If I live that long, I shall be one hundred and five years old!" I said.

'Mr Hannibal Fogg slapped me on the back, and promised that I would live. He said it with such certainty that over the years I almost wondered if he had seen the future.'

'What instructions did he give you?' asked Will.

As if summoning a stream of memory, Tewodros pressed a hand to his wrinkled brow.

'He told me to make my way to the Presidential Palace in the afternoon, and to look for a young man — a white man.' Tewodros sighed. 'I'm getting old,' he said sorrowfully, 'and as you have seen it's chaos. So I sent my grandson, Solomon, to find you.'

Emma turned to Will.

'How could he have known?'

'I know… it's incredible, even for Hannibal.'

Tewodros touched a hand to his throat and began coughing. He coughed so long that the others thought his time might have at last come. But the coughing eventually eased.

'And now,' he said, 'I will take you to the room.'

'Which room?'

'The one you have come to see.'

Will looked at Tewodros.

'I don't know what you mean,' he said. 'What room?'

'Mr Hannibal's Abyssinian Chamber of course.'

Fifty-two

SOLOMON PRISED OPEN A storm grate in the Mercato quarter of town. Two hundred yards to the south of where he was crouched with a crowbar there was carnage.

Kitted out in third-rate riot gear, a dozen soldiers were attempting to stave off droves of looters and hold their ground against the legions of protestors. Molotov cocktails and debris were flying through the smoke-tinged air, cries of rage drowning out the military sirens.

Once the storm grate was open, Solomon motioned to Emma and Will.

'Get in there quick!' he barked, just as a vigilante Jeep reeled full tilt towards them.

Dropping to his knees, Will shuffled up to the hole, swivelling the lower half of his body inside. Rusted iron rungs were set into the concrete casing. His hands grasped them, and were at once covered in roaches.

'God damn it!' he shouted, lowering himself down into the darkness.

'Miss Emma, you next!'

'What about Tewodros?'

Solomon let out a grunt, an expression of brute strength.

'I'll carry him down.'

Once Emma had disappeared behind Will, the old man curled both arms around his grandson's back, and together they descended — Solomon's giant hand heaving the storm grate back into place just in time.

'How far down is it?' called Will, his voice echoing up the tunnel.

'Just keep going!'

Solomon's words were lost in the roar of the vigilante Jeep rattling over the storm grate above.

One hand after the next, they descended. Will was thankful for the darkness. It prevented him from actually seeing the cockroaches, or the rats — which were everywhere.

In a frail voice Tewodros cried out, instructing Will to wait at the bottom.

A moment after that, all four of them were in the sewer pipe, their feet slipping in sludge.

Solomon clicked on his torch and, gagging, Will wished they were in darkness again.

'Just a little further,' Tewodros intoned.

'How can you be sure it's still there?'

The old man shrugged.

'I can't.'

'When were you last down here?'

'With Mr Fogg.'

'But when?'

Taking the torch from his grandson, Tewodros staggered ahead.

'In the summer of 1936,' he said.

Reaching back, Will felt for Emma's hand. He squeezed it reassuringly.

'Here's the passage,' said Tewodros, aiming the light's arc high. 'This one, off to the left.'

One at a time, they followed, the stench of raw sewage unbearable.

'Here it is.'

Tewodros rapped a knuckle to an iron door. Fumbling, he pulled out the key hanging around his neck.

'I've worn this almost my entire life,' he said with a sigh. 'It's three keys in one.'

'Quickly, open it,' Will pleaded. 'I'm covered in roaches.'

The lock's mechanism clicked and a steel bolt slid back.

Gently, Tewodros pulled the handle.

The steel door swung open on greased hinges.

In single file they entered.

When the door was firmly shut and locked behind them, Tewodros pushed open a second portal. The rats and the cockroaches were gone now, replaced by a clinical room. Small and bare, it smelled of ammonia and was lit by electric lights.

'Is this the Abyssinian Chamber?' asked Will, a tone of disappointment in his voice.

Tewodros pointed at a third portal. Unlike the first two doorways, it was made from stone.

'In there,' he said. 'Mr Fogg sealed it to prevent decay or corrosion.'

Stooping down, he slid the key into the lock and turned it twice.

A gushing sound came and went.

'What was that?' asked Emma.

'The hermetic seal being broken,' Tewodros replied. 'The air's rushing back in.'

He signalled for Solomon to open the door.

Stepping forwards, his grandson wrenched the handle downwards and pulled with all his might.

The door was immensely heavy — crafted from a single slab of granite — balanced perfectly on a complex hinge mechanism. As it swung open, Hannibal's

Abyssinian Chamber was revealed.

Fifty-five feet square, it was bright, illuminated by shafts of natural sunlight searing in through blocks of glass set into the roof. Tewodros entered first, blinded by the sudden light.

The others followed close behind. As their eyes adjusted to the light, they caught a first glimpse of the equipment.

There must have been fifty crates filled with expedition gear, weaponry and specialist supplies. All of it in mint condition and monogrammed; it was a time capsule of ingenuity.

'Hannibal!' cried Will in disbelief. 'You've done it again!'

Tewodros fluttered a hand at the crates dismissively.

'Tip of the iceberg,' he said with a toothless grin.

'Huh?'

'Follow me.'

The old man cocked his head at a stack of crates piled up against the far wall. 'Get those away,' he said.

Will and Solomon did as they were told, revealing a low door.

Tewodros punched a number into a mechanical display. A system of gears unlocked, and the door opened.

A moment later, he and the others were standing in a far larger room. Much of it was taken up with equipment. But it wasn't the gear that caught Will's attention.

In the middle of the chamber, its tyres raised an inch

off the ground, was a vehicle.

Emma burst out laughing.

'This has been the wildest day,' she said.

'How the hell did he get this old thing down here?' asked Will.

'Old?' said Tewodros. 'What are you talking about? It's brand spanking new!'

Circling it as in a dream, Will took in the cloth top, the bucket seats and the running boards.

'What make is it?'

Tewodros reached out and, brushing his fingers against the driver's door, he breathed in.

'It's a Rolls-Royce,' he said.

Fifty-three

1936

A SEMI-CIRCLE OF THATCHED huts stood in the middle of the plain, their baked mud walls affording little shade from the blistering African sun.

A stone's throw from the hamlet, some boys were tending the clan's sheep, the parched mud beneath their bare feet a shattered mass of cracks.

It hadn't rained in the Afar Desert for years.

Hannibal Fogg was seated in a chair under a sprawling thorn tree — the only natural shade for a hundred miles. He was dressed in khaki, a safari outfit of his own design. On his lap was a notebook, the pages ruled in neat columns, each one filled with phonetic symbols.

Standing an arm's length away was a tall Ethiopian man of about twenty. Unlike Hannibal, he appeared distressed by the sweltering heat.

'Tell me, Tewodros, what's the Amharic word for buffalo?'

'It is *gosh*, Mr Fogg.'

'Ahh, that's right. And tell me, how does one say, "How long does it take?"?'

'Sent gizea yiwesdal.'

Tewodros had turned his back to Hannibal's chair.

He was standing stock still, as if listening to the wind.

'What do you hear?'

'It's not what I hear, sir.'

'Then what?'

'I smell the Danakil, Mr Fogg.'

'Oh hush, there's no Danakil for fifty miles.'

'Where Danakil are concerned it is unwise to take a chance, sir.'

Hannibal circled a phonetic notation with his pen.

'And what does *kulfu* mean?'

Slanting his face into the breeze, Tewodros breathed in through his nostrils.

'I must plead with you, sir,' he said. 'I can smell them very clearly. They are near.'

'Nonsense!' said Hannibal. 'Come on… *kulfu*…?'

Tewodros had nothing but respect for his employer

and would not normally have made a fuss. But the Danakil were not a normal tribe.

'I believe you know what they prize more than anything else, sir.'

'*Testicles?*' said Hannibal, the word rolling off his tongue with delight.

'Yes, sir. But there's one kind of testicle they prize above all others, for their trophy necklaces.'

'And what kind of testicle is that, Tewodros?' asked the Englishman studiously.

'A white man's, sir.'

Groaning, Hannibal went back to his notes.

'You know I don't believe that mumbo jumbo,' he said.

Tewodros was at the point of pleading.

'Danakil can follow the scent of a lion crouching on the savannah three horizons away,' he said.

Glancing up from his notebook, Hannibal seemed distracted. He was about to reply, when something caught his attention — the frozen mask of terror wrapped over Tewodros's face.

He looked at the horizon.

In the distance, sweeping over the plain at impressive speed, were a thousand Danakil warriors. They looked like a plague of insects at first, one blurred into the next.

But, as they got rapidly closer, Hannibal could make out their rhino-hide shields, and the elongated spears wielded ferociously above their heads.

As they drew even closer, he discerned the individual faces and the strands of human testicles worn around their necks.

In a single deft movement, Hannibal lurched up from the chair, tossed down the notebook…

…and ran for his life.

Fifty-four

'MR FOGG HAD THE Rolls-Royce modified for Abyssinia,' Tewodros explained. 'It started out as a Silver Ghost Tourer, but was stripped down to the chassis and completely rebuilt. The engine is a straight-six, the suspension reinforced and the panelling is fully armoured.'

'Armoured?'

Hannibal's former assistant tapped a fingernail to the bodywork, the details crystal clear to him despite his advanced age.

'Bullet-proofing all round,' he said. 'But that's just the start. There are stun grenades in the doors and a water-cooled Vickers .303 machine gun mounted under the bonnet. You pull that lever when you're ready to deploy it.'

'How did he ever get it down here?' asked Emma, for a second time.

'More to the point, how do we get it out?' said Will.

Tewodros gesticulated at another stack of crates.

'There's a door behind those,' he said. 'Takes you on a purpose-built track... comes out near the Church of Saint George.'

NEXT MORNING, AFTER A night stretched out on the floor of the safe house, Will, Emma and Solomon set off in the Rolls-Royce, driving north out of Addis Ababa. The vehicle had started on the first go, filling Fogg's secret Abyssinian Chamber with fumes.

In the hours of darkness, the Presidential palace had been burned to the ground, the ancient wealth of the Ethiopians looted.

Steering through the suburbs, Solomon zigzagged between the bodies of dead protestors, and others caught in the crossfire.

As the vehicle progressed into the wealthier suburbs, Will spotted the plumes of smoke rising from the mansions where the President's henchmen had lived in luxury until a few hours before. Some of them had escaped to neighbouring Djibouti or even to Europe, as their leader himself had done. Those less fortunate were hanging from the trees, trussed up by their ankles by the mobs of vigilantes baying for blood.

Leaning back, Will tested the ropes holding the luggage. He had followed Solomon's advice and taken along only what they could be certain to use.

As Solomon explained, in a war situation, nothing

was so precious as provisions or fuel. The Rolls-Royce was laden with plenty of both, its mighty engine growling under the weight of it all.

The suburbs gave way to the open road, and Will's thoughts turned to the Ladder of Mithras.

As if the task of locating it wasn't challenging enough already, Ethiopia's political situation was disintegrating hour by hour.

Wishing them well on their journey, Tewodros had revealed one last nugget of information entrusted to him in person by Hannibal Fogg:

'Seek out the Cross of Lalibela,' he had said, 'and the Ladder will be near.'

A day and a half of jolting and juddering, and the Rolls-Royce swerved west off the main road. The last fifty miles had been strewn with bandit positions, and many more bodies strung from the trees.

While Solomon deployed the stun grenades and opened up the Vickers to clear the path, Will took the wheel.

'Lalibela's only a few miles now,' said Solomon.

'Thank God for that.'

'Oh, no...'

'What is it?'

Solomon cocked his head to the distance.

Will had been so busy swerving around the potholes, some of them as deep as a man's height, that he had forgotten to keep his eyes on the road ahead.

Two hundred yards beyond them was a roadblock. Beside it, a beer truck was burning on its side.

Solomon pulled the Vickers into position.

'Hold tight!'

Emma thrust out a hand from the back seat.

'They're just kids!'

'This is war,' Solomon countered.

'I'll ram it.'

Will's voice was lost against the sound of the Rolls's engine gaining speed.

As they approached the barricades, the child soldiers raised their weapons in disbelief.

'They've got AKs!' Solomon yelled. 'They'll shred us!'

Will forced the accelerator to the floor.

'Heads down!'

Aided by the gradient, the Rolls-Royce picked up speed.

It was pushing sixty by the time it struck the burning barricades. Against the clatter of Kalashnikov fire, the Rolls barrelled ahead, its bodywork raked by razor wire.

'We're through!' Emma shrieked.

Will breathed out, whooped, and got a flash of the predictable life in San Francisco he had left behind.

An hour later, the Rolls-Royce reached Lalibela.

'So where's the Cross?' Emma asked.

'This way, in the Church of Saint George,' Solomon said.

It was then they caught a first obstructed view of the

rock-hewn church. Like all the others in Lalibela, it was carved into the pancake-flat plateau — every inch of it hollowed in a true wonder of pious dedication.

If the church had been anywhere else on earth there might have been security cordons and tourists.

It being Ethiopia, there was gunfire instead.

'Maybe this isn't such a good idea,' Will said, clambering out of the vehicle.

Solomon unclipped a stun grenade from its mooring in the driver's door.

'Be prepared for anything,' he said, leading the way to the viewpoint.

Once at the edge, he held up a hand to halt Will and Emma. Together they peered down at the Church of Saint George. A singular feat of architecture and endurance, it was carved from the rock plateau in the shape of a perfect cross.

'This is it,' said Solomon. 'The Cross.'

'Not quite what I had in mind,' said Will.

One by one they climbed down to the door of the church. Inside, a group of priests were performing a ritual in the darkness, the rock-hewn interior pungent with the smoke from burning myrrh.

'We should speak to the priest,' said Solomon.

'Which one is he?'

'That one over there, reading the Bible.'

Emma was about to add something, when a white man in military camouflage leapt through the door, a long-shafted mace grasped between outstretched hands.

Lunging at Will, he missed his shoulder by an inch.

Solomon pulled the pin on a stun grenade, but held back from hurling it. They would all have gone down if he had.

Will ran out of the door into the blinding light. The assailant was after him, the mace twirling above his head like a lasso.

Stumbling, Will fled behind the church.

The hit-man was closing in.

Zigzagging left, then right, Will ran fast, like a gazelle hunted on the savannah. Turning, he looked back in utter consternation.

The attacker was lying dead on the ground.

His throat had been torn open below the Adam's apple, the blade had gone all the way through the neck.

Will felt adrenalin surge through his bloodstream.

He fell to his knees.

'What the…?!'

Sprinting up fast, Solomon kicked the assailant over with his boot.

'Thank you,' screeched Will.

'I didn't kill him.'

'Then who the hell did?'

Emma reeled forward, her eyes wide open in shock.

'I threw the knife,' she said, her voice trembling. 'Don't know how I ever hit him.'

'You saved my life,' said Will, straining to breathe.

'I killed a man,' Emma replied in horror. 'I can't believe I killed a man.'

'He wasn't local,' said Solomon.

'He was coming for me,' Will added. 'Oh my God, he must be the enemy Hannibal warned me about.'

'Who?'

'The Magi.'

Fifty-five

THE PRIEST SEEMED UNSURPRISED at there being an attacker in the church compound. Wizened, with a balding head, his body was gnarled, wrapped in linen robes.

In Amharic, Solomon asked him about the Ladder of Mithras.

The lids lowered over the priest's eyes, and he thought for a long while.

'The Ladder will only be found by the man who does not search for it,' he said.

Will rolled his eyes.

'That's just great,' he said sarcastically.

The priest uttered a line of Amharic with slow deliberation, pronouncing each syllable as though vitally important.

'What's he saying?'

'That the Ladder of Mithras connects Man with his destiny.'

'But *where* is it?'

'Above the mines.'

'What mines?'

'The gold mines of Ophir.'

ANOTHER FULL DAY OF driving through choking dust, and the Rolls-Royce Tourer reached the starvation camps.

On Presidential orders, thousands of tribesmen and their families had been herded together in pens. The government's fear was for the world to once again catch sight of the stark truth — starvation in the Highlands of Ethiopia.

Word of the President's inglorious departure had spread rapidly from mouth to ear. As it did so, the army deserted en masse. The starving clansmen of the Highlands might have fled too. But, with no food, there was little chance of escape.

'Was Live Aid for nothing?' Emma asked reflectively.

Solomon huffed.

'D'you really think that money ever reached these people?'

'What happened to it, then?'

'The Derg — Mengistu's dictatorship — that's what happened. Most of the cash was siphoned off to Switzerland long before it ever reached Ethiopia.'

'What's the hope?' said Will.

'There isn't any.'

'So?'

'So they'll die here,' Solomon remarked, his voice even and cold.

'We can share out our supplies,' said Will, realising at once the stupidity of the remark.

'Feed fifty thousand people with a few tin cans?' Solomon said.

'What's gone wrong here?' Emma asked.

'These people you see are from the wrong tribe.'

'What do you mean?'

'They're not Tigrayans — not from the dominant tribe.'

'So what?'

'So they've been abandoned on the scrap heap of life and left to rot.'

Fifty-six

THREE HOURS BEYOND THE starvation camps, the track came to an abrupt end.

Far in the distance stood a freestanding outcrop of rock, a slender plateau running its length. Solomon thrust an arm in its direction.

'We'll walk from here.'

'Do you know the way?'

'That way.'

Hours of stumbling followed, over boulders and

through parched scrub. They had hidden the vehicle in a thicket of thorn trees. As they left it, traipsing off in the direction of the horizon, Will wondered if they would ever see it again. In a landscape so devoid of luxury, a Rolls-Royce made for an incongruous travelling companion.

Eventually, as they neared the plateau, they caught the muffled hum of voices.

'Don't see anyone,' said Emma.

Solomon patted the air in front of him.

'Wait.'

Approaching the plateau's base cautiously, they curved around it from the far side. The boulders gave way to a steep slope. Scrambling up it, they found themselves staring down into a man-made canyon.

It was filled with people.

Thousands of them.

Men, women and children — all digging with their hands.

'My God,' said Will. 'It's like something out of the Old Testament.'

'The mines of Ophir,' Solomon said, 'where the ancient Egyptians got their gold, and King Solomon, too.'

Dressed in little more than rags, the miners paid no attention to the outsiders. They were far too engrossed in their work — gleaning a few grains of gold dust from the alluvial lode.

'The system hasn't changed in four thousand years,' Solomon explained. 'Not since the time of the Pharaohs.

Look at the sluices — those were invented in ancient Egypt.'

Will nudged a hand over to the far side of the pit.

'What's going on over there?'

'They're digging shafts. They send the children down because the tunnels are so narrow. It's dangerous work, and there are frequent cave-ins.'

The timing of the remark was uncanny.

For, at that moment, one of the miners began yelling. The sound preceded a frenzy of commotion. Everyone stopped digging and hurried over to a bore-hole.

From a distance Will, Emma and Solomon watched as the miners scrabbled to save a young life. One group frantically dug a second tunnel down through the clay. Another opened out the original hole.

But it was too late.

A woman's voice ripped through the canyon. The shrill sound of anguish — a mother's instinct. Somehow she already knew her child was dead.

A few minutes passed.

Then, the limp body of a boy was heaved from the ground. The miners dropped their shovels and froze. Careering through the mud, the mother collapsed on reaching her son.

Despondently, Solomon shook his head.

'All this for a few pennies' worth of gold,' he said.

The body was carried from the pit at shoulder height, dozens of miners following behind, heads bowed in respect.

An hour or so passed and the digging began again, the atmosphere more sombre than before.

'We must get up there,' Solomon said, pointing at the sheer rock face.

'How the hell do we do that?' asked Will. 'It's a vertical climb. We'll need ropes and harnesses, and that gear's back in the car.'

Nearing the cliff face at its widest point, they shielded their eyes from the dazzling afternoon sunlight.

Will spat on his hands.

'We could try climbing without ropes.'

Solomon laughed.

'Who are you, *Spiderman*?'

Just then, a man's voice called down from the top of the plateau. They looked up into the sun.

'What's he saying?'

Solomon cupped a hand to his ear.

The voice came again, a little louder.

'He says to wait down here.'

Little by little, a thick leather rope slithered down the precipice like a great fawn-coloured serpent.

One at a time, they tied the rope around their waists, and were heaved up the sheer cliff face.

Will went first.

As the rope jerked him higher and higher, he looked down at the sprawling canyon, the miners no more than specks in a no man's land of sludge.

Up on the plateau, he spotted a clutch of crude stone buildings, and half a dozen priests heading to their shade.

Solomon began the prolonged greetings that tended to accompany the arrival of a visitor.

'Ask about the Ladder of Mithras,' Will whispered urgently.

'First we must take coffee with them.'

They were led to a spacious reception room, decorated with cartoon-like murals of King Solomon receiving the Queen of Sheba. At length, coffee was served, the colour of straw. Drinking it, they praised the taste and gave thanks.

Another hour of greetings slipped by.

Then Solomon cleared his throat. Sitting up, fumbling awkwardly, he posed a question while motioning something long and thin with his hands. The priest appeared concerned. Standing up, he bowed, and walked backwards to the door.

'Something's going on,' Solomon said.

'What?'

'Not sure.'

Outside, there was indistinct conversation, and the *pat-pat-pat* of bare feet running fast.

More voices. More running.

Will glanced at Emma.

'I can't stop thinking about that man down in Lalibela,' she said. 'The thought of taking a life is so dreadful.'

'But he would have killed me.'

'I know, but even so.'

Will stared at the mural of Solomon and Sheba, his vision blurring as he remembered the attack.

'The Magi,' he said in a chilled voice. 'I didn't believe they existed.'

Dusk approached, ebbing into darkness.

'Looks like we'll have to sleep up here,' said Solomon.

Will got up and strode to the doorway.

He peered out.

'A priest's coming,' he said.

Fifty-seven

FATHER ANTHONY HAD THE physique of a weightlifter, his squat muscular frame furled up in a white cotton vestment. As soon as he spotted the visitors, he welcomed them cordially in English.

'I have been told you have come for the Ladder,' he said once introductions were over.

Will nodded.

'We were told that you keep it here.'

Father Anthony scratched a hand to the back of his neck.

'Our community has existed up on this plateau for a thousand years,' he said. 'The monastery was founded to protect the Ladder. We have always known that one day an outsider would come and ask for it. Such is the legend. But you must forgive our surprise that this day has at last arrived.'

'Can you give it to us?'

The priest dipped his head.

'Are you ready to receive it?'

'Yes we are,' said Will firmly.

'Then come with me.'

Emma and Solomon got to their feet.

'Your friends must wait for you at the bottom of the cliff.'

'They can't come?'

'No. Only you may stay here. Your friends must leave.'

WILL FOLLOWED FATHER ANTHONY across the plateau, Simien wolves howling in the darkness far below.

'How big is it?' Will asked as they walked.

'I do not know.'

Will frowned.

'You've never seen it?'

'None of us have.'

'Why not?'

'Because it's a sacred relic.'

Edging around to the plateau's rear, they crossed a field of alfalfa, and reached the mouth of a cave.

'This is the place,' said Father Anthony, leading Will to a sacred alcove set into the side of the cave. Lit by burning torches fuelled by ghee, it was thick with smoke and packed with handwritten volumes in Ge'ez.

The priest tugged a burning torch from its bracket and handed it to Will.

'You will find the Ladder at the end of the passageway,' he said. 'I wish you luck.'

'Aren't you coming?'

In silence, Father Anthony turned and left.

Cautiously, and with small steps, Will paced down the rock-hewn passageway, his hand stretched out, the torch vanquishing the dark. Cold air streamed over his face, the flames rippling in the draught.

Filled with the stench of bat excrement, the passageway narrowed.

Will staggered ahead.

Another fifty feet and it was too low to stand. Straining to keep the flames from his face, he shuffled ahead, to a stone doorway.

Scrambling through it, he emerged into what seemed to be a natural cavern, the ceiling thick with bats. Alarmed at the intruder and the light, they swooped to and fro.

Offset in the chamber there was an altar.

A hand protecting his head, Will approached it. As he did so, the torch's fire was snuffed out. He swore, the exclamation lost against the screech of the bats.

A voice was calling out in his head, reminding him to use the night-vision goggles. Hannibal had patented the invention under the name 'Darkness Dispelling Viewing Device'.

Fumbling in the daypack, he grabbed the goggles and pulled them on.

A flick of the switch and darkness was replaced by turquoise light.

Will drew closer to the altar, squinting to get a view of its upper surface. Laid out on the stone slab was a pair of human skulls, a silver orb and a bronze box upside down — each object smothered liberally in centuries of bat droppings and grime.

Lifting the box in his hands, Will turned it over. Fixed to the top was a sheet of card, adorned prominently with Hannibal's monogram. Under the card was a keyhole.

Fishing the key from under his shirt, he inserted it into the lock and turned twice.

The box opened.

Inside, wrapped in a disintegrating scrap of velvet, was an object — a double helix crafted from solid silver.

'The Ladder!' he bellowed. 'Hannibal! I've got it!'

At that moment the bats fell silent.

Stuffing the helix under his arm, Will looked up.

The altar fell away, plunging into an abyss, followed by much of the floor.

Will screamed out for help, but there was no reply.

Summoning courage, leg muscles clenched tight, he prepared to jump to the other side.

Something stopped him — Hannibal's voice.

Do the unexpected.

Huh?

Jump!

What?!

Panicked, Will gaped down through the turquoise mist. There was no way of telling how far the drop could be. It looked like certain suicide.

Sorry, Hannibal, but I'm going with gut instinct.

Once again, he clenched his leg muscles, readying himself to leap across the void.

But, wait.

Flame and shadow were racing down the passageway from where he had come, the light flaring through the goggles. Enraged at the prospect of losing their relic, the priests were pouring into the cavern in a blur of turquoise rage.

Will looked down into the abyss.

What to do?

No time to deliberate.

Hugging the helix to his chest, he took a deep breath, and jumped.

Down.

Down.

Down.

The rock streaked turquoise as he fell, his voice a single prolonged shriek of terror.

Suddenly, he plunged into ice-cold water.

A pool.

Instinct told him to flail his arms. But the helix — he had to keep hold of it.

Struggling with all his strength, Will swam upwards into the dark, the relic clutched tight in his hand.

Ripping off the night-vision goggles, he swam to the edge of the pool and struggled out. A voice echoed somewhere in the darkness. Will opened his mouth a fraction to hone his hearing, as his father had taught him to do.

He listened. Must be the priests coming for him.

His chest tightened with fear.

But it was a woman's voice. What's more it was speaking English.

Thank God. It was Emma.

Fifty-eight

BY THE TIME THE Rolls-Royce reached the safe house a full week had passed since they had left it. Life in Ethiopia was now so precarious that Solomon almost suggested Will and Emma flee north over the border to Eritrea, or even to Djibouti.

But there was a reason Solomon insisted they drive back along bandit-infested roads to Addis Ababa — the secret his grandfather had guarded for so long.

On the way through the capital's war-torn suburbs, the Rolls was strafed by small arms fire, the bullets hardly making a mark. Pulling out the Vickers, Will opened it up into the darkness. It was the first time in his life he had ever fired a real gun.

As the vehicle ground to a halt outside the safe house, Tewodros appeared.

'Thank God you're alive,' he said having heard their voices.

'All thanks to Solomon,' said Will.

'It's his duty,' the ancient replied. 'Now, come inside and rest.'

A feast of *njira* and *wot* was served on a low raffia table. Clustering around, Will and Emma followed Solomon's example, tearing the sheets of *njira* in their right hand and using it to scoop up the stew.

When the meal was at an end, Tewodros reached into his jacket pocket.

'I have kept something from you,' he said. 'A last instruction from Mr Fogg.'

'What is it?'

'Before he left Ethiopia the last time, he asked me to give you a letter — if you survived your journey.' Tewodros swallowed abruptly. 'I mean *when* you had finished your journey.'

'He'd seen the future,' Will muttered under his breath. 'He knew we'd make it.'

Tewodros passed over the envelope which was crumpled and filthy from all the years he had protected it.

Will ripped it open. Inside, he found a letter written in familiar green script — Hannibal's unmistakable hand.

Unlike his previous messages, this one was encoded.

'I'll use the CODEX,' Will said, pulling open the case. 'Can you read it a line at a time?'

Emma held the letter into the light.

'Ready?'

'Yeah.'

'Here goes: AFSYS73JS WTWH7DL9 QUQ.'

Typing in the sequence, Will hit 'return'.

Inside the CODEX, the rotor wheels and gears engaged.

A decoded string flashed up on the main display.

'What does it say?' asked Emma.

Will glared, his brow furrowing.

'It's gobbledegook. Maybe it's not meant for the CODEX.'

Emma glanced at Hannibal's device.

'I once read a book about the German Enigma,' she said. 'The cipher machines they used in World War II. Before they could be used, they had to be primed with a "day code".'

'And where d'you get that?' asked Will gruffly.

Emma held the letter to the bare bulb hanging from the ceiling. In the top right hand corner was an elaborate watermark.

'Try this,' she said: 'RTRRKFJ7.'

Will entered the code. As soon as he hit 'return' the CODEX chimed.

'I think it's worked.'

Fifteen minutes later, after some effort, he had read out half the decrypted message:

'If Tewodros has given you my letter it will mean you have succeeded in regaining the first component. My congratulations.'

'*First* component?!' Will spluttered. 'What the hell does he mean?'

Emma read the second half of code.

'Here it is…' said Will, typing faster than before.

'To complete the task and enable the Alexander Mechanism to be reassembled, you must collect all seven components. Only by doing so will the Fogg family name be restored.'

Emma choked.

'*Seven*?!'

'Hannibal, you're a maniac!' hissed Will.

'You sure it says "seven"?'

'Positive.'

Will stood up, steadying himself against the concrete wall.

'That's it,' he said. 'I'm ready to go back to my quiet old life. I'm done with Hannibal's psycho zone.'

In slow motion Tewodros got up and rested his hand, its skin loose with age, on Will's shoulder.

'Mr Fogg told me that when you read this letter you would be most concerned,' he said tenderly. 'Now that I have dispatched the duty I promised to undertake, I have no reason to live.'

Will began to say something, but Tewodros urged him to be silent.

'It's impossible for you to understand the responsibility on your shoulders,' he said grimly. 'The decision is yours to make, and yours alone.'

Taking in the ancient's sagging face, eyes frosted with cataracts, skin creased as elephant hide, Will's expression warmed.

'You've been a loyal friend to my family,' he said.

Tewodros raised the tip of his walking cane in the air.

'Now it's your turn,' he replied, 'to fulfil the duty expected of you.'

'How would we ever locate the second component?' asked Emma.

'With the CODEX,' Will replied fast.

He tapped in the last line of code from Hannibal's letter.

A new set of grid coordinates flashed up on the display:

'13°03'37.50N 80°14'58.68E.'

'Where the hell's that?'

Launching Google Maps, Will looked up the reference.

'India,' he said.

'But what *is* it, the second component?'

Will's fingers twisted the main scrolling wheel clockwise and a second line of text appeared.

'The component…' he replied. 'It's the Hands of God.'

Fifty-nine

ALL SIXTEEN COUNSELLORS OF the Order of Zoroaster had been summoned to an extraordinary and unexpected conclave. As before, they had travelled from all corners of the earth.

Once his brethren had taken their places on the horseshoe of golden thrones, the Proctor swept in. Rapt with shock, his face was hidden by his cassock's hood.

Seating himself, he greeted the distinguished counsellors.

'Never before in the long history of our assembly,' he began, 'has the Council been recalled before the interval of one hundred years. Please understand it is only in the most exceptional circumstances that the measure to reconvene our Order has been taken.'

A Brazilian counsellor raised his hand.

'What is the reason for this session, Master?'

On his gilded throne, hands upturned before him, the Proctor explained:

'News has reached us,' he said solemnly. 'News that affects each one of you as indeed it does the entire human race.'

A Russian counsellor raised his sleeve.

'Pray tell us without delay!'

The Proctor drew breath.

'As you are all aware, the Order of Zoroaster conceived and built a machine in the farthest limits of history — a machine known by most as the "Alexander Mechanism".'

'I have heard of it, Master,' an Oriental counsellor declared, 'but please elucidate for us... pray tell what does the Mechanism do?'

The Proctor, who abhorred direct questions, held up a hand — the emerald ring on his finger catching the light.

'A colossal machine,' he uttered gravely. 'Created by our fraternity for the purpose of uniting mankind with the Lord's own realm, the Elysium of Paradise. In its own way, it is the supreme secret of Man — irrefutable proof that God exists.'

A Danish counsellor called out:

'Where is the machine?'

'Concealed.'

'But why?'

The Proctor was surprised at such elementary questions. But, as he pondered it, there had never been a need for the Order's counsellors to be fully briefed.

Not until now, at least.

'Following Alexander's tyrannical conquest of the East,' he explained, 'our Order dispatched the Macedonian king, took possession of the Mechanism once again, and concealed it.'

'Where?' questioned a voice.

'In a brutal location.'

Signalling for the counsellors to calm themselves, he went on:

'Before the Mechanism was hidden, seven key components were removed,' he said.

'Where are they?'

'Embedded within human culture.'

An Indian counsellor raised her hand.

'What do you mean "embedded"?'

The Proctor regarded his brethren one by one.

'The key components were concealed as religious icons within disparate faiths,' he said.

'Where?'

'All over the earth.'

Silence prevailed.

As the counsellors made sense of the information, the Proctor raised both hands above his head.

'We have learned that the Mechanism may at last be about to be reassembled,' he said.

'By whom?'

'By the Bloodchild.'

As a hum of anticipation swept through the hall, an African counsellor spoke:

'Who is the "Bloodchild"?'

Wiping the perspiration from his brow, the Proctor explained:

'A man whose line was chosen by our Order in antiquity,' he said. 'We understand he has located the first of the components.'

'Which one?'

'A double helix known as "the Ladder of Mithras".'

The Russian called out again:

'What chance he will succeed, Master?'

Pressing his palms together, the Proctor looked down at the floor.

'Alas, almost no chance at all,' he replied.

Sixty

WITHIN A DAY AFTER reaching Addis Ababa, Will and Emma flew to New Delhi, having made Solomon the proud owner of a second-hand Rolls-Royce.

Theirs was the last commercial plane out of Bole Airport before armed vigilantes took over. Hunting for government officials, they rampaged through the departure terminal, slaughtering passengers and staff in a crazed killing spree.

At Indira Gandhi International, a bevy of porters heaved six luggage-laden carts out to Arrivals, beyond an ocean of dark heads. Will wondered why he had bothered to pay extra to bring so much of the equipment along.

But, as he reflected, locating the Hands of God could call for all manner of specialised gear. And, as ever, Hannibal seemed to know better than anyone else what was going on.

Once they were out of the terminal building, the heat hit Emma and Will like the door of an oven being drawn back. By the time they were in the taxi's icy air-conditioning, their clothing was drenched.

'Where are we going to stay?' Emma asked for a third time.

'I told you already, it's a surprise.'

The cab stop-started its way through gridlock, eventually reaching the sprawling boulevards of Lutyens's capital. Being in India got Will thinking about Chaudhury. He wondered what the ancestral manservant from Cooch Behar would be doing, and why he had hurried them out of Marrakesh as he had.

Amid a cacophony of honking, the Sikh driver swerved a left onto Janpath, and turned left again, down the palm-lined driveway of the Imperial Hotel.

After the rigours of Ethiopia, Will thought they had both earned a little pampering.

A team of bellboys heaved the luggage up to the Royal Imperial Suite, hovering in the hope of generosity.

'Are you being newlyweds, sir?' their leader asked, not because he was interested, but because honeymooners tended to be the most munificent.

'Just on vacation,' Will replied, handing over a folded five hundred rupee note.

Taking the connecting room, Emma sprawled out on the bed. Beside the phone she found a card advertising spa treatments, and studied it hard.

'I'm going to get a facial,' she said, 'and a manicure, and a pedicure as well. And after that I'm going to get packed in aromatic mud.'

'Sounds revolting!'

They both laughed.

'Thank God you didn't know me in my former life,' Will groaned.

'Were you *so* different?'

'I was a geek,' he said.

Emma smiled.

'You still are.'

'Yeah, but I was a geek with hysterical tendencies.'

'Such as?'

'Well, for my entire life I had this weird feeling I was being followed.'

'When?'

'All the time.'

'That's nuts.'

'I know… well, I know that now. But back in Frisco it was all I'd ever known.' He swallowed. 'Close my eyes and I can still hear the footsteps.'

'Who d'you think it was…?'

'Dunno. Just someone out to get me.'

'The Magi?'

'Guess so.'

Plumping up a pillow, Emma leaned against the headboard.

'What happened back in Ethiopia,' she said. 'Those guys who tried to kill you — they weren't part of any secret brotherhood. They were just part of a country in freefall.' Nudging a strand of hair away from her eyes, she smiled again. 'We're in India now,' she said. 'I'm sure everything's gonna be fine.'

Sixty-one

1891

A SERVANT WAS STANDING to attention to the left of the dais, his frail form wrapped partially in a white cotton lungi, bare feet splayed apart for balance.

A strand of brown parcel string had been tied to the index finger of his right hand. Every ten seconds he tugged the string, powering a fan which in turn cooled the room.

Upon the dais, his legs crossed in the lotus position, was Hannibal. He was meditative, as if his mind were on a higher plane.

His manservant padded in, a hookah in one hand and a bowl of burning coals in the other. Placing the pipe near his master, he uncoiled it and set to work with the coals.

'Tell me, Chaudhury,' enquired Hannibal, eyes closed. 'Has Professor Maa arrived?'

'Yes, sir. He is awaiting you in the study.'

Hannibal reached down and raised the mouthpiece to his lips.

'Very good,' he said, 'send him in at once.'

Chaudhury exited, returning soon after, an anxious-looking man with pigtails following close behind.

'Professor,' Hannibal said, inhaling a lungful of apple-flavoured tobacco. 'Very good of you to come to Calcutta to meet me. I trust your journey from Peking was satisfactory.'

'Quite so, Mr Fogg. I am grateful to you arranging such comfortable passage.'

Uncrossing his legs, Hannibal reclined on a bolster. He rolled another in the direction of his guest.

'Would you be more comfortable speaking Mandarin?'

'Thank you, but I am well acquainted with your language,' Maa responded.

'Excellent. Now, I would like to know what you can tell me about a matter of mutual interest.'

'What do you wish to know about?'

'The Hands of God.'

Professor Maa lay back, his bony elbow hardly making a dent in the bolster. A second hookah was brought in by Chaudhury.

The academic had wondered why the celebrated English explorer had sent for him so urgently.

'The Hands of God — supreme symbol of the Vandals?' he asked.

Fogg drew on his pipe.

'Yes.'

'A Germanic people who sacked Rome in the fifth

century regarded the symbol as a kind of ideogram.'

'And the actual relic, where is it now?'

The professor held the hookah's bit in his teeth and inhaled slowly, the smoke bubbling up through the water.

'As I understand it, the relic of which you speak was acquired by the architect Sir John Soane.'

'For his private museum in Lincoln's Inn Fields?'

'Indeed.'

'When?'

'Back in '25, I believe.'

'But I've spent half my life at Soane's and have not seen a record of it.'

'Of course not,' whispered Professor Maa.

'Why is that?'

'Because a month before Soane's death the relic was sold to a dealer in Berlin — a Herr Gutemann.'

'Doesn't make sense,' Hannibal responded studiously. 'Soane never traded artifacts, especially one so important as this.'

Regarded as a foremost expert on the esoteric, Professor Maa raised an index finger as if about to make a point.

'It seems that Soane regarded the Hands as cursed. He held them responsible for the tumours on his back.'

'An absurd suggestion,' countered Fogg.

The professor's index finger wagged left to right.

'Perhaps not as far-fetched as it may sound,' he said.

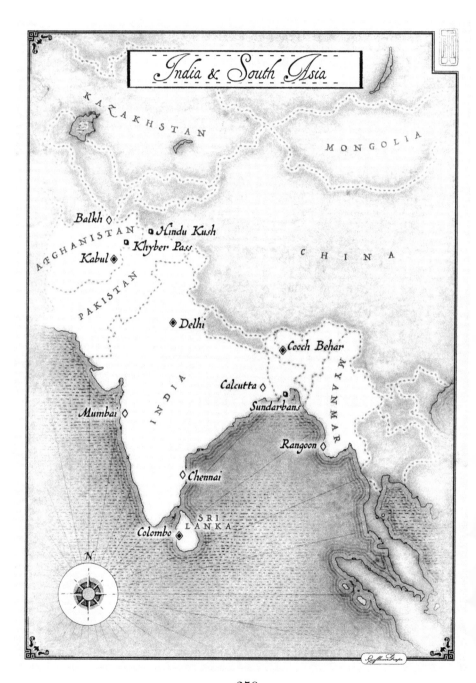

'How so?'

'The illness may have in actual fact been caused by the relic's unusual mineral composition.'

'Oh?'

'The Hands are believed to contain a high percentage of bismuth.'

'Fascinating,' Hannibal affirmed, sitting upright. 'And what of Gutemann?'

'He sold the Hands on at once — to a Polish collector. He in turn presented them to his teacher.'

'Who was who?'

'The Russian-born mystic, Madame Blavatsky.'

'I've heard of her,' said Hannibal, his brow warming with interest. Motioning for the servant to tug the string a little harder, he grunted. 'Heard she's started some kind of a cult down in Madras.'

'Indeed,' Maa replied. 'It's called the Theosophical Society.'

'It's not too far away.'

Professor Maa drew on the pipe, apple-flavoured smoke spilling into his lungs.

'I shall make you an introduction to Madame Blavatsky if you wish.'

Exhaling, Hannibal Fogg gave thanks.

'Now, do tell me, Professor,' he asked, 'how would one obtain a supply of bismuth?'

Sixty-two

EMMA SPENT THE AFTERNOON enveloped in medicated mud, scraped from the upper banks of the Jumna.

While she was undergoing the pampering of her life, Will sat on his bed with the CODEX and a stack of Hannibal's canvas-backed maps. The grid reference was somewhere in Chennai, a city known as 'Madras' until the recent preoccupation with erasing old place names of the British Raj.

Will checked the exact location on Google Maps.

The pin had come down on a colossal hulk of Colonial brick and masonry.

Squinting, he strained to read the tiny print beside it. 'Central Post Office.'

When Emma came back from her spa treatment, Will ran over, his face brimming with an ear-to-ear smile.

'We're going to Chennai!' he said. 'To the Central Post Office.'

Emma regarded him with a poisonous glance.

'*You* are!' she riposted caustically.

'So are you — *right*?'

'No I'm not!'

'What are you talking about?'

Emma slapped her hands together hard.

'Will, I need a break from you!'

'*What*?!'

'You heard me!'

Will stepped forwards, but Emma stepped back.

'Don't touch me!' she screamed.

A minute later, she had grabbed her few possessions and left, slamming the suite's door behind her.

Perched on the corner of his bed, Will tried to make sense of what had just happened. He felt hollow inside, confused and cold, as if there'd been a terrible misunderstanding.

A few minutes slipped by. He took a beer from the refrigerator and slugged it down fast.

'Women!' he cried.

Sixty-three

THAT EVENING, WILL TOOK the Grand Trunk Express from Hazrat Nizamuddin Station. A herd of red-shirted porters ferried his luggage on their heads to the first class compartment at the rear of the train.

In more usual circumstances, he would surely have been shocked by the tumultuous frenzy of life that consumed every inch of the station, a micro-universe of mayhem.

But Will's mind was on Emma and her impromptu departure. Unable to understand what he had said or done to upset her, he replayed their last conversation over and over in his head.

The Grand Trunk Express reeled out of Hazrat

Nizamuddin, clattering and groaning through the slums. Will glanced out of the window, the tinted glass making it impossible to get a clear sense of anything. A stench of sewage hung over the first fifteen miles of track. Then the air-conditioning kicked in, turning the compartment into an industrial freezer.

Will lay on the bunk, his thoughts still on Emma. A thirty-five-hour train journey would give him time to mull it over. In life he had had a never-ending stream of crushes, but had not once felt a real connection.

Kicking off his shoes, he bolted the door and flicked off the light. His face eased into the pillow and, within a minute or two, he was in deep sleep, the carriage grinding south towards Chennai.

A handful of hours must have passed.

All the carriage lights were out, and the dining car shut down for the night. Will turned in his sleep, his left hand caressing the side of the pillow.

The train's wheels locked.

Screeching, screaming, the rolling stock skated down the track.

The wheels sparked like angle grinders gnawing through steel. Hurtled from sleep, the passengers were flung about. Before there was time to question what was going on, gravity and the sharp curve took over.

One by one the carriages tumbled over the edge.

Will was catapulted over and over against the ceiling, floor, window and door, as the compartment careened down the steep embankment.

The riot of twisted metal, smashed glass and noise ended as suddenly as it had begun.

Lying face down on the ceiling, Will sensed a breeze ripping through the darkness. Too stunned to move, he lay there, his ears picking up the distorted sound of a woman screaming. The injured and the dying were smothered by the stench of smoke and burning fuel.

Will forced himself up, his body mangled, cut and bruised. Crawling out from where the window had been, he set about helping to free the other survivors.

In the next compartment he pulled out a woman and her twins, and a blind man from the one after that. They gave thanks, but all Will heard was the grating of steel against steel.

As he staggered to the next carriage, a pair of muscular hands grabbed him from behind.

He struggled to turn, but couldn't.

Forcing him to his knees, the hands snatched his wrists back, binding them with a nylon cable tie.

A sackcloth hood yanked down over his face.

Clenched into a fist, one of the hands slugged him in the jaw.

Sixty-four

WHEN HE CAME TO, Will was lying spreadeagled in daylight on a stone floor. His wrists had been untied, the hood pulled away. Raising his head a little, he did his best to scan the room. It was ten feet square, with six iron bars over a single window mounted high on the wall.

With all his strength, Will leapt at the bars, pulling himself up.

Outside he spotted a line of mottled grey battlements. They ran along a ridge, as far as the eye could see. It seemed to be a stone fortress.

A pair of uniformed soldiers were standing guard, both armed with Uzis. Nearby, partially obscured by a screen of poplar trees, was a lovely garden. The lawn was manicured, set for croquet, a peacock strutting between the hoops.

Will touched a hand to his face. It was the first time he had been knocked out cold.

Keys jangled on a ring.

The iron door opened.

A towering Sikh guard strode in, and grabbed him by the neck.

'Where am I?' Will asked.

'The Nawab is waiting.'

The throne hall's floor was black and white with chequered marble tiles, the walls hung with raw silk, the colour of pomegranate juice. An enormous room by any standards, its ceiling was so high that the fine details of the Baroque murals were lost.

Along one side ran a gallery, lined with steel cages. In each a prisoner was crouching, wrists bound with nylon cable ties.

At the far end of the hall, some distance from the cells, a glass partition rose floor to ceiling. Behind it stood six identical wooden desks, a suited member of staff at each speaking urgently into a phone.

Between the glass wall and the cages stood a golden throne. Upon it, reclining in thought, was His Highness Nawab Jaswant Singh.

Dragging Will to the throne, the guard thrust him to the ground.

Winded, he pushed himself up and caught a first look at the Nawab. Aged somewhere between fifty and sixty, his face was cruel and rather haggard, as though shaped by the pain he had caused others to endure. His nose aquiline, his eyes were black and cold, and his regal form coutured in an embroidered robe, worn with jodhpurs and knee-length riding boots.

'My apologies for waking you last night,' he said in impeccable English. 'But how could I have let you go by without receiving you?'

Will regarded his host with disdain.

'What the hell's going on?!'

The Nawab's nose crumpled as it sniffed.

'You have something that I need.'

'Are you the Magi?' Will asked point blank.

The Nawab clicked his fingers, barking at the henchman, who hurried out.

'No, no, Mr Fogg, I am but a humble collector.'

The strong man swept back in, his feet hardly touching the marble as he bounded over it.

In his hand was a silken cushion, the silver helix upon it.

The Nawab watched as Will glared at him.

'I've spent thirty years searching for this object,' he said with a smile. 'The Ladder of Mithras. Quite a coincidence. You see I had a team scouring Ethiopia for it this very month. All they brought me was some worthless Imperial bric-a-brac.'

'Give it to me!' Will snapped defiantly.

Nawab Jaswant Singh climbed off the throne, the soles of his boots treading over to the glass partition wall.

'Have a look back there,' he called, turning. 'My staff are acquiring artifacts at auctions all over the world. *Why?* Because I get whatever I like.'

He glanced at a magnificent gold Patek Philippe on his wrist.

'A sale of rare European clocks opened ten minutes ago at Christie's, Hong Kong...'

His sentence was interrupted by the sound of steel-tipped boots clattering over marble.

A dozen guards flooded through the north door into

the throne hall, each carrying a packing crate. One at a time the lids were prised off. An assortment of treasures were removed, chips of polystyrene packaging spilling out onto the floor.

The Nawab went over to inspect the latest arrivals.

The first crate contained a jewel-encrusted sword made for King Henry VIII. The second, Napoleon Bonaparte's cavalry boots and the third, a crude golden crown. Will recognised it from the treasure vault in Addis Ababa — the Crown of Emperor Menelik.

'There's no single serious collector who would not kill for the Ladder,' said Jaswant Singh. 'I congratulate you but…'

'But I won't leave without it!' Will bawled.

Snatching the helix, he held it to his chest, before the guards instantly snatched it back.

The Nawab scowled.

'A click of my fingers and Ram here will slit your throat. Simple as that. No discussions. No fuss.'

The henchman clicked his neck, indicating he was ready.

'You look sensible to me,' said Jaswant Singh. 'So I propose we make a compromise.'

'What do you mean?'

'We shall play a game… a nice little game of chess. He who wins gets to keep the Ladder.'

'Chess?'

'Yes.'

Will got a flash of the Chess Club at SFSU, otherwise known as 'Geek Central'.

'Chess… OK… sure. But if I win, I get to leave with the Ladder?'

Agreeing, the Nawab clapped his hands.

'Do you have a board?' asked Will.

Again, the Nawab smiled. He pointed to the throne room's floor.

'There's one,' he said.

Sixty-four squares were marked out with a twisted golden cord.

'What about the pieces?'

Jaswant Singh jerked his head up at the cages.

'Ram, get me thirty prisoners down.'

Keys turned in locks and cage doors opened and closed. Blindfolded and bound, a stream of convicts were led down and into the throne room. Some were cowering, others whimpering as though sensing grave danger.

The Nawab thundered ferociously in Hindi, and their outbursts ceased.

'What d'you say?'

'That if they didn't pipe down, I'd eat them for lunch.'

The henchman approached with two sets of hoods. Fifteen were white, embroidered with black chess-piece motifs. The same number again were black, embroidered in white.

'Playing with live pieces is so much more agreeable,' the Nawab explained.

'I've got the feeling you've done this before,' said Will.

Nawab Jaswant Singh strained to look meek.

'You be white,' he said.

Before they began, the henchman handed Will a pair of adjustable spikes.

'Slip them over your shoes, please.'

'Why?'

The Nawab waved his hand reassuringly.

'Makes the marble less slippery.'

Will fitted the spikes.

'But we're missing the kings,' he said.

Jaswant Singh raised an index finger as if testing the wind.

'You and I,' he said.

Taking his place as the white king, Will could smell the prisoners' fear. He could only imagine the depths the Nawab would stoop to in order to win. After all, he had sent dozens of innocent passengers to their deaths only the night before.

Will began to play:

'Pawn to E4.'

The henchman led the white pawn two steps ahead.

'Knight to C6,' replied the Nawab at once.

Again, one of the prisoners was shuffled into place.

Will recognised he was playing the unusual Nimzowitsch Defence. Moving his knight to F3, the Nawab countered by advancing a bishop — thereby threatening Will's own bishop.

Would he do a bishop swap so early? Will wondered as he castled.

The Nawab boomed:

'Bishop takes bishop!'

As the words left his mouth, the henchman stepped up and slit the throat of Will's bishop, washing the floor in blood.

Rooted to the square, Will did a double take.

He couldn't believe what he was seeing.

'I, I, I... I can't play...'

'Oh but Mr Fogg, I assure you that you can, and that you will. You see, failure to finish the game and your king will fall. Need I inform you what that means?'

Inhaling, Will smelled the scent of fresh human blood spilling over the marble. An overpowering wave of anger warmed his arms. He heard his father's voice: 'Channel the rage, Will, use it, harness it.'

Stepping off the board, he considered the game from the sidelines. The Nawab had brought out his queen, laying himself open to attack, and leaving his king — himself — unguarded.

The challenge was to achieve checkmate without taking or losing any more pieces.

Captured pieces meant prisoners would die.

Jaswant Singh advanced his knight into the middle of the board.

Will countered by defending his queen.

'Check,' said the Nawab.

'Huh?' *Damn! Didn't see that coming.*

Will blocked check with a pawn.

'Check again!'

The Nawab's queen lined up with the knight.

Again, Will blocked.

Nawab Jaswant Singh took a white pawn with his queen.

The henchman's blade tore left to right through another throat.

'Relax,' the Nawab said frivolously, 'they're only prisoners.'

Will's eyes narrowed in anger and concentration.

'Bishop to D5.'

'You're walking on thin ice, young Mr Fogg.'

'Huh?'

Jaswant played a bishop, and glanced back at the throne on which the helix was sitting.

'You're about to lose your neck,' he grinned conceitedly.

Will's mouth tasted bitter and cold. Through a series of convoluted associations, the sensation stirred a memory.

A variation on a match he had studied back in high school.

Adrenalin surging down his back and through his arms, he saw it crystal clear — Game 6, Fischer vs. Spassky, Reykjavik '72.

'Queen to F4,' Will whispered, attacking the square on which his opponent was standing.

The Nawab's fists clenched in rage.

His eyes trained on the blood-drenched board, Will sniffed in disgust.

'Checkmate,' he said.

Sixty-five

1891

A SADHU WAS SQUATTING on a platform fashioned from packing crates, an audience watching. Comprised of Indian gentry and a smattering of foreigners, they were standing in a circle around him.

The holy man had a long white beard, tiny maniacal eyes, and almost no body fat at all. His waist was furled in a grubby loincloth, and his head wound in a turban made from a length of jute.

The only person not on their feet was a European woman, seated on a low wicker chair, her arms by her sides. She was fifty, with dark eyes set in a plain face, the kind that would be lost in a crowd.

When the audience could wait no longer, a child of about nine or ten began beating a drum, slow and rhythmic: *Tack! Tack! Tack!*

As the strikes grew harder and louder, the sadhu took a meat skewer, forcing the sharp end into his cheek. Oblivious to any pain, he threaded it through to his mouth and out through the other cheek.

After that, he walked across a pit laid with burning embers and, then, swallowed a box of glass marbles, gulping them down as if they were boiled sweets.

In the interval, Professor Maa made the introductions.

'Madame Blavatsky, I should be delighted for you to be acquainted with Mr Hannibal Fogg.'

The European woman held out a hand so that it might be kissed.

'My pleasure,' she said in a severe Russian accent.

Hannibal bowed, pressing his lips delicately to the bleached white skin.

'The pleasure, Madame, is all mine.'

With the interval over, the god-man ripped a long strand of jute from his turban, the width of a household bandage. With due care, he began to swallow it.

Having heard of the routine, Hannibal looked on with interest.

'What's he doing?' one of the spectators asked.

'He is cleaning his digestive tract,' answered another.

'Whatever for?'

'Wait and see,' whispered Professor Maa.

The sadhu withdrew the cloth, and again squatted in the lotus position on the dais. Breathing heavily, he closed his eyes, palms upturned on his knees.

A yard or two away, Hannibal made out the god-man wheezing. He wondered if the feat, which had made him famous, would kill him this time.

After ten minutes of forced breathing, the holy man

stood up, flipped his ears inside out, and clambered into a sturdy wooden box.

The audience chattering among themselves, posing questions and craning their necks for a better view.

Three assistants strode up. One of them fastened the box's lid, securing it with a Chubb padlock.

'Now they will bury him,' said Maa.

'Where?'

'In the hole they have dug. Look, it's six feet deep.'

The box was lowered into the grave, the mound of earth beside it used to fill in the hole. One of the assistants sprinkled a handful of grain, splashing water over it from a bucket.

'What now?' asked Hannibal, raising an eyebrow.

'Now,' Madame Blavatsky replied, 'we return in a month, when the barley has grown.'

Sixty-six

JASWANT SINGH REPAIRED TO his private apartment to wash the blood off his feet. He was steaming at having been beaten as much as he was for having lost the Ladder of Mithras.

Before going up to change, he had given the order for the remaining chess pieces — black and white — to be taken out and shot. He regarded it as bad luck to use the same set twice.

Having removed his jodhpurs, he looked at himself in the mirror, sponged a spot of blood from his cheek. What to do with the boy? No question of allowing him to leave with the relic, or leave at all. The game had been an amusement, a diversion to pass the time, but certainly not something to be taken seriously.

The Nawab stepped calmly over to a refrigerator beside his bed, the kind found in hotel rooms. Its miniature shelves were packed with strips of pills, medical equipment and apothecary bottles.

Nudging a hand back behind a clutch of hypodermic needles, the Nawab withdrew a single glass phial, two inches in length.

Holding it to the light, he tapped the top.

Around the base three or four words were engraved into the glass, almost too small to read with the naked eye.

Jaswant had no need to see its name. He knew the phial's contents full well — *Calebas curare*, lightly chilled.

Staring at the clear contents, the phial held between forefinger and thumb, he flinched, as though startled.

He turned.

The curtains were dancing in the light breeze.

His attention back on the poison, he grimaced at his plan.

Outside, an intruder swept over the battlements, moving deftly along the parapet. Seconds later, the figure had slipped unnoticed through the window, into the Nawab's apartment.

Placing the phial on a neatly folded handkerchief, the Nawab crossed the room to where his evening clothes were laid out.

A set of fingers pressed into the soft flesh behind each ear.

His head twisted to the right.

But his body didn't move.

Jaswant Singh fell to the floor, dead.

Sixty-seven

1891

A FULL CALENDAR MONTH after the burial, the same audience reconvened on the banks of the Hoogli. As before, Madame Blavatsky was seated and, once again, Hannibal Fogg and Professor Maa stood nearby.

The barley had been tended by the sadhu's grandson, the boy with the drum. With sunshine and plenty of water, it had grown quite high.

'Now for the moment we have been awaiting,' said Maa.

'I bet he's dead,' heckled an Englishman at the back.

Hannibal's weight fell onto the front of his boots.

The assistants exhumed the box with their shovels.

Although a little dirtier, it looked much the same as it had done a month previously.

The lock was unfastened, the lid furled back.

Inside, lying quite motionless in the box was the

holy man.

'Dead,' intoned Maa with disappointment, 'I knew it.'

Hannibal Fogg cocked his head to the left.

The sadhu opened an eye.

'He's alive, by George!' burst out the man who had doubted it.

'Of course he is,' sniffed Hannibal, as the god-man was heaved up onto the grass.

'Why do you say that?' asked the professor.

'Because almost anything is possible with a little self-discipline,' Hannibal replied.

Sixty-eight

GUESSING NAWAB JASWANT SINGH would be a sore loser, Will expected him to play dirty, especially as he had lost at chess.

After the game, he claimed the silver helix from its resting place on the throne. Having unstrapped the spikes from his shoes, he washed his hands and face. To his surprise, his daypack was hanging from a hook in the washroom. Snatching it, he made his escape through the kitchens.

The chef and a legion of minions were preparing water buffalo, garnished with dragon fruit. They didn't notice as Will slipped past them and out through a service door.

Leaping into the back of a delivery truck just as it was leaving, he touched the Ladder to his face. In the very same moment, the Nawab's henchman discovered his master's body.

As the truck rumbled onto the open road, sirens blared out. Dug down under the tarp, Will had no idea at all.

A DAY AND A half later, he reached Chennai.

Reeling after the long bus journey, he was thankful beyond belief at having escaped the Nawab's murderous pleasure dome with his life.

In a café he opened his daypack, the only piece of luggage he still had after the train crash. Back in Addis Ababa he had bought an identical pair of them — one for Emma and the other for himself.

Will delved a hand inside the pack, touching the Ladder's curved stems. He sighed with relief. Thank God it was safe, as was the stash of banknotes. But worth far more than the cash was the irreplaceable CODEX.

Digging it out, Will switched it on.

He double-checked the grid reference on Google Maps. As before, it flashed up as the General Post Office.

Soon after, Will was standing inside an architectural tour de force from the days of the British Raj, a celebration of a waning Empire's might.

Ceiling fans sliced languidly through stifling pre-monsoon heat. Will approached the counter.

The clerk glanced up quizzically from the horoscope page of the newspaper.

'You want postage stamp?'

'Um, er… well…' Will stood there, staring blankly. He wasn't actually sure why he'd come, except that Hannibal had wanted him to be there.

'I have come to collect something,' he said.

Sullenly, the clerk waved a hand towards the next room.

'In there. Counter fifteen.'

'What is?'

'The *poste restante*.'

Another clerk was manning counter fifteen, a clone of the first. Like his colleague, he was busy studying the daily horoscope.

'I've come to collect a letter,' said Will.

'Name?'

'William Fogg.'

'Spell?'

'F-O-G-G.'

Turning, the clerk rooted through racks of pigeonholes arranged over the wall behind him.

'Nothing by that name.'

Will touched a hand to his chin in thought. Had Hannibal meant him to come to the post office in search of something else — a postage stamp perhaps? It was possible. Thanking the clerk, he was about to leave, when an idea hit him.

'If there's no letter for William Fogg,' he asked, 'is there one for *Hannibal* Fogg?'

The clerk looked up.

'Repeat name, if you please?'

'Hannibal Fogg.'

The clerk scuffled away into a cavernous storeroom behind, its door to the right of the pigeonholes. He was gone a long time, so long that Will wondered if he had forgotten.

After half an hour the clerk scuffled back.

Clasped in his birdlike fingers was a letter. It was black with dirt.

'Time it was collected,' he said.

'How long's it been waiting?' Will asked.

'Since 4th January 1926.'

Sixty-nine

IN THE TWENTY YEARS he had spent on the travel pages of the London *Times*, Richard Matheson could hardly remember a day when he wasn't dispatching journalists on trips of a lifetime. While they crisscrossed the globe, he was stuck at his desk on Pennington Street, Wapping, dreaming of adventure.

Over the years, Matheson had become an avid reader of the great nineteenth century travellers — men like Livingstone, Stanley and Burton. He didn't much care for modern travellers, but envied them all the same.

Then, one morning on the tube ride to work, he had an idea. He would propose a series of articles about the forgotten greats of Victorian exploration. The editor gave it a thumbs-up at the mid-week meeting.

Wasting no time, he got down to research on Wikipedia.

One page linked to the next and, by lunchtime, Matheson had zigzagged a route through the golden age of exploration.

He was about to head out to the cafeteria, when an obscure website caught his eye. Dedicated to conspiracies, it featured a short biography of an Edwardian explorer — Hannibal G. Fogg.

Seventy

OPENING THE ENVELOPE, WILL fished out another encoded letter. As before, he set the CODEX to the letter paper's watermark. The decrypted message instructed him to go to the Theosophical Society outside Madras, and to locate the Hands of God.

At the bottom of the letter, written in Hannibal's familiar cursive script in green, were three words: *Omnia causa fiunt.*

Will translated them out loud:

'Everything has a reason.'

Seventy-one

WHEN MATHESON TYPED IN the name almost nothing
came up. Only by following a series of obscure links did
he eventually arrive at a long biographical entry:

> **HANNIBAL GARRETT FOGG** (Born in Loch Lomond,
> 26th December 1868 — disappeared Manchuria 25th
> December 1939). Eldest son of Sir Uriah Fogg and Baroness
> Esmeralda Lascelles. Diplomat, explorer, soldier, author, spy,
> Fogg was born into a wealthy landowning family, with estates
> in Perthshire and Somerset, and extensive property in central
> London.
>
> **Education:** Educated at Wellington School and at Balliol
> College, Oxford, from where he was sent down.
>
>
>
> **Career:** Through family contacts, Fogg secured a commission
> with the Royal Engineers, but soon relinquished the notion
> of a military career. Fogg was for a time private tutor to the
> children of Tsar Alexander III, until dismissed because of
> a scandal. Throughout his life Fogg undertook numerous
> explorations — both on his own behalf and for foreign
> dignitaries and governments. The precise details of these
> missions are unknown — having been expunged from
> recorded history during the Great Foggian Purge.
>
> **Marriage:** While on an expedition up the Volga River in
> 1902, Fogg attended a slave auction near Samara, where he
> bought an enslaved princess, Alina Pasternak. The couple
> were married and enjoyed numerous adventures together until
> Alina Fogg was poisoned in 1923.
>
> **Children:** Alina Fogg bore a single son, Wilfred Fogg
> (1904–1951), who emigrated to New York and died in
> poverty. Wilfred Fogg married an Irish woman and had three
> children — Richard, Edith and Helen, who all moved out to

California in their youth.

Awards: Fogg was awarded numerous honours, including *the Most Exalted Order of the White Elephant of Siam, the Imperial Order of the Lion and the Sun of Persia,* and *the Order of the Tower and the Sword of Portugal.*

Interests: Fogg was regarded as an authority on ethnography, the Classics, swordsmanship, clockwork mechanisms, cartography and on rare postage stamps. He was an accomplished linguist, speaking more than twenty languages with fluency — including Albanian, Russian, Japanese, Mandarin, Serbo-Croat, Maori, Hindustani, Arabic and Esperanto. As well as being a proficient swordsman and martial artist, Fogg was a renowned pianist, and the inventor of numerous mechanical machines. Of these, the most celebrated were a series of mechanical animals which he referred to as 'Viventem Machinis'.

Memberships: Fogg was a member of the Athenaeum and the Travellers in London, and the Cercle de l'Union Interalliée in Paris — until the time of his disgrace. He was known to have dabbled in Freemasonry, having belonged to Lodge 349 in Calcutta. As a young man in Damascus, he was initiated into the Order of the Peacock Angel through his mentor Sir Richard Burton, a fraternity to which he was faithful his entire adult life. It is for his association with the Order of the Golden Phi that he is best known, although he never spoke publicly about membership, and little of it is known. He was also a member of the Worshipful Company of Clockmakers, the Ancient Order of Odd Fellows, the Ancient and Mystical Order of Rosae Crucis, the Brotherhood of Lost Souls, and the Order of Sanctified Hope.

Acquaintances: Fogg was acquainted with a number of famous and infamous characters of the time, including Freud, Zamenhof, Crowley, Conan Doyle, Hemmingway, Graves, Einstein, Shackleton, Tolstoy, Hitler and Blavatsky.

Disgrace & Purge: In November 1928, Hannibal Fogg was arrested and imprisoned in the Tower of London for treason to the Crown. The following month, on 2nd December 1928, a bonfire of Fogg's collected work was set alight on the Victoria Embankment near Cleopatra's Needle. A Royal Commission headed by Lord Rothermere subsequently found that Fogg had been engaged as a spy, having received orders from Hitler himself.

Exile: Upon a request from Sultan Abdelhafid of Morocco, Fogg was exiled to North Africa in 1929. Little is known of his years in exile, except that he undertook a series of missions concerned with exploration, necromancy and mechanical machines.

Lost journals: Fogg is known to have kept a journal through his life, as well as a set of encoded expedition journals which, it is believed, contained the locations of five treasures. As with much information surrounding Fogg's life and work, it is not certain whether such material ever existed at all.

Publications: Hannibal Fogg was the author of numerous books and academic monographs. Precise details on many of his works were lost during the Great Purge and in the years that followed it. Despite exile Fogg continued to publish privately, although in almost all cases the editions were seized and destroyed. Fogg's published works are thought to have included *Lost Years* (1890), *The Pain of Silence* (1891), *Twixt Hell and Marshland* (1892), *Ballads of Hope and Anguish* (1894), *Advanced Techniques in Swordsmanship* (1896), *Experiments in Metallurgy* (1897), *A Poem of Love* (1898), *Considerations on the Subject of Desert Fauna* (1899), *Short-blade Weaponry* (1899), *Warfare in the Tribal Context* (1899), *Elementary Mechanics* (1900), *Electro-Mechanics Made Easy* (1901), *Variants of Shaolin Kung Fu* (1901), *An Evaluation of the Nile and Its Sources* (1902), *Joy on the Volga* (1903), *Flight in Ancient Times* (1904), *Lichen Growth and Its*

Unique Specification (1912), *Destinations Unknown* (1913), *Methods and Mysteries of Shrinking Heads* (1913), *Siamese Bronzes* (1913), *Philatelic Irregularities* (1914), *Sexual Dysfunction Among the Hema Tribe of the Belgian Congo* (1914), *Letters to Satan* (1914), *Why?!* (1915), *Philately of Empire* (1915), *A New Approach to Mechanics* (1916), *In Search of Hidden Animals* (1916), *The Orisha Stone and Its Role in Cultural Ethnography with Reference to the Human Leopard Society of Sierra Leone* (1916), *Perfidious Albion* (1917), *Advanced Maori Etymology* (1918), *Accelerated Learning Techniques* (1919), *Penis Sheaths of Oceania* (1920), *Common Misconceptions in the Study of Oriental Folklore* (1920), *Forty Truths Regarding Advanced Palaeontology* (1921), *Cartographic Conundrums* (1922), *Manx Birdlife* (1923), *Horror of War* (1923), *Ancient Egyptian Necromancy* (1925), *Encoded Mnemonics* (1925), *Further Ancient Egyptian Necromancy* (1926), *Cyclonic Ciphers* (1926), *A Short Treatise on the Study of Mechanical Instrumentation* (1927), *Unexpected Phobias* (1927), *Collected Poetry* (1928), *Mathematic Brevity* (1928), *Finite Infinity* (1929), *Studies in Assyrian Masonry* (1930), *Eleven Poems* (1931), *A Bibliographic Appraisal of the Dark Arts* (1931), *Travels in Disguise* (1931), *An Eye to the Future* (1932), *An Investigation into the Nocturnal Practices of Three-toed Sloths* (1933), *Palaeontology for Beginners* (1934), *Berber Love Magic* (1934), *Spells of the African Hinterland* (1934), *Myths and Legends of Central Africa* (1934), *Ceremonies in Black Magic* (1935), *Advanced Philatelic Considerations* (1936), *Carpology and Its Uses* (1936), *Astronomy and Related Cartography* (1937), *Social Rethinking* (1938), *Forced Ineptitude* (1938).

Legacy: Fogg's life and achievements continue to be studied and celebrated by a number of groups throughout the world. These include the Association for the Study of Foggian Adventure (New York), and the Fogg Institute (Cape Town).

The longest remaining association devoted to the explorer's life and work is the Hannibal Fogg Society, founded in London in 1954. The Society is believed to consist of several chapters, most of which continue in secrecy for fear of condemnation. At the time of writing there appear to be chapters in Tirana, Arusha, Havana, Ibarra, Manaus, Ushuaia, Alice Springs, Swakopmund and Vladivostock. In addition, the Association for Foggian Research (Stockholm), was established in 1941, but is thought to have been disbanded soon after. Similarly, the Society for the Advancement of Foggian Thought (Berlin) was shut down in 1952, its premises having been burned to the ground. On the rare occasions that items thought to have been owned by Fogg are sold at auction, they command high prices. Foggian afficionados believe that with time the truth about Hannibal Fogg will come to light and, along with it, the body of lost work leading in turn to treasure. Perhaps the most intriguing aspect of the interest in matters 'Foggian' is a series of novels and encoded notebooks published by Tahir Shah, a British author, based on the life and adventures of Hannibal Fogg.

Seventy-two

THE THEOSOPHICAL SOCIETY WAS set in acres of parkland on the northern outskirts of Chennai. Will arrived there by auto-rickshaw, a stream of sky-blue smoke spewing out behind him like a vapour trail. The driver stopped at the gates. When asked to keep going down the long shaded drive, he refused, and drove away.

Will walked the half mile to a plain white colonial building of whitewash and stone. He was still thinking about Emma, and why she would have left so inexplicably. It didn't make any sense. But then neither did the train crash or the bloodthirsty reception in the palace of Nawab Jaswant Singh.

The only thing for certain was that the Ladder was as precious to collectors as it was to the mysterious Magi.

A voice startled Will from his thoughts.

'Have you come for the tour?'

He looked up.

A lady was standing behind him on the path. She was wearing a silk sari, her wrists jangling with glass bangles.

'Um, er, yes I'm visiting,' Will said.

'It's this way. I'll show you.'

Will followed the woman into a spacious hall. It was curved, almost circular, and cool inside. On each wall was displayed an oversized symbol — a cross, a coiled serpent, a swastika, and the Star of David.

'You are the only visitor today,' said the woman. 'So we shall begin.'

She asked what Will knew of the Society.

'Very little.'

'That's good, it means you will not have a mind clouded with misconceptions.'

She explained how the Society had been founded by the clairvoyant Madame Helena Blavatsky and her companion, a bear-like American called Colonel Olcott, and how it was dedicated to the Universal Brotherhood of Humanity.

As she led the way through the sacred meeting rooms, she explained how theosophy was based on the fusion of symbols.

Will was going to ask about the Hands of God, when the guide tapped a door-frame with her palm.

'This is where we keep the relics,' she said.

'*Relics?*'

The guide gestured to a glass display case, lacquered mahogany, the varnish cracked with age.

'This is the swastika from Nagpur,' she explained. 'And this a cross from Jerusalem. As for that…' she motioned to a curious object the size of a side-plate, comprising a cross made from four stylised hands. 'That was brought here by Madame Blavatsky shortly before her death.'

'What is it?'

'It is called the "Hands of God".'

Will stared at her, as though hoping to coax an explanation from her.

'A powerful spiritual device,' she said, 'it is believed once to have belonged to the Vandals of the Volga.'

Advancing to the display case, Will got a good look at the relic.

Crafted with intricate care, the black metal was covered by a green-grey patina. He almost asked for it right then, declaring the Hands to be his birthright.

Smiling, the guide said the tour was over.

'Come again,' she said.

'I may do that,' Will replied.

Seventy-three

BEFORE HE KNEW IT, Will was sitting alone in an ordinary hotel room, uncertain what to do next.

He got a flash of his great-aunts.

Aunt Edith was scowling, as though mortally offended. Close beside her, aunt Helen. Unlike her sister, she was a bundle of cheer, an oven-warm cherry flan in her hands.

Scrolling back to the birthday tea, to the conversation about Hannibal Fogg and the gift wrapped in Little Bo Peep, Will found himself humming the '*Rhyme of Ernest Pie*'. In the memory, aunt Helen winked, glancing down at the coffee table. The album. Will fished a hand into the daypack, wondering if it was still there.

His fingers touched the canvas boards, a little more rubbed than before from adventure. Pulling it out, he rifled through the sheets of postage stamps.

Such order in a time of chaos.

Three or four pages from the end, he came to a series of Indian stamps dating from the British Raj. A good many featured King Edward VII. But it wasn't they that caught his eye, but rather another series, featuring pristine colonial buildings — the great landmarks of Bombay, Delhi, Calcutta and the Madras Presidency.

Will recognised the Chennai Railway Station and the city's General Post Office. A third stamp depicted the Governor's Mansion; a fourth, the Royal Madras Yacht Club.

The strange thing was that, whereas all the other cities had five stamps, the Madras selection had just four.

There was a space where the missing Madras stamp ought to have been. Will checked that it hadn't been slipped in somewhere, or fallen out into the bag. It hadn't.

Then he had an idea — a long shot.

Pulling out his iPhone, he did an image search.

A few seconds and he found it, a large red sandstone building in the Mughal style, known to scholars as 'Indo Saracenic'. The caption beneath read, 'The Literary Society of Madras, Founded 1812'.

Will thought about it. Strange that such a complete album should be missing the one stamp that might be relevant. Could it have been a clue in reverse? A building made conspicuous by its absence?

Leaving the hotel, Will hailed a rickshaw and was soon standing outside the Literary Society, a grand sandstone pile on College Road. Less pristine than on the stamp Will had found online, it was pretty much the same — although instead of bullock carts, there were cars outside.

Crossing the street, he went inside.

There may have been dazzling sunshine out on the street, but the Literary Society was shadowy and dark. The central hall was lit by dozens of neon tube lights and arranged with hardwood desks, at which sat rows of students and members of the public. An air of gravity hung over the vast book-lined library, along with a sense that it had been forgotten by time.

Ancient ceiling fans clicked round on the slowest setting, disturbing what would have otherwise been utter stillness. The bookshelves were crafted from the same wood as the desks, a recurring fishtail motif carved into the vertical supports.

The books themselves were in a sorry state. The bindings warped, glue perished from damp, oily dust staining the cloth.

Will reproached himself. He ought to have gone straight back to the Theosophical Society instead. After all, that was where Hannibal had apparently wanted him to go.

Making his way to the door, he gave the reading room a last glance. A time capsule of the colonial age, it was the epitome of faded grandeur.

As he approached the entrance, Will noticed an epigraph etched into one of the flagstones: 'IN RAIN, IN FOGG, IN SHINE'. It was followed by a reference in subscript — F333 — as though it were a quote.

The misspelling may have been an error but, in the circumstances, it looked to Will like the work of his ancestor. Making his way over to the index, he opened the drawer marked F300 TO F400.

As worn as the books they listed, the cards were grubby from decades of moistened thumbs. Flicking his way through the numbers, Will mouthed out a string of author names: FALE, FAUCH, FELTON, FINCH.

Card F333 was different from the others — not only back-to-front but upside down.

Removing it, Will sighed with pleasure as he read the card:

TITLE: *The Pain of Silence*
AUTHOR: *Hannibal G. FOGG*
DATE: *First published 1891*
PUBLISHER: *Sampson Low & Co., London.*

HAVING ESCAPED THE GREAT Foggian Purge, the book had lain undisturbed for decades. After a prolonged hunt Will discovered it filed three shelves too high — no doubt the reason for its survival.

Taking it over to one of the desks, he flicked through it.

The book detailed early adventures through the Far East, India and Ceylon. Will found himself reading an account of a sadhu undergoing what Hannibal described as 'human hibernation':

The audience was most impressed with the god-man; none more so than Madame Helena Blavatsky, a Russian-born psychic and mountebank. She claimed the man had superhuman powers which came from a diet of sacred figs which he had acquired in the Himalayas. With great interest I watched the burial, and then the disinterment thirty days later. It was immediately clear to me how the feat had been accomplished.

On careful examination, once the audience had gone,
I noticed that the home-made coffin had a false bottom
made from beech, and that a concealed passage ran from
the grave to a nearby field.

Will turned the page. He was about to read on, but the binding had disintegrated, the individual segments loose. As he squared the volume on the desk, a slip of printed paper fell out.

Something was scribbled in green ink on the reverse.

22/ St Mary's.

Quickly, Will looked the address up on Google Maps.

There it was...

St Mary's Road, bang in the middle of town.

Returning the book to its place on the shelf, he slung the daypack onto his shoulder and hurried out into the blazing sunshine.

Seventy-four

1902

A STORM HAD RAGED all afternoon, forcing the pair of birch-bark canoes to take shelter on the banks of the Volga, at its confluence with the Oka River.

Hannibal and his companion, a thickset Englishman

named Ernest Beauchamp, had been searching for a set of lost wax tablets containing scriptures dating from the tenth century.

A specific text had long preoccupied Hannibal — the so-called 'Apocalypse of John'. His interest was so great that he had mastered the Old Novgorod dialect. Despite following every lead, the quest had come to nothing. As a consolation, he had suggested a canoe trip down the Volga.

Heaving the craft up onto safe ground, they went in search of shelter.

They soon found themselves at a village on the outskirts of Novgorod. A throwback to the medieval age, its wattle and daub homes were set around a central square.

After spending the night at the village inn, they explored the surrounding area on foot, as the river's waters were still too turbulent for them to continue. The landlord had directed them to a spring fair a short distance away, held each year when the Oka thawed.

Rows of tents were pitched along the riverbank, offering all manner of delicacies and locally made wares. Hannibal sampled a good caviar from Astrakhan, and ate a bowl of ognivo, a thick soup made from fish fins. He was about to try some cheese, when his companion motioned to a crowd forming in the distance.

Hannibal asked the stall keeper in Russian what was going on.

'They are selling off prisoners,' he said.

'Slaves?'

'Yes, sir.'

Drawn by curiosity, the pair went over to have a look.

Thirty men and women in rags had been jammed into a small pen. Some were weeping; others had collapsed from exhaustion.

One of them caught Hannibal's attention.

A young woman with an alabaster complexion and a mane of flaxen hair, she immediately stood out. Yet it was not her beauty that captivated Hannibal, but her serenity. Standing tall, her grey-green eyes stared down at the ground beneath her feet.

Hannibal stepped closer.

Rising by degrees, the woman's gaze ranged through the blur of spectators and came to rest on Hannibal's face. Her lips eased upwards in the faintest hint of a smile.

The auction began.

Two lame prisoners were sold off first for ten pieces of gold to a man with a whip. The next pair went for half as much. Then a woodcutter and his wife were sold and, after them, a cluster of destitute children.

Towards the end of the slave auction the blonde woman was led through the crowd. Her wrists were bleeding where the twine had cut into them, her arms bruised from a beating she had received that very morning.

Bidding began at three gold pieces and quickly

increased to ten times as much.

Tears welling in his eyes, Hannibal felt a sharp pang of pain in his heart. Never in his life had he wanted something so much — not because of greed, but through a sense of destiny.

Pushing to the front, he raised his hand forcefully.

'A hundred pieces of gold!' he cried.

Seventy-five

221 Sᴛ Mᴀʀʏ's Rᴏᴀᴅ didn't exist. Where it ought to have stood — between a McDonald's and a KFC — lay a patch of waste ground. If the address had been a clue, thought Will, then Hannibal had misjudged the ongoing Indian preoccupation with levelling buildings left over from the British Raj.

He went into the McDonald's, ordered a Maharajah Mac Meal and sat down to eat it facing the corner. As he popped fries into his mouth, he thought about Hannibal's passion for the cryptic. He looked at the address again. Was it plausible it could have meant something else? Perhaps. But it seemed more likely Hannibal had got it wrong.

The door opened and a gaggle of schoolgirls streamed in, ordered Happy Meals, and paid for them in small change. Before the door had swung shut, another customer entered. Will didn't notice as the man bypassed the counter where the girls were waiting for their order, hightailing it round to the toilet.

Kicking open a locked cubicle, the man made eye contact with a woman inside. Clutched tight in her right hand was a switchblade and, just visible through her light cotton blouse, was a tattoo — a double-spiral helix.

Expertly, the man severed the woman's jugular with his own knife. Such was his skill that the spray was directed at the floor. Not a single droplet of blood touched him.

The woman folded down, her chest wheezing in death.

A moment later, the assailant escaped through the kitchen. Seconds after that, the restaurant's front door opened again.

Another wave of schoolchildren flowed in and, along with them, came a woman.

She had spotted Will from the street, and had raced inside.

'We have to leave,' she said fast.

Will leapt up.

'Emma! Where have you been?'

'C'mon, quick!'

Emma grabbed his arm at the wrist, like a mother scolding a child.

'Where have you been?!' he demanded, more forcefully the second time.

But Emma didn't answer.

'We've gotta leave!'

Will's face was dark with indignation.

'What the hell's going on?!'

'I don't know!'

They ran out and hurried down an alley behind the McDonald's.

'What's happening? Where the hell have you been?'

'I needed time,' Emma said.

'Time for what?'

'Time for myself!'

'How the heck d'you find me?'

'Had a hunch.'

Will froze, taking in Emma's eyes.

'Don't believe you.'

She smoothed a hand back over her hair.

'Trust me.'

'I can't.'

'Didn't you see the police cars back there? There's something going on.'

Again, Emma grabbed Will's wrist, dragging him after her. They emerged at the far side of the alley.

Will dug his heels into the tarmac.

'This is where it must have stood!'

'What?'

'Number 221.'

'So?'

'Hannibal left me a clue — 221 St Mary's.'

A siren wailed by as another armoured police car

swept down St Mary's Road in the direction of the McDonald's.

'Told you,' said Emma. 'There's something big going down and this is the wrong place to be.'

'Another hunch?'

Emma's eyes were drawn and fearful, as though she knew far more than she was letting on.

'Something like that,' she said, hailing a rickshaw.

Clambering in, Emma barked something at the driver, and the ramshackle vehicle sped off.

'So what is it this time?' Will shouted against the noise of the two-stroke engine.

'What's what?'

'Your hunch.'

Emma blew Will a kiss.

'Wait and see,' she said.

CROSSING THE CITY, THE rickshaw hit the brakes outside an Anglican church, one of the oldest buildings to survive from British India. Proud above it, the steeple had originally been designed to repel cannon balls.

'My hunch is that he didn't mean St Mary's Road,' said Emma, 'but St Mary's Church.'

'What about the number — 221?'

Emma led the way into the cemetery.

'Look at the graves… they're numbered,' she said.

Will checked the ornate headstones, their lettering worn away by centuries of monsoon wind and rain.

'Looks like the numbers go in a clockwise direction.'

'This is one-ninety,' said Emma, 'Admiral Sir Stanley Hood, died 1814.'

'And that's Lady Jane Russell.'

They both spotted grave 221 at the same moment.

Will broke into a smile.

He ran a hand over the top edge of an impressive tomb in weather-worn Portland stone. Grander than the other graves, it appeared to be newer as well.

Emma read out the inscription:

'Jocus Fogg. Born in Gloucester 8th March 1876, died 9th August 1914.'

'Jocus,' said Will.

'The Latin word for "joke".'

'Hannibal's unmistakable sense of humour?'

'Funny. Haha.'

'So what do we do? Smash it open, and exhume the body?'

Emma shook her head.

'No need. Look, there's a panel.'

Mounted on the rear of the monument, a little above ankle height, was an iron cover. Will prised it open.

'There's something in here.'

Sliding his fingers in, he felt the sides of a steel box padded in cobwebs. Straining, he slid it out, into the light. Even before it was clear of the tomb, he saw the monogram.

'HF,' said Emma.

Staggering under the weight, Will carried the box to the rear side of the church. He made sure no one was watching, then forced off the top. It took some time, as the box was sealed with lead trim.

Inside was a tan leather portmanteau. He lifted it out, struck by the weight.

'Here goes,' said Will, clicking the catches open.

He swung the lid back.

'I don't believe it.'

Emma shrugged.

'What is that?'

'It's the Hands of God,' he said.

Seventy-six

AN AFTERNOON SPENT AT the National Archives at Kew pulled up a series of files, most of which dealt with the Purge of Hannibal Fogg.

At the acquisitions desk, a clerk handed Richard Matheson a wad of uncompleted requests.

'These aren't declassified yet, sir,' she lisped.

'When will they be?'

The clerk checked the computer terminal.

'In 2056.'

Trawling through the files, Matheson tried to piece together the fragments of Hannibal's life. What struck him was that there was so little known about a man who had been very famous indeed.

Next day, back at his desk on Pennington Street, Matheson again trawled the net for mentions of Fogg. There were almost none — except for a few haphazard claims he was a work of fiction, dreamed up by a British travel writer.

Matheson closed Google and launched a lesser known browser — dogpile.com. If indeed there had been a purge against Fogg, then there was a chance it was continuing. Years as a hack had taught Matheson to rely on less than mainstream methods.

Typing 'Hannibal Fogg' into dogpile, he hit 'return'.

The same claims of fiction flashed up.

But they were supplemented by an additional reference:

Three years before, Christie's South Kensington had auctioned a pith helmet belonging to the explorer. It had sold for €36,000.

In his lunch hour, Matheson took the tube down to the auction house.

A little flirting with the pretty young woman at the reception, and *The Times*'s finest came up trumps.

Scribbling the details of the pith helmet's buyer on a compliments slip, the receptionist turned it over. She jotted down her mobile number, slid it over to Matheson, and winked.

Seventy-seven

'WHAT I CAN'T UNDERSTAND is why Hannibal would send me to the Theosophical Society if he already had the Hands of God,' said Will, when they were back at his hotel.

'Maybe they aren't actually the Hands,' Emma replied.

'They sure look like them.'

'What if they look like the Hands of God, but are a fake?'

'A substitute?'

'Precisely.'

'So all we have to do is to switch them with the real thing.'

Emma was only half-listening. She was trying to work out why the case was so heavy, even when the Hands of God were taken out. The answer was that all four sides were reinforced with thick sheets of metal. The top edge of each was embossed with a reference: LU-71.

'Mean anything to you?' she asked.

Will shook his head.

'But look at that...'

'What?'

Reaching over, he pulled away a strip of rubberised padding. Yet more ready-made shapes had been cut into the case's lining.

'What's all that for?'

'I guess the Ladder goes here.'

Taking it out of his daypack, Will slipped it into place.

'A perfect fit,' he said.

Seventy-eight

COMTE OSCAR DE MALLOIS and his pair of albino Pekinese resided in a magnificent first-floor apartment on Avenue Franklin Roosevelt. With splendid views out towards the Grand Palais, the building, number 29, had originally been constructed for Napoleon III's mistress — an English woman named Harriet.

The salon was well proportioned. Laid in Versailles parquet, the floor was adorned with exquisite Turkoman rugs. Set at opposing ends of the room, magnificent trompe l'oeil mirrors reflected each other above fireplaces of white veined carrara.

The Comte was taking a little Earl Grey from a blue Limoges cup when the doorbell sounded. Impeccable in a chequered sports jacket, a cravat and corduroy trousers, he had dressed for the winter rain.

He glanced at his watch.

Eleven-fifteen.

Must be the Englishman — the one who had telephoned the day before.

Pressing the entry buzzer, he waited for the antique wrought iron lift to ascend from the ground floor. A few moments passed and the journalist appeared.

Comte de Mallois introduced himself, shook his guest by the hand and apologised for the din the dogs were making.

'They're a damned nuisance,' he said.

'Thank you so much for receiving me at short notice,' Matheson spluttered. 'I promise not to take up too much of your time.'

The Comte motioned to the salon.

'Earl Grey?' he asked.

Thanking him, Matheson struggled with small talk — the weather, Hausmann architecture, lapdogs and Oriental rugs.

Only when his host seemed satisfied with pleasantries did he pull out a notepad, and enquire about Hannibal Fogg.

The Comte smoothed down an eyebrow with a moistened fingertip.

'What do you know of him?'

'That he was an explorer; that he was disgraced.'

De Mallois offered his guest a second cup of Earl Grey, inhaling the tea's bergamot oil aroma as he poured.

'Hannibal Fogg was far more than that,' he replied. 'He was a genius in the true sense of the word, a polymath, a man of astonishing ability. A confidant to world leaders, a member of secret societies, a brilliant linguist, swordsman, and lover to the most beautiful woman of his time.'

'A lover?' echoed Matheson.

'Indeed. To the one and only woman in his life. His true love.'

'Who was she?'

'Her name was Alina Pasternak,' said the Comte. 'Born a princess, she was enslaved, until rescued by Fogg.'

'Where?'

'On the Volga.'

'When?'

'Early last century. I've heard it said Fogg paid a king's ransom for her.'

The journalist looked up from his notepad.

'Is that true?'

'I suspect it is.'

'I believe you,' said Matheson awkwardly.

In a delicate movement, the Comte cocked his head quizzically to one side.

'Might I ask you, sir, why you are interested in the life of Hannibal Fogg?'

Touching the chewed end of a disposable biro to his lips, the journalist cleared his throat.

'Researching a series I'm doing,' he said. '"Forgotten Victorian Explorers".'

Comte de Mallois got up from his chair. Striding over to the tall windows, he looked out at the chestnut trees.

'I am a student of history,' he said, shooing the Pekinese from his heels, 'but never have I encountered a man who excelled such as Fogg.'

'Excelled in what?'

'In absolutely everything.'

'I've read he was a spy.'

'Of course he was,' riposted the Comte. 'He lived in a time of spies. Everyone was spying on everyone else. But I tell you there was no basis in the accusation he was working for the Nazis. That's a lie.'

Richard Matheson took a sip of his Earl Grey. He was cherishing the change from his routine in Wapping. There was nothing quite like foreign trips for claiming on expenses.

'The pith helmet,' he said. 'Might I see it?'

De Mallois pointed to a display cabinet.

'It's in there, along with a few other Fogg relics.'

'Could I take a look?'

'Help yourself.'

Matheson opened the cabinet and removed the hat. Turning it over, he read the label inside — Lock & Co., Hatters of St James's. As with all the other relics, it bore the HF monogram.

'Following the purge, a great deal of Fogg's property was destroyed,' the Comte explained. 'A little remains in private hands. The contents of that cabinet have taken me half a lifetime to collect. I once heard a rumour that Fogg's Marrakesh mansion still survives, but I have come to understand it's nothing more than legend.'

Richard Matheson pointed to a marquetry box on

the middle shelf.

'Might I ask what's in there?'

Reaching up, the Comte opened the lid.

Inside was a pressed flower.

'This is perhaps the most special of all the relics,' he said tenderly. 'It was worn by Fogg on the evening that he married his beloved princess.'

Seventy-nine

1902

THE DAY AFTER THE auction, Alina described how she had been captured the year before by bandits, and sold into slavery up the Volga River, near Samara. Her family had been slaughtered in the attack, her father's eyes gouged out as he struggled to save his favourite daughter.

That evening, as Hannibal walked along the riverbank, Alina close to him, his hand reached down and touched hers. In all his years of adventure and war he had never been so moved by a tale of suffering. He whispered something in her ear.

Alina looked into his eyes.

The dusk light fading behind Hannibal, she kissed his cheek.

As they walked back in the direction of the village, Alina picked a peony, and threaded the stem into her saviour's buttonhole.

Within the hour they were standing at the altar of the Orthodox Church, a priest before them. Ernest Thomas as witness, the service was no more than a minute or two.

When it was at an end, Hannibal kissed his bride.

'You have made me the happiest man on earth,' he said.

Eighty

THERE WAS MUCH ABOUT Emma that Will didn't trust. Her sudden reappearance in Chennai, her hunch at the cemetery, or the fact she had tracked him down.

It didn't add up.

Will found himself wondering what her ulterior motive could be. Was it money?

Perhaps.

But if she had wanted to rob him there had been plenty of chances.

Back in Ethiopia, she had told of how she grew up living as an ambassador's daughter — a fact that explained her knack at languages, as well as her extraordinary knowledge of cultures and history. She had claimed her father had been honoured in Vietnam, that her brother was a Rhodes Scholar and a rising star in Texan politics, and that her mother was on the board of Amnesty.

Will waited for Emma to come down from her room for dinner. The hotel's restaurant was nondescript —

vinyl tables and plastic plants, halmaddi incense to keep away the flies, trucks rumbling to and fro out on the street.

A stream of moonlight broke through the gap in the curtains, playing shadows over the walls, giving the ordinary a tinge of magic.

After forty minutes, Emma appeared. They ordered dosas, savoury south Indian pancakes served with spicy chutney.

Emma took a bite of her dosa and gulped a glass of water down in one.

'That's what I call HOT!' she said, choking.

Will didn't seem to notice the spice.

'Tell me again, where were you born?' he asked casually.

'Told you, in DC.'

'And after that…?'

'We lived in Holland, then Japan… and in Spain after that.' She took another sip of water. 'Didn't I tell you this stuff?'

'What about the winters? Did you come home for vacation?'

'Yeah, we'd spend time at my aunt's near Austin, a suburb… West Lake Hills.'

'I see.'

Emma paused, and looked at Will hard.

'What is it?' she asked.

'You tell me.'

'Huh?'

'I don't get what's going on…'

'I'm not reading you.'

Will put down his dosa and wiped his fingers.

'Well let me be loud and clear.'

'About what?'

'How did you know where I was?'

'Told you, it was a hunch.'

'Do you really expect me to buy that?'

'Do if you want to, and don't if you don't.'

'So tell me something…'

'Tell you what?'

'Anything, anything about yourself.'

Emma put down the glass on the table. There was pain in her eyes.

'How dare you?' she said, tears rolling down her cheeks. 'I don't give a damn if you believe anything I've ever told you.'

Will stuck his ground.

'That's great,' he said. 'Because I don't believe you! All I know is that there's some crazed reason you feel it necessary to hide behind lies!'

Eighty-one

AT TEN NEXT MORNING, the first tour of the day was held at the Theosophical Society. A group of visitors from Mississippi had come to Chennai for a medical conference. One of them had read online that Hitler acquired the swastika as a symbol through his interest in theosophy. Although not fans of Hitler or of the Nazis, they couldn't resist having a look.

As they toured the halls, learning about the Universal Brotherhood of Man, Will made his way through the parkland, to the Theosophical Society's building. Over one shoulder hung his daypack, the object from grave 221 inside.

To his surprise, there were no guards on duty. Hurrying down a long corridor, he entered the room with the relics. A moment later he was standing over the cabinet in which the Hands of God were kept.

To his shock and delight it was unlocked.

Having swapped the original relic with Hannibal's copy, Will made his escape. As he ran back down the long corridor, he heard a voice calling him.

Panicked, he turned.

At the far end of the corridor, half-shrouded in shadow, was a young priest. His face was honest, his expression calm. Dressed in a saffron robe, he was barefoot. In his right hand he was holding a lengthy iron shaft.

Will stood there, frozen to the spot.

The priest stepped forward into the light.

'We have waited,' he said with slow intensity.

Will faltered.

'Waited for what?'

'Waited for you,' replied the priest, advancing.

His back warming, Will prepared for confrontation.

'I have to leave,' he said sternly.

The priest kept on coming, until he was no more than a man's height away. However hard Will tried, he couldn't muster the courage to run.

'Where are you going?' the priest asked.

'I don't know.'

'Then stay with us.'

'I can't.'

Taking a final step forward, the priest was within arm's reach.

Inches away from him, Will was cold, his hands and face damp.

He was about to turn and flee, when staring him in the eye, the priest thrust out the iron staff.

Holding it in both hands, he turned it.

As Will watched, the ritualistic standard at the end rotated into view:

The monogram of Hannibal Fogg.

Eighty-two

IN THE EARLY AFTERNOON Will made his way back to the hotel, where Emma was waiting in her room.

As she opened the door an alarm sounded. It was coming from Will's daypack.

'Sounds like your clock's ringing,' Emma said.

Quickly, Will fumbled with the zip.

'It's the CODEX!'

Jerking back the cover, he checked the dials, which had come alive with a grid reference.

13°03'36.30N 80°13'51.22E

'Hold on... I'll check Google Maps,' Will said, spinning round. Pulling out his phone, he tapped in the coordinates.

'Wow!' he cried.

'Where is it?'

'Peru!'

Eighty-three

THE MONASTERY OF SAN Francisco was a five minute walk from Plaza de Armas, Lima's central square. Completed in the eighteenth century by the Conquistadors, it was the product of an age defined by the Spanish Crown's lust for gold.

On the long journey westwards from India, Will had checked the CODEX's grid reference again. The reference appeared to mark the Monastery of San Francisco as the target.

Will had no idea where the component might be hidden, let alone what he was searching for.

Hannibal's stamp album had been no help at all. Its pages contained no Latin American postage stamps. The only clue, indeed if it was one, was a pair of letters the CODEX had spewed out while Will and Emma waited for a connecting flight at Amsterdam's Schiphol International.

OS.

'Must be a glitch,' Emma had said.

'It's unlike Hannibal to deal in glitches.'

Will had followed a line of high school kids weaving their way through the rows of fixed airport chairs.

'Bone.'

'What?'

'*Os*, it's the Latin word for bone.'

'*So*?'

'So nothing. Just thinking aloud.'

AT THE MONASTERY, THEY paid an entrance fee and strolled in through a cobbled yard, teeming with pigeons and tourists. An organ grinder was playing in the background against the sickly scent of candyfloss.

A French woman on her way out had marvelled

loudly about the library.

'Shall we start with that?' Will suggested.

'Sounds like a plan,' Emma replied.

They climbed to the upper level, the stone staircase as imposing as it was graceful. Above it hung a fabulous geometric cedarwood ceiling, Moorish technology brought to the New World by the Conquistadors.

Down a long cloistered corridor, a turn to the left, and they entered the kind of library scholars dream of at night. Rectangular and dark, it was musty, as though ripened through centuries of solitude.

A pair of lecterns stood at the front, displaying an oversized hymnal and a Bible. Tropical hardwood shelving ran the length on either side, crammed with vellum-bound tomes, some more than five centuries old.

An upper galleried level looked as though it was about to collapse. Two thirds of the way along, a pair of exquisite spiral staircases wound down to the floor.

'It's the Ladder,' said Will.

'Huh?'

'The double helix — the Ladder of Mithras.'

Emma smiled.

'Think there's a connection?'

'Don't know,' Will said. 'But it's *my* turn for a hunch.'

'What?'

'Think we're in the wrong place.'

Will led the way back down the stone staircase, through an Andalusian courtyard resonant with the sound of tumbling water, along a passageway, and down yet more steps.

In silence, they descended well below the monastery.

'I've got a feeling this is off the tourist route,' said Emma.

'Does that bother you?'

She grinned.

'Not in the least. Where are you taking me anyway?'

'Told you, it's a hunch.'

A line of low-watt bulbs ran the length of a vaulted cloister, with passageways leading off to the catacombs.

As she walked, Emma brushed her shoulder against the lichen-encrusted wall.

'Stinks, doesn't it?'

Will might never have been to the Monastery of San Francisco or to Lima before, but he felt something guiding him. He found himself remembering a story great-aunt Edith had once told — of a mischievous boy who had strayed into the catacombs under Rome and lived there his entire life. She had claimed it to be true, a cautionary tale to little boys everywhere.

The cloister continued a long way under the Plaza de Armas, before coming to an abrupt halt.

A few feet before it ended, a set of uneven spiral steps descended.

The low-watt bulbs continued down the steps.

'And what exactly do you expect to find down there?'

'Os.'

'Bones?'

Before Will had time to reply, Emma got her answer.

In front of them, filling what looked like the top of a broad well shaft, were thousands of human bones. They had been arranged artistically, skulls in the middle, long femurs radiating outwards like bicycle spokes.

'If only the dead could speak,' Will said.

'It's the ossuary.'

'The what?'

'When the cemeteries used to fill up, they'd dig up all the bones and shove them in a kind of storeroom like this.'

'A charming tradition,' said Will, taking the CODEX from his daypack. 'Now for my hunch.'

'You think it's made a mistake?'

'No.'

'Then?'

'Something's playing over and over in my head.'

'What?'

'A story.'

'How does it go?'

Will touched a knuckle to his chin.

'Once there was a boy who ran away from his mom and climbed down a ladder into the catacombs under Rome. He found a lost city there: miles and miles of streets. And he lived on lichen scraped from the walls. His whole life was spent living alone in the darkness. Then…'

'*Then…?*'

'Then one night when he was old, he stumbled on a secret ceremony — priests in long hooded robes, and...'

'*And*...?'

'And he turned into stone.'

'Nice ending,' said Emma, screwing up her face.

Will clicked on the CODEX.

Whereas he usually kept it safe in its case, something had prompted him to remove it. Holding it up to the twenty-watt bulb, he turned it slowly. Under the unit he located a button, the size of a penny coin.

He pressed it.

A miniature compartment snapped open.

'What's that for?'

Will didn't reply. As Emma watched, he detached what looked like a microscope's glass slide, and scraped it gently over the lichen on the wall. When it was tinged khaki-green, he slipped it back into the machine.

The CODEX started whirring. The lamps illuminated and the display flashed up with some text.

'How d'you know how to do that?!' Emma screeched.

'Got round to reading the instructions when you disappeared,' said Will.

'You must have missed me terribly.'

'Not a bit... the instructions kept my attention.'

'Bet they were scintillating.'

'Sure were.'

In the dim light Will strained to read the display.

'Is it in code?'

'No.'

'What does it say?'

'Something about the component.'

'Read it out.'

'"My dear William, again I commend you. As you have no doubt understood, the lichen was programmed as a key. It is *Culbersonia americana*, specific to the catacomb in which you are standing."'

'That's incredible!'

'There's more,' said Will, scrolling down to the next chunk of text. '"Now that I have you in Lima, I can tell you why I lured you here to Peru. I need you to locate the golden Tumi of the Incas. As you no doubt know, the Tumi was a dagger, used for sacrifice.

'"Centuries ago, when the Conquistadors swept across Peru searching for gold, the Incas retreated into the jungle. Fearing the conquerors would get hold of their most sacred object, the Incas sent it deep into the Amazon, where they entrusted it to a warlike tribe, the Shuar. They vowed to keep the dagger safe in return for the one thing they wanted…"'

'What was that?' asked Emma.

'"A supply of Spanish heads".'

Eighty-four

THE ORDER OF ZOROASTER'S Supreme Council had convened in a second exceptional conclave. As before, the Proctor greeted the members, waiting for them to take their seats on the arc of gilded thrones.

When absolute silence prevailed, he rose to his feet.

'Our faiths ensure the equilibrium of Man,' he intoned. 'If harnessed between us, the Mechanism would strengthen each of our faiths. Imagine it: unequivocal proof of the existence of the Divine!'

'Have you called us here to inform us merely of this?' asked a member from Iberia, his tone bordering on ire.

'Indeed I have not,' replied the Proctor. 'You have been summoned to receive news.'

'What news?'

'That the Bloodchild has acquired the second component.'

'Excellent!' declared an Aboriginal counsellor who had travelled from Alice Springs.

'How long before he locates all seven components?' asked another.

The Proctor spoke:

'There is no clear way of knowing,' he replied. 'But such is the danger shadowing him, he is unlikely to complete the task ahead.'

'What can we do to ensure he survives?'

'Ought we to pray for him?'

'Indeed we must,' said the Proctor on reflection. 'Yet while in prayer, we must strive to eliminate the dark forces.'

The Chinese member raised his hand.

'Who are they?' he asked.

The Proctor cleared his throat.

'Half the known world,' he said.

Eighty-five

1903

 CALLING IN A FAVOUR owed to him since tutoring at the Winter Palace, Hannibal Fogg secured himself ninety minutes in the Apostolic Archives of the Holy See.

The door was opened to him at three minutes past eight by the papal majordomo, who was entrusted to fulfil the favour on the highest authority.

Hannibal had only been to the Vatican once before, while on an official journey as a messenger for the Ottoman Sultan Abdulhamid II. He didn't like the place one bit, regarding it as being steeped in pomposity.

The reason for his return to the Holy See was simple: to locate the document describing the treatment of captured Conquistadors by the Shuar of the Upper Amazon.

Rarely were outsiders permitted access to the miles of secret shelving hidden away in the Apostolic Archives.

The favour owed to Hannibal reflected the weight of the good deed he had himself discharged. For, using all the connections at his disposal, he had succeeded in saving the neck of a Roman Catholic cardinal sentenced to death by the tsar.

Once in the Apostolic Penitentiary, a little north of the Piazza Belvedere, Hannibal moved fast. Experience had taught him that, when against time, he should not take the obvious route, but follow his gut.

In this case, it meant shunning card catalogues and relying on pure Zigzag Think.

Less than an hour after crossing the threshold, Hannibal was ploughing through an encoded memoir written in the hand of the seventeenth century priest Antonio de la Calancha. Simple to crack, the code employed was the Caesar Cipher — in which letters are shifted forward or back according to a set algorithm. A little more challenging was the turgid Latin of the time, heavy with metaphor and elaboration.

Hannibal feared that after locating the manuscript with relative ease, he would be unable to track down the passage needed.

But then he saw it:

> *The Jivaro or Shooa tribe of the Amazon jungle have exacted a terrible revenge on our God-fearing community. They have slaughtered as many as a thousand members*

of our Church, including a great many of the clergy. As if this were not abomination enough, these savages severed the heads of their victims and, in their grotesque tradition, reduced them to the size of apples. We must on no account allow word of these atrocities to reach the ears of our countrymen, for fear that they will encumber our monumental quest for gold.

WHEN HIS TIME WAS up, Hannibal hurried from the gates of the Vatican, ordering the carriage driver to take him straight to the Appian Way.

Chaudhury was at the reins.

An accomplished horseman in his own right, the Indian manservant drove so swiftly that they reached the designated spot twenty minutes ahead of time.

Once in position, Hannibal tugged off his boots and rubbed his feet with lavender oil, while his trusted retainer prepared a little supper.

The carriage had been based on the dormeuse designed for Napoleon Bonaparte. The central compartment was bullet-proofed and could be filled with poisonous chlorine gas if a passenger was hostile. Crafted from vulcanised rubber, a single mask was cunningly concealed in one of the cushions, with a tube leading to a canister of compressed air hidden under Fogg's seat. The apparatus was a modified version of the Pressurised Respiration Apparatus he had used at Antikythera Island.

With the pull of a lever, the compartment could be transformed into a dining-room, a bathroom, a bedroom, or even a map room. Rarely content with existing plans, Hannibal had improved on Napoleon's design.

He had added electric lighting, a heated floor for winter, and had even managed to have a surgeon's operating table installed.

Once his master was relaxed, Chaudhury served his specialty dish, toad in the hole, complemented with a glass of chilled Bollinger 1886.

After the meal, Fogg put on a pair of waxed canvas boots, anointed his hair with brilliantine and tied a cape around his shoulders. He called for Chaudhury, who drew back a hatch set into the floor.

The carriage had been parked over a drain cover.

Lowering a grappling hook with chain attached, the manservant heaved the iron cover away by means of a mechanical winch.

Descending through the trapdoor, Hannibal slipped unnoticed from the comfort of the carriage, down into the Crypt of the Popes.

The entrance had been revealed to him twenty years earlier by the late Giovanni Battista de Rossi, the archaeologist credited with discovering the catacombs.

Far below street level, in the Catacomb of Callixtus, the walls were lit with burning torches — one every twenty-seven feet. Hannibal strode briskly towards the far end of the passageway, his head stooped to avoid colliding with the low ceiling.

Unlike most who ventured down into the catacombs, he had no difficulty in navigation, for he had been presented with a master plan to the tunnels by de Rossi himself — decades before even hearing of the Order of the Golden Phi.

On this occasion, as Hannibal made his way into the central catacomb, the lichen on the walls caught his eye. It possessed an unusual phosphorescent quality, which appeared to be more than a simple reflection of the flames.

Well aware time was short before the assembly of the Order of the Golden Phi, Hannibal scraped a sample of the lichen into his snuff box to be studied when he was in less haste. A consideration of the material was later to lead to the publication of a monograph entitled *Lichen Growth and Its Unique Specification*.

Sales may have been modest, and every copy in existence had been destroyed during the purge. But Hannibal had no interest in securing a wide readership for the paper, or for any of his work. As far as he was concerned, one ought to write to satisfy oneself alone — which is exactly what he did.

Eighty-six

ONE REASON THAT THE monograph on lichens was received with limited public interest was that Hannibal's research was decades ahead of its time.

He had discovered that lichens, feeding off their local surroundings, provided an individual locational-fingerprint unlike any other type of flora. By decoding the sequence of the lichen make-up, it was possible, he found, to determine exactly where a specific sample had been obtained.

And, by using the information in reverse, it could be employed as the basis for a revolutionary type of security system — an elaborate flora-based key.

Will appreciated his ancestor's preoccupation with clues and codes, but he had no real comprehension of its depth. Hannibal had devoted years of painstaking research to devising methods by which information could be concealed in absolute secrecy.

The catacomb beneath Lima's Monastery of San Francisco had prompted the CODEX to spout out a swathe of background information.

'Looks like we hit the jackpot,' said Will.

'What?'

'The CODEX has been spewing all afternoon.'

Still recovering from jet lag, Emma had only just woken from a long siesta.

'What's it been saying?'

Will scrolled back to the top line on the mechanical display.

'Listen to this: "For a thousand years the Fogg family has strived to locate the Alexander Mechanism's components, beginning with Friar Benedict of Faugg in the twelfth century. Each subsequent generation has accumulated additional information, in an effort to locate the components. All the while, danger has shadowed us. For this reason we have been forced to keep the discovered components in situ until the appropriate time to collect them is reached. But now, William, the moment has come for all seven components to be retrieved, and fitted into the Alexander Mechanism. Follow my instructions and collect the golden Tumi."'

Eighty-seven

VIEWED FROM THIRTY THOUSAND feet, the trees blended together into an endless mantle of emerald green, broken only by the river — a great serpent of sludge-brown water.

A bizarre anomaly of human history, Iquitos was a city slapped down right in the middle of the jungle. It had been founded on greed and greed alone — avarice for the instant wealth derived from rubber trees.

At its height, in the late 1800s, the city was in a league of its own when it came to showing off. The rubber dealers lit their cigars with flaming $10 bills, bathed in chilled champagne, and imported shiploads of luxury from Paris and New York.

On the Sunday afternoon Will and Emma arrived, a curtain of torrential rain fell, easing the insufferable tropical heat. At the bars overlooking the Amazon River, on the once-glorious Esplanade, the beer was flowing fast.

While Emma went in search of waterproof shoes, Will took a seat in El Malocca, ordered a lager, and opened the flight case. He didn't dare leave it in the hotel room.

Folding back the leather flaps, he caught sight of the inch-thick metal sheets that gave the case both its rigidity and weight. It seemed odd that Hannibal would have used such a heavy metal.

As he sat there pondering the case's design, he noticed once again the inscription — LU-71 — embossed into the leading edge of each metal sheet. Tapping the letters into Google, he checked their relevance. An answer flashed up:

> LU: Chemical symbol of a key rare earth metal LUTETIUM (pronounced 'lew-TEE-shee-um'), whose atomic number is 71. One of the rarest and most valuable metals in existence, Lutetium has applications in electronics for which it is highly prized. Lutetium is currently valued at approximately six times the value of gold.

WILL WAS JUST ABOUT to click on another link, when a burly foreigner swaggered in from the Esplanade. Six foot three and lean as a racehorse, he was dressed in camouflage fatigues, his face gaunt and tanned. In his left hand was smouldering a damp cigarette and in his right was a razor-sharp machete. Slipping down into a seat just inside the door, he ordered a Pilsner.

When it came, he knocked it back in one.

South African by birth, his name was Walt Spieler. Or, rather, that was the name printed in his current passport — the document issued by the Republic of Guatemala in part payment for a job he had done. As with most of the other baby-boomers residing in Iquitos, Spieler was lying low from the world, and from his past.

Hiding places didn't get much better than the Peruvian Amazon.

Like everyone else, he had been seduced by the unrealistic gender ratio — six women to every man, by the cheap beer and by the jungle.

Back in the '60s, Spieler had enlisted as one of Colonel 'Mad' Mike Hoare's 'Wild Geese', the most successful and feared band of mercenaries operating on the African continent. He had broken free a couple of times, gone home to Transkei, got married, divorced, married and divorced again, before returning to the business he knew best of all — the coup d'état.

Jungle was in his blood, whether it be in Africa, the Far East, or South America. In the '90s he had run guns in Bolivia, cut-price cocaine in Colombia, and had done time in a Venezuelan jail. It had been there he got the tip-off of a lifetime: Iquitos, an Amazonian paradise of unequalled allure and vice — the Saigon of South America.

As if the girls and the beer weren't enough, a third commodity made the city irresistible — fresh-faced eco-tourists.

When Spieler wasn't knocking back Pilsner or sleazing it up with underage girls, he was prowling the Malocca bar for customers.

That's where he first caught sight of Will.

'Need a guide, gringo?' said Spieler, tugging off his Ray-Ban Aviators, the end of a cigarette screwed into the corner of his mouth.

'Er, um,' Will faltered, his head jolting up. 'Yeah, kind of... we need to go upriver.'

A second later, Spieler was sitting across from him, in his hand an empty glass, dried foam crusted down the side.

'If you're buying, I'll have another,' he said with a smile.

'Sure, yeah...'

A fresh round was slapped down by a teenage waitress. She fluttered a hand over Will's shoulder as she left. Blushing, he fished out a canvas-backed map and motioned to a slim blue vein on the sea of green.

'The Rio Tigre... that's where we need to go. D'you know it?'

The South African nodded.

'Sure I do.'

'Really?'

Walt Spieler laid his right hand down on the table, glancing hard at the knuckles and the scars.

'Know it as well as that,' he said.

Eighty-eight

RICHARD MATHESON HEARD FROM Comte Oscar de Mallois that Hannibal had kept a series of expedition journals during his life. They had been mentioned in the biographical entry the journalist had read online. Along with most of the explorer's possessions and publications, they had apparently been destroyed during the Great Foggian Purge.

At their meeting in Paris, de Mallois mused that the notebooks were most likely written by Hannibal for his son, Wilfred.

Matheson asked about the journals themselves.

'I once heard that they were encrypted documents,' said the aged aristocrat, pouring a pair of glasses of green chartreuse. 'That they contained all the material needed to locate seven treasures — treasures Hannibal had found, but left untouched.'

'Why would anyone leave a treasure if they found it?'

The Comte sipped again.

'You must remember,' he said, 'Fogg was not your

average man. He wasn't interested in wealth for the sake of wealth. Money didn't excite him. Of course he was never without it, but for him it was nothing more than a means to an end.'

Peering out at the trees, Matheson leaned back.

'Sure, but a treasure...'

'Whatever the truth,' said the Comte, 'it's a great sadness the journals were lost, or destroyed, for they might have contained extraordinary material — clues to the workings of Hannibal's mind.'

Sipping the liqueur, Matheson yearned for numbers.

'How much do you think the journals would be worth?' he asked.

The Comte swilled the chartreuse around the cut crystal glass and grinned like a Cheshire cat.

'An incalculable amount,' he said.

'Really?'

'Of course.'

'How much?'

Draining his glass, Comte Oscar de Mallois shrugged.

'If Fogg's hat sells for tens of thousands, the lost notebooks would fetch millions,' he said.

ELEVEN DAYS AFTER HIS return from Paris, Richard Matheson was back at his desk on Pennington Street, sipping a cup of watery coffee from the vending machine.

Hannibal Fogg had slipped into his life so much that he was unable to get down to any proper work.

The landline rang. He picked it up.

'Travel desk.'

'I should like to speak to Mr Matheson,' said a cultivated French voice.

'This is he. Is that…?'

'Le Comte de Mallois.'

'Good morning, sir.'

The Comte disliked making small talk on the telephone, regarding conversation as being far more satisfying face to face.

'I have learned something which may be of interest to you,' he said.

'Oh?'

'That next week, Sotheby's will hold an auction of travel manuscripts at the Hotel Negresco in Nice. A late addition, Lot 361, has been described as *The Manchurian Journal of Hannibal Fogg*.'

'How interesting,' said Matheson, reaching for his notepad. 'Does it give a reserve?'

'Indeed it does… a hundred thousand euros.'

'That's steep.'

'Perhaps I shall see you there,' said the Comte, as he rang off.

Matheson smiled. Nice would be nice. His mood brightened, he went to the Negresco's website and booked himself a junior suite.

He was on expenses after all.

Eighty-nine

SEVEN DAYS AFTER PUSHING out into the jungle, with Walt Spieler as their guide, all Will and Emma could think of was lost luxury.

For Will it was the fantasy of a hot meal, one without insects stirred in, and for Emma, a recurring image of a piping hot bath lathered with bubbles.

Spieler had hired a boat, a rotten hulk named *Luz*, infested with rats, roaches and lice. The crew were made up of misfits — a couple of gringos scooped up from the bars along the esplanade, and a handful of Peruvian derelicts.

During the day, Will and Emma stretched out on the roof, watching the undergrowth ease by. And through the long infernal nights they lay in their hammocks down below, listening to the jungle devouring itself, as they waited for the first strains of dawn.

When he was not out of his mind on flora-based hallucinogens, Spieler regaled his captive audience with tales of the Seychelles coup — the one which had gone so horribly wrong.

'Those frigging war movies have it all wrong,' he said bitterly.

'How's that?'

'They never tell you the truth.'

'So what was the truth?'

Spieler lit a local cigarette, sucking hard on the end. 'War's the greatest kick imaginable!' he said.

THE JOURNEY ABOARD *LUZ* was followed by a week of insufferable hardship — hacking through jungle in torrential rain. Will lampooned himself for having complained at the river journey and for being so poorly equipped. Giving in to Spieler's tall tales and bravado, he had allowed the war veteran to buy provisions and basic equipment. As a result, he had paid three times the going rate.

Had Will thought about it, he might have wondered why Hannibal hadn't planned for the river journey. After all, meticulous forethought was his hallmark.

By downloading digital maps onto his iPhone, Will had missed a vital clue. Scrawled over one of the cloth-backed maps, in invisible ink, were encrypted instructions which detailed the location of Hannibal's Amazonian Chamber. Containing a full range of equipment for a grand expedition, it lay twenty feet beneath the ornate bandstand in the Iquitos market at Belen — a structure designed by Gustav Eiffel for the 1889 World's Fair.

Inside the expedition chamber there were six inflatable boats of Hannibal's own design, eleven tents made from rubberised canvas, machetes crafted from Sheffield steel, waterproof cases of provisions, rifles and ammunition, calcium phosphide flares, and sackfuls of glass beads for paying off the tribes. There was even a seaplane which Hannibal had designed for reconnaissance over the jungle.

On the morning of the fourth day, Spieler gave the order for the ragtag expedition to pack up camp. Although it was still early, shortly after dawn, he claimed to have smelled smoke in the night — signalling that a tribe was close by.

Will had found himself wondering if Spieler was the real thing, or a sham, all talk. Everything about him was clichéd, from his soundbite lines about being under fire, to his preoccupation with South African whores.

That evening, when they reached a jungle encampment, a roasted sloth was provided as a peace offering. An arm was ripped off and presented to Spieler. Without any surprise he got down to eating it.

'The best one I've had in years!' he said.

Ninety

1904

THE EXPEDITION CLEAVED A path through a stretch of jungle sixteen miles due west of the Rio Tigre.

In the lead, a Japanese *wakizashi* blade in his gloved hand, a pith helmet crowning his head, was Hannibal Fogg. Directly behind him, a similar weapon in her clasped fingers, followed Alina.

Streaming out behind in single file for over a mile were more than eighty porters, camp staff, hunters and guides.

Where possible, Alina insisted on joining her husband on his journeys despite the danger. Proving herself as tough as anyone else, she had become something of a legend after pulling an arrow from her thigh during a Dyak ambush in the jungles of central Borneo. When offered rubbing alcohol, she had shunned it, declaring that the loss of blood would make her stronger.

In torrential rain, the expedition reached a clearing at the base of an escarpment. Hannibal gave the order to camp in the lee of the sheering granite rock face.

The men were exhausted.

Although he never mentioned it, not even to his beloved wife, Hannibal had begun to fear the porters might mutiny.

From his time with the Royal Engineers, he had learned the ins and outs of keeping a team motivated and avoiding mass desertion. In his opinion, nothing boosted flagging spirits like a plentiful supply of hot food. A vicious circle of course — the more food brought along, the more porters needed to carry it.

For this reason, Hannibal tended to dispatch teams of hunters in advance. They would slaughter giant tapirs, known to the tribes as *sachavaca*, then butcher and hang the meat, ready for the arrival of the expedition.

As camp was prepared, Alina explored the nearby

rockface, and was the first to spot the petroglyphs.

Rising like a curtain from the jungle floor, the granite wall was adorned with ancient symbols incised into the stone. Some looked like faces, others meaningless squiggles, yet more were wavy lines — the route of the river, or the form of a great snake.

As soon as they set eyes on the wall, the porters began wailing in terror, as though a terrible curse had been exacted upon them. Dropping their loads, some tore back through the undergrowth the way they had come.

Hannibal immediately gave the order to serve up some of the precious pemmican. Packed in fat, the meat rations had been transported all the way from London's East End.

As the steel cans were chiselled open, a lookout sounded the alarm.

'What's he saying?'

'There's a scout approaching.'

A minute later, a small-boned native wearing a toucan-feather crown was before them. In his left hand was a bow fashioned from *chonta* palm; in his right, a roasted sloth.

He presented the animal to Hannibal.

Without faltering, the explorer ripped off the creature's head, smashed it against a rock and sucked down the brains. Tearing off the right arm, he passed it to Alina, who sank her front teeth into the biceps.

The scout turned, and beckoned them. Leaving the

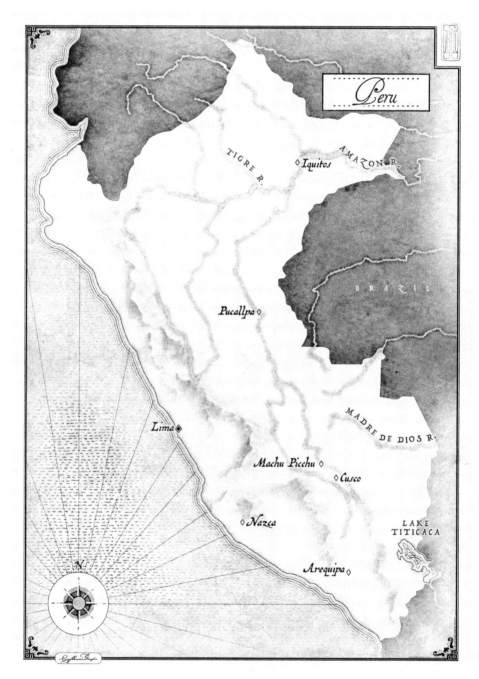

others to make camp, Hannibal and Alina followed him into the forest.

After a short distance they came to a second clearing in which the Shuar village lay. All around it, low branches hung with the shrunken heads of their vanquished enemies.

The Foggs were received in a longhouse by the chief, on his head a crown of scarlet macaw feathers. Having presented him with a bag filled with glass beads, they were served a white milky beverage in return.

'*Masato*,' said Hannibal with loathing, as Alina held the gourd to her lips.

'What is it, dearest?'

'Manioc,' he said. 'It's chewed by the old crones and fermented in their saliva.'

Alina winced. The eyes of the village elders on her, she took a long hearty draught.

The refreshment was followed by other delicacies: toasted leaf-cutter ants, grilled hornets and a nest of roasted pink-toed tarantulas.

Plucking one of the spiders from the banana leaf plate, Hannibal showed Alina how to extract the flesh from the arachnid's abdomen. He shelled it as if he were peeling a shrimp, and reached down for another.

After the feast, Hannibal presented the Shuar chief with yet more gifts, including a brand new Remington shotgun and a box of cartridges. Alina presented each of the chief's six wives with fifty yards of calico and a sack of cane sugar.

Much grinning ensued.

'Ought we to hasten back to the camp now that it's getting dark?' she asked cautiously.

'No, not yet.'

Hannibal nudged his face towards the far end of the longhouse, where a forlorn-looking man was busily stirring a cauldron.

'What's that?' whispered Alina.

'I suspect it's *ayahuasca*.'

'What might that be, dearest?'

'The Vine of the Dead.'

For an hour the shaman stirred the brew, reducing its volume over heat until no more than a pint of nut-brown liquid was left.

When it had cooled, he poured it into a gourd, blew tobacco smoke over it and held it to Hannibal's lips.

The explorer drank, and after him, Alina.

Nothing happened at first.

But, gradually, Hannibal felt the base of his back warming. The sensation continued until his spine was ignited with a penetrating heat. At the same time, the longhouse contorted, its bamboo floor and sides melting like wax. Streams of brilliant colours bombarded his vision — vibrant purples and electric blues.

Hannibal sensed he was growing wings, and flying.

All around the jungle slept.

As he circled higher and higher above the forest

canopy, he heard a noise. Shrill, it was coming from the direction of a lone kapok tree.

Plunging like an eagle at its prey, he plummeted to the base.

Then, flexing his fingers, he began to dig.

Down through soft soil and roots, they touched something…

…Something cool and hard.

Ninety-one

THE SOUND OF SINGING wafted over the jungle encampment, spilling out from a longhouse set apart from the rest. The voice of a boy broke into a solo in what sounded like a hymn.

'The damned missionaries have a lot to answer for,' replied Spieler with disgust.

Emma strolled through the clearing until she reached the church's simple wooden steps. Inside, thirty villagers were waving their hands aloft in devotion.

'They used to shrink human heads,' she said to Will, who had caught up with her. 'And now they're Seventh Day Adventists.'

Will, Emma and the South African were led into the chief's longhouse, where they sat cross-legged on the bamboo floor. Once the Adventists had finished their service, the chief and his family prepared a feast.

The meal began with a creamy white beverage, served in the bottom half of a gourd.

'Tastes bitter,' said Emma as she quaffed it down. 'Wonder what it's made from.'

An old hag came over, a clutch of loose teeth doing little for her smile.

'Think she wants you to finish it.'

Will drained the bowl. The beverage was followed by a banana leaf piled high with roasted specks of black. The chief invited his guests to eat. Her face screwed up, Emma tossed a handful into her mouth.

'Those are ants,' said Will. 'That one's still alive.'

The ants were followed by grub worms, and the grub worms by roasted tarantulas.

Will's face fell.

'Really don't think I can stomach those.'

The chief leaned over, peeled him a tarantula abdomen and plopped it in his mouth.

Will swallowed.

'Look down there,' Emma said.

'What?'

'That guy's cooking something up.'

'Looks like tea.'

Fifteen minutes later, the shaman served the nut-brown liquid.

It tasted strong and sour, like herbal-based mouthwash.

'This meal's getting worse and worse,' said Will.

The next thing he knew, the base of his back was

growing warm, and he experienced an overpowering sensation that wings were sprouting from his shoulders. His vision clouded by bright colours — vibrant purples and electric blues — he found his perception was altering.

He was a magnificent eagle soaring above the jungle, wings aloft on the breeze.

Circling higher and higher, he heard a noise. A piercing wail coming from the direction of a kapok tree.

His wings swept back and he plunged — down through the sky, through the branches, creepers and bromeliads, until he was at the base of the kapok tree.

He was still an eagle, but he had human hands. Not knowing quite what he was doing, he used them to dig.

Soon his fingers were holding something fashioned from gold.

NEXT DAY, WILL WOKE to find himself lying on the forest floor. Covered in mud and filth, he was shaking like an addict gone cold turkey.

'What the heck was that all about?' he said to himself, struggling to stand.

He looked round for Emma, but couldn't see her.

With so many trees and so much foliage, it was all conjured together to form a single entity.

But, one tree stood out from all the others — a sprawling kapok — the very same one from Will's dream.

Picking up a flat-edged stone, he started to dig down through layers of dead leaves, gravel and roots.

After three feet of excavation, he reached something wrapped in waxed canvas cloth. He dug it out. Although it was disintegrating, he made out a symbol painted on it — Hannibal's distinctive monogram.

Ripping the cloth away, Will found himself holding the rounded hilt of a golden dagger.

The sacred Tumi of the Incas.

Ninety-two

SHORTLY BEFORE SUNSET, A Piper Navajo seaplane landed into the wind on the island of Praslin in the Seychelles archipelago. The twin propellers grew louder in volume before the pilot powered down.

A moment after that, the single passenger was ashore, walking briskly over the platinum sand towards the shadowed entrance of a luxurious beach house. He was of Asian appearance, his skin leathery from years of exposure to the tropical sun.

Once inside the building, he was greeted by a man and a woman, both younger than he. All three were wearing an identical emerald ring on the middle finger of their left hand.

'Thank you for making the journey, brother,' said the woman. 'Although a little inconvenient, Praslin is equidistant for us all.'

'I came as soon as I received your message.'

'Time is of the essence,' said the man. 'The Bloodchild has collected three of the components.'

'But have our agents not brought his mission to an end?'

'Not yet.'

'Each one has failed.'

'Then we shall have to double our efforts.'

The newly arrived counsellor stroked a hand down his chin.

'There is surely no need to remind either of you of the danger we face. Should the Bloodchild succeed, organised faith as we know it will be doomed. The very thought of it… mankind in direct communication with God. It is preposterous to even contemplate it.'

'Immense wealth accrued over centuries will evaporate,' said the woman. 'Our communal lands, our treasures, our influence… all will be lost in the blink of an eye.'

The younger of the men twisted the ring on his finger to the right.

'The Proctor is exciting spirits with talk of the Alexander Mechanism and the damned Bloodchild.'

'There is one course of action,' responded the second man.

The woman looked out at the sun disappearing below the horizon.

'We must send an agent to terminate him,' she said.

Ninety-three

IN THE NEGRESCO BALLROOM three hundred gold banqueting chairs had been arranged in rows. Sotheby's staff were flustering about making final preparations for the sale.

Along the sides of the room, a series of glass cases had been set up, in which rare objects relating to travel were on display. In one was a handwritten manuscript of *The Seven Pillars of Wisdom*. In another, a signed letter from Stanley to Livingstone. And, in the display case nearest to the podium, Lot 361, *The Manchurian Journal of Hannibal Fogg*.

Richard Matheson had arrived at the celebrated hotel on a British Airways flight from Heathrow in the early afternoon. He had ordered a club sandwich with extra french fries, washed down with a bottle of Hautes-Côtes de Beaune, and fallen into a deep slumber on the king-size bed.

Soothed by drink, he overslept.

By the time the Fleet Street hack had woken up, showered and made his way down to the ballroom, there was standing room only.

On the way in, a member of Sotheby's staff asked Matheson if he would like to register for a paddle.

'No thank you, I'm a journalist,' he said haughtily.

The Comte de Mallois was poised discreetly in the back row. Immaculate in evening dress, he wore a fresh pink peony in his buttonhole. Catching Matheson's eye, he smiled vacantly, and left it at that. An experienced member of the auction circuit, he believed in fraternising only when a sale was at an end.

On the stroke of eight, the auctioneer stepped to the podium, adjusted the microphone and tapped his gavel twice.

'Mesdames et Messieurs, allow me to welcome you to this sale — devoted to rare and unusual objects relating to travel. This evening we have the privilege of representing some of the most sought-after items of exploration ever to come under the hammer. And so Mesdames et Messieurs, let us begin.'

The auctioneer took a sip of water, adjusted his horn-rims and observed the giant digital display board. Twenty currencies were reset to zero, and the staff on the telephones indicated they were ready.

'Lot one,' called the auctioneer, 'a rare autograph manuscript by Sir Richard Francis Burton. Shall we start the bidding at thirty thousand euros?'

Ninety-four

SUBDUED BY THE EFFECTS of the hallucinogen, Will staggered to the river, where Emma was lying in the water. Climbing down the bank, he slipped in, his feet sinking into the silt.

'That was the wildest thing ever,' he said.

'You can say that again!'

'I had a dream I was a great eagle, soaring over the trees.'

Emma smiled, her eyes ringed with dark circles.

'And I was a butterfly,' she said.

In a voice no louder than a whisper, Will mumbled something.

'Huh?'

'I found it…' he said, a little louder.

'Found what?'

'The dagger.'

Emma looked up.

'What?! Where?!'

'It was buried at the base of that huge kapok tree over there.'

Thirty feet from where they were wallowing, Walt Spieler was watching them. Certain they were not about to move, he strode up into the longhouse barefoot. The chief and his family weren't there. They were back in church singing a Shuar rendition of '*Onward, Christian Soldiers*'.

Moving fast over the bamboo floor, Spieler passed a crate of missionary Bibles, and the carcass of a newly slaughtered caiman, its tail boiling in a pot nearby. Making his way over to Will's daypack, he rooted through it.

First, he pulled out a wad of fifty-dollar bills. But as

soon as the dagger's hilt touched his hand, he tossed the money back. Marvelling at the craftsmanship, he stuffed it down the front of his camouflage fatigues.

Thirty seconds after that, Spieler was in the undergrowth behind the village. Against strains of Shuar singing, he turned on his phone, waited for the unit to register and engage the satellites. Once patched on, he spoke quickly, leaving a succinct encoded message on a voicemail system.

Stowing the twelve-inch antenna, the veteran mercenary clicked off the power and slid the satellite phone back in its pouch.

He was about to hurry away, when a muscular hand reached out from the undergrowth, an upturned blade extended from its fist.

In a perfect practised movement, the knife was wielded low and fast — slicing a deep arc from the left ear to the Adam's apple.

The South African's body was covered with a leafy branch hacked from a cecropia tree. A day or two and the voracious Amazonian ants would have it stripped down to the bone.

The dagger was replaced in Will's daypack, as the tribe launched into yet another hymn.

Soon after, Will and Emma were back from the river.

'Look at the Tumi!' said Will, pulling it out.

'It's so beautiful,' Emma cooed, running her fingers over the exquisitely moulded hilt.

Will looked up, his face trained on Emma's.

'What d'you say you saw in *your* dream?' he asked.

She swallowed, her expression sour.

'I saw treachery,' she said.

IN THE LATE AFTERNOON the villagers left the church, their service at an end. The children ran out first, darting between the shacks. Then came the women, Bibles wrapped in red plastic envelopes given to them by the missionaries. After all the others came the warriors, each resplendent in a macaw feather crown.

Will was asleep, his face pressed down onto the bamboo floor, Emma curled up nearby. They didn't hear the chief and his family enter, or notice them begin the elaborate process of heating stones at the far end of the longhouse.

It was only when an iron bucket of river sand was placed on the fire that Emma opened her eyes.

She looked up.

'Smells like something's burning.'

The chief and his family were standing in a circle, armed with sharpened machetes.

Emma slapped Will's leg.

'Wake up! Wake up!'

'Huh? What...?'

Will opened his eyes sleepily, and jolted back.

'What's... what's going on?!'

'Not quite sure,' said Emma. 'But I have a feeling it's got something to do with our heads.'

Will did his best to stress friendship. The chief blinked an order. His warriors leapt up and bound their visitors with vines.

'Where the hell's Spieler?' Will shouted. 'He should be watching out for us!'

'God knows,' replied Emma. 'Probably stoned out of his mind.'

The chief had found the golden dagger.

Will watched as he performed a purification ritual around the sacred object.

'I'm sorry, really sorry,' he said.

'Don't think that's going to calm him down.'

A rusted machete in the chief's right hand, his shadow fell over Will. A clutch of baked stones were brought over from the fire, clicking with heat.

'They're gonna smash our heads in?'

'Don't think so,' said Emma. 'The stones…'

'Huh?'

'But what are the hot stones for?'

'For shrinking our heads.'

'Great,' said Emma, taking a deep breath.

'Stay calm.'

'Stay calm and do what?'

'Stay calm and pray.'

Before Emma could reply, the chief's wife grabbed

her by the shoulder. Holding her down she punched her in the face. Then she struck her chest, ripping her blouse.

The chief's wife fell back, screaming.

Suddenly, the chief dropped his machete. Taking a step back, he got down on the bamboo floor and, begging for his life, chopped the bindings away.

'What's going on?!' Will whispered urgently.

Dazed from the attack, Emma strained to make sense of the situation.

'Think it's got something to do with my tattoo.'

The chief raised the Tumi in line with his eyes.

Halfway down the hilt was the same spiralled design as on Emma's shoulder blade.

Ninety-five

LOT 360 WAS HELD up by one of Sotheby's porters: a sketch of the Zambezi made by David Livingstone. It failed to reach the reserve of eleven thousand euros. The display board was reset, the unsold item whisked away.

'Lot 361,' announced the auctioneer, pressing a hand to his paisley bow tie. 'This, Mesdames et Messieurs, is, I might say, one of the stars of the evening. The "lost" *Manchurian Journal of Hannibal Fogg*.'

A wave of murmuring swept through the room.

Standing near the back, Matheson had a good view of both the auctioneer and the art-collecting crowd.

The Manchurian Journal was removed from the glass display case and held up by the porter wearing white cotton gloves.

'Until now,' the auctioneer intoned, 'it was believed by many experts that the journals of Hannibal Fogg had been lost, or destroyed at the time of the Purge. This may be true in part, of course, but the Manchurian Journal — which has been held in a private collection for almost a century — is, in itself, a fabulously rare treasure of exploration.'

More murmuring, followed by a hushed wave of anticipation, undulated through the ballroom of the Negresco.

The auctioneer announced the sale once again, adding:

'A reserve price of one hundred thousand euros has been attached to this item. And so shall we start the bidding there?'

He clicked the gavel to the top of the podium and the auction began.

'A hundred thousand,' blurted out a voice in the front row.

'One hundred thousand euros,' echoed the auctioneer, the display board flashing the amount in a dozen currencies.

'Do I hear an advance on one hundred thousand?'

'Five hundred thousand!' called out a man in Jordanian desert robes.

'Five hundred thousand, with the gentleman at the front.'

'A million.'

'Five million.'

'Seven million euros.'

The auctioneer dabbed a starched linen handkerchief to his brow. In his long career, it was the first time he had ever sold anything ascribed to Hannibal Fogg. Until the week before he had never even heard the name.

'We have seven million euros,' he said, taking a sip of Evian. 'Any advance?'

At eight million a betting paddle waved left and right — a paddle held in the right hand of the Comte de Mallois.

'Nine million,' said the voice at the front.

The Comte's paddle waved again — at ten million.

'Eleven million,' called out the Jordanian.

'Twelve million.'

'Twelve million euros against you, sir,' said the auctioneer, attempting to maintain his composure. 'Are there any other bids in the room?'

Silence.

THEN, STANDING UP, THE sharp heels of her Jimmy Choos pressing hard onto the parquet, a young Russian woman raised her paddle.

'Fifteen million euros!'

Matheson swivelled round fast. Aged about twenty-five, she was ravishing — russet-brown eyes set in the kind of face that drives honest men mad.

'Is there any advance on fifteen million euros?' asked the auctioneer.

Tense silence.

'Well there we have it, Mesdames et Messieurs, an extraordinary price, for an extraordinary object.' The auctioneer clipped the gavel on the podium again, announcing: 'Fifteen million euros for the "lost" *Manchurian Journal of Hannibal Fogg.*'

Ninety-six

THE SHUAR CHIEF CLAPPED his hands, signalling his wife to prepare another gourd of creamy white *masato*. When she was gone, he bowed. His head low, he presented Emma with a Bible that had been translated into Shuar in Mobile, Alabama.

All Emma could think about was the tattoo parlour in Austin. She had gone there aged eighteen with her best friend, an English girl called Jolie. After looking through pictures, she planned to get a gecko lizard done in scarlet. But at the last moment she changed her mind. Jolie had said that in England the Celtic spiral warded off evil.

A gallon of *masato* was held to Emma's lips. Once she had drunk as much as she could, the gourd was presented to Will.

'Looks like the universe has dealt us a new hand,' he

said, before taking a long satisfying draught of the brew. 'Can't place the taste. I wish I knew how they made this stuff.'

As he drank, the Shuar chief strode the length of the longhouse, bamboo slats clicking underfoot. He rummaged in the rafters before returning, hands outstretched. Between them was the disintegrating cloth bearing Hannibal's monogram.

Ceremoniously, the chief presented the Tumi to Emma, before pointing out to the forest.

'What's he saying?'

'No idea.'

The chief descended the steps, turned, and beckoned.

'Think he wants us to go with him.'

They followed, the scorching afternoon light blinding them as they crossed the village and pushed into the coolness under the forest canopy. The chief moved like a ballerina through the trees, his feet hardly touching the ground. Struggling to keep up, Will and Emma got more tangled up with every footstep.

Well outside the village they came to a clearing, shaded by a lofty breadfruit tree.

The chief gestured towards it.

Will and Emma took in its trunk.

Halfway up, cupped in the branches and overgrown by vines, was a tree-house.

Leaving them to investigate alone, the chief squatted down on the ground and lit his pipe with *mapucho*, black tobacco from the jungle.

Will climbed up first.

As his right foot touched the first rung of the ladder, he guessed the secret.

'Bet it was built by Hannibal,' he said.

'What?'

'Look at it… there's Fogg written all over it.'

Forcing open the door, they found a room strewn with belongings and campaign furniture. The climate had taken a heavy toll, but the tree-house was very much as the explorer must have left it.

In the middle stood a magnificent monogrammed brass bedstead, rotting mosquito nets clinging to the frame. On a long table under the glazed window were a dozen insect specimens pinned out in glass frames. Near to them stood an assortment of laboratory equipment and a medicine box covered in grime. And, staring down from the timber wall was an oil portrait of a blonde woman with a gentle complexion.

'Must have been his wife,' said Emma.

'It's incredible to think he was here.'

'I wonder how long he stayed.'

'Long enough to build this place.'

'Oh my God, look at that.'

Emma was pointing to a foldable desk.

Laid out on its surface were a pair of curious trophies.

The first was a gold goliath-sized pocket watch. On the reverse were inscribed the initials 'SAC', along with what looked to Will like a grid reference: 25°46'27.31N 80°11'24.94E. The second object was a shrunken human head in a bell jar.

Will pulled away the jar and picked up the head. Examining its miniature features, he noticed how the mouth and eyes had been sewn with twine.

'It's so grotesque.'

'It's so alluring,' Will replied.

'The face is strangely familiar,' said Emma. 'I wonder who he was.'

Will moved over to the bed. Under the shredded mosquito net was stuffed a mass of rotten bedding.

'Look, there's something on the pillow,' said Emma.

'What is it?'

'Looks like a big bug.'

Pinned out in a glass frame was a colossal beetle, an entomologist's tag attached.

'Can you read it?'

Will leaned in.

'*Titanus giganteus.*'

'Think it's a clue?'

'How could *that* be a clue?'

Will took the CODEX from his daypack. Turning it on, he tapped in the name of the insect. The mechanism whirred, chimed, and a grid reference appeared:

8°33'22.89N 12°47'39.04E.

The CODEX began to chime again. Will looked closely at the display.

'What does it say?'

'It says "Orisha Stone".'

Ninety-seven

MATHESON FOLLOWED THE RUSSIAN from the ballroom, observing from a discreet distance as she paid at the sales desk. Taking into account the buyer's premium of twelve per cent, the total cost for the Manchurian Journal came to €16.8 million.

Dressed in a Gucci two-piece sailor suit, she paid with a Centurion American Express card — the fabled black card unfettered by a preset limit. Printing out a receipt, the clerk slipped it into a cream Conqueror envelope. A porter stepped up and handed the customer a Sotheby's carrier bag with a smile.

Outside, a graphite-grey Bentley Azure was waiting, the peak of the chauffeur's cap barely visible from the kerb. The woman allowed the Negresco's doorman to open the rear door to the vehicle. She slipped in, having perfected, at finishing school in Geneva, the art of getting into a limousine without spreading her legs.

Richard Matheson waited for the Bentley to purr away, before hailing a cab. He followed at a distance, having already scribbled down the Bentley's number plate — S364, from nearby Monaco.

The limousine sped east down Promenade des

Anglais, circumvented the port, and paused at the traffic lights just short of the marina.

The jet set's luxury yachts were moving in the evening swell, in a world of champagne and crystal.

In his best schoolboy French, Matheson had asked the taxi driver to hold back. The last thing he wanted was to be spotted. Scanning the waterline, he wondered which boat the Bentley Azure was heading for.

In the back, the woman twisted the top off a Chanel lipstick and applied a coat of Barcelona red.

The lights changed to green.

The chauffeur eased his foot from brake to accelerator.

As he did so, there was a violent explosion.

His window open, Matheson caught the blast on his cheek. Where the Bentley had stood seconds before, was a seething heap of twisted metal.

Thrown clear of the wreckage, lying in the gutter, was the Chanel lipstick in Barcelona red.

Ninety-eight

HIS BACK RAMROD STRAIGHT, Chaudhury opened the door to Dar Jnoun from the inside as Will's hand reached for the knocker.

'Good afternoon to you, sir,' he said.

As he entered, Will gave the manservant a hug.

'Sure it's safe to be here?'

'As I said in my text message, sir, the danger has passed.'

'Glad to hear it.'

Crossing the threshold, Emma pecked Chaudhury on the cheek. 'Good journey, miss?' he enquired, embarrassed by the attention.

'There were ups and downs.'

Having put the flight case and daypack on the floor, Will breathed a heavy sigh of relief.

'A life without steep learning curves would be no life at all,' he said.

THE AFTERNOON CALL TO prayer rained out over Marrakesh as Chaudhury ferried the luggage in from the street. Once he had unpacked, he served tea with slices of lemon on the side.

Will slumped into one of the leather club chairs in the south salon and fished out Hannibal's canvas-backed map of West Africa.

'I'm happy to be home,' he said.

'*Home?*' echoed the manservant.

Will smiled.

'Well, you know what I mean.'

Turning on his iPhone, Will checked the grid reference against the paper map.

'Fifty miles south-east of Freetown, Sierra Leone.'

'I am pleased to see you are resorting to tried and tested methods, sir,' said Chaudhury approvingly.

'Huh?'

'Printed cartography, sir.'

The servant excused himself, and Will's attention slipped down onto the Afghan rug. Although passionate about all things digital, he sensed that Hannibal's methods concealed clues — clues which he might well have been missing.

'I'll bet Hannibal has it all figured out,' said Emma, strolling into the salon, her hair damp from the shower.

'We've got three components, only four more to go.'

'You're making it sound like a parlour game.'

Will got to his feet and looked out into the courtyard.

'The question is how the Orisha Stone fits into it all,' he said.

'D'you have any idea what it is?'

'No... and Google's been a fat lot of good.'

Chaudhury padded back through.

'I do believe Mr Fogg wrote a monograph, sir.'

'*Monograph*? What the hell's a monograph?'

'On what subject, Chaudhury?' asked Emma.

'As I recall, it concerned the Orisha Stone of Sewa Delta, miss.'

Padding away into the north salon, he returned a minute later, a silver tray on an upturned palm. Upon it was a slim volume bound in lizard-green leather.

Will opened it at the title page.

'*The Orisha Stone and Its Role in Cultural Ethnography with Reference to the Human Leopard*

Society of Sierra Leone,' he read out loud. 'By Hannibal Garrett Fogg, published in London, 1916.'

'Catchy little title,' said Emma.

Will sat up in the chair.

'Listen to this,' he said.

'"The Human Leopard Society of the Sewa Delta regarded a spherical agate orb with great reverence. They believed the stone to have supernatural powers, and that to preserve it, the sphere had to be anointed day and night with human blood. The stone was thought to have been taken to West Africa in the 1500s by an Egyptian Copt, named Theodore, who traded it to the natives for diamonds. He himself had acquired the relic from thieves, who had robbed it from an ancient Greek tomb in Carthage. Theodore never managed to leave West Africa, however. In a bizarre ritual involving sharpened gastropod shells, he was devoured by members of the Human Leopard Society."'

'Don't like the sound of West Africa!' said Emma bitterly.

'Nor do I, but it looks like we're off the hook.'

'Why's that?'

'Listen: "In 1788, a great many members of the Human Leopard Society were captured en masse, and transported to plantations in South Carolina. Wary of the fact that the agate orb required regular anointing, they concealed it, taking it with them to the New World."'

'So, it's in America?'

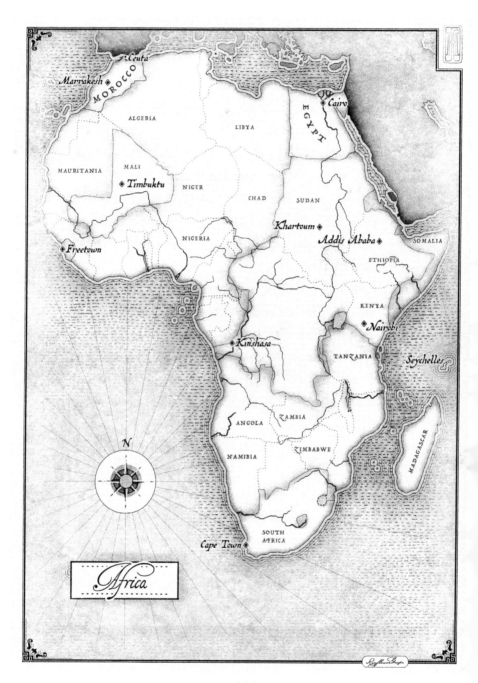

Will nodded.

'Sounds like it.'

'But why would Hannibal have planned to send you to Sierra Leone?'

'A red herring?'

'Must have been.'

Will chewed his lower lip in thought.

'What if it was a miscalculation on his part... one which Hannibal never managed to successfully correct?'

Pacing over to the delicate study of a woman's face looking down from the wall, Will touched a hand to the gilt frame.

'Picture it,' he said. 'Hannibal leaves the head-shrinkers, retraces his steps through the jungle and sails back to Marrakesh. Then he realises he's got the coordinates wrong. The Orisha Stone isn't in Sierra Leone at all, but somewhere else, in the US.'

'So why didn't he just re-jig the clue in the CODEX?'

'He couldn't,' said Will.

'But why not?'

'Because there's a built-in security mechanism. It's obvious if you look at the gearing arrangement. The ratchets don't allow the cogs to reverse.'

'So what does that mean?'

'That once the CODEX is programmed, it can't be changed.'

Emma balked.

'So he'd have had to traipse back to Peru and hack

his way up the jungle again?'

'Returning to the Rio Tigre would have taken months.'

'Why not send someone else then... someone he could trust?'

Will slammed a hand on the table.

'Exactly.'

'But who to send?'

At that moment, Chaudhury came in holding a plate of toast spread lightly with Marmite. He had acquired a taste for the savoury yeast extract while at boarding school in Ajmer. A jar was always included in the parcels he received from the family palace in Cooch Behar.

'There was the sad case of my great-uncle,' the servant intoned, having apologised for listening in.

Will and Emma looked up.

'Who?'

'My great-uncle,' Chaudhury said. 'He was sent to the headwaters of the Amazon by Mr Fogg.'

'And... what happened to him?'

'Never returned, sir. It was a terrible blow to my great-aunt Anjali.'

'Why was your great-uncle sent up the Amazon, Chaudhury?'

'I believe that Mr Fogg had wanted him to pin an identification tag on a beetle, sir. It seemed a curious request at the time.'

'What was his name?'

'Chaudhury, miss.'

'No, his first name?'

'Sanjay, Sanjay Ashok Chaudhury.'

Will rooted about in his daypack.

'SAC.'

'Indeed, sir.'

'Then this belongs to you, Chaudhury,' he said, handing over the gold watch.

Visibly moved at seeing the monogrammed object, the manservant gave thanks.

'I don't suppose you heard mention of Great-Uncle Sanjay, sir?'

Will and Emma exchanged an anxious glance.

'*No!*' they both said at once.

Switching on the CODEX, Will entered the grid reference from the pocket watch. It was decoded into a new reference.

He plotted it on the map first, then on his iPhone.

'Miami,' he said.

Ninety-nine

1906

THE STIFLING NIGHT AIR alive with mosquitoes and bats, a dozen men were busy dismembering their human prey. Cloaked in leopard skins, they chopped the bodies apart, tossed the limbs in one pile, the heads in another and the torsos in a third.

Thirty yards away, the ground had been laid with banana leaves and sprinkled with fragrant flower petals. Crafted from iron and laden with drywood, a row of charcoal braziers sent sparks spitting into the night.

Three hundred members of the Society were already in attendance, each of them dressed in leopard skins, curved steel claws masking their fingers. A sense of primeval danger prevailed as the roasting began.

The only figures not attired in leopard skins were Hannibal and Alina Fogg. It was the first cannibal banquet either had attended, and their inexperience and anxiety were conspicuous.

Hannibal did his best to make small talk with the chief, speaking Krio with an accent, the result of learning the language entirely from a book while sailing down to Freetown.

The first platters of meat were served — a selection of charred human limbs. The chief took a blackened foot and, holding it as one might a piece of roasted chicken, stripped the flesh from the heel with his teeth.

A dish of internal organs was then ushered forth, sizzling from the grill. Tiring of conversation, the chief waved a hand at a platter of human brains.

'One last question,' said Hannibal, hoping to avoid the delicacy through conversation. 'Where exactly is the agate sphere?'

The leader of the Human Leopard Society

snatched half a brain greedily and sunk his teeth into the cerebellum.

'The slaves took it across the water,' he said.

Hannibal's eyes glazed over.

Leaping to his feet, he snatched his wife's hand and gasped:

'We are in the wrong country, my dear!'

Excusing themselves, they hurried away into the night.

One hundred

WILL FELT A PANG of anxiety as Air France flight AF72 landed at Miami-Dade. He had been away so long, the thought of being back on American soil at last had got him worked up. Unbuckling her seatbelt, Emma squeezed his arm affectionately.

'Can feel you trembling,' she said.

At Immigration they handed over their passports, Will's first. As he rifled through the pages, the Homeland Security officer made a face.

'Well you've certainly been on the move,' he said, clicking down the stamp.

Emma slid her passport over the counter. The officer swept it under the UV lamp, then scanned it in the reader.

Frowning, he looked up.

'You got a criminal record, miss?'

Emma flinched.

'Excuse me?'

'Would you please answer the question, looking into the camera?'

'Um, er.'

'It's a yes or no question, miss.'

'Um, yes... I do.'

Will did a double take.

'*You what?*' he whispered.

'Served time, miss?'

'Er, yes, yes I did.'

The officer didn't look up; he was opening Emma's file.

'How long?'

'Three years.'

A long pause was followed by the click of the Immigration stamp.

'OK. That's fine. You're free to go, miss.'

As soon as they were away from the Immigration desk, Will snapped:

'Why didn't you ever tell me you were in jail?'

Emma's face flushed flame-red.

'Because...'

'*Because?*'

'Because it was none of your goddamned business!'

Will wasn't ready to let it drop.

'What were you in for?'

'I don't want to talk about it, OK?'

'C'mon! Tell me!'

Emma's expression flipped from embarrassment to rage.

'*No!*'

Taking a deep breath, Will exhaled it in a sigh.

'OK, OK,' he said.

FROM HANNIBAL'S MONOGRAPH, WILL learned that the West African slaves brought their own deities with them to the New World, concealed in the guise of the Catholic Trinity. The publication had revealed another valuable strand of information as well — that the Orisha Stone was sacred to a secret group within Santeria, a sect known as Santo Pandera.

A little surfing online, and Will came up with the address of a local botanica — a shop specialising in Voodoo and Santeria goods.

Emma and he had spent the night at the Best Western on South Beach. As always they took two rooms, at Emma's insistence. The duty clerk slipped a key to each of them. But, after checking her room, Emma had asked Will to switch. She wanted a bathroom with a hairdryer.

Since the episode at Immigration she hadn't seemed herself, and Will had felt betrayed. To make matters worse, his precious iPhone had mysteriously gone dead in the night. None of the usual tricks coaxed it back to life.

Before breakfast he slipped down to use the motel's free computer terminal, set in the corner of the dining-room. For twenty minutes he trawled every detail Emma had told him about herself — starting with her family.

Just as she said, her father had been honoured in Vietnam, with no less than the Congressional Medal of Honour. After leaving active duty, he had served as an ambassador in Amsterdam, Tokyo, Madrid, as well as at the UN.

As for Emma's brother, he was indeed a Rhodes Scholar and an up and coming Democratic hopeful, while her mother had been on the board of Amnesty for a decade or more.

Will was just about to leave the Amnesty website, when he felt a hand brush over his shoulder.

'You doing what I think you're doing?' said Emma accusingly.

Will spun round. As he did so, she reached for the mouse and clicked on the 'history' tab.

'So let me see,' she said forcefully. 'You've been checking on my mom, my dad, my bro… *all* of us!'

'You have to listen to me!' Will countered defensively. 'I can explain…'

'You're going to explain your paranoia?!'

'I'm so, so, so sorry!' said Will. He stood up, stretched out his hands but as he did so, Emma stepped back.

In the afternoon, they visited the botanica, a sense of unease hanging heavy between them. They hardly exchanged a word between the motel and the store.

At the shop, the window display was jampacked with statues of the Virgin Mary, Jesus, and with a farrago of bric-a-brac and saints. To anyone unfamiliar with Santeria, it might have appeared like just another store dealing in Catholic wares. But once they were through the door, the veil of Catholicism was washed away.

There were books of black magic and divination charts, talismanic powders, scented candles, Yoruba masks and feather chains, amulets and aromatic oils, bark stripped from jungle trees, and miniature glass phials of musk.

Uncertain how direct to be, Will came straight out with it and asked the woman behind the counter about Santo Pandera. To his surprise, she wasn't fazed by his interest in the subject.

'Every night at eight,' she said in a Cuban accent, a long scarlet fingernail motioning towards a flyer pinned to the counter.

'Is it open to tourists?'

The woman glanced out at the street.

'They'll take anyone they can get,' she said.

One hundred and one

FOLLOWING THE EXPLOSION, MATHESON had driven straight back to the Negresco. The Sotheby's staff had all left for the night, the golden banquet chairs stacked up in the ballroom and the unsold lots taken back to secure storage.

Matheson went to the bar, perched himself on one of the high stools and ordered a single malt. He knocked it back in one, ordered another and knocked it back as well.

Then he had an idea.

He went to the house phone and asked for de Mallois's room. It was unlikely the Comte would be staying anywhere else. The Negresco suited his style.

The operator connected him immediately, putting the call through to the Presidential Suite.

'It's Matheson, from *The Times*,' he said. 'I'm sorry to call so late. Do you mind if I come to your room?'

Comte de Mallois was wearing a pair of indigo-blue pyjamas, a touch of ruby-red on the collar. He looked quite exquisite in the soft light, his skin pallid as a porcelain doll.

'The journal,' Matheson said as he entered the Comte's suite, 'it's been destroyed. Blown sky high, along with the woman who bought it.'

The Comte widened his eyes.

'What are you talking about?'

'I followed her after the sale. A limo with Monaco plates took her in the direction of the marina. But as she neared it, the car blew up.'

'I thought I heard a sound,' said de Mallois, 'but put it down to a storm approaching.'

'Who would have wanted to destroy the journal?'

Comte de Mallois pinched his moustache.

'Plenty of people.'

'But why?'

'Because of the treasure,' he said.

One hundred and two

THE MEETING ROOM'S WALLS were shrouded in cheap Chinese-made silk printed in leopard skin; a cement floor was hidden by bloodstained sheets of hand-woven raffia. Halfway down the hall stood a rectangular bird cage, packed with white chickens. By the time Will arrived, at a quarter past nine, more than twenty followers were chanting at the far end of the room.

Having complained of a headache all afternoon, Emma had opted to stay behind in the motel. For once Will was happy to go on without her.

He had found the building with ease and parked the rental Chevy Aveo at a nearby underground parking lot, scribbling the bay number on the back of his hand.

At the door a squat Cuban man in cowboy boots

waved Will in.

The next thing he knew, he was sitting cross-legged on the raffia matting with the followers.

An hour went by.

Will felt his legs go to sleep, pins and needles punctuating the numbness.

The chanting continued, a melodic droning hum. As it did so, a Latin woman entered. She was about thirty, almond eyes framed in an overbearing face. In her hand was a polished orange stone the size and shape of a softball. The surface was scored with concentric lines, like the rings of Saturn.

As soon as they saw it, the audience broke into tumultuous wails of delight.

One of them, an ancient man, struggled to his feet. Stumbling through the hall, he kissed the stone passionately.

Another devotee opened the rectangular cage, yanked out a chicken by the neck, ripped off its head, and directed the spout of blood over the stone.

The Latina who had brought the object in sat cross-legged on the floor. Her hands cupped the Orisha Stone in her lap, her eyes firmly closed.

One by one the devotees approached. An aide to the woman handed each of them a chicken snatched from the cage. Without thinking, they tore the heads off the birds, allowing the blood to spurt over the Latina and the stone.

Another hour slipped by.

Will was wondering how he would get his hands on the sacred object, and how many more chickens were going to be killed. But then, the Latina got up and placed the Orisha Stone on a blood-soaked cushion padded in faux leopard skin.

The aide unscrewed the top of a five-gallon plastic container and poured the contents — a cold brown brew — into a chalice fashioned from beeswax and bone. Lining up again, the devotees took it in turns to drink the liquid, before breaking into a chorus of song.

Passing up the chance to take part in the ceremony, Will watched from a safe distance.

Ten minutes after the brew had been consumed, it began to take effect.

Containing datura, a powerful hallucinogen from the upper reaches of the Peruvian Amazon, it sent the members of the Santo Pandera sect into a catatonic state of collapse.

In the middle of where they were all lying, contorted and foaming at the mouth, was the sacred Orisha Stone — brought to the New World by enslaved members of the Human Leopard Society.

Seizing the moment, Will leapt up, snatched the stone and fled.

One hundred and three

1907

RMS CAMPANIA WAS ON the third day out, en route from Southampton to New York. The winter swell had been so acute that the promenade deck was closed. Ginger capsules had been made available to first class passengers to counter the violent listing of the ship.

Alina was snoozing in the bedroom, having been unable to sleep the previous night. Asleep beside her was little Wilfred, who had turned three the week before. Next door, in the stateroom's luxurious salon, Hannibal was seated in a gilt cabriole chair.

Putting on a blindfold, his back was to Chaudhury.

'That's been a full minute. So I'll begin.'

Unlike Fogg, the manservant was prone to the effects of seasickness, his face having turned a worrying shade of olive. He was standing over a fine marquetry chessboard, swaying gently back and forth on his heels.

Sixty-four postage stamps were laid out on the squares, one in each. Beside the board stood a stack of albums, bound in lizard-green leather.

'Are you ready, sir?' enquired Chaudhury, choking back a mouthful of bile.

'Quite.'

'Then I shall begin with A-8, sir.'

'That's easy, it's an Austrian Red Mercury.'

'Correct.' The servant cleared his throat. 'D-7.'

'A Mauritius Penny Blue.'

'Correct again, sir.'

'Come on, Chaudhury, try to challenge me!'

'F-8, sir?'

'That's an ordinary Penny Black, a cancellation stamp dated 14 Oct 1840.'

'Indeed it is, sir.'

Hannibal ripped off the blindfold. Testing his memory was a favourite pastime.

'Lay out a fresh batch,' he said, 'and double them up this time. Two stamps on each. After that I'll have a go at three.'

Chaudhury was picking the postage stamps from the board, when there was a knock at the cabin door.

Slipping on his white gloves, he strode out into the vestibule. It would not of course have been seemly for a gentleman to open the door to a visitor.

The manservant reappeared with a salver, a visiting card face up upon it.

'A Chinaman named Mr Yang sends his compliments, sir, and asks you to join him to discuss a matter of "national interest".'

Hannibal raised an eyebrow.

'At what time?'

'Right away, sir.'

'His cabin?'

'C31,' said Chaudhury. Pausing a fraction of a second, suggesting displeasure, he added, 'I believe it is in second class, sir.'

His curiosity piqued, Hannibal combed back a strand of stray hair. He took a pinch of Macouba, and paced to the door.

'Please inform Mrs Fogg I shall be back in time for sherry at six,' he said. 'In the meantime lay out the stamps and don't forget to double them up.'

'Very good, sir.'

To HANNIBAL'S ACUTELY HONED sense of smell, the second class corridors were tinged with the odour of sewage. He made a mental note to bring the matter up with the captain when they dined at his table that evening.

Port side, cabin C31 was set halfway down a long corridor. Hannibal observed that the door handle was an inferior model to the one on his cabin door, and that the door itself was second-rate beech rather than premier-quality teak.

He knocked gently.

The door was opened by a Chinese manservant.

Hannibal introduced himself, presented a visiting card and was invited inside. As the servant disappeared into an adjoining room, Hannibal turned to the porthole to survey the second class view of the sea.

He clicked his tongue, turned ninety degrees.

Then he fell to the floor with a thud.

Standing over him, the handle of a lead cosh gripped in his fist, was Mr Yang.

One hundred and four

AT THE PRECISE MOMENT Will was grabbing the Orisha Stone, there was a rap on Emma's door. With nothing more than a bath towel wrapped around her, she had opened it, expecting to find Will.

But a would-be assassin was standing in the doorframe instead.

His expression calm, his well-developed upper body was squeezed into a jet-black muscle shirt. An elaborate tattoo was poking from the right sleeve: a yellow flambeau and the motto 'Honneur et Fidélité', the crest of a feared brotherhood — the French Foreign Legion.

In the hit-man's right hand was a WASP hunting knife, a canister of compressed gas in the hilt. Grasping Emma by the hair, he forced her into the bathroom.

As she struggled, the former legionnaire — in the occasional employ of a Balkan agency — unfastened his belt. Under his immense strength, Emma felt herself fold to her knees. No amount of squirming could break her free.

Lying against the clinical white tiles, her back was forced up against the wall, her body shaking, as the assailant's knee jammed into her ribs, winding her.

Satisfied his victim was defenceless, the legionnaire tied her wrists with cord and spread her legs. As he did so, Emma writhed like an animal in a last pitiful display of fight. Her mind was ordering her to give in, to resign herself to the ordeal.

Her body went limp.

Somehow she managed to wriggle her hands free.

Without knowing where she got the strength, she jerked the knife's point away from her neck, forcing the assailant to stab himself just above the groin.

Instinctively, Emma's hand squeezed his fingers. In doing so, the button on the WASP's hilt was pressed. The canister was pierced and a stream of frozen gas surged into the legionnaire's intestines.

The result was an explosion, followed by entrails being spattered across pristine bathroom tiles.

Emma collapsed.

Crying, shaking and hyperventilating all at once, she slumped into the corner. Her body was smudged in fragments of torn human flesh.

For more than an hour after that, she lay in the same position — too spent with exhaustion to move.

Finding the door to her motel room open, Will had burst in jubilantly, the Orisha Stone in his hands.

Emma's room was dark and silent. Noticing the bathroom light was on, Will stepped past the twin beds and peered in.

'Oh my God!' he roared in horror. 'What on earth happened here?!'

Emma didn't reply. She couldn't speak. Will took a towel, wrapped it around her and crouched down close, his hand coaxing her head to his chest.

'It'll be fine,' he said tenderly, glancing over at the legionnaire's dismembered remains.

'He was going to kill me,' said Emma in a whisper.

Will helped her through into the bedroom.

'We switched rooms, remember? He must have been after me.'

'We'll have to report the body,' Emma replied, breaking into tears again.

'If the Magi know we're here,' Will said, 'we're not safe.'

He opened the leather flight case and nudged the Orisha Stone into the latex moulding.

Another exact fit.

As soon as it was in place, the CODEX began chiming.

'Sounds like another destination,' said Emma in little more than a whisper.

Will scowled.

'To hell with it… After what you've been through, it's meaningless.'

Putting her head on Will's shoulder, she rested it there for a long time. She thought back to the comfort of her childhood, and to the blazing winter sunshine at Cape Cod.

With dread, she wiped her eyes.

'Go and have a look,' she said. 'It's important — very important.'

'You sure?'

'Yeah.'

Picking up the CODEX, Will checked the dials. The display was showing another grid reference: 34°15'53.57N 108°56'39.35E.

'My iPhone's dead,' Will said.

'Check the maps.'

Will was already on it. Moving into the lamplight, he opened the master sheet.

'Where is it?'

'Peking, or rather "Beijing".'

Will laid the CODEX on the bed.

'I'm so sorry for ever doubting you,' he said.

'So what are we going to do?' Emma countered. 'We've got two hundred pounds of dead meat in there. Sure you don't want to go to the cops?'

Will wiped a hand over his face.

'Imagine how it'll sound,' he said. 'They'll eat us alive. Besides, we have something in our favour.'

'What's that?'

'Well I'm betting no one's going to report the loss of their muscleman.'

'So...?'

'So we clean up the mess and dump the body.'

'Like where?'

'There are bushes back there.'

Emma frowned.

'Listen to what you're saying!'

Will shrugged.

'I once had a friend who worked part time at a cleaning company,' he said. 'Can't remember its real name, but everyone called it "Death's Janitor". My pal spent his time mopping up after gangland killings, suicides, and dealing with bodies that'd been rotting for weeks. He taught me some tricks of the trade.'

'Such as?'

'Ammonia,' replied Will, fast. 'There's nothing quite like it for breaking down blood.'

One hundred and five

DISABLING THE SURVEILLANCE CAMERA outside Emma's room, Will hauled the legionnaire to the bushes at the back of the motel, with a fireman's lift. He picked up every single fragment of flesh, bone, skin and internal tissue, as well as the contents of the assailant's stomach.

Then, Will sprayed the bathroom in ammonia, from a nearby pharmacy. He had bought three gallons of it, mixing it with household bleach. The quick-fix solution found online claimed to break down the DNA like nothing else.

The taxi driver steered onto the Dolphin Expressway en route to Miami-Dade. Much quieter than usual, Emma started sobbing, muffling the sound with the sleeve of her dress. Cuddling up to her on the back seat, Will did his best to give comfort.

Once they arrived at the airport, he unbuckled his money belt and counted the cash.

'Christ! We're down to three hundred bucks. Not enough for flights to Chicago let alone China.'

Emma looked at him and blinked, her eyes red.

'Hannibal would have known.'

'Known what?'

'That your funds were low.'

'Why didn't he do anything about it, then?'

For some reason Will thought of the secret study and the row of marble busts arranged in a row.

'Franklin,' he said.

'Huh?'

'The Z-Grill...' he muttered, hunting through his wallet. 'I can't believe it!'

Emma leaned over

'What's the matter?'

'Must have left it in Marrakesh.'

'The question now is whether Hannibal actually saw the future,' said Emma. 'Or if he merely planned for how he imagined it would be.'

'I've no doubt he saw it,' Will countered. 'Frame by frame.'

'So he knew we'd be standing here in urgent need of help?'

Will smiled.

'In need of his help and *cash*.'

'You think?'

Will nodded.

'Bet you there's a safe deposit box a stone's throw from here stacked with gold bricks.'

'That'd be nice.'

'Maybe he's left something else to sell.'

'He did,' Emma said. 'The silly little stamp.'

'But he would have known I left it on the nightstand in Marrakesh.'

'Pity.'

Will froze.

'What d'you just say?'

'That he left you the Z-Grill.'

'No, no, before that. You said he might have left a safe deposit box…'

'…Stacked with gold bricks.'

Will reached down to the flight case.

'What about another metal?' he said, clicking the catches open.

'Are you really thinking of selling the components?' Emma asked in disbelief.

'Not them.'

'Then what?'

'These…'

One by one Will pulled out the metal plates.

'Don't want to be a pessimist, but I'm not imagining you'd get very much for scrap iron.'

'This ain't any old iron,' Will riposted.

'Then what is it?'

'Lutetium.'

'*Lu-what*?'

'Lutetium.'

'Never heard of it.'

'Granted, it's kinda obscure — they use it in electronics.'

'So what do we do with god-knows-how-many-pounds of rare metal?'

'We sell it,' said Will without hesitation.

One hundred and six

1907

IN THE BOWELS OF RMS *Campania*, against the thunderous roar of the triple expansion engines straining to maintain twenty-two knots, lay a makeshift torture room.

Inside, lit by a pair of paraffin lamps, were Yang and his henchman, Yao. Trussed up before them, his jacket, necktie and shirt stripped away, hung Hannibal.

His wrists had been bound together with jute twine, hitched over a hook mounted high on the wall. By stretching, the tips of his toes just about managed to touch the floor.

'A last chance to answer the question, Mr Fogg,' said Yang, 'or we will begin our work.'

Hannibal didn't reply. Slowing his breathing, he calmed his racing mind with a vision of serenity — spring daffodils in Perthshire.

'Where are the components for the Mechanism, Mr Fogg?'

Yang counted down from ten to one.

'Very well…'

Mumbling something in Cantonese to his henchman, he unscrewed the lid of a glass gallon jar.

'*Hirudo medicinalis*,' he intoned balefully.

Hannibal hardly needed to be reminded of the scientific name for the common swamp leech. Regarded as the leading expert on the species, his monograph on its taxonomy and reproduction was the standard work available.

Rolling up his sleeves, Yang began placing the leeches on the prisoner's back. Well aware that by struggling he would force the little creatures to reposition their triple rows of teeth, Hannibal remained quite still.

It took just five minutes to cover his back, chest and arms.

From the moment the first leech was in place, Hannibal sensed the blood flowing out, the weight of the leeches increasing as they gorged.

The torturer relished the treatment.

'Would you like to talk now, Mr Fogg,' he asked,

'while you still have blood in your throat muscles?'

Still, Hannibal said nothing.

He was busy calculating.

How long would it take Chaudhury to work out he had been abducted and that he was being tortured in the depths of the ship?

The odds were against him.

From the start, Yang had expected Hannibal to be an unobliging informant. His legendary tolerance of pain suggested he would reveal nothing at all. He glanced approvingly at the jar. Plenty of leeches left.

Just as he delved in to withdraw an especially fine example, the door to the torture room swung open.

Standing in the frame, an automatic double action revolver in each hand, was Chaudhury.

A pair of simultaneous blasts.

Yang and his henchman fell to the iron floor — both shot straight through the centre of the brow.

'Good show!' Hannibal moaned.

Apologising for his tardiness, the manservant cut his master down.

'How did you know to find me here?'

Draining one of the lamps, Chaudhury used the paraffin to remove the leeches.

He sniffed, straining to avoid eye contact.

'One might call it a servant's intuition, sir,' he said.

One hundred and seven

ARRIVING AT WACHOVIA BANK on Miami's 8th Street, Will and Emma waited in line until the next teller was free. They had spent a day and a half negotiating a sale for the lutetium to a non-ferrous metal dealer downtown. Fortunately for them, a recent breakthrough in robotic Swarm technology had led to a severe shortage in the metal. Its price had quadrupled in the previous month alone, resulting in a cashier's cheque made out for $842,623.

Elated at having serious cash only the second time in his life, Will slid the cheque over to the young woman at counter number four.

'I'd like to cash this, please.'

The teller held the cheque to the light, before slipping it into the fraud detector.

'We'll require you to open an account,' she said.

'Sure,' said Will.

The teller picked up the telephone receiver hanging above her desk and dialled an extension. Sitting in his office at the far end of the banking hall, branch manager Kevin O'Donnell was on the phone to his mistress when the secure line buzzed through.

'I'll call you back, babe, I promise.'

Peering through the glass partition into the banking hall, he jerked the receiver to his ear.

'O'Donnell.'

'It's Marti at counter four.'

'What's up, Marti?'

'Mr O'Donnell, there's a gentleman here with a cashier's cheque. He'd like to open an account.'

Fifty-five minutes later, Will had a savings account, a platinum credit card and fifteen thousand dollars in cash.

'At the Wachovia Bank we aim to please, Mr Fogg,' O'Donnell gushed. He scribbled down a number on the back of his business card. 'Here's my cell. Always here for you, 24/7.'

As they left, Will got a flash of Rosario back at the bank in San Francisco.

'Looks like my luck's changing,' he said.

One hundred and eight

1901

A LONE FIGURE WAS limping through the cold winter rain down Peking's Morrison Street. His indigo cotton jacket soaked through, the conical straw hat offered little protection from the downpour. Pausing at a street hawker's stall, he ordered a box of Wulong tea in faultless Mandarin.

The sound of a woman screaming behind caused him to turn.

Heading right at him was a mob of young men

wielding swords and long Wushu canes. A similar group had surrounded a Mercedes-Benz and were rocking it back and forth. Inside, a prim English woman and her children were begging for mercy.

Taking the tea from the street hawker, the figure in the blue jacket limped away fast down Morrison Street. He turned left into the maze of hutongs, threading his way quickly down the telescoping lanes until he came to a battered bamboo door.

Only when he had made quite sure the coast was clear did he slip inside. Bolting the door top and bottom, he hurried through into a room at the rear, drawing back a triangular trapdoor.

He jumped down.

INSIDE WAS A SPACIOUS, lavishly decorated salon, replete with antique wall silks and Louis XVI furniture. A small library had been set into the far wall, housing a few hundred leather-bound books. On the dining table was a proof copy of a new monograph, *Variants of Shaolin Kung Fu* and, hanging over a trestle desk, was a rack of exquisite opium pipes in carved tortoiseshell.

One corner of the salon had been turned into an artist's studio. There was a jar filled with calligraphic brushes, and an assortment of unfinished sculptures. Among them, models in clay, moulds, and the bronze study of a woman's face.

Standing to attention to the left of a fireplace was

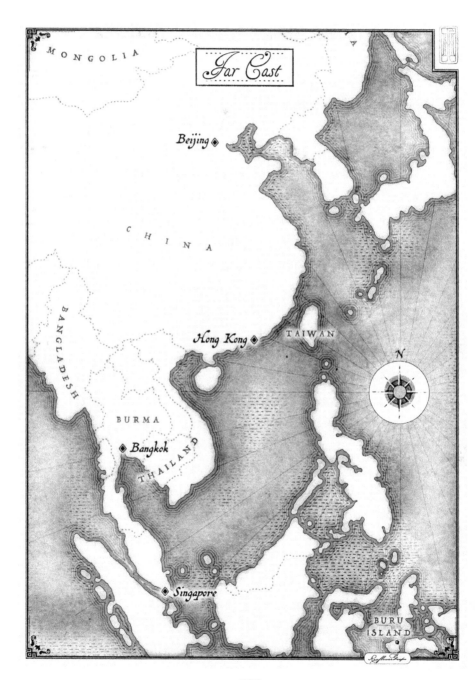

Chaudhury. Dressed in tweeds, he had resisted the temptation of going native — unlike his master.

'Warm yourself, sir. I shall fetch your dressing-gown at once.'

With a sigh, Hannibal removed the damp jacket.

'The Boxers are gaining in strength,' he said. 'I fear the worst. It will be days at most before the entire city goes up.'

'I almost forgot, sir,' said Chaudhury, a bamboo platter held between his hands.

'A letter arrived this afternoon by private messenger.'

Hannibal looked up fast.

'Who's it from?'

'Forgive me, but I do not read Chinese, sir.'

Snatching the envelope, Hannibal scanned the characters drawn down the front.

'At last!' he exclaimed. 'News from Professor Maa!'

Ripping open the envelope, he regarded the columns of text.

'Excellent! The professor has located it!'

'Located it, sir?'

Hannibal put down the letter and warmed his hands over the flames.

'The Prayer Wheel of Kublai Khan,' he said.

One hundred and nine

THE GRID REFERENCE HAD led the way to an antique shop on the south side of Liulichang Street. A sign above the entrance bore the name 'Dragon Moon Anteeks', and was complemented with an image of a Ming vase and another of Chairman Mao.

The front display window had been blacked out, except for a tiny circular hole, about the size of a bottle top.

Will peered in.

'See anything?' Emma whispered.

'Nothing.'

'Let's go in.'

Reaching forwards, Will brushed a hand over Emma's elbow.

'Like I told you back in Miami, there's no pressure on you to follow the trail. You've been through enough,' he said.

Emma swallowed, her eyes tired and drawn.

'I told you — I want to be part of it,' she said, pushing open the door.

DRAGON MOON ANTEEKS WAS packed floor to ceiling with remnants from the Glory Days of Empire — the *British* Empire. The inside smelled of cabbage soup, the result of it being located beside a cut-price noodle shop.

Shelves lined each wall, packed with pre-war European objets d'art.

There were Bohemian crystal decanters and terrestrial globes, porcelain dolls with cracked faces, sedan chairs complete with carrying bars, Prussian helmets, rows of medals from the Afghan Wars, Georgian urns, snuff boxes engraved with double-barrelled names, piggy banks and Queen Anne chairs.

'All this stuff looks as if it's come straight out of Hannibal's home,' Will said.

'Perhaps it did.'

They glanced at each other and smiled.

'You think its Hannibal's Peking Chamber?'

Emma swivelled one-eighty, turning to face the door.

'You feeling what I'm feeling… that it's here?'

'What is?'

'The thing you're supposed to find.'

Will nodded in agreement.

'Hannibal would have made sure it was something I'd appreciate,' he said. 'Something that links me with him.'

Spreading out, they struggled to put themselves in the right mindset.

Imagining himself strolling through his ancestor's Marrakesh home, Will overlaid the memory with the antique shop.

But it was Emma who noticed the sculpture first. Her delicate hand pointed at it.

'Reminds me of the one in Hannibal's bedroom,' she said.

'What…?'

'That… the bronze of three heads.'

Will went over. Emma was right. He couldn't say precisely why, but there was something about it, something distinctly Foggian.

Turning it over, Will made out a rectangular slot on the base, along with three familiar initials: 'HGF'.

One hundred and ten

SIR LANCELOT BEAUCHAMP WAS waiting in the lobby of his London club, the Travellers on Pall Mall. Since his wife passed away, fifteen years before, he tended to take lunch there most weekdays, at the members' table.

Most of Sir Lancelot's generation were long gone. The few contemporaries of his who had cheated death were locked up in retirement homes, and weren't nearly as well preserved as their distinguished friend.

Aged a hundred and one, Sir Lancelot was one of the longest serving members of the club. He had been a member since his nineteenth birthday, having been proposed by his godfather, Stanley Baldwin.

At one o'clock precisely, Richard Matheson was shown through by the hall porter. The introduction had been made the week before by Comte de Mallois.

An acquaintance, Sir Lancelot was the one man the French collector had ever met who had known Hannibal Fogg personally.

'Shall we go in to luncheon?' Beauchamp bellowed, pushing down onto his walking canes. 'You'll have to speak up. I'm a little deaf, don't you know?'

Over a grouse lunch, Sir Lancelot explained how he had been tutored by Hannibal through childhood in Hausa, Swahili and Mandarin, and how he had regarded him as a mentor. A lifelong friend and travelling companion, his father — Ernest — had stuck by the disgraced explorer through the Purge. When Hannibal was exiled, he sent young Lancelot to stay with him in Marrakesh, and to accompany him on his expeditions.

'He was a member here until the great disgrace,' Sir Lancelot said. 'Liked to dine at that table over there beside the window.'

'Do you believe Fogg was guilty — that he spied for the Germans?' Matheson asked.

'Of course he wasn't! He was, as they say in America, "framed".'

'Who by?'

'Good Lord knows. By the establishment, I suppose. You see he was a rebel of the first order — the kind of man who made enemies far more easily than he did friends. His genius put other people's noses out of joint, you see.'

'Did you ever travel together?'

Sir Lancelot's eyes glazed over.

401

'Frequently. Accompanied him on trips from childhood. We trekked through Africa, the Australian Outback, and down the Yangtze once or twice. One winter we trekked across Tibet by yak. There was nothing Hannibal liked more than a good yak.'

The sommelier poured Sir Lancelot a second glass of the '96 St Estèphe.

'Could you tell me about Fogg's disappearance?'

'Don't know much about it I'm afraid. He was of course broken by the death of his wife, his beloved Alina. There was talk of his disappearance in Manchuria being suicide. But anyone who knew him was certain of the impossibility of that.'

'He spoke Mandarin, did he not?' Matheson asked.

'Like a native. Knew the country inside out. He was in Peking during the Boxer Rebellion. God knows how he ever survived.'

Matheson sipped his Perrier.

'What was he doing in China during the Rebellion?'

'A mission… something about a sacred prayer wheel. You know, one of those Buddhist things. Just as he was about to get his hands on it, the Boxers struck. They hurled the entire treasure over a cliff.'

'Did Hannibal ever find it?'

Sir Lancelot drained his Bordeaux.

Hands out in front of him, palms up, he shrugged.

One hundred and eleven

1901

FOR MONTHS PROFESSOR MAA had worked on tracing the lost hoard of Kublai Khan.

His network of informants were spread like a spider's web across China. They had each been briefed: deliver information that might enable the treasure to be found, and they would strike it rich. Maa had paid out a fortune in bribes, leading to nothing but dead ends.

Then a chance tip-off had changed everything.

An old chef from Xi'an named Hu Jiang, employed in the Grand Hôtel de Pekin, had been walking home from his job, when he noticed something strange.

Three carts had drawn up outside the building opposite, a sprawling stone mansion set in half an acre of garden. It was the property of a German-born entrepreneur, Baron Gustav Bönickhausen. There was nothing particularly unusual about the carts, the shire horses that drew them, or the fact that the guards supervising the delivery were armed with new German Mausers, bayonets fitted.

What was less usual were the wooden crates being carried hurriedly up the marble steps into the mansion. They may well have contained weapons, but something told Hu Jiang that there was more to the delivery than met the eye.

He had sent a query to the professor, and the system

of checking and counter-checking had kicked in. A backhander was paid to find someone in the mansion prepared to spy.

A day later, the information was forwarded to Maa.

The crates were said to contain the fabled hoard of Kublai Khan.

No stranger to the Peking Legation Quarter, Hannibal Fogg had known it well in the days before the Boxers went on the rampage. He had often enjoyed a fillet mignon at the Grand Hôtel de Pekin, washed down with a glass or two of Chateau Latour 1883. The dining-room boasted the best wine cellar in the Orient. Indeed, it was so well stocked that people were known to have travelled all the way from Malaya to indulge.

But since the Boxers had begun their slaughter of Chinese Christians, and were now killing foreigners as well, Hannibal preferred to keep a low profile. In any case, the Dowager Empress Cixi had singled him out as a special threat to national security.

She had put a handsome price on his head.

For an extra fee, the spy — a woman from Shandong — had risked her life in jemmying open some of the crates in her search for the Prayer Wheel. Discovering it wrapped in a muslin bag, she had immediately sent word to Professor Maa, using the designated code phrase — 'the Lotus bud is open'.

The next day, Hannibal was dressed in his indigo jacket again, limping through the Legation. He had just heard that the Dowager had doubled the bounty on his head.

Maa had instructed him to wait outside the Grand Hôtel with a rolled-up newspaper pointed at the ground. He was standing there, doing his best to appear inconspicuous, when he heard the report of a cannon firing nearby.

The doorman ushered a European businessman inside.

'Quickly, monsieur! The Boxers are coming!'

Bolting the doors, the doorman didn't give a moment's thought to the foreigner wearing an indigo jacket outside.

A minute or two later, a swarm of young men surged down past the Forbidden City in the direction of the Legation Quarter.

At that moment, Hannibal noticed the frail figure of a woman leaving the mansion opposite. From the way she was stooping, it seemed she had something tucked under her shawl.

Adrenalin readied Hannibal for flight or fight, his brow moistening. Jerking the newspaper up and then down, he signalled that he was the contact.

The woman seemed to nod.

A HUNDRED YARDS AWAY, she was moving steadily in his direction.

Shifting his weight onto his back foot, Hannibal prepared to flee as soon as the handover had been made.

The woman was in the middle of the street. He could see her face, delicate and pretty. He saw her necklace, too; hanging from it — a large silver cross.

One of the Boxers had spotted the necklace as well.

From where he was standing it was an impressive feat of vision. But he saw it all the same.

In a dexterous movement, he leapt up, wielding his Wushu baton with full force.

Hannibal could only watch as the poor woman's skull caved in from the blow, her lifeless body slamming down onto the cobbles.

The sacred Prayer Wheel was discovered, carried off by the Boxers.

Hannibal's heart sank.

He had been so close.

One hundred and twelve

THE BRONZE SCULPTURE HAD cost the equivalent of £7,300 which, in the circumstances, seemed cheap at the price.

When the object had been wrapped up in brown paper, Will carried it back to the curiously named Three Legged Frog Hostel. Although they possessed abundant funds, Emma had insisted on it — attracted by the low-key atmosphere and the peculiar name. Although in the mood for luxury, Will had agreed to stay at the hostel

406

if Emma didn't frown on him splashing out on a new iPhone.

Once in his room, he unwrapped the bronze scultpure and examined it with care. Other than Hannibal's initials, no obvious clues leapt out. The faces didn't look like anyone in particular. Rather, they seemed more like caricatures than accurate representations of actual people.

The first was that of a man with deep-set eyes and a sloped lantern jaw. The second was the face of an elderly woman who appeared to be missing one eye. As for the third, it was that of a child with a long, almost comical nose.

Placing the sculpture on the scuffed coffee table, he put on the standing lamp. Then he walked around it, observing the features as well as the way light played over them. He squinted, in the hope that partial vision might reveal a deeper layer of information. But it didn't. Taking off his shoe, he tapped it, and listened to the hollow sound of lost wax bronze.

Something prompted Will to turn it over again.

Tilting it into the light, he tried to see if anything had been stuffed in through the oblong slot. As far as he could make out, there wasn't anything inside.

The more he scrutinised it, and thought about it, the more Will wondered whether he had found one of Hannibal's clues at all. As Emma had said, just about anything in Dragon Moon Anteeks could have belonged to the explorer at one time or another. No surprise in that, as Hannibal had spent a great deal of time in old Peking.

The only clue was the monogram.

Will went to bed early, tossing and turning as Hannibal's world circled through his dreams. Waking, he got out of bed, opened the flight case and looked at the components collected so far:

The Ladder of Mithras.

The Hands of God.

The Golden Tumi of the Incas.

The Orisha Stone.

Snapping the case shut, he sighed, and pushed a hand hesitantly back through his hair. Then, sighing again, he knocked gently on the dividing door between his and Emma's room. After a minute or two, the door opened. Emma was standing in its frame in her night dress, eyes screwed up against the light.

'Can't sleep,' said Will. 'Going crazy.'

'Let's go back to the antique shop in the morning,' Emma said, reading his mind.

Will reached down and touched her hand. He did it silently, his eyes staring into hers. He was desperate to kiss her, but didn't have the nerve.

'Go back to sleep,' she said.

Will strode over to the coffee table and clicked on the cheap standing lamp. Well illuminated, the sculpture looked somehow different — softer and much more refined.

Picking it up, Will rotated it again. If Hannibal's previous clues had taught him anything, it was to look at an object in ways that were not immediately obvious.

With closed eyes he ran a hand over the sculpture, allowing the sense of touch to take over where eyesight had failed. The sculpture had evidently been cast in two separate halves. Will's fingertips could just about feel the seam — almost burnished away once the two hemispheres had been joined. Opening his eyes again, he turned the bronze round and round, trying to crack what he could only imagine was a code.

Then something occurred to him: if he could slip the end of his new iPhone into the slot on the sculpture's base, he might be able to scan the interior surfaces. He had once downloaded a free sonographic app, but had never managed to find a use for it.

Opening the app, he set it to scan mode. Then, carefully, he pushed the top of the iPhone in through the slot. It fitted exactly. Emitting an ultra-high frequency, the device scoped out the inside of the bronze. By the time it was done, the app had charted a 3D layout of the interior.

'Incredible,' he said as soon as the scanned image flashed onto the display. 'I've got to cut the sculpture in half.'

Emma had walked through into Will's room and was staring at him, perplexed.

'If this is a clue,' he said, 'then there's one thing for

sure. It's anything but a sculpture.'

Using his penknife, Will worked away at the seam. While it appeared to be strong, it wasn't, and the two halves came apart with ease, as if they were supposed to be separated.

Emma was about to say something facetious, but she sensed he was on to something.

'This isn't a sculpture at all,' he said with absolute certainty.

'Then what is it?'

'It's a map,' said Will.

One hundred and thirteen

1901

HANNIBAL RESORTED TO USING Professor Maa's network of informants a second time in an effort to locate the prayer wheel. Over weeks and months there had been sightings, dead ends, information and misinformation.

No amount of bribery had led to the whereabouts of the wheel.

The professor believed the prized object had been simply trampled underfoot. But he didn't dare reveal his theory to Hannibal Fogg — who had refused to leave China until the Prayer Wheel of Kublai Khan had been found.

As the weeks passed, spring easing into summer,

Hannibal threw himself into his studies. He taught himself Malay, mastered the violin, and would spend hours at a time pushing the boundaries of mnemonics. By September, he could remember the order of six hundred postage stamps laid over the squares of a chessboard, having viewed them for no more than a minute and a half.

Chaudhury began worrying for his master's sanity. Each day the explorer grew markedly more eccentric, his behaviour increasingly bizarre.

Hannibal took to writing secret notes in microscopic script, with a nib he had made himself. He would chatter to himself in Aramaic for hours on end each day, and only walk backwards — that is, if he moved about at all. Most of his serious work was done at night, in the light of fifteen beeswax candles, while standing on one foot. And, although he refused most food, he allowed the manservant to prepare infrequent dishes of poached eggs garnished with octopus entrails.

Whenever Chaudhury suggested they return to the Occident, so that his master might be reunited with his family, Hannibal flew into a rage. Over and over, he vowed not to leave China until he knew the location of the Prayer Wheel of Kublai Khan.

Many months passed.

Then, one morning, a letter arrived and was presented on the bamboo salver. Hannibal opened it in a lacklustre way. He had hardly any energy, and seemed uninterested

411

in life.

Allowing the paper to slip onto the floor, he let out a deranged cry of joy.

'Good news, sir?' Chaudhury probed.

Whooping, Hannibal danced a jig.

'He's found it! The wheel… he's found it!'

'Might I enquire where it is, sir?'

'Read it for yourself,' he said. 'It's in English.'

Chaudhury picked up the letter and read it aloud:

'"My dear Fogg, forgive me. I have not contacted you until now, because there has been no reliable news at all. Even now there is something to tell, I present it with a heavy heart.

'"The good news is that the prayer wheel was not destroyed in Peking last spring. After extensive consultations with my informants, I have assembled a detailed picture of what took place. The wheel was of course of no value to the Boxers. So it is not surprising they discarded it right away. By chance it fell into the hands of an unscrupulous scholar named 'Wa Ming'. This is the unsavoury news. Having realised what he had in his possession, he sold it for a small fortune.

'"The new owner was a wealthy man from Shanghai, himself sympathetic with the cause of the Boxers. A collector of sorts, he had amassed numerous objects from religious sources. For a reason I do not quite understand, he believed the prayer wheel to be associated with the Christian church. His rage against

Christianity stoked, he gave the order for the object to be hurled into the depths of the caves at Miao Keng.

'"And so, my friend, I must inform you that, although technically located, the prayer wheel is no more. The profundity of the caves is so great that there is no hope whatsoever of retrieving the sacred relic. I am so sorry. Yours most sincerely, H J Maa."'

One hundred and fourteen

WILL HAD ONLY NOTICED the two slender grooves set into the old woman's chin because of the way the shadow played over them. Hardly thinking of what he was doing, he removed the CODEX from its case and slotted it into the indentation. As with so many things from the mystifying realm of Hannibal, it fitted perfectly. Once in place, the CODEX switched itself on, the gears turning.

A message rolled onto the display.

'What does it say?'

'Don't know why, but this one's in cipher,' answered Will, reaching for a pen and notebook.

Scribbling down the text, he set about decoding it.

Emma sat on the edge of the bed, tapping her fingertips together impatiently.

'Any ideas?'

'Something about a cave.'

'Huh?'

Underlining every third word in his notebook, Will read them out loud:

'"The Prayer Wheel of Kublai Khan was hurled into the depths of the Miao Keng cave system. The bronze map will guide you."'

Emma groaned.

'Sounds appropriately cryptic.'

'Told you it was a map!' Will responded. 'Now all we have to do is find the caves.'

Right on cue, a grid reference appeared in the CODEX's window:

28°11'46N 112°20E.

FOUR DAYS LATER, WILL and Emma reached Miao Keng in Guizhou Province.

In the nearby village of Tian Xing, they bumped into a veteran Dutch speleologist named Sebastian van den Bosch. He was nursing a fractured arm and a pair of shattered legs. Having spent a month exploring caves at Miao Keng, he had almost perished inside them.

'No one's ever got down to the bottom of the structure alive,' said Sebastian darkly.

Will asked for tips on making the descent.

'You in the mood for suicide?' Sebastian asked.

'Guess I must be.'

'Then you'll need first-rate equipment and training. Hope you've got both.'

The Dutch expedition had transported an entire

container to Miao Keng — packed with the latest equipment. But even that had proved insufficient. Sebastian said the caves were off the scale, beyond an Extremely Severe E14 rating.

'Never seen anything like it,' he said, 'and I've been up K2 twice.'

THE CODEX GRID REFERENCE turned out to be a dingy guesthouse about a mile away from the cave entrance. It was called 'Hotel Deluxe', but luxury was only in the name. The rooms were cramped — windowless with bare brick walls and plenty of damp rot.

Lying back on his bed, Will slipped his iPhone into a waterproof housing he had bought in Miami. For no clear reason, he thought of the equipment room at Dar Jnoun.

He had sent Chaudhury a text: *did Hannibal leave caving equipment?*

At once a reply came back: *advise coordinates.*

Will checked the CODEX and tapped out his grid location — *28°11'46N 112°20E.*

He hit 'send' and waited for a reply.

But none came.

TAHIR SHAH

One hundred and fifteen

THE PROCTOR TOOK TEA in his private apartment thirty minutes after the end of evensong, a single candle burning on a table beside his chair, an iron cross hanging on the wall behind.

Holding the porcelain cup to his lips, he sighed long and hard.

Then, falling to his knees, he bowed his head in silent prayer. A lifetime of devotion, and this was a defining moment in petitioning the Almighty for help. Until then prayer had often been automatic, something he guided others to do, standing as a mediator between the mortal world and the divine.

The Council's network of informants had passed on the news: the Bloodchild was close to acquiring the fifth component. The Proctor prayed for the Mechanism to be restarted, so that all doubt could at last be removed as to the existence of the Almighty.

As the Proctor kneeled in prayer, lids drawn down over his eyes, the candle's flame flickered in a draught. The shadow of a Balkan hit-man moved through the chamber, skimming over the simple furniture and the flagstones.

The Proctor finished his prayer.

He was about to rise from his knees, when the iron cross was snatched from the wall and used to knock in the back of his skull.

One hundred and sixteen

FOR A SOLID WEEK it rained, hailed, and even snowed.

The onslaught continued day and night, the tin roof of Hotel Deluxe clattering as if the end of the world had arrived. Taking directions from the injured Dutch caver, Will made his way to the cave entrance at the end of the week during a break between downpours.

As Sebastian had said, there was an opening on the east side of a sheer granite spur, a mile's walk from the guesthouse. From the thick vegetation it was evident that visitors were few and far between.

Will had taken the bronze sculpture with him to the cave. But without any equipment, going inside would have been instant suicide.

Backtracking to Hotel Deluxe, he found Emma down at the reception. She brushed a hand over his cheek and smiled.

'There's a surprise for you,' she said.

'What?'

'Wait and see.'

'Where is it?'

Emma pointed to the second floor landing.

'Have a peek in number six.'

Narrowing his eyes, Will climbed the stairs and knocked on the door of room 6.

It was opened by a familiar figure in tweeds.

'Chaudhury!'

'Good afternoon, sir.'

'What on earth are you doing in China?'

'I thought you might be in need of a little back-up, sir.'

The manservant took a step to the side.

Stacked behind him were fifteen steamer trunks piled one on top of the next, each one monogrammed with Hannibal's initials.

'What the heck are they?'

'Mr Fogg's caving equipment,' said Chaudhury.

One hundred and seventeen

WILL SPENT TWO DAYS sorting out the gear. Chaudhury had searched the storeroom and found the equipment ready and waiting. He had known at once what his duty involved. Next to the steamer trunks was a large sign. It read: 'Chinese Caving Expedition'.

What struck Will was how Hannibal had overcome limitations in existing technology. He hadn't had access to nylon, polyester, Kevlar, or high spec fluoropolymers, carbon fibre, or synthetic fuel. But in an unprecedented display of characteristic genius, he had improvised.

The ropes were strengthened with aciniform silk from the black widow spider, a species that uses the fibre to bind prey. After months of trials and testing, Hannibal had found it to be as strong as tempered steel.

418

The only drawback was in securing sufficient quantities of spider silk. The problem had eventually been overcome by establishing an arachnid farm on the outskirts of Marrakesh. Supplying sufficient silk for the Miao Keng descent had taken more than three years and cost the equivalent of a Rolls-Royce Silver Ghost.

Hannibal had lavished as much care and attention on the other equipment as well. The climbing harnesses were made from yak leather sourced from western Tibet, and the helmets padded with albatross feathers brought specially from Easter Island. As for the climbing boots, they had been prepared as a special order by Ede & Ravenscroft, former robe makers to Queen Victoria.

The great explorer had left nothing to chance.

So preoccupied was he by the tremendous drop of the Miao Keng cave complex that he developed a special winching system to lower Will down onto the cave floor. It had been his intention that his great-great-grandson would take up rock climbing in childhood so as to prepare himself. But the plan had fallen through — a consequence resulting from the sudden death of Will's parents.

An industrial-strength vacuum escape system had ensured that the steamer trunks were kept hermetically sealed. Since being packed in the 1920s, the climbing gear had remained in mint condition in its airless environment. Hermetic sealing had only been possible by using reinforced steel cases and a special form of rubber vulcanisation, the secret ingredient of which was octopus ink.

Once laden, the trunks were so enormously heavy that Hannibal had invented an inbuilt conveyance system. A set of wheels could be unfurled from the side of each case, driven by crankshafts and powered by galvanic cells.

When the gear had been sorted, checked and double-checked, Will, Emma and Chaudhury went to scope out the cave itself. They took with them Hannibal's powerful headlamps — modified from the standard issue on a Rolls-Royce Twenty. They had taken the bronze sculpture along, too.

Torrential rain had fallen for thirty-six hours, the water gushing along the conduits running through the limestone. A government official employed to guard the cave entrance had deserted his post, no doubt because of the deplorable conditions.

Using the sculpture as a three-dimensional map, Will led the way into the cave. A flick of the switches on the headlamps' battery packs, and the cavern's entry was illuminated in the most spectacular way.

In single file the three visitors proceeded cautiously down a long vaulted tunnel. A natural cathedral of stone, it curved sharply round, doubling back on itself.

A series of sloping natural steps followed, lined with contours.

After another thirty yards, Will caught a first sight of the colossal limestone wall that was Miao Keng.

Rising up above them like the bulwark of a medieval Crusader castle, the exterior surface was rippled, shaped by millions of years of erosion.

So distracted was he by the height, that Will hadn't noticed the depth.

Roping them both together, Chaudhury secured a position on the wall with a spring-loaded cam. As he did so, Will took another look at the sculpture. He allowed his fingers to trace the contours of the shaft, taking in its elliptical form.

'The cord is secure, sir,' Chaudhury reported.

'You really think it'll take a man's weight?'

'I do believe it could support an Assamese elephant, sir.'

Taking up the slack, Will edged on to a narrow limestone parapet. The heels of his climbing boots engaged with notches worn into the stone's surface.

To go rock climbing had always been his dream. More than once his father had promised to take him, but he had perished the very week they had been due to go.

Will shuffled out twenty feet along the wall's leading edge. Having reached as far as he could, and with Chaudhury supporting his weight, Will tilted the headlamp downwards.

Utter darkness.

He moved his head in an arc, but the beam hardly illuminated more than a few feet.

'Whoa!'

'Are you able to see the bottom, sir?'

421

From where Will was standing, his back thrust hard against the limestone, Chaudhury's question seemed farcical. Will was about to shoot back a sarcastic reply, when a blast of freezing air shot up the shaft, knocking him to the side. Steadying himself, he calmed his breathing and began to shuffle backwards along the parapet.

'Hannibal's a nutcase!' he yelled, as he neared Chaudhury. 'There's no way I can get down there, let alone find the Prayer Wheel!'

The manservant undid the knot which had hitched them together.

'Have a little faith, sir,' he said.

One hundred and eighteen

A FULL AFTERNOON WAS taken up in transporting all of Hannibal's equipment to the entrance of the Miao Keng caves.

Fortunately, the official guard was still far away from his post. Emma said she had seen him down in the village, spying on the Dutch caving team. He appeared to earn more by providing the authorities with tipoffs than he did by doing the job for which he was actually employed.

At one of the village noodle shops Emma had learned that, during the Cultural Revolution, hundreds of people from the surrounding region had disappeared — their bodies tossed unceremoniously into the Miao Keng caves.

Shortly after dawn, Will, Emma and Chaudhury reached the cliff face, their headlamps turned up to full power, copper cables running down to battery packs on their belts.

Torrential rain had continued to fall through the night. The limestone was glistening, the air far cooler than on the previous day.

Once they had checked the equipment one last time, Chaudhury took out a single harness. In taut silence Will slipped it on and tightened the straps.

'Where's mine?' asked Emma indignantly.

'No, no, no!' Will shot back. 'You're *not* coming down with me!'

'Why not?'

'*Because…*'

'Because what?'

'Because I need you up here giving Chaudhury support. Someone's got to be ready to yank me back up.'

Reaching into the trunk, Emma grasped a second harness.

'Try and talk me out of it,' she said, 'and I'll make sure Chaudhury cuts the rope.'

'You'd never do that!'

Emma grinned.

'Try me,' she said.

Will glared at her so forcefully that she backed down.

One hundred and nineteen

MATHESON HAD MANAGED TO persuade a stringer for
The Times in Monaco to exert his influence with the
royal bodyguard, the Compagnie des Carabiniers du
Prince. The result was the full ownership details of
the Bentley Azure, including a copy of the original
deed of sale.

The limousine had been bought by Fabergé
Communications, a Monte Carlo registered company.
A little more delving, and Matheson got access to the
firm's files. There was only one employee — not bad
for an annual turnover of €311 million. The owner was
a Ukrainian energy tycoon named Leonard Dmitri
Polkovich. As for the employee, she was his wife, Svetlana.

Matheson ran a background check, searching the
internet for any mention of Polkovich. He came up with
a string of stories from the financial press. The Ukrainian
oligarch had been involved in a stream of unscrupulous
deals relating to energy commodities in the Balkans and
Uzbekistan.

According to a recent report in the *Financial Times*,
Polkovich had purchased one of the most valuable
properties in London as his private residence. The
house, at 10 Kensington Palace Gardens, had cost
him more than £100 million. What the report failed
to mention was that Polkovich had spent half as much
again turning the mansion into a fortress.

One hundred and twenty

A<small>FTER SECURING HIS HARNESS</small>, Will set up the winching device. It may have been ninety years old, but it was in pristine condition, perfectly greased and balanced along both the horizontal and vertical axes.

With care, he threaded the arachnid rope into the mechanism, making sure to double it back through the safety gate.

Tying the rope onto his harness with a figure-eight knot, he closed his eyes, and focused.

'Ready,' he said, his voice dry from fear.

Just then his iPhone started vibrating.

'A hell of a time for a phone call,' said Emma.

'Surprised I'm getting a signal in here.'

'Can't it wait?'

Will glanced at the display.

'No. Gotta take it,' he replied, clicking the phone on. 'Hello! Aunt Helen... yeah, everything's fine. You both OK? That's good. Listen... it's a little hard to speak right now. Just in a meeting. I'll call you later. I promise.'

Chaudhury approached with the backpack Hannibal had designed for the descent. Exceptionally heavy, it had a series of hexagonal lead seals along the edges — designed to prevent the pack from being opened by accident.

'Put your arms through, sir,' said the manservant, straining to hold the pack up at chest height, 'and now strap on the helmet.'

Emma, who was standing behind them, looked disdainful. As Will edged up to the parapet, she silently slipped on a harness as well.

Then, as Chaudhury began to pay the first few feet of cord through the mechanism, she jumped into Will's path. Before he could object, she tied herself to him with a Carrick Bend.

'You'll never get that off,' she said.

Will allowed his glower to ease into a smile.

'What am I going to do with you?'

Emma adjusted her harness.

'What does that mean?'

'It means you're impossible.'

'Not that... *that*...'

'What?'

She jerked her head at the rim of Will's helmet.

The words TERMS UNIT were inscribed on it on a brass plaque.

'What's a TERMS UNIT?'

'Beats me... Chaudhury, you know?'

'I cannot say that I do, sir.'

Will let out a blast of laughter.

'Think it's a Foggian witticism,' he said.

'Huh?' replied Emma.

'It's an anagram: "TRUST IN ME".'

'Most reassuring, sir,' said Chaudhury as he began to lower away.

As the cord took Will and Emma's combined weight, it creaked, the silk fibres stretching tight.

'Christ… you think it's going to hold?' Emma whispered.

'Let's do as he said.'

'Trust in him?'

'Yup,' Will replied.

The winch mechanism turned a full rotation, belaying the cord a foot at a time. They tilted their headlamps upwards, so as not to blind each other. Will was staring into Emma's face, her features lost in shadow.

He dug out his iPhone, launched a measuring app and pointed the device straight down towards the bottom of the cave. It took five seconds to give a reading.

'Three thousand, two hundred and twenty-one feet, six and a half inches to the bottom,' he said.

Emma gulped.

'That's more than half a mile!'

'Then we'll die together.'

'In a suicide pact?'

Peering down at his feet, hanging against a backdrop of black, Will resigned himself to fate. Hanging by a thread — on a cord of spider's silk — he knew the only hope of survival was to place himself absolutely in Hannibal's hands.

All the while, the cord wound down.

…And down.

As they descended, the air grew cooler, the wet

undulating wall in the distance striated and bleak.

Fifty yards of slow and steady descent, and there was a sudden forceful jolt.

'What's happening, Chaudhury?!' Will called up.

'A slight problem with the mechanism, sir, I may have to pull you up.'

'What's wrong?'

'It's jammed, sir.'

'Oh, Christ!'

Then the winch mechanism abruptly lost its hold.

The cord span out.

Emma and Will plunged fifty yards in a second and a half.

The cord jammed.

They bounced upwards, then plunged down again, before dangling mid-air against the blackness.

Craning his head back, Will voiced his panic, but the manservant from Cooch Behar didn't answer.

'Think that was supposed to happen?'

Emma leaned in, her lips an inch from Will's. They stared into each other's eyes. Neither of them had ever felt so close to anyone.

'We're going to make it,' she said. 'He'll get the winch working.'

Like a pendulum straining for motion, Will began shifting his weight from one side to the other.

'What're you doing?'

'Trying to get to that ledge.'

'Where?'

'Way over there.'

'Are you crazy? We'll never make that.'

'We won't if we don't try.'

On the fifth or sixth go, the tip of Will's right boot brushed against the limestone. A few more swings and his heel jammed down.

Will pulled Emma tight to him.

'What do we do now?'

'Guess we wait for Mr C to sort himself out.'

Emma scanned the darkness.

'What's that?'

'What's what?'

'That ring-pull thing.'

Will groped a hand to his right shoulder.

'Dunno. Feels like a handle.'

'Didn't notice it before.'

'Me neither.'

'Pull it and see what happens.'

'But what if…'

'If it screws us up even more than we are already?'

Will heaved the handle hard.

Detaching itself, the cord swung out into the abyss, leaving them stranded on the ledge.

'Oh my God.'

Pressing her back against the limestone bluff, Emma dared not move. Beside her, staring certain death squarely in the face, Will broke into laughter.

'Hannibal, I put all my trust in you!' he wailed, the words echoing back at him.

'Think this is the moment we give up on dear Hannibal Fogg!' Emma snarled.

'Have to tell you something,' Will said.

'What?'

'A confession.'

Emma managed a smile.

'So this is the *Thelma & Louise* moment?' she grinned. 'Just before we go out in a blaze of glory.'

'That might be overdoing it a tad,' Will replied.

'So what was it… the confession?'

'It's about you.'

Emma rolled her eyes.

'Yeah?'

'Yeah.'

'What about me?'

'I never believed you,' Will said. 'Not from the start.'

'Yeah?'

Will nodded.

'Why not?'

'Because there were gaping holes in your story.'

'Which part?'

'All of it.'

'Thanks,' said Emma.

Reaching out, Will thumped a hand to the rock wall.

'But being here with you has renewed my faith.'

'In me?'

'That's right.'

'A kinda hefty price to pay for renewed faith!'

They looked at each other, laughed, and hugged.

Just then Will's backpack began hissing, as though it were about to explode.

'What the hell's going on?'

'It's doing something.'

'Sounds like compressed gas.'

Exploding open, the backpack deployed a pod. Shooting high above them, it burst open, releasing an oval-shaped balloon. Fashioned from pale-green waxed silk, it was open at the bottom and fastened to a slender copper frame that had elevated itself from the backpack.

As they watched, a gearing mechanism moved into place.

Will sniffed.

'I can smell gas.'

Emma grimaced.

'Me too!'

'It's coming from the backpack.'

'Oh my God, it's warming up... can you feel that?'

'Yeah... it's roasting.'

'We're gonna be cooked alive.'

Throwing his head back, Will caught a fleeting glance of the mechanism.

'It's a burner!'

His words coincided with a tremendous roar as the

machinery sparked into life.

The green silk balloon grew tighter and tighter with hot air, the copper frame beneath it clicking from the heat.

Inches above Will's head, the burner fired again, and then a third time.

'Oh my God!' Emma shouted, as the soles of her shoes lifted gently from the ledge.

'We're going up!'

Little by little the balloon rose into the abyss. Hovering in space, it hung there like a celestial lantern.

Then, gently, it began to descend.

The burner fired automatically in short bursts, its deafening roar shattering the tranquillity.

As they floated downwards, the flame bathed the walls of the vast cavern in spectral orange light. Neither Will nor Emma dared to wonder how they would ever get back up to the surface.

Instead, they forced fear aside and savoured the miracle.

Peering down, the void beneath their boots lit by the burner's flare, they were awed in equal measure by the terror and the beauty of Miao Keng.

'Look down there!' Emma screamed.

'We're nearly…'

Will's reply was cut short.

The burner had gone dead, the balloon collapsing into a billowing envelope of limp silk.

'Brace yourself!' Will cried out as they plunged the final thirty feet. With tremendous force the soles of his boots slammed down, the weight of the backpack doubling the impact.

Rolling sideways onto the gravel, Will pulled Emma down onto him to break her fall. Bruised and battered, he struggled to stand.

Once upright, he flicked his headlamp around and scanned the cave floor.

All around them, shielded from the main gallery by a natural rock wall, were hundreds of shattered human skeletons.

Tilting his headlamp downwards, Will noticed a tangle of golden objects glistening among the bones scattered down the gravel beach.

'See that?'

'My God!' Emma burst out, her headlamp illuminating the gruesome landscape. 'Treasure!'

Grabbing a gold coin, Will wiped it clean and stuffed it into his pocket.

'Look! Over there!' Emma shouted, pointing to a pile of rocks in the distance.

As though placed for them to find, there was an object on top of them.

Will scuttled forwards.

A wooden shaft led to a bronze wheel adorned in ancient Sanskrit:

The Prayer Wheel of Kublai Khan.

One hundred and twenty-one

THE ELATION OF FINDING the sacred object was utterly wonderful but short-lived.

Exhausted from having cheated death, Will had collapsed to his knees. He clambered out of the harness, his face drained and pale. Emma and he were at the bottom of a shaft somewhere in rural China, half a mile beneath the surface. They may have located the prayer wheel, but there was no way back up.

What sounded like a freight train hurtling through the dark caused them to look up.

'Water!' screamed Emma.

'Where?'

'*There!*'

As they flipped round, their headlamps lit up the crest of a tidal wave surging through a nearby tunnel.

Instinct told them to run.

Sprinting along the gravel, they got about fifty yards.

Will paused at a second natural wall, assuming it would offer some protection — after all, the skeletons and the treasure hadn't been washed away from the gravel.

Emma noticed a niche hollowed out in the rock, a natural sanctuary.

She called out.

A survival raft had been tethered inside. Made from balsa, it was pinned together with aluminium nails.

Will reeled in disbelief.

'Hannibal must have been here and found a way out.'

Unleashing the raft, he dragged it beyond the protective wall and pulled Emma on, as a second surge barrelled headlong towards them.

Scooped up by the flow, twisting and jarring, the raft was buffeted against the passage walls.

Emma and Will held on for their lives.

The raft gathered speed as the river's gradient plunged.

Will spotted something in the water.

'What the hell's that?'

Emma peered down.

'What?'

'*That!*'

Flush with the waterline was a reptile with ruby-coloured eyes.

'There's another one…!'

'And another!'

'The water's infested with crocodiles!'

Ripping through gorges and tunnels, the surge propelled the raft forwards at what seemed like lightning speed. Frozen to the bone and drenched, Will and Emma struggled to keep hold.

The balsa raft may have appeared low-tech, but it wasn't — for it was strengthened by high-tensile steel bars. Hannibal had arranged for it to be designed by a team of Swiss technicians from Gstaad. Impressed by their record-breaking bobsleighs, he had brought them to Miao Keng for a test run with the raft on his third and final visit to the caves.

As ever, the inimitable explorer had thought of everything.

Or, rather, almost everything.

For, as the raft reached high speed, battered against the walls, it struck an angled stone buttress three feet beneath the water's surface. Despite numerous trial runs, Hannibal and the bobsleigh engineers had failed to notice it.

The raft flipped upside down, tossing its passengers into the water. Their headlamps were ripped away in the force while Will and Emma clung on, both struggling desperately to turn the raft over again.

A red-eyed crocodile lunged from the darkness.

With the little strength he had left, Will launched himself at the reptile, jabbing a thumb into one of its eyes. Half-blinded and flailing, the reptile was carried away by the current.

More twists and turns, then another buttress approached.

Thinking fast, Will vaulted up onto it. And, in a deft movement, he hurled himself over the raft, levering it the right way up.

Clambering aboard, he pulled Emma up.

Without any strength to speak, she threw her arms around his neck.

After being buffeted left and right, the raft broke out

from the caves into blinding sunshine.

Overwhelmed with euphoria, Will roared with joy. Miraculously, both the prayer wheel and his precious iPhone had survived the ride, tucked under his belt.

Widening, the river curved sharply to the left and disappeared.

'What the…?!'

The raft plunged over a waterfall, a sheer vertical drop of two hundred feet.

One hundred and twenty-two

On Saturday morning Richard Matheson received a phone call at 6.43. He didn't recognise the number and so assumed it was an emergency.

'Matheson here,' he said, half asleep.

'Good morning to you, Matheson.'

'Who's that?'

'Beauchamp.'

'Oh, Sir Lancelot…' Matheson sat up, caught the display of his digital clock and glared. 'How nice to hear your voice.'

'Remembered something,' Sir Lancelot Beauchamp said.

'Oh?'

'Something about Hannibal.'

Matheson swivelled his feet onto the floor.

'Oh, yes?'

'Like to feed ducks, do you?' Sir Lancelot asked.

THAT AFTERNOON, MATHESON MADE his way as directed to the seventh bench along the south side of the Serpentine, in Hyde Park. He found Sir Lancelot Beauchamp scattering pieces of wholemeal bread on the ground.

Half a dozen ducks had been lured out of the water and were feeding.

Matheson held out a hand.

'Good to see you again, Sir Lancelot.'

'Ah, there you are my boy. Here, take some of this bread.'

Together, they tossed the pieces until the loaf was gone. Having waited so as not to seem impolite or pushy, Matheson cleared his throat.

'On the phone you said something about having had a memory, Sir Lancelot.'

'What? What's that?'

'A memory... you remembered something — something about Hannibal Fogg.'

Sir Lancelot stared down at the ducks.

'Funny little creatures, aren't they?'

Matheson forced a smile. He was going to say something, when the old man lifted a finger and wagged it at his chest.

'In the years before his public disgrace, Hannibal became increasingly eccentric,' he said. 'Some people thought he was going potty.'

'Can you be a little more specific, Sir Lancelot?'

'In his later years he became ever more secretive. He trusted no one, none that is except his manservant… an Indian chap called Chaudhury. He was certain someone was out to get him. He never walked the same route twice, and took to sterilising his food with potassium permanganate. He rigged his bedroom door up with a revolver, too. Terribly dangerous it was. On one occasion Chaudhury was shot in the shoulder, although he was very sporting about it. Damned good fellow he was.'

'Who did he think was trying to get him?'

'A sect of some kind. He believed they'd stop at nothing until they gained certain information — information known only to him.'

'What was the sect called?'

Sir Lancelot Beauchamp peered down the shaft of his walking cane as though it were a rifle.

'Believe he called it the "Magi".'

'*Magi?*'

'That's right.'

'D'you know anything about it?'

'Not really, no. But what I can tell you is that Hannibal went to extraordinary lengths to hide information from them. For a great many years he was engaged in accumulating a number of components.'

'What kind of components?'

'Pieces of some sort of machine. He regarded it as

439

the greatest mission of his life. He would never tell me about it.'

'Why not?'

'For fear that I might be captured and tortured.'

'Sounds like something out of James Bond.'

Sir Lancelot straightened his necktie.

'Perhaps it was,' he said. 'But the thing about Hannibal Fogg was the ever-present bedrock of truth.'

Matheson took in the Serpentine and cocked his head to the side.

'Was Hannibal mad?' he asked.

Sir Lancelot balked at the question.

'Even in those dark days clouded by eccentricity,' he replied, 'I knew he was quite sane. As for the thing I remembered, you'll find it in the topographical section of the London Library.'

'What is it?'

'A clue perhaps, if it's still there. You see, he asked me to hide it for him.'

Wondering what Sir Lancelot was going on about, Matheson looked at him hard.

'To hide what?'

'A book.'

'Which book?'

'*Fire and Sword in the Sudan.*'

One hundred and twenty-three

SPLASHDOWN!

Smashing into a plunge pool, the raft disintegrated into balsa matchwood, leaving no other sign of movement or life.

Suddenly, a hand shot up through the water, fingers splayed.

Behind it, Emma's mouth thrust to the surface, gasping for air. Breathing deep, she jerked herself around.

'*Will! Will!*'

No reply.

Swimming fast to the edge of the pool, Emma pulled herself up. Her face covered in a veil of blood, she held a hand to the gash on her head. Scanning the water and the debris, she wept.

Without warning, a dry blanket was wrapped over her shoulders from behind. She turned fast, hoping for Will's face.

'Are you all right, miss?'

'Chaudhury?'

'Pleased to find you safe, miss.'

Hysterically, Emma grabbed the manservant's shoulders.

'Where is he?!'

His expression one of gloom, Chaudhury threw a second blanket onto the ground. With gritted teeth, he ran down the riverbank searching the waters. Emma followed, clambering over the rocks and through ankle-deep mud.

But there was no sign of Will.

Chaudhury was about to suggest they search elsewhere, when something caught his eye. The tip of an elbow poking out of the water — an elbow curled tightly around a splinted stave of balsa wood.

Following his line of sight, Emma checked for crocodiles, leapt into the water and caught hold of Will.

Having heaved him ashore, she administered CPR.

Coughing out a lungful of river-water, Will gasped for air.

'Thank goodness!' Chaudhury exclaimed. 'I feared we had lost you, sir!'

Will nuzzled his face against the dry ground.

'Paradise,' he groaned.

The manservant pulled him to his feet.

'If you would both follow me, I have prepared a light luncheon,' he said.

Leading the way back to the waterfall, he escorted them to the shade of a sprawling acacia tree. Beneath it, a fabulous meal was awaiting. A picnic hamper from Fortnum & Mason had disgorged its contents over a red and white gingham tablecloth laid on the grass. Among the delights on offer were Serrano ham sandwiches, foie gras on squares of toast, Scotch eggs, and a bottle of vintage Roederer Cristal, perfectly chilled.

Without a word, Will and Emma slumped on the

edge of the tablecloth. Both wondered how the ancestral manservant had known where they would emerge from the caves and how he had got there so fast.

'Care for a slice of Melton Mowbray pie, miss?' asked Chaudhury courteously. 'I believe it's rather good.'

'Thank you.'

Will looked round.

'How did you do it?'

'Do what, sir?'

'All of it.'

'All of…?'

'You know… getting out of the cave, finding us here… setting up this little banquet.'

Chaudhury gaped up into the acacia's branches, his gaze lowering onto Will's face.

'Mr Fogg left instructions,' he said.

'Instructions?'

The manservant grinned.

'Instructions on a rather satisfying shortcut, sir,' he said.

Will didn't reply.

Instead, he stared out at the waterfall. In the weeks since learning of his ancestor, he had lived many lifetimes in one. Cupping his hands over his face, he tried to imagine anything but the all-consuming world of Hannibal Fogg.

It was then that he remembered the gold coin.

Stuffing his hand in his pocket, he felt for it, but it was missing. He cursed.

'Lost something?' Emma asked, giving him a sideways glance.

'Er, no... nothing of importance.'

Just then the CODEX chimed.

'I took the liberty of bringing it down here,' said Chaudhury, 'along with Mr Fogg's maps.'

Will didn't answer at first. His expression growing sullen, he looked at the decryption device.

'I can't do this any more,' he said.

Sprawling back, Emma sank her front teeth into a Scotch egg.

'Neither can I.'

'Then perhaps you would allow me, sir,' said Chaudhury.

Will shrugged.

'Help yourself.'

Fumbling with the CODEX, the manservant drew back its leather cover and read out the coordinates — 48°51'24.00N 2°21'03.55E.

'I wonder where that is...'

'I don't,' Will replied firmly.

Chaudhury unfolded the master map, an index fingertip halting over Paris. Opening an individual plan of the French capital, he checked the CODEX's display, and raised both eyebrows.

'Place de la Concorde,' he announced.

One hundred and twenty-four

1919

WHENEVER IN PARIS, HANNIBAL and Alina would stay in the Duc de Crillon Suite at the Hôtel de Crillon, on Place de la Concorde. The lavish furnishings were supposedly inspired by the Salon de Mars at Versailles. Although they were a little over the top for Hannibal's taste, he regarded the hotel's service and its history as without equal.

The French capital was abuzz with intrigue and talk of recrimination as the Peace Conference got under way. The Foggs had been in Paris for a month, with Hannibal taking an interest in various matters of state associated with the outcome of the Great War.

In a sense they were refugees, as their newly acquired home in London's Kensington was being completely refurbished.

In what had seemed to Alina like an act of obsession, Hannibal had chosen a mansion on a pleasant tree-lined street running between Bayswater and the Kensington Road.

Refusing to consider any other property, he had eventually cajoled the owner, the elderly Second Viscount Portman, to sell it to him. The figure paid by Hannibal was three times the asking price. But, as he so often reflected, money was of little consequence. What mattered to him was not wealth, but rather sticking to a perfectly conceived plan.

IN THE BEDROOM OF the Duc de Crillon Suite, Alina was seated at the dressing table, her breakfast tray left untouched. Grooming her blonde hair with a monogrammed brush, she was even more pale than usual. Unknown to her husband, she was taking tincture of opium twice daily, prescribed by Dr Horatio Foost of Harley Street.

Hannibal stepped into the salon, where Chaudhury was waiting with a salver. Upon it was a letter which had arrived at the Crillon by private messenger only moments before.

Breaking the seal, Fogg inspected the lines of impeccable handwritten script, and sauntered back through to the bedroom.

'An invitation my darling, to dine at the home of Comte de Camondo this evening,' he said. 'He sends apologies for the short notice, but suggests there is a matter of urgency he wishes to discuss. I dare say it has to do with the Conference.'

'I do hope the Comtesse will be there,' said Alina softly. 'She is a most striking lady. And I have heard much talk of their new home; that it contains many extraordinary contrivances.'

'Well, a lack of funds is surely not a problem they would have encountered,' said Hannibal.

446

Shortly after nine, a brand new Rolls-Royce Silver Ghost pulled up at 63 Rue Monceau, in the eighth arrondissement. Chaudhury was at the wheel, the Foggs seated comfortably behind on the studded red leather banquette. The Indian manservant welcomed the opportunity of spending the evening outside, in the car.

He was distracted following the sudden death of his youngest brother, Sunil. His parents' favourite child, Sunil had drowned a week earlier — when the ocean liner on which he was bound for America had struck a pair of mines left over from the War. Travelling first class with twenty servants and seventy sea-trunks — almost all of them packed with food — he had set out from India to see the world.

The transatlantic voyage was the second leg of the young prince's journey. Undeterred by the last throes of the Great War, he had set off from the ancestral palace in Cooch Behar five months previously, making stops in Cairo, Rome, Marseilles and London — where he had taken an entire floor at The Savoy.

The intention was for him to travel from New York to San Francisco by train, in the Maharajah's state carriage, which had been shipped from Bengal in advance.

Before being laden aboard the cargo ship at Calcutta, the railway carriage had undergone the necessary adjustments, reducing the gauge from 5'6" to 4'8½".

Waiting outside the Camondos' mansion, a liveried servant ushered the Foggs inside and then through into the grand salon. Decorated in opulent eighteenth century style, the room was adorned with medieval European tapestries, the parquet floor hidden by exquisite Persian rugs.

Abundance was the order of the day.

Multiple Chinese cloisonné vases sat on tables inlaid with walnut veneer, and Rodin sculptures were illuminated in the light of Bohemian crystal chandeliers, the room glistening with miles upon miles of gilt.

Comte and Comtesse de Camondo swept into the salon to greet their distinguished guests.

'My dear friends,' gushed the Comte, 'what joy it gives us that you accepted our humble invitation.'

'The honour is ours and ours alone,' Hannibal responded impeccably, dipping his head in a bow.

A servant stepped up with a tray of flutes filled with chilled Ruinart.

'Allow me to propose a toast,' said the Comte, raising his drink. 'To old and trusted friends!'

They touched glasses, the sound of Czech crystal and laughter filling the salon.

A sumptuous meal was served:

Terrine of hare, followed by pepper crusted rack of venison with morel sauce, washed down with a rare Chateau Pétrus — served at exactly seventeen degrees Celsius.

After the meal, the Comtesse led Alina into her

parlour for a little discreet conversation. Nothing in the world gave her more pleasure than gossiping with a confidante — not even the masterpieces her husband showered on her conjured by the hands of Lucien Gautrait.

When the ladies had withdrawn, Comte de Camondo beckoned with a finger discreetly in Hannibal's direction.

'Would you come with me into the library? I have something rather special to show you,' he said.

Over Armagnac and Montecristos, they discussed the founding of the League of Nations, in which both men had played a significant role. Draining his glass, the Comte stepped from the fireplace over to a Louis XIV writing desk. From a secret compartment located on the left side, he removed a miniature silk purse.

'My dear Fogg...' he said, 'nineteen years ago you asked a favour of me. You may have imagined I had forgotten, but I made you a promise then that I would do all in my power to assist.'

For the sake of politeness, Hannibal pretended to be uncertain what his host was speaking about. But in reality he remembered perfectly well. After all, Hannibal Fogg rarely forgot anything, especially matters as important as this.

On a freezing winter night in 1900, he had requested the Comte to use his connections in India to acquire a certain gemstone.

At arm's length Camondo held the silk purse in his guest's direction.

'I must commend your patience,' he said, pressing the purse into Hannibal's hand.

'My God, how on earth did you manage to…?'

The Comte held up a hand. Then, drawing on his cigar, he replied:

'The Maharajah of Jaipur happens to be on the Level.'

'A Brother in the Craft?' asked Hannibal quizzically.

'Indeed. Grand Lodge of Bombay.'

'What good fortune!' Hannibal uttered, as he eased the stone through the purse's neck. Taking his time, he held it to the gaslight, marvelling at the flawless nature and the cut.

Awaiting approval, Camondo looked at his friend.

'Perfectly magnificent!' said Hannibal. He slipped the gemstone back into the silk purse and returned it to the Comte.

'Now I need to ask you another favour,' he said, his tone grave. 'As my most trusted friend, I ask for you to keep it safe until such a time that I come for it.'

Comte de Camondo frowned. Then, nodding, he broke into a smile.

'Anything you ask,' he said.

One hundred and twenty-five

WITH LIGHT WINTER RAIN glistening on its windscreen, a Mercedes limousine headed down the Champs Elysées. Spiralling round the obelisk at Concorde, it came to a gentle halt outside a grand classical building.

'Est-ce que numéro dix?' Chaudhury asked the driver in passable French.

'Oui monsieur, numéro dix — l'Hôtel de Crillon.'

'Well, well,' said Will. 'This is the first of Hannibal's coordinates I actually approve of.'

In a feat of both diplomacy and shrewd logistical coordination, Chaudhury had talked the others into travelling to Paris, arranged transport, shipped Hannibal's climbing equipment back to Marrakesh and had a pair of extra-large steamer trunks sent to meet their flight at Charles de Gaulle.

As soon as the Mercedes had stopped, a pair of liveried doormen opened the passenger doors.

'Welcome to the Hôtel de Crillon,' they said in unison.

'You have no idea how happy we are to be here,' said Emma with widened eyes as she stepped into the building.

At the reception desk Will slid his credit card over the counter and asked for three single rooms.

The duty manager swanned up with effusive salutations, attending to the reservation himself.

'May I say what a great pleasure it is to have you with

us at long last, Mr Fogg?' he said. 'As I am sure you are aware, the booking was made quite some time ago, and was paid for in cash by a Mr...' the manager glanced at his register.

'Let me guess,' said Will smiling. 'By another Mr Fogg.'

'Precisely, monsieur. And I am happy to say that your namesake had rare and impeccable taste. He requested we reserve for you three of our signature suites, including his own personal favourite, Suite Duc de Crillon.'

One hundred and twenty-six

HAVING BORROWED A COLLEAGUE'S membership card, Richard Matheson was admitted into the historic London Library at 14 St James's Square. He was directed by the librarian to the left of the old catalogues, through a doorway leading into the stacks.

After getting profoundly lost in the rabbit warren of shelving, Matheson found himself in Topography. Fifteen minutes after that, he located the volume Sir Lancelot had mentioned — *Fire and Sword in the Sudan* by Rudolf Slatin Pasha.

A hefty book, the spine two inches across, it was bound in speckled calf.

Wheeling over the librarian's footstool, Matheson climbed up, and pulled the volume down. Opening it to the title page, he flicked forward through the chapters.

It looked like any other book — although a very dusty one, the binding rather lose. From the withdrawal slip pasted into the prelims, it appeared the volume was hardly in high demand.

It had last been taken out in 1951.

As he flicked through a second time, Matheson noticed that a sheet of paper had been cut to the exact size of the other pages, and bound in towards the end. It caught his eye because it was not printed, but rather handwritten.

Strange, he thought — for the page appeared to be a sales receipt for a pair of men's shoes, from John Lobb of St James's, bootmakers to royalty.

It was not the receipt that so surprised Matheson, but the name of the customer — H G Fogg.

One hundred and twenty-seven

EMMA SPENT THE ENTIRE afternoon in a bubble bath in the Bernstein Suite. Next door, in the Louis XV Suite, Chaudhury wrote a clutch of letters home on the hotel stationery. Despite his appreciation for technology, he had been brought up to maintain the traditions of a pre-digital world.

Down in the Duc de Crillon Suite, Will lay back on the couch with his eyes closed tight. He had tried to put the horror of the Miao Keng caves out of his mind, but it kept creeping back. Through the afternoon, he was touched with equal pangs of wonder and trepidation, as he struggled to make sense of Hannibal Fogg.

The clock on the mantelpiece struck five.

As though summoned by it, Will sat up and went over to the flight case. Opening it, he took out the components and placed them on the coffee table.

Now there was tranquillity, he considered each one in turn: Ladder, Hands, Dagger, Stone and Prayer Wheel. Each was both bizarre and magnificent. But, far more importantly, they were all cornerstones in the business of belief.

As Will handled them, turning each one with care, observing details, Hannibal's words ran through his mind like a ticker-tape: 'I shall reveal to you what is necessary when necessary, or when you are ready to understand.'

What Will couldn't understand, though, was how Hannibal could be in such control of a world he must have left long before. No one appeared certain when he had actually died. As Will pondered it, in all likelihood he perished soon after his disappearance in Manchuria, back in 1939.

Striding over to the window, Will stared out at the ordered beauty of the French capital. The only question in his mind was how Hannibal could have known the future.

'If you've seen it all,' he said aloud, 'then you have

seen me standing here at the window in the Duc de Crillon Suite... asking this very question at this exact moment.'

Just then the clock on the mantel chimed again. But, instead of falling silent, it went on and on.

Will turned, his attention moving from the streets of Paris, over gilded fauteuils, the coffee table and the components and up onto the grey marble mantel.

Set squarely in the middle, between crystal candle-sticks, was an ornate eighteenth century rococo clock, an expression of golden opulence.

Stepping up to it, he took in the Roman letters inscribed into the porcelain face. As he did so, the chimes fell silent.

Hannibal's doing, Will thought to himself.

With both hands, he lifted the antique timepiece from the mantel, carried it over to the desk and put it down. Will could almost smell the scent of Hannibal. But, despite it, there was no obvious clue.

Not yet at any rate.

Something was nagging at Will, coaxing him to turn the clock over.

He did so, and found a little metal flap, screwed down with a wing-nut: the hatch through which the clockmaker could adjust the speed of the movement.

Two twists and the flap was open.

Rolled up inside was a miniature scroll.

Will shook it out, unrolled it and found a message.

A message from Hannibal Fogg:

Indeed you are right, my dear William, that I have seen you sitting there, enjoying the elegance of the Duc de Crillon Suite. As you may know, it was once the private chapel of the Crillon family. Many a time I have sought refuge there with my dearest Alina, and joyous times they were!

I am sensible of the fact you prefer beer to champagne, but I urge you to take a sip of the Roederer Cristal that I have asked to be brought for you. It should be there in a minute or two. In my lifetime the vintage was a little harder to come by, reserved for the tsar's family and others in positions of privilege. I understand that in your world, the vintage has become the preferred beverage of musicians whose inability to perform is matched only by their inordinate success.

It would be remiss of me to not lift the curtain on how I know what I do. The answer is simple. The Hands of God possess energy of a particular frequency that allows an empty mind to conjure the future, just as it does the past.

But before you take advantage of this instrument, I advise you to leave it alone. For, knowing the future tends to corrupt the present.
Affectionately yours,

Hannibal

One hundred and twenty-eight

At seven o'clock on the evening of Will's arrival in Paris, Comte Oscar de Mallois stopped by the Hôtel de Crillon — the first time he had visited since the grand redecoration. Under his arm was a black leather Louis Vuitton case from the firm's Epi collection.

At security, a guard took a look inside and waved him through. Making his way to the concierge desk, de Mallois introduced himself.

'I should like to ask the occupant of the Duc de Crillon Suite to join me for a glass of champagne in the bar,' he said.

The Crillon prided itself above all on its sense of discretion, but the Comte was well known to the hotel, and an extremely valued client.

At once, the concierge picked up the house telephone, and called the Duc de Crillon Suite.

Ten minutes later Will was sitting at a corner table in the bar with the Comte.

'I would not have disturbed you,' said de Mallois, 'but I think you may be interested in what I have to say.'

He waved a hand at the waiter.

'*Oui monsieur?*'

'Dom Perignon, the '92.'

'At once, Comte de Mallois.'

'If you don't mind, I would prefer a beer,' said Will. 'Budweiser, if they have it.'

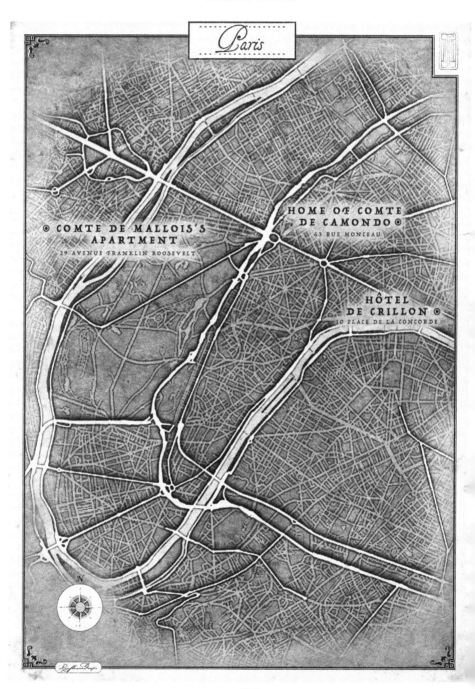

Smiling, the Comte seemed pleased.

'Never lose touch with reality,' he said. 'It is a golden virtue.'

The waiter returned with the chilled bottle of champagne and a Bud Light.

Sipping his beer, Will eased himself back into his chair, and listened.

'Some months ago I bought at auction a pith helmet that had once been owned by the explorer Hannibal Fogg,' the Comte began. 'I should explain that I have been for many years a great admirer of Fogg's work and, where possible, I have collected memorabilia relating to his life.

'On purchasing the pith helmet, I received with it a pamphlet, guiding the hat's owner in its appropriate use. The pamphlet was issued by its maker, Lock & Co. of St James's in London. Written on the back, in Fogg's hand, was a message.'

De Mallois took a sip of Dom Perignon, allowing the bubbles to fizz on his tongue.

'A message?'

'Indeed.'

The Comte reached into the Louis Vuitton case and removed the pamphlet.

'You can see for yourself.'

Will glanced at the paper. Written in Hannibal's hand was a single sentence of text:

If you are in possession of this pith helmet on Monday 12th June 2017, please take it to the Duc de Crillon Suite, l' Hôtel de Crillon, Paris.

The elderly aristocrat reached into the case a second time.

'I am merely doing what has been asked of me,' he said, placing the hat on the glass table.

Will grinned.

'Incredible, isn't he?'

'Do you have an idea of what is expected?'

'I believe so,' he replied. 'I'm no expert, but I am getting used to the way Hannibal thinks.'

Will signalled for the waiter, who arrived instantly.

'Can you please bring me a sharp knife?'

'At once, *monsieur.*'

A steak knife was fetched from the kitchen and brought through into the bar on a starched napkin, the napkin on a salver.

'You must forgive me for doing this,' Will said sombrely, looking into de Mallois's eyes.

Then, taking the knife, he applied the blade to the pith helmet's lining. The Comte watched, a little horrified and a little amused, as Will carved an arc into the lining and pulled away the flap of cloth.

'There it is.'

'What?'

'The paper I expected to find.'

Reaching in, Will pulled out a folded sheet of letter paper bearing Hannibal's distinctive monogram.

My dear William,

I can hardly express the depth of my gratitude, or my genuine sense of wonder at your achievements. There is some information that is now relevant to pass on to you. It concerns a rare blue diamond sacred to the aboriginal people of the Great Australian Desert.

They believed that the clear blue stone kept the world in balance, in what they referred to as 'Dreamtime'. Although disregarding the stone as valuable in any way, they believed it possessed a sacred power.

In 1881 an Afghan cameleer stole the gem and sold it to the Indian Maharajah of Jaipur. He in turn presented it as a gift to a French banker, the Comte Moise de Camondo, in the year 1919. A gesture of affection from one Brother Mason to another.

If my calculations are correct, the gentleman sitting across from you at this very moment will be in a position to inform you on the whereabouts of the stone. I wish you God's speed and great luck.

With affection,
Hannibal

When the Comte had departed with his prized pith helmet, Will took the lift back up to the Duc de Crillon Suite.

As he pressed the button for the second floor he smelled the scent of sandalwood, no doubt a trace of lingering cologne. At once, the aroma made him think of his father, who adored it. The thought of his father was inseparable from the memory of the accident — an event so terrible that Will almost never allowed it onto the stage of his mind. But now he was in a position to revisit the sequence of events, and witness what had taken place.

Hannibal may have warned of the danger of knowing the future, but he had said nothing about visiting the past. It was there that Will needed to travel if he were to have an answer to the one detail that tormented both his dreams and waking hours.

Stepping over to the coffee table, he took hold of the Hands of God. Then, closing his eyes, he strained to imagine.

His ninth birthday.

Raw anticipation and excitement.

Even with the Hands of God, he couldn't see more than the usual fragmentary loop of memory played over and over.

Will re-read the note he had found in the clock. Was there a clue almost at the end: '… allows an empty mind to conjure the future, as it does the past'.

An *empty* mind.

The Hands of God in his own hand, Will swept his mind clean, forcing out the detritus that tended to fill it.

Little by little, the past came into focus as Will remembered how it began.

29th April 2005.

Early morning, sunlight streaming through a gap in Apollo-13 curtains. A voice wafting up the stairs. The scent of Oscar Mayer's bacon and hot-buttered toast.

Leaping out of bed, Will shuffled on his slippers, slid down the banister, kissed his mum, then his dad, jumped for joy, and spun round and round.

'D'you want them now or later, darling?' his mum asked sweetly.

'Now! Now! Now! *Pleeeease!*'

His dad laughed.

'Open these now, and you'll get the big one later, OK?'

'Yeeeeeees, Dad!'

Will sped over to the breakfast table, ripping his way through half a dozen packages.

'Oh, wow! A Tamagotchi! Lego! Thank you! Oh, cooooool! Buzz Lightyear!'

Jerking Buzz out at arm's length, Will raced around the kitchen.

'To Infinity and Beyond!'

'Quickly eat your breakfast, there's not much time before we have to leave.'

'OK, Dad!'

Will's memory skipped fast-forward.

They were in the Volkswagen Jetta heading over the Golden Gate to Sausalito. Will's dad was singing 'There's a Hole in My Bucket' at the top of his voice, while his mother checked the signs for Route 101.

Fast-forward again.

The car was rumbling through Clam Beach.

And on again…

Will's face was covered in chocolate ice cream. His dad was doing an impression of a drunk octopus, while hunting for the exit back onto 101.

Then the moment it all changed:

The front right wheel hit a dip in the road.

Will's dad over-compensated.

The VW rolled down an embankment, spinning over and over.

Clutching his stomach, eyes tight shut, Will confronted the memory — the one he had never dared know:

Unscathed in the back, he was covered in ice cream.

Motionless in the front were his parents, all covered in blood.

One hundred and twenty-nine

JOHN LOBB & Co. hid behind one of the least assuming shopfronts on St James's Street. For well over a century the family firm had equipped emperors, kings and maharajahs, opera supremos, literati and business tycoons, with the finest handmade shoes money could buy.

A variety of traditional leather footwear was arranged neatly in the window — polo boots, monogrammed slippers, and Oxfords — in assorted shades and grades of leather.

Richard Matheson arrived at the shop a little after lunch. Stepping across the threshold he felt intimidated, fearful at entering a world reserved firmly for the elite.

Lacquered dark varnished cabinets lined the walls, displaying a veritable museum of fine footwear. A sense of sombreness hung heavy in the main salon. Unlike normal shoe shops, there were no price tags. Lobb made shoes strictly to order. Customers who felt it necessary to ask the price were most likely in the wrong place.

The Lobb family had turned the creation of exquisite shoes into an art form. Laborious by any standards, the process began with sculpting the client's foot, mapping out every bump and curve, and ended, a year or more later, with a pair of shoes set to last a lifetime.

Since his undergraduate days at Oxford, Hannibal Fogg had worn Lobbs. Like other gentlemen of a discerning nature, he regarded the expense as well worthwhile. Over the years he had ordered more than two dozen pairs of shoes from the firm, often supplying his own leather, which he sourced while on expeditions.

A sales assistant was standing behind a low display cabinet at the far end of the shop. In the forty-two years he had served at Lobb, he had learned everything there was to know about shoes and feet. The moment someone walked in through the door, he could tell whether they were serious about their shoes. *The Times*'s finest was certainly not such a customer. He was wearing a pair of worn-out Timberland's.

Intimidated, his mouth bone-dry, Matheson approached.

'Good morning,' said the journalist, straining to be far more posh and polite than he actually was. 'I wonder if you might be able to assist me. I have an old sales receipt for a pair of Lobb shoes.'

Matheson, who had torn the page out of the book at the London Library, placed it on the glass display case.

'It seems, sir, that these shoes have been waiting some time,' the salesman said.

'Yes, as I said — it's rather old.'

'They are marked as being ready for collection since 7th September 1923,' stated the salesman without breaking into a smile. 'Might I ask, sir, whether you are a descendant of the gentleman who placed the order?'

'Er, yes, um. He was my great...great-grandfather.'

'Well, sir, if you would give me a moment I shall go and look for them.'

Matheson blinked.

'You mean to say they were never collected?'

'It appears not, sir.'

'How can you tell?'

'Well, although the order was paid for in advance, there is not a signature denoting collection.'

The salesman disappeared into a back room, where he hunted through dozens of uncollected orders. The length of time between ordering and delivery, coupled with the fact that Lobb appealed to a rather mature clientele, led to many pairs of shoes never being collected at all.

Ten minutes later the salesman reappeared.

In his hands was a wooden box with the word 'FOGG' stencilled in large letters on the side.

'Here you are, sir, a pair of crocodile leather brogues…' Pausing, he glanced at a note stapled to the side of the box. 'Seems as if Mr Fogg requested to take charge of his own lasts.'

'Is there a problem?' Matheson asked.

'Well, sir, it is unusual for the lasts to ever leave the premises, but I shall get them for you.'

Again the salesman disappeared, traipsing into another storeroom. Filled floor-to-ceiling with racks, each was piled with the wooden moulds of feet.

After a great deal of searching, he located Fogg's lasts.

Like all the others, they were strung together with parcel string, a number written on the heels.

Carrying them back into the shop, the gnarled grain caught his eye. He couldn't be sure, but they didn't look like maple, beech, or hornbeam, the preferred choice for durability. Rather, they appeared to have been fashioned from a root. The salesman touched the right last to his nose.

It smelled of tangerines.

One hundred and thirty

THE COMTE DE MALLOIS had an abiding fascination with anything connected to the Comte Moise de Camondo, a distant relative on his mother's side.

Having heard the year before that an important blue diamond formerly owned by Camondo was coming up for auction, he had attended the sale.

The gemstone had been listed in the catalogue as 'the property of a lady'. A lengthy blurb had described how de Camondo's daughter, Beatrice, had been sent to the Nazi death camps during the Second World War. After passing through various hands, the blue diamond of the Australian aboriginals was acquired by a member of the Italian aristocracy. Having fallen on relatively hard times the current owner had decided reluctantly to part with it.

No one except for the Comte de Camondo had ever had cause to wonder why Hannibal had not taken the gem on the evening they had dined in 1919. Complex in the extreme, the reason for leaving the diamond in Camondo's possession involved a blind Indian fakir, a sack of boiled ox bones, and the lost treasure of King Nebuchadnezzar.

At the auction the Comte de Mallois watched with considerable surprise as the rare blue diamond was sold to a bidder on the telephone for an astronomical sum — €45 million. He had learned from an acquaintance that the buyer was a secretive financier who planned to use it in an elaborate case of insurance fraud.

Having handed over the pith helmet, the Comte had described the diamond and its owner to Will. He in turn had mentioned it to Emma at breakfast next morning.

Her curiosity piqued, she googled Polkovich and learned that he had recently diversified from energy into an even more lucrative activity — weaponry. But not of a conventional variety. Rather, his laboratory in Kiev had developed an ultra-fast-acting form of bubonic bacteria to be used on the battlefield.

The morning after de Mallois had brought the pith helmet to the Crillon, Emma had received a secret report detailing the Ukrainian's business affairs and his private life.

When she showed it to Will, he asked how she could

have come across such sensitive material. She smiled at him benignly.

'I dated a guy in the Ukrainian Secret Service,' she said.

NEXT MORNING THEY TOOK the Eurostar from Paris Gare du Nord to London St Pancras. Chaudhury had booked them seats in a first-class carriage, and handled getting the luggage on board. To ride the train between Paris and London had been his secret ambition since childhood.

During the journey, Emma flicked through a copy of *Vogue*. Beside her, Will sat with the CODEX on his lap, the flight case at his feet. Tapping in names and numbers, he noted the results on the back of a receipt.

When he typed in 'POLKOVICH', the display came up with: 'CITROPSIS ARTICULATA'. He read the words out.

Chaudhury raised an eyebrow.

'Mean anything to you?'

The manservant shook his head.

'Looks like gobbledegook, sir, or an anagram.'

'What about you?'

Leaning over her magazine, Emma peered at the display.

'As I remember,' she replied, 'it's the Linnaean term for the African cherry orange, otherwise known as the omuboro tree.' She paused, touched the top of

470

the magazine to her chin. 'In central Africa the root's considered an aphrodisiac.'

Will looked across at her quizzically.

'I told you, I like to read,' she said, blushing.

'Wikipedia?'

'Yes, but that little jewel of information was culled from a monograph written by Hannibal.'

'Really?'

'It was sitting on the window ledge in the guest room at Dar Jnoun. As I remember it was rather racy in places.'

'What was it called?'

The Eurostar entered the Channel Tunnel, daylight was replaced by darkness.

Emma smiled.

'It was entitled *Sexual Dysfunction Among the Hema Tribe of the Belgian Congo,*' she said.

One hundred and thirty-one

1922

SEATED WITH HIS BACK towards the glass cabinets arranged with samples from the company's past, Hannibal Fogg reclined as a fitter measured his feet in intimate detail. His father, Uriah, had first introduced him to the House of Lobb.

Aged eighteen, Hannibal had been measured for his first pair of lasts. Sculpted from aged beech, they were

471

still in good condition, but the explorer had decided to order a new pair. He had provided a block of wood for the purpose, the very first customer in the history of Lobb to have done so.

When the measurements had been completed, Hannibal stood up.

'As usual I shall pay you in advance,' he said, 'and I should be obliged if you would make me a pair of Oxford brogues in this.'

Fogg placed a packet of supple leather on the counter. The manager opened it, running his thumb over the grain.

'Crocodile, sir?' he enquired.

'*Tribolonotus gracilis*,' Hannibal replied, 'a giant sub-species of the red-eyed crocodile skink. Although it's more usually found in New Guinea, I came across this particular example in central China.'

The manager inspected the leather, holding it into the light at the front of the shop.

'If I may say so, sir, it is especially fine,' he said. 'As for the tanning, it is quite exceptional.'

Hannibal almost gloated.

'Tanned it myself,' he replied.

'When exactly would you like the shoes to be ready, Mr Fogg?'

Hannibal thought for a moment.

'No hurry at all,' he said. 'Indeed, it will be quite some time before the shoes are actually collected.'

One hundred and thirty-two

THE SECRET SERVICE DOSSIER on Polkovich revealed the Ukrainian's three overwhelming passions.

The first was hunting the endangered Asiatic black bear in the forests of eastern Siberia with a crossbow.

The second was high altitude freefall jumping.

And the third — an obsession with rare postage stamps.

At the age of nine the oligarch had developed an interest in philately while living with his grandfather. They shared a wretched unheated room on Kiev's Esplanadna Street. Through the long winter nights there was ice on the inside of the windows, and the stink of raw sewage. Postage stamps had been a way for young Polkovich to escape abject poverty.

As a connoisseur of rare stamps, Will knew Polkovich would be unable to resist the lure of the Franklin Z-Grill. The little blue one-cent stamp was so rare there was almost no chance the arms dealer already had one, and every chance that he would rise to the bait. Chaudhury had been dispatched on a flight to Marrakesh in order to retrieve it from Will's night stand.

Posing as a high-end philatelist, Emma had contacted Polkovich's private secretary, a sullen-sounding Cossack named Alexei Yenisei. He had hung up the phone, promising to call back that afternoon. To her surprise he phoned her five minutes later, his voice flustered.

Polkovich had asked for the stamp to be brought to him at 7 p.m.

Lined up on the forecourt of 10 Kensington Palace Gardens were a pair of Lamborghinis, a Bugatti Veyron and a Bentley Hunaudières concept car — all of them in oyster grey.

Dressed up to the nines, Will and Emma arrived at the mansion on time, crossing the street to the east side. Even before they had reached the forecourt, a pair of security guards stepped out and frisked them.

Spitting out a line in Russian, one of the guards radioed to the control room, then waved them over to the entrance.

A side door opened electronically.

A second pair of towering security guards greeted them and swept them for metal and explosives before escorting them into a waiting suite. Considering it was the home of a billionaire, the decor was surprisingly down at heel. The sofa was tatty Ikea, the fitted carpet stained with splotches of dirt.

'You're sure you've got the stamp,' Emma whispered, as they sat waiting to be seen.

'Yeah, right here in the file. I've checked a hundred times.'

At 7.19 a shortwave radio hissed in a back room, and yet another guard appeared. He had a scar running from his left eye to the base of his chin.

'You come with me!'

After passing through three armoured security doors, they reached Polkovich's drawing room.

The salon was as grand as the waiting room had been plain. The walls were hung in old masters, enormous works bought for size rather than composition. Half a dozen bronzes by Damien Hirst were dotted around, a matching pair of Blue Period Picassos hung on either side of the fireplace and, opposite it, the entire wall had been decorated in Warhol soup cans.

All Will could think of was how he would ever retrieve the blue diamond and make it out alive.

The building was a fortress.

Snipers were positioned in the front and back gardens, as well as on the roof. The windows were glazed with armoured glass, and the external masonry was fortified. Polkovich had even had a bombproof basement installed. The Swiss manufacturers claimed it could withstand nuclear, chemical or biological attacks, including the oligarch's own strain of bubonic bacteria.

It was clear Polkovich was on his way into the room because of the sound of feet scurrying fast over the parquet. A pair of burly security guards preceded him, as well as Yenisei the Cossack, and a manicurist. Bringing up the rear were another three guards, each of them armed with an SPS pistol — a model developed specially for Polkovich's elite security team.

'Have very little time,' said the oligarch, his accent heavy on the consonants. 'Understand from Yenisei you have Z-Grill. Correct?'

Will removed an envelope from the leather file.

'I will show it to you,' he said.

Opening the envelope, he tapped the stamp out onto the surface of the file.

Polkovich clicked his fingers.

A magnifying loupe was immediately passed to him.

Squinting through it, he observed the stamp with extreme care, rotating it slowly in an anti-clockwise direction.

'Good,' he said without moving his eye from the loupe. 'How desperate you are?'

'How *desperate*?'

'How much you want?'

Will had been so engrossed in getting access to the Ukrainian's mansion that he hadn't really thought about the actual sale of the stamp.

'Two other collectors are already interested,' he said, thinking fast. 'At this stage I am open to offers.'

Polkovich put the loupe on the table.

'Always get what I want,' he said angrily.

Will swallowed.

'So do I.'

The arms dealer smiled. Nothing pleased him more than meeting someone with a backbone.

'Last Z-Grill sold was...'

'Traded back in 2005 for a set of four Inverted Jenny stamps,' Will broke in. 'They were valued at $3 million.'

Polkovich sniffed.

'I double it.'

Will glanced over at Emma, and back at Polkovich.

'You'd have to double it again,' he said.

One hundred and thirty-three

1923

ON THE MORNING OF their departure, Hannibal rose at 4.15 a.m. and went through the proofs of his new publication, entitled *Horror of War*.

The volume, about the Great War, set against a wider consideration of conflict, had been the most challenging work of his literary career. Almost nothing in life had shocked Hannibal quite as severely as the futile slaughter of young lives in Flanders' fields. He hoped to rock the establishment to its very foundations with a scathing attack on the British military system. His publisher, John Long of Paternoster Row, planned to launch the book in time for Christmas.

Alina was sipping a cup of orange pekoe when Hannibal came down for breakfast. Kissing her head, he swept around the table and sat at his usual place, with a view down Kensington Palace Gardens.

'Chaudhury will take charge of the luggage,' Hannibal said, 'and we shall leave for Dover at ten.'

'Very good, my dear.'

Chaudhury padded silently into the dining-room, placed a letter in front of Alina, bowed, and crept away.

'I wonder who it's from; the stamp looks Italian.'

Opening it with a butter knife, she glanced at the page and frowned hard, her eyes welling with tears.

'What is it, my dear?'

'It's...'

'Yes?'

Alina stood up, pressing a hand to her chest as though she were suffocating. Jumping to his feet, Hannibal vaulted round the table.

His beloved Alina fell to the floor, dead.

The burial at Kensal Rise was private, limited to Hannibal, their son Wilfred and to five close friends.

As the pall-bearers bore her coffin over the frost-clad ground, Hannibal broke down, choking tears into a linen handkerchief. He had never known such despair.

For thirty minutes he had tried to resuscitate her, even continuing when it was quite clear she was dead. He had held her in his arms on the dining-room floor for a whole hour, his face a gnarled mask of grief.

Inconsolable, he turned his attention to the reason for Alina's death. He had looked at her face. Pale as marble, it was utterly serene. The fact that her lips had turned aquamarine suggested poisoning of some kind.

With a napkin, Hannibal had picked up the letter and glanced at the text. It was written in Cyrillic and appeared to be from a childhood friend, someone who shared a memory of Astrakhan in the spring.

Hannibal had held the letter to the window. There was no watermark. The paper was bonded and unremarkable except that the script had spread slightly, as if the ink had been diluted.

He had touched it to his nostrils — breathing in the faintest scent of geraniums.

By the morning of the funeral, Hannibal had isolated the poison or, rather, the poisons. There were two of them, painted over both sides of the letter. The first was the venom of the inland taipan from central Australia. The second was lewisite.

Now that he knew what had killed her, Hannibal wanted to know who would have wanted his beloved Alina dead.

He was certain the Magi were to blame.

With the funeral over, he returned home, ordering Chaudhury to sew all the curtains shut.

In almost darkness, he went up to his study. Once inside, he closed the door, took off his jacket, and removed a revolver, a Russian-made Nagant M1895, from a secret compartment in the roll-top desk.

Loading four of the seven chambers, he spun the cylinder, and opened his mouth.

Then, he pulled the trigger.

One hundred and thirty-four

LEONARD POLKOVICH HAD ONLY ever once been swindled in business. The project was a high-profile gas concession in Uzbekistan. So enraged was the oligarch at being duped, that he had made sure his entire team were publicly disgraced. As though humiliation were not enough, he had then made sure they were framed for crimes they didn't commit.

A young American philatelist was small fry compared with the Central Asian thugs he more usually did business with. Even so, he was willing to offer a fair price — $11 million. After feigning displeasure, Will had agreed.

The exchange was planned for the next afternoon.

'Hannibal knew Polkovich would own the gem,' said Will, as he and Emma made their way back to their hotel.

'Even if we had enough cold hard cash to buy it,' Will replied, 'Polkovich wouldn't sell. He's the kind of man who values something merely because of its rarity.'

'A game for the high rollers,' said Emma.

Will's eyes might have been on Piccadilly's traffic, but his mind was picking its way through Hannibal's world.

'He's always five steps ahead,' he said.

'I'm sure he would have left a plan,' Emma responded.

'I'm sure you're right — we just have to find it.'

AT BROWN'S HOTEL, CHAUDHURY was cleaning Will's trainers with a brush which had belonged to his grandfather, Mohan Chaudhury. The bristles had last been replaced in the 1920s, using hair from a herd of Tamworth pigs Hannibal had acquired a year before his dramatic fall from grace.

Will was still sure that a clue was awaiting him.

'I bet you we've missed it,' he said.

'Missed what?'

'The clue. He was meticulous. I'm certain it's right here under our noses.'

'If it exists we'll find it,' Emma said.

'If Hannibal had somehow seen the future — *my* future — he'd have known I'd stay here in London,' said Will.

'In this hotel,' Emma added.

'In this suite.'

'So it stands to reason he would have put the clue right here, doesn't it?'

'In this room.'

Emma sighed.

'But it would have been discovered long ago.'

'Not if it was concealed with appropriate care.'

Chaudhury laid the brush down on the floor and untied his butler's apron.

'If I may speak up, sir,' he said. 'Many hundreds of guests must have stayed here since the days of Hannibal Fogg.'

Will strode over to the dressing-room. Opening the cupboard's double doors, he rooted about at the back.

'What are you doing, Will?' asked Emma.

481

'Searching,' said a muffled voice.

'What for?'

There was a loud thud, as if a false wall had been knocked out. Will reappeared holding up a padded envelope caked in dust.

'For this,' he said.

'My God, I can't believe it.'

'Well, I can,' Will replied, tearing the envelope open.

Stuffed inside was an encoded letter, the blueprints to a building, and a long steel key.

Using the CODEX, Will started decrypting the letter, scribbling the decoded version on a hotel notepad.

'"My dear William, I had at first been unsure whether you would locate any of the clues I placed around London to guide you to this letter. The fact that you are reading it suggests you found at least one of them.

'"As you have no doubt established, the blue diamond is kept at my former home, number 10 Kensington Palace Gardens."'

'Hannibal lived at Polkovich's mansion?!'

'Yes, he did,' said Will. 'Listen to this: "During my residence there, I installed a safe of my own design, which I believe will still be regarded as impenetrable in your time. Of course, the current owner will have added extra security provisions. I have taken these into account. By following the directions enclosed, and by using the equipment stowed in the cupboard where you found this letter, you should succeed in the heist."'

Will went back to the cupboard and rooted about again. He located a wooden packing crate disguised as a water tank.

Labelled 'X19', it was filled with Hannibal's burglary equipment.

One hundred and thirty-five

ON THE ROOF OF Polkovich's mansion, between equidistant chimney stacks, was a triangular aerial device. Written in large white letters was the initialism 'PSCC'.

Will had spotted it while scoping out the billionaire's home from the other side of Kensington Palace Gardens. Another palatial mansion on the market there. It was the former residence of a Greek shipping magnate who had lost his fortune, having been blackmailed by an unusually vindictive mistress. As luck would have it, the mansion was located directly opposite Hannibal's former home.

While touring the property, posing as the son of a Texan oil tycoon, Will managed to get a few shots with a camera fitted with a telephoto lens.

Back at Brown's, he enlarged an image of the roof on his laptop.

Emma pointed to the triangular antenna.

'What's that — a satellite TV aerial?'

Having squinted at the image long enough to copy

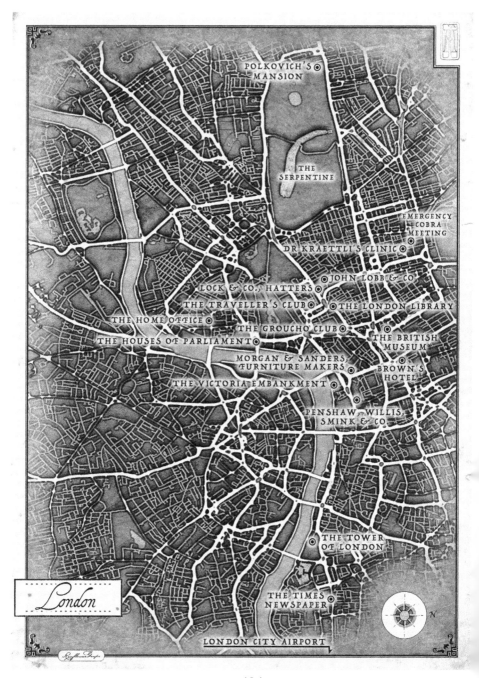

POLKOVICH'S MANSION

THE SERPENTINE

EMERGENCY COBRA MEETING

DR KRAETTLI'S CLINIC

JOHN LOBB & CO

LOCK & CO. HATTERS
THE TRAVELLER'S CLUB
THE LONDON LIBRARY

THE HOME OFFICE
THE GROUCHO CLUB
THE BRITISH MUSEUM

THE HOUSES OF PARLIAMENT

MORGAN & SANDERS FURNITURE MAKERS
BROWN'S HOTEL

THE VICTORIA EMBANKMENT

PENSHAW, WILLIS, SMINK & CO

THE TOWER OF LONDON

London

THE TIMES NEWSPAPER

N

LONDON CITY AIRPORT

down the initialism, Will searched for it on the web.

A few seconds later he had the answer.

PSCC was the cutting edge in private surveillance. Its site advertised the fact that the firm — based in Liechtenstein — handled security for billionaires the world over. Their speciality was a system they called 'Guard Force Technology'.

The network's selling point was the way it created a '*Bodyprint*' of anyone permitted to enter one of their secure properties. Without being added to the system, there was no hope at all of ever getting inside. The only way of being added was by logging in via PSCC's secure portal, using one of their own specially calibrated computers.

Having surfed the site, Will gave a heavy sigh.

'Looks like a serious case of Game Over,' he said. 'There's no way I can get into this.'

'Thought you were supposed to be a geek,' said Emma.

'There's geeks and there's geeks, and this stuff is Geekhood: The Next Generation.'

'Forgive me for overhearing, sir,' said Chaudhury, leaning in, 'but might I peruse the website?'

'Go ahead, it's all yours.'

The manservant sat down at the laptop and typed commands so fast his fingers blurred. Within less than a minute he had cracked the login page. A minute after that he had used a Trojan worm to penetrate the security interface's first and second levels.

'Way to go!' exclaimed Will, his mouth wide open. 'How did you do that?'

'Just a little programming trick, sir,' said Chaudhury. 'I had a great deal of down time while I was waiting for you to arrive up in Marrakesh.'

'Do you think you can get through the back door?'

'Possibly, sir, but we will need some hardware. PSCC provide their own to clients directly. It says here they build it themselves.'

'What does that mean?' asked Emma.

'That we need to go shopping,' Will replied.

 BY THE EVENING HE and Chaudhury were back at Brown's. They staggered in through the main door with a dozen bags packed with tools and equipment.

It wasn't long before they had set up the work desk. Arranging the tools in order, Will laid out the key apparatus.

'I'm guessing PSCC designed this wild,' he said. 'If they had any of the usual stuff they'd be using a standard PC.'

Emma came over from her suite and groaned at all the gear.

Chaudhury got down to assembling a tower computer from scratch, an LED headlamp mounted on his forehead. She watched him slotting in the components at high speed, following a guide hacked from the dark web.

'Where exactly are you getting this information?' she asked.

The manservant coughed into his hand.

'From a source, miss.'

'You never saw any of this,' Will added.

Chaudhury looked up from the motherboard, the headlamp blinding Emma as his face swung round.

'It's not the first time I've been in here,' he said with uncharacteristic informality. 'Anyway, it keeps them on their toes.'

Within an hour and a half the tower computer was ready. His hands typing even faster than before, the manservant ran the set-up sequence.

'How's it looking?' asked Will.

'So far so good, sir. Next step is to get a mole.'

'D'you have one in mind?'

'Oh yes.'

Chaudhury used a VPN to send a double-encrypted email. A second later, a single line of raw code appeared on the screen.

'You can always rely on the GIA.'

'You mean *CIA*?' Emma said.

'*GIA*,' the manservant repeated.

'Who're they?'

'The Mongolian Secret Service.'

'Is that it?' asked Will. 'The Master Key?'

'Shouldn't be more than a minute or two now, sir.'

Pasting the code into the system's portal, Chaudhury hit 'Enter'.

An LED warning lamp flashed orange, then green.

'Looks like we're in!' said Will.

'Please type in this string, sir,' Chaudhury replied.

'Ready.'

'FFGUTDS973339881.'

Tapping in the code, Will hit 'Enter' again.

'Platinum Clearance,' he said. 'Now we just need to breach the last firewall.'

Chaudhury flicked a hand at the motherboard.

'Easy,' he said. 'Re-enter the code backwards: 188933379SDTUGFF.'

Will began tapping in the sequence. But a warning alarm sounded.

'Oh my God!' he said. 'What's it asking for?'

'For the exponent quotient of pi.'

'What?!'

Chaudhury held his face.

'We've got fifteen seconds…'

'Try to stall it.'

'Are you joking?'

'We're going to be locked out!' shouted Will.

'Five, four, three, two…'

Just before it reached zero, Chaudhury jabbed a hand at the keyboard, typing something super fast.

The countdown stopped.

Will looked at Emma, then at the manservant from Cooch Behar.

'What the heck was that?'

Chaudhury smiled.

'A digital skeleton key I've been keeping for a rainy day,' he said.

By the evening, Will's *Bodyprint* had been loaded into the system.

Pecking them both on the cheek, Emma went to the door. Just before heading back to her suite, she paused.

'You two are awesome,' she said.

One hundred and thirty-six

1924

THE CHAMBER HAD BEEN empty, fate decreeing that Hannibal should live.

Packing the Russian revolver in its drawer, he had sat back in the low club chair and thought about the first time he had set eyes on Alina.

For six months he had hardly ever left his study. Having dragged a mattress inside, he would sleep under the window. The only person who ever saw him was Chaudhury. Such was his grief that he gave strict instructions to turn all visitors away — including his own son, Wilfred.

Hannibal took to studying the black arts, immersing himself in works on the occult. With the door to his study double locked, the darkness illuminated only by beeswax candles, he attempted to summon Alina's spirit.

On some occasions, Chaudhury would rap discreetly on the study door, begging his master to pull himself from melancholy.

But there would be no reply.

Then, one morning in early summer, Chaudhury ascended the stairs to the second floor, only to find the study door wide open. The curtains had been drawn back, the windows flung open.

Hannibal was standing in the middle of the room, his eyes wide open, his face bearded.

'We must leave at once!' he roared.

'Do you have a destination in mind, sir?'

'Of course I do!' exclaimed Hannibal. 'We're going on the Orient Express!'

One hundred and thirty-seven

THE NIGHT BEFORE THE heist, Will lay awake in bed, the window open, the curtains rustling in the breeze. It wasn't worry that was keeping him from sleep, so much as a longing to be with Emma. A voice in his head was urging him to get up and make the first move.

Will chewed the inside of his lip, trying as best he could to pluck up courage. Then he had an idea. Why not use the Hands of God to see the future? Right away he would know whether she would embrace his advance or spurn it altogether.

Clambering out of bed, he opened the flight case and gently eased the Hands from their niche. Then, getting comfortable on the couch, he held the icon firmly, as he had done before — when it had shown him the crash.

With closed eyes he cleared his mind.

Darkness melted into waxy yellow sunlight, the air fearfully still. Alone against a bright blue sky, a black cormorant was soaring out to sea.

Panning down, he glimpsed a lighthouse poised on rocks at the far end of a sleek ribbon of sand. The beach was deserted. As his line of sight moved towards the lighthouse, Will spied a great jagged chunk of driftwood, gnarled and blackened.

The lens moved over the wood's surface and, as it did so, Will noticed a couple huddled on its leeward side.

A man and a woman.

He didn't see their faces. Not at first.

The man was bent down over the woman, in an unnatural posture, a long knife grasped in his right hand. The blade was dripping in dark ruby blood. Inches from it, the woman lay on her back, lifeless and cold, her chest hacked open.

Changing its angle, the lens focused tight on the

wound. In slow motion it pulled back, revealing a blood-soaked floral print dress, and Emma's face, all bleak and grey. As the lens moved again, Will saw himself.

Gasping, he dropped the Hands of God.

They fell to the floor.

He sat there, his eyes swollen in grief for a crime that hadn't yet been committed.

One hundred and thirty-eight

MATHESON DINED AT HIS favourite table at the Groucho Club on Dean Street. He had been joined by one of his colleagues, Samantha from the Sports desk.

A buxom girl, she had a mane of blonde hair and expensive stilettos. Matheson's plan was to ply her with Pinot Grigio and lure her back to his bachelor pad in Camden Town.

Things were going well.

They were on their second bottle and had begun to cuddle up close, both flirting shamelessly. Samantha from Sports hunted for her phone, which was ringing. It was an old flame — a bank clerk with prospects and a second-hand Alfa Romeo with racing stripes.

From the side of the conversation Matheson could hear, it seemed as though the ex-boyfriend was in London.

Fuelled by the stream of Pinot Grigio, Samantha cooed into her phone romantically. Listening in,

Matheson came to understand that the ex-flame was actually only a couple of streets away.

Struggling to find her stilettos, kicked off under the table, Samantha gave Matheson a hug and was gone.

Furious at being duped, he sat there swearing under his breath, nursing his sorrows in the last gush of Pinot Grigio. The Groucho was a shark pool of celebrity, in which a down-on-his-luck travel editor had no stock value at all.

After feeling sorry for himself for fifteen minutes, Matheson downed the last glass, paid the bill and reeled towards the lobby.

On the way out, the porter recognised him.

'Mr Matheson?'

'Yes?'

'There's a letter waiting for you, sir. It just arrived.'

Snatching it, Matheson glanced at his name on the front.

'Yeah, that's me,' he said, stuffing it into his jacket pocket.

The next morning, while taking the tube to Tower Hill he cursed Samantha from Sports, and then Pinot Grigio for giving him such a terrible hangover.

As the District Line train rumbled through Blackfriars, he dug a hand in his pocket, felt the letter, frowned, remembered, and tore it open.

Squinting at the curiously old-fashioned handwriting, he read:

10 Kensington Palace Gardens, SW
10th August 1923

Dear Mr Matheson,

I am grateful to you for collecting my shoes from Lobb. I would now be indebted if you would take the lasts over to Brown's Hotel on Albemarle Street, and leave them there, for the attention of a

Mr Chaudhury.

You will find a second sheet of paper folded in the envelope in which you received this letter. Please enclose it along with the lasts.

As for the shoes, they are a particularly fine pair of Oxford brogues crafted from a rare species of giant Oriental skink.

As a gesture of goodwill, I invite you to keep them. They are made for a foot a little wider than your own but, all the same, they ought to be very comfortable indeed.

Yours truly,

Hannibal C Fogg

One hundred and thirty-nine

THE MORNING AFTER SEEING the future, Will used the steel key to unlock the front of a raised ventilation hole, halfway down Kensington Palace Gardens. Once the hatch was open he jumped inside.

Although apprehensive, he was prepared, dressed in the protective suit Hannibal had designed for the heist. It came with a range of accessories and tools. The suit's inner surface was lined with a web of capillary tubes, the outer layer rubberised mackintosh. A full set of instructions had accompanied the blueprints and the equipment. Having studied it for hours, Will committed the plan to memory.

At the same moment that he was climbing into the tunnel, Emma was arriving at the mansion.

Hannibal's blueprints contained not only the design of the house itself, but a detailed diagram of the entire street's subterranean layout.

Following the path Hannibal had intended him to take, Will made his way through what appeared to be a large storm conduit. After a few minutes of walking, the headlamp's beam trained in front of his feet, he spotted the doorway.

He leant down, opened the backpack and took out the CODEX. Hannibal's instructions directed him to remove the device from its casing and to slot it sideways into the recess at the centre of the door.

He did so.

The CODEX display rotated to read 5-4-7-8-2. Inside it, the gears whirred, and the door clicked open.

A second passageway lay ahead.

Will went through the instructions. After twenty-five feet, he was to turn the valve on his suit to the second notch, allowing the capillaries to fill with freon. The cooling system was needed to overcome the mansion's temperature-sensitive security system.

After continuing to the trapdoor at the end of the passageway, he was to open it by tapping the numerical sequence displayed on the CODEX — the one gained by opening the first door.

As Will crawled towards the trapdoor, his iPhone started vibrating. He took it out, checked the name, groaned and put it to his ear.

'*Hello... Aunt Edith...* great to hear your voice too,' he said in a forced whisper. 'The reception's bad because I'm in a tunnel. Er, no I'm not in a car... I'm actually on foot right now... well almost on foot. That's right. *Where?* In London. Yeah... No, no it's not foggy here. Aunt Edith, I'm going to have to call you back. You're breaking up... Love you too...'

Will clicked his phone off, stuffed it away, sighed, and shuffled down the tunnel. A moment or two later and he was at the trapdoor. As he crawled through it, Emma was being cleared by security up at ground level. This time, she was taken directly into the drawing-room, where Polkovich was waiting.

'Forgive me for coming alone,' she said. 'My colleague, Mr Fogg, was tied up with some important business.'

The arms dealer looked at her hard.

'More important than eleven million dollar deal?'

Emma didn't respond. She opened the dossier.

'Would you like to see the Z-Grill again, Mr Polkovich?'

The Ukrainian clicked his tongue.

'Have seen it enough. We will wire the money. Give Mr Yenisei bank details.'

The Cossack handed Emma a notepad and a solid gold pen.

Twenty feet below the spot where she was sitting, Will was crawling on his stomach, his body frozen by the refrigerant gas pumping through the capillary suit.

Inching down a slender ventilation duct, he turned right at the end.

Another five yards and he came to a vertical shaft. While preparing the mansion for this day, Hannibal had concealed it by building it onto the back of the chimney flue.

Will struggled to stand upright.

As he did so, his head touched a rope. Hannibal hadn't failed him. The rope was connected to a pulley mounted at the top of the shaft. The instructions were to haul himself up until level with the second floor hatch.

Downstairs, Emma had provided the account number and was waiting for the transfer to be made.

Polkovich was standing near the fireplace, speed-reading a test report on the N2G1-6 strain of ultra-fast-acting bubonic bacteria. He barked something in Russian at his Cossack assistant, who got down on his knees and begged for forgiveness.

An inch at a time Will pulled himself up the shaft, his muscles frozen by freon.

It took ten minutes to get to the hatch, six more than Hannibal had expected. But in his tests he had always had Chaudhury standing by at the top.

Just as Hannibal had maintained, there would be a series of clips holding the hatch in place. As instructed, Will unfastened them in opposing order.

The hatch came away, hanging on its own retaining line.

Will clawed his way through the hole and into the anteroom.

He worked at the door for ten minutes with a lock-pick. However hard he tried, he couldn't turn the barrel inside.

Have you screwed up on this, Hannibal?

A voice in his head replied, telling him to try the handle.

He did so. The door swung open.

It hadn't been locked.

Twisting the refrigerant knob to the third notch as instructed, Will felt his muscles jarring with pain. He dug into the backpack and pulled out a pair of rubber surgical gloves and a small mechanical device.

Like everything else in Hannibal's burglary kit, it had been designed with absolute attention to detail. Once he had strapped it to his wrist, Will measured the ambient temperature.

Emerging from the shaft, he found himself in Polkovich's bedroom. Spacious and light, it was decorated in magnificent Tibetan textiles mounted in frames. There was a display cabinet filled with samurai swords, another with fossilised dinosaur eggs, and there were numerous rare species of orchid on ornate ceramic stands. The bed itself was solid silver, the headboard monogrammed in great golden letters with Polkovich's initials.

As he moved towards the window, Will observed himself from a distance. He was planning to crack a safe in the bedroom of one of the wealthiest men on earth. Get it wrong and the henchmen downstairs would carve him up and feed him to the dogs.

But the strange thing was that he was totally calm.

HANNIBAL'S NOTES HAD EXPLAINED that the safe was located behind a picture, adjacent to the window. Will went over to the wall. A life-size Impressionist study of a child hung awkwardly off-centre. Lifting the frame away, he found it easily. A tempered steel safe, with a combination dial and a pair of symmetrical keyholes hidden by ornate escutcheons.

Removing the CODEX from his pack, Will turned it on and touched it to the front of the safe. It snapped hard to the side, kept in place by electromagnetic force. Checking the ambient temperature, Will turned up the refrigerant another notch.

Although the safe had been designed to be programmed by its current owner, Hannibal had built in a secret master-code to be used in conjunction with the CODEX, one which could never be superseded.

A name quite impossible to forget.

W-I-L-L-I-A-M.

Will tapped the code into the CODEX, swung the handle down, and the door clicked open.

His gloved hands quickly rifled through the contents.

There were what looked like bank bonds, a semi-automatic pistol, various jewellery boxes, and a dossier of photos showing businessmen and politicians engaged in compromising situations.

But no blue diamond.

Downstairs, Polkovich was growing impatient.

'Transaction made or not?!' he barked.

Yenisei the Cossack dabbed a handkerchief to his brow.

'Minute or two more, sir.'

Emma sensed her face beading with perspiration.

Polkovich said her name.

She turned.

'Excuse me?'

'You philatelic dealer for long time?'

Emma's gaze ranged up from the laptop and over onto Polkovich's face.

'Not for as long as I would have liked,' she said with a smile.

The private secretary slapped the desk.

'It is done!'

'Excellent,' Polkovich beamed. 'Confirm money reached correctly.'

'Of course.'

Emma stepped over to the laptop, accessed the login page for the Wachovia Bank and entered Will's account number.

She was hit with a sinking feeling.

Will had forgotten to give her the password.

Swallowing in fear she tried to imagine what Will would have used. The names of his aunts? They would have to be joined together to make up the minimum eight digits. But was it EDITHHELEN or HELENEDITH?

Emma pulled her hands from the keyboard.

She could have simply trusted Polkovich, or asked for a delay. But neither were acceptable alternatives.

What would Will have chosen for the password?

In the circumstances there was only one likely choice.

HANNIBAL FOGG.

As soon as her fingers had typed the name, the account's balance displayed. There it was. A deposit of $11 million from Fabergé Communications, registered in Monte Carlo.

'Thank you, yes, it has reached our account,' said Emma primly, passing over the Z-Grill.

The arms dealer's face clenched tight in a fake smile.

'Mr Yenisei will show you to door,' he said.

Emma was about to leave when a woman strode in.

Elegant in a cruel way, she was wearing a Chanel suit, complemented by an orchid-inspired hat by Louis Mariette.

Weighted down in her cleavage was an immense ocean-blue diamond hanging on a chain.

One hundred and forty

EMMA HAD BEEN IN her suite at Brown's for an hour when Will returned. His face was ashen, his eyes ringed with dark circles.

'Managed to get into the safe,' he said. 'But the diamond… it wasn't there.'

Emma stood up and gave him a hug.

'I've got two pieces of news for you,' she whispered in his ear. 'The first is that, as of 4.57 p.m. this afternoon, you are eleven million dollars richer.'

Will didn't flinch.

'Don't give a damn about the money.'

'That's why I think my second bit of news will be of interest.'

'Yeah?'

'I've found the blue diamond.'

Will's face lit up.

'Where is it?'

'Hanging around Madame Polkovich's neck.'

One hundred and forty-one

WHILE WILL HAD BEEN cracking the safe in Kensington Palace Gardens, Richard Matheson had discharged the duty left to him by Hannibal Fogg.

He was touched by a twinge of pride mingled with an undercurrent of bewilderment. No amount of thinking explained how Fogg could have known of his existence.

As soon as he got to the office, he had put on the Lobbs. Hannibal was right — the wide fitting was suited to his own feet.

Having bundled the lasts up in a plastic Tesco carrier bag, along with the letter, he dropped in at Brown's, handing the package to the doorman.

The lasts were taken up to Chaudhury's room.

That evening, when Will was back, and the heist equipment put away, the manservant brought out the bag.

'This was apparently delivered in the afternoon, marked for my attention, sir.'

Will opened the plastic bag.

'What are these?'

'They appear to be shoe lasts, sir, together with a note from Mr Fogg.'

Will read the letter:

> I take it that you did not read my monograph entitled 'Sexual Dysfunction among the Xema Tribe of the Belgian Congo'. I had left a copy for your attention at my home in Marrakesh, but books do have a way of being moved or tidied back into the shelves.
>
> No matter. I should explain, therefore, that in the Belgian Congo there is a tree known as the 'Omuboro', or the 'African Cherry Orange Tree'. The lasts may be prepared into a decoction, by boiling both pieces of wood in a gallon and a half of water, and evaporating off until only a third of a pint is left. The resulting essence is an exceedingly potent aphrodisiac, a cause of much celebration in long African nights.
>
> It is said that no woman who tastes the beverage can resist the amorous advances of even the most wretched specimen of manhood.

'Hannibal's gone loopy,' said Emma.

'You mean he *went* loopy,' Chaudhury added casually.

Will held the wooden lasts to the lamplight, taking in their gnarled grain.

'He knew the diamond wasn't in the safe,' he muttered coldly.

'What are you talking about?'

'I could have been killed.'

'Well, why then did he go to such great lengths to set up the heist? He even bought the mansion to get you a clear route in.'

Will pushed back his hair and sighed testily.

'All the while he knew the gem was hanging around Mrs Polkovich's neck. And if that wasn't bad enough, he's now sending me wooden feet.'

One hundred and forty-two

THE DAY AFTER HIS visit to Brown's, Matheson opened the morning's *Times* at his work on Pennington Street, only to find a long obituary of Sir Lancelot Beauchamp. The text revealed that Sir Lancelot, who had slipped away in his sleep, had been a British spy.

Picking up the phone, Matheson dialled de Mallois's number. He wanted to break the news to the Comte. It would also be an opportunity to tell him of the letter he had received from Hannibal Fogg.

The phone rang, and rang, but no one picked up.

Perhaps he had gone out to walk the dogs, thought Matheson.

Little did he know that the Comte de Mallois was lying in his salon, face down on the floor, the back of his head smashed in by a Balkan hit-man.

Whimpering, the albino Pekinese were sitting at his feet.

One hundred and forty-three

EVEN IF WILL HAD brewed up the aphrodisiac tea, the question was how he would ever persuade Svetlana Polkovich to drink it.

He and Emma were brainstorming the subject, when Chaudhury asked whether he might have the evening off. He wanted to visit an old school friend, he said, who was living in Elephant and Castle.

Before leaving, he proposed an idea.

'A humble suggestion, sir,' he said respectfully. 'But I believe I may know one temptation that might draw Mrs Polkovich.'

'And what would that be?'

'Every woman's dream.'

'Huh?'

'Eternal youth, sir.'

Will looked the manservant in the eye.

'And how exactly would we arrange that?'

Chaudhury brushed a hair from his lapel.

'Leave it to me,' he said.

One hundred and forty-four

1925

FOR A YEAR AND a half Hannibal Fogg travelled with Chaudhury as his companion. He later described the journey as 'the ultimate exorcism of melancholy'.

Their expedition began on a balmy June morning at Waddon Aerodrome on the outskirts of London. Hannibal had been presented with a captured German biplane, a Fokker D.VII, in the last month of the Great War. Having never had time to fly it, he had always relished the opportunity of getting behind the controls.

On a turbulent flight he piloted the aircraft to Paris, flying low enough to see the rooftops of Amiens, over which Chaudhury disgorged his breakfast.

They stayed in the French capital a single night, dining at Le Train Bleu at Gare de Lyon, before continuing on the Orient Express via Vienna to Constantinople.

An aficionado of railway travel, Fogg had taken the Orient Express so frequently that its bar served a special cocktail bearing his name. A *'Hannibal Fogg'* was equal parts gin, vodka and Cointreau, with a splash of iced vermouth.

Hannibal composed a short ditty, entitled *'Rattle of the Wheels'*, to be played on the bar's grand piano while he sipped the cocktail. The strong beverage proved extremely popular. It was, however, withdrawn at the time of the Great Purge.

Hannibal had taken a pair of compartments — one for himself and another for his manservant. Each one was upholstered in crushed blue velvet and lit by a fashionable crystal chandelier from the House of Lalique.

The train had been delayed by six hours, reaching the Turkish capital in the nick of time for a rendezvous at the Dolmabahce Palace. Having heard of Hannibal's impending arrival, the President, Mustafa Kemal Atatürk, had given orders for a state banquet to be held in his honour.

It was during this sojourn in Constantinople that Hannibal acquired an abundant supply of the rare metal lutetium, from a dealer with offices on the Asian side. He had first heard of the element from his friend, Baron Carl Auer von Welsbach, a noted Austrian mineralogist.

A few years previously, the baron had isolated the metal as an impurity in the mineral ytterbium. Fearful that the lutetium might be mislaid on the continuation of their journey East, Hannibal had it shipped to his home in Marrakesh.

From Constantinople, Chaudhury and he had continued by land to the Caspian Sea, south through Persia, and on eastward to Afghanistan. They had spent eight months in the kingdom, most of it holed up at the northern city of Balkh, the former capital of Alexander the Great.

Hannibal excavated what he believed to be an oracle and, beside it, a fabulous marble pleasure dome. Among the ruins he came across a block of Greek text etched into porphyry. The tablet described the great victories of Alexander, declaring that the Macedonian king had learned the 'Supreme Secret of Man'.

From Afghanistan, they journeyed east up the Khyber Pass into India. Travelling by camel, elephant and in a borrowed yellow Rolls-Royce Tourer, they crossed the subcontinent, reaching Rangoon on the anniversary of Alina's death.

Although still distraught, the explorer appeared to be returning to his old form.

One morning, after they had inspected a factory making lacquer betel boxes in Mandalay, Chaudhury watched as his master shinned up a palm tree and tossed down the coconuts.

There was warmth in Hannibal's voice once again.

One hundred and forty-five

BY CHARMING THE NIGHTSHIFT'S sous chef, Chaudhury secured himself access to the kitchen at Brown's from midnight until six.

He took a large urn, placed the wooden lasts inside, and boiled them as instructed. After several hours of staring at the pot, he was left with a pungent-smelling liquid, the colour of sarsaparilla.

Once it had cooled, he poured it into a Baccarat

crystal decanter which had contained royal jelly bubble bath until a moment before.

At 9 a.m., he picked up the hotel's landline and took a deep breath. Having made a promise to his master, he pulled every imaginable string he could muster in the butlering trade.

Svetlana Polkovich relied on an English servant named Dawes who had been wrongly accused of drunkenness the month before, and was bristling for revenge.

Dawes had let it be known to Svetlana that a brilliant young physician from Switzerland, a Dr Kraettli from Zug, was about to arrive in London with a proven elixir for treating advancing age. Distilled from a rare jungle root, the decoction had been found to strip away years from even the weariest face.

Svetlana Polkovich had risen to the bait, only to be informed blankly that the elixir was so scarce she would have to wait a full year before a dose could be made available to her.

Incensed at having to wait for anything at all, she had given orders for the Swiss doctor to name his price if — and only if — she could be treated that very day.

With Dawes acting as intermediary, it was agreed that Madame Polkovich would come to a private clinic on Harley Street at 4 p.m. the same afternoon, if she agreed to an additional surcharge. The surgery had been rented by the hour, a practice not unusual for visiting quacks.

Giving the security detail the slip, Dawes had escorted Madame Polkovich in the Bentley, having double-checked the blue diamond was hanging around her neck. Fortunately, there was nothing the arms dealer's wife liked more than wearing the gem when out and about.

Arriving at the clinic, they were armed with a leather Gladstone bag, weighed down with wads of crisp £50 notes. As the wife of an arms dealer and energy mogul, Svetlana was used to shopping with undeclared cash.

The surgery itself contained a simple white examination table, a desk, and a chaise longue upholstered in ivory vinyl.

Chaudhury received Madame Polkovich straight away. He had upgraded his butler's uniform for the starched white coat of a physician, straining hard to fill the role of Swiss chemist.

Laid out neatly on the desk were a ruled notebook, a calendar, a cut glass tumbler and a vase of purple gladioli. Turned to face the window so that the crystal caught the light, was the Baccarat decanter.

The arms dealer's wife seemed uninterested in a medical spiel Chaudhury had spent hours rehearsing. She asked only how long it would take for the elixir to work, and whether there would be any side effects.

In a faux Swiss accent, the doctor delivered the appropriate answers.

When he broached the subject of money, Madame

Polkovich opened the Gladstone bag and asked Dr Kraettli to name his price.

'The express treatment is £60,000,' he said, his words sharp with Swiss inflection.

'Help yourself,' replied Svetlana Polkovich.

Having put the money on the desk, Chaudhury poured a tumbler full of the brown liquid, wincing at the foul smell.

The patient knocked it back in a single gulp, grimaced, then burped.

The next thing Chaudhury knew, Madame Polkovich was pulling him onto the chaise longue, her mouth pressed against his. Although he regarded himself as attractive, his looks had not before been rewarded with such instant and infatuated attention.

With Dawes dozing in the waiting-room, the man-servant from Cooch Behar indulged his fantasies and satisfied the tycoon's wife in ways she had not imagined possible.

Then, pledging his own affection for her, the Swiss physician asked whether she would commit to provide him a memento of their tryst. As he posed the question, his fingers brushed against the blue diamond.

Without the slightest hesitation, Madame Polkovich untied the gemstone. Kissing him passionately on the mouth, she pressed the blue diamond into the good doctor's hand.

One hundred and forty-six

EXCUSING HIMSELF SO THAT the patient could dress, Chaudhury hurried into the waiting-room, woke up Dawes and dropped the bundles of banknotes in his lap.

'You've earned this,' he said. 'But if you want to keep it, I suggest you get out in the next fifteen seconds.'

Madame Polkovich's butler charged out onto the street.

As the clinic's door slammed back on its hinges, Chaudhury slipped a hand into the pocket of his white coat and felt the cool, perfect edges of what may well have been the most valuable gemstone on earth.

At that moment, he heard the deranged voice of a woman calling out from behind the closed surgery door. She was begging for another dose of the doctor's miracle medicine.

A wave of primal fear surged through Chaudhury's body, from the top of his head down to his toes.

He had just seduced the wife of one of the most vindictive and dangerous men alive. But far worse than the illicit encounter was the small matter of a €45 million gemstone.

Rushing into the street, Chaudhury hailed a black cab and called Will, instructing him to bring Emma and meet him at the airport.

'Which one?' Will asked.

'Er…' the manservant tried to think.

Polkovich would be on to them within the hour —

that much was certain. After all, you don't get to be an A-grade Russian oligarch without being able to work out super fast what was really going on.

'London City Airport, sir,' he said. 'We will have to get a private jet.'

At Brown's, the senior doorman hailed three black cabs and supervised as the luggage was loaded aboard. In all his years on Albemarle Street, he had never seen such a bizarre accumulation of hand-made suitcases and steamer trunks.

Slipping him a folded ten-pound note, Will was just going to climb into the first taxi, when he heard a commotion on the other side of the street.

He turned.

A woman was lying on the ground, screaming. Bearing over her was a mugger, his face hidden in a hood. One hand was clutching the hilt of a knife, the other grabbing the woman's handbag.

Will got a shot of déjà vu — Market Street, San Francisco, a stone's throw from the Union Bank of California.

Vaulting round the taxi, his right fist clenched, he socked the mugger in the jaw.

'You're the last gentleman alive,' the woman said as Will helped her up and gave her the handbag.

'Happy to help, ma'am,' he said.

LESS THAN AN HOUR after leaving the clinic, Chaudhury had met the others at London City Airport. While

Will signed the paperwork at the Air Charter desk, the luggage was taken away and screened.

Chaudhury looked over in the direction of the toilets.

'Would you mind accompanying me over there, sir?'

Moments later, they were in a cubicle together with the door bolted.

'What's this about?' asked Will.

'Security, sir.'

'As in…'

'As in the fact that Mr Polkovich will hunt us like there's no tomorrow, sir.'

'And…'

'And, he will rip us limb from limb once he finds us.'

Chaudhury breathed in deep.

'Now, would you do me the honour of opening the flight case, sir?'

Clicking the catches, Will pulled back the flaps.

With the case open, the manservant reached into his jacket pocket, and pulled out the stone.

Grabbing his face by the cheeks, Will kissed the top of his head.

'You're a frigging magician!'

Blushing, Chaudhury stiffened his back and regained his composure.

'I must admit that retrieving the stone was not entirely unpleasant, sir.'

As soon as the gem touched the lining of the case, the CODEX started to chime.

Closing the case, Will opened the device and checked the main display:

2°53'00.500N 73°33'00.00E.

'Any guesses?' asked Will, launching Google Maps on his iPhone.

'I would postulate it is in Indonesia, sir.'

Will peered at his iPhone, which was showing an island somewhere off Sumatra. 'How the hell did you know that?' he said. 'And don't give me any baloney about a butler's intuition.'

Chaudhury smiled.

'I shall tell you once we're aboard, sir,' he said.

One hundred and forty-seven

THE CESSNA CITATION X taxied to runway 27 at London City Airport. With its Rolls-Royce engines pushed to full power, it took off over the Thames, banking right into the evening sun.

As the jet's landing gear retracted, a pair of henchmen in the Ukrainian arms dealer's employ reached the Air Charter desk. They demanded to see the roster of flights out that afternoon. When refused on grounds of privacy, they threatened to blow the receptionist's head clean off her shoulders.

The fastest civil aircraft on earth since the retirement of Concorde, the Citation was soon cruising high above the clouds on the long flight east.

It was the first time Will, Emma or Chaudhury had ever been in a private jet. The extra luggage allowance was an obvious perk, especially for anyone travelling with Edwardian steamer trunks.

Another advantage was the service.

The stewardess was an Australian girl with long red hair and the kind of smile toothpaste firms sign up for their advertisements. She served a bottle of vintage Veuve Clicquot wrapped in a starched white cloth. Will took one sip, winced, and asked for a beer instead.

'Don't you like champagne?' she asked.

'Not so much.'

The stewardess laughed.

'You're the first gentleman I've ever had up here who didn't want to drown himself in the stuff. How about some beluga caviar?'

Will was going to shoot her a smart reply, when he remembered what Chaudhury had said back in the cubicle.

'So how did you know we would be heading for Indonesia?' he said.

The manservant took a gulp of champagne, the bubbles fizzing out through his nose. He had been remembering his recent seduction of the Ukrainian billionaire's wife. As if the day hadn't been pleasing enough already, he was now being wined and dined on champagne and beluga caviar.

'Because of something Mr Fogg once told my antecedent, sir,' said Chaudhury.

'What?'

'That his great-great-grandson would one day have possession of the most valuable gemstone in existence, and with it he would fly from Europe to Borneo at almost the speed of sound.'

Will held up his glass of beer.

'A toast,' he said. 'To real friends.'

The three of them clinked glasses.

Chaudhury took another swig of Veuve Clicquot.

'The strange thing is that I never actually believed it would come true,' he said.

THE CITATION REFUELLED TWICE en route, at Cairo and then Colombo. As it soared once again into the blinding sunlight, Chaudhury raised his seat and leant over to Emma.

'I have something for you, miss.'

Emma broke into a smile.

'Is it a big blue diamond by any chance?'

'Not quite as grand, but all the more precious.'

Emma's brow creased quizzically.

'I'm intrigued,' she said.

Chaudhury opened a hidden compartment in the bottom of the flight case and took out a black velvet pouch.

'Instructions were left for me to give you this once we left Colombo.'

'Who's it from?'

'From Mr Fogg.'

Emma seemed overcome. Her eyes welling with tears, she held the pouch in her hand.

'Have a look inside.'

Emma's fingers spread the drawstring apart.

'It's a rosary... an exquisite rosary.'

'I believe that Mrs Fogg prayed with it every day, miss,' the manservant said.

Emma wiped her eyes.

'Well, I shall do the same,' she said.

One hundred and forty-eight

THE CITATION TOUCHED DOWN at Namlea Airport on Buru Island at 6.29 p.m. the next day. After the luggage had been unloaded, Will consulted the CODEX. The machine hadn't yet provided a clue about the final component.

'We've come all this way,' he said vacantly, 'and I have no idea why.'

'Have you tried BURU?' suggested Emma.

'Yeah, but it didn't work.'

Chaudhury cleared his throat.

'Might I suggest CAVIAR?'

Tapping in the word, Will shook his head.

In her pocket, Emma's fingers fondled the rosary.

'Alina, try A-L-I-N-A,' she whispered.

As soon as the name was entered, the CODEX's mechanism came alive.

The display showed a grid reference and the word: G-A-R-U-D-A-M-A-S-K.

FOLLOWING THE COORDINATES, THEY arrived next day at a desolate beach on the southern coast of Buru Island. The sand was pure white, rough to the touch and peppered with fragments of coral-pink seashell.

Fifty yards from the waves, separated by a perfect beach, lay the jungle. Will could hear it loud and clear, a cacophony of birdsong and vibrating insect wings.

Their bare feet disappearing into the sand as they walked, the three travellers made their way down to the water's edge.

Will looked out to sea, paused, and got down on his knees, Emma and Chaudhury standing behind him. Opening the CODEX, he observed the display. Then he checked the iPhone and, after it, Hannibal's cloth-backed map.

'Think I've made a mistake,' he said. 'The grid reference isn't here on the beach.'

'Then where is it?' asked Emma.

Will motioned to the water.

'About two miles that way.'

'Perhaps we ought to double-check it, sir,' urged Chaudhury.

'Have already — twice.'

'Hannibal must have got his bearings off,' said Emma. She looked at the others, realising how unlikely that would be.

As the three of them stood there, staring out at the waves, a hollowed-out wooden canoe made its way silently around the cove. Two men were paddling in time with each other, the sweat on their bare shoulders glistening, home-made oars in their hands.

One of them looked like a local. He was thin and sinewy, his body the product of its environment. The other was a foreigner — as out of place as his companion was at ease. Balding, he had wire-rimmed glasses, and a thick meaty body all covered in sores.

Will, Emma and Chaudhury watched as the pair jumped out in the shallows and rammed the canoe up onto the sand.

Reaching back into the canoe, the local pulled out half a dozen fish, hooked together at the mouth. As soon as he spotted other people, the foreigner made his way over to where they were standing.

'Can't remember the last time I saw gringos down here!' he called, his voice a heavy southern drawl. 'You here for big game fishing?'

Will introduced himself.

'Not exactly,' he said.

'Frank Pittzer, with double a "T". Happy to show you around, or help you get a boat.'

'That's good of you,' said Emma.

'If you can keep up you're welcome for a cocktail.'

'Where's the bar?'

Pittzer jabbed a thumb at the undergrowth.

'In there. 'Bout three miles.'

'Is there a hotel?'

'*Hotel*? You crazy?! I live with the tribe.'

'*Tribe*?' echoed Chaudhury dispiritedly.

'That's right. The Garuda.'

PITTZER'S HOME WAS A shack he had built himself from thick staves of black Java bamboo, dried palm fronds laid on top. It was offset from the centre of the village, and had an improvised terrace tacked onto the front.

'I'm an anthropologist by trade,' he said, pouring bamboo cups of home-brew. 'Been here three years now.'

'What're you researching?'

'The Garuda customs.'

'And do they have any curious ones?' asked Emma. 'You know, any freaky stuff…?'

'They have Sin-eaters,' said Pittzer, 'and you don't get much freakier than that.'

'What are they?'

'In every village there's the shaman who'll swallow the sins of the guilty… for a price.'

'How does that work?'

'Means you can swear, fornicate, drink till you drop, or even kill — and have your sins completely absolved.

522

Hell, it's even better than a Confession booth in church.'

'I could imagine that catching on back home,' said Will.

Pittzer pointed to a hunched figure walking between a nearby row of huts. His face was peppered in pustules, the skin on his back gnarled and burned. His right hand was missing entirely.

'That's him,' he said.

'Jesus Christ.'

'All that from swallowing a few sins?'

Pittzer slugged down a cup of home-made firewater and burped.

'Who said it was a few sins?' he said.

In the silence which followed, Will tried to work out why Hannibal had sent them to a remote island in a forgotten archipelago.

'Do they believe in God?' he asked all of a sudden.

'They put their faith in Mar-ram-ap.'

'What's that?'

'The Great Being, the Balance of the World.'

'Do they worship him?'

'It's beyond worship,' said Pittzer. 'The Garuda are utterly preoccupied with him. They regard him as their communal father, the husband to their wives, their teacher, priest — an all-powerful deity.'

'How do they worship him?'

'They believe he's around them, but they feel his presence most strongly in the temple at Mulam-ya.'

'Where's that?'

'That way… up in the hinterland.'

Pittzer poured another round of drinks.

'Most people have never been to the temple, and certainly never inside.'

'Why not?'

'Because it's filled with giant hornets. Get stung and even the Sin-eater can't help you.'

'So what do they do if they can't worship at the temple?'

'They worship an icon instead — say it represents the power of Mar-ram-ap. You find it everywhere in the village: carved into the doors, on the altars in homes, tattooed on chests and backs.'

'How does it look?'

'It's kind of rectangular, and almost looks like a monogram of an F and an H.' Pittzer pulled back his sleeve. 'Got one done as a way of blending in.'

As soon as Will saw the symbol, he knew they were in the right place. When Pittzer stepped out to greet the tribal chief, Will leaned over to Emma.

'Not an F and an H, but an H and an F,' he said.

One hundred and forty-nine

1925

LAID OUT ON THE floor of a grand longhouse, the building camouflaged in dense foliage, was a banquet fit for a god.

There were roasted piglets, giant-sized lobsters, grilled Borneo shark, and banana platter leaves adorned with exotic fruit — papaya, mangosteen and rambutan.

Seated on a carved wooden throne looking down at it all with disinterest, was Hannibal. He was wearing a feather headdress, his body smeared in war-paint.

A scantily clad maiden scooped out the eye of the shark and dropped it into his mouth. At the same moment, a second maiden entered the longhouse and set about massaging the explorer's shoulders.

All the while, members of the tribe trooped past the longhouse, bowing down as they neared the door. Some of them bore gifts of food, others offered simple objects whittled from coconut shells.

When Hannibal could eat no more, the remains of the feast were bustled away, to be distributed among the destitute.

As soon as the last platter had gone, a straight-backed man ascended the steps into the longhouse. He was barefoot, wearing what appeared to have once been tweed trousers, his chest clothed in a fibrous shirt.

'The chief has requested the honour of an audience with you, sir.'

Hannibal opened one eye, yawned, and pulled himself upright.

'Very well, send him in, Chaudhury.'

Cowering, a tribal warrior crawled into the longhouse, his face a mask of worry. So fearful was he of the

Englishman, that he dared not make eye contact with him.

Reclining back on his throne, Hannibal greeted the chief in the Garuda tongue and motioned for him to approach. The tribal chief crouched low on the floor, a short distance from the base of the throne.

As was the tradition, silence prevailed until the Mar-ram-ap, the Great Being, was ready for the palaver to begin.

'Yes, my chief,' Hannibal said at length in Garuda. 'What is your concern?'

Averting his eyes, his face flushed with fear, the chief replied:

'Oh Great Being, Exalted One, forgive me for troubling you with the trepidations of mortal men, but there is a matter I wish to address.'

Hannibal Fogg gazed listlessly out at the jungle.

'Speak!'

Cowering like a dog kicked hard in the belly, the chief stammered:

'Oh Supreme One, in the time of the ancestors, when the ocean swallowed our world, we moved to higher ground. And now, there have been omens that the Great Wave will once again devour us.'

Hannibal listened, his face expressionless. After all, it would not have been appropriate for a deity to show emotion.

After a prolonged hush, he asked what exact omens

had been seen in the village.

The chief's eyes widened with terror.

'A pig was born without any feet,' he said, 'and a chicken was found to have two hearts.'

The Great Being remained remote and emotionless. Eventually he replied in a deep voice:

'To protect against the danger,' he said, 'you will build a temple in the hinterland according to precise plans which shall be provided. One single deviation and…'

The chief looked up, making eye contact with the Great Being for the very first time. Such was his sense of anticipation that his heart missed a beat.

'…and the end of the world shall befall you!' boomed Hannibal Fogg.

One hundred and fifty

PITTZER LED THE WAY through the jungle into the island's hinterland, his machete chopping vines and foliage as he went.

Will, Emma and Chaudhury followed behind in single file, moving clumsily through the tangled undergrowth.

It took two more hours to reach the rocky promontory on which the temple had been built.

There was a sense life had stood still there for decades, since the stone blocks had been heaved up from the makeshift quarry below.

By the time they reached the sanctuary, they were all drenched in perspiration, their backs covered in sweat beads. Climbing up on to the outcrop, they got a clear view over the jungle and out to sea.

Pittzer halted short of the temple itself — which was another thirty feet up a granite bluff.

'This is where I leave you,' he said.

'Are you frightened?'

'You bet I am,' the anthropologist crowed. 'This is forbidden ground. Don't forget,' he said, turning, 'it's protected by hornets.'

Will touched Emma on the shoulder.

'You and Chaudhury go back with him,' he said. 'I'm doing this one alone.'

'Are you crazy? Of course we're coming!'

'I'm immune to insect stings,' Will explained. 'Don't know why, but I am.'

Emma sighed.

'I'm sure we'll be fine.'

'No,' said Will firmly. 'You've both gotta leave me. I'll see you back at the village when I'm done.'

Leaning forward, Emma hugged him, crushing his ribs.

'You take care,' she said.

'Holler if you need us, sir,' added Chaudhury.

A minute or two later, Will's boots were searching for footholds among the rocks, his fingers digging into leverage points as he scaled the bluff.

The humidity didn't make the task any easier. Stifling his breathing, it caused his head to spin. He got a flash of his great-aunts sitting in their comfy chairs back in Oakland, breathing in the scent of honeysuckle. Then, pulling himself up the last few feet, he saw his dorm room in SFSU. He had almost forgotten the life left far behind.

Cloaked in a screen of palms, the temple's ash-grey walls were overgrown in vines. Twisted and contorted, they doubled back on themselves — layers upon layers. A great monument of stone, the construction must have been fifty feet high. The rear was lost in foliage, the front bathed in stems of yellow and red heliconia flowers.

Cautiously, Will made his way towards the portal.

Set in the middle, at chest height, was the sacred sign of the Garuda tribe — a symbol known to him as the monogram of Hannibal Fogg.

A little lower down, offset to the side, was a second symbol: a rectangular box bisected by a line — the Egyptian hieroglyph for 'house'.

Glancing at the back of his hand, Will looked at the lapis lazuli ring Hannibal had left him. Working out what to do, he nudged it to the hieroglyph on the door.

Nothing happened at first…

But then, very gradually, the great portal began to draw back, against a rasping sound of stone on stone.

Wedging a rock in place so that the door could not be sealed behind him, Will stepped inside.

The temple had a long tapered hall, a wooden roof

and polished stone floor. At the narrow end was a raised altar, crafted from a vast slab of pumice.

But it was the walls which caught Will's attention.

Set into them, on either side of the nave, was a series of impressive stained glass windows, through which jungle sunlight streamed.

Moving down the nave, Will took in the scenes one at a time.

The first depicted a church — not in the jungle but lodged at the top of a precipice. Beside it was a double helix: the Ladder of Mithras. The next window showed the Hands of God, set against a backdrop of human symbolism. The third portrayed the Tumi dagger of the Incas and, the fourth, the Orisha Stone.

Will turned to the opposite side of the nave, where the symbols continued.

As he stepped over to focus on the detail of the Prayer Wheel of Kublai Khan, the temple filled with butterflies — thousands of them, cascading out from fissures in the walls.

Lost in a blizzard of multi-coloured wings, Will caught a glimpse of the blue diamond depicted in stained glass.

Beyond it was a last panel.

Surrounded by Prussian-blue waves was a mask fashioned in the shape of a magnificent bird.

Another step forward and the butterflies vanished.

Approaching the altar, Will wondered whether they had existed at all.

Ascending a flight of white marble steps, he reached the altar itself.

Lying on the surface of the volcanic rock was a cylindrical tube, crafted from silver.

TAKING IT IN BOTH hands, Will twisted it, scrutinising the strange repeating pattern etched into the surface. For some reason it reminded him of his parents' funeral, and of the first time he had looked into Emma's eyes.

Prising off the end, he found a letter.

It was written in English in a familiar hand.

My dear William, were there more time, I would regale you with tales of how, by strange coincidence, I have become regarded as a deity in the eyes of the Garuda tribe.

But, alas, time is of the essence.

I must ask you to read the directions on the reverse of this letter only once you have reached the shrine.

Leave at once!

The reason is simple: to prevent the wrong person from appropriating this amulet in the decades that separate us, the tribesmen down in the village believe — quite rightly — that, by entering the Temple of the Great Being Mar-ram-ap, they will release a swarm of Vespa mandarinina, the giant Asian hornet.

Although aware of the fact that, like all males of our line, you will most likely be immune to their sting,

*I would imagine that encountering the swarm would
be exceedingly unpleasant.*

*By the time you have spent a little time regarding
the artwork between here and the door, opened this
cylindrical container and read thus far, the hornets
will have woken from their slumber.*

So, grasp the letter, and run like the wind!

Affectionately yours,

Hannibal

WILL'S EARS FILLED WITH the sound of insect wings.

Not a drowsy summer meadow bumble-bee buzzing, but a ferocious orchestra of raw terror.

He swivelled round.

Careering at him from all directions were tens of thousands of giant hornets, the size of golf balls. The temple was filled with them.

Overcome with a sense of panic, Will tossed the cylinder to the floor, grabbed the letter and fled.

The hornets followed.

He scrambled back down the rocks into the under-growth, through the twisting vines and over fallen trees. Tripping, regaining his balance, charging, arms flailing.

The buzzing grew louder.

And louder.

Then, as he clambered over a tree stump, the first of the hornets made contact with his flesh.

It was like being slugged with a cricket bat. The first sting was quickly followed by another… and another… and by twenty more. He screamed out in pain as he ran.

Miraculously, the swarm vanished.

His head twitching left and right in shock, Will crumpled into a ball at the foot of a coconut palm.

A full hour passed before his breathing calmed.

Once near the village, he pulled out the letter, turned it over, and read:

I do hope the suffering was not too terrible, William. As you have no doubt already learned, there was once a city located a little due south of the beach, submerged by an earthquake in antiquity. The ruins lie deep under the ocean. Despite numerous attempts, and having employed my own aquatic breathing mechanism, I have been unable to dive down to a sufficient depth. My efforts have been hampered by toxic levels of hydrogen sulphide, released from the sea floor by volcanic action.

If my calculations are correct, there will be a small window of time in which the sacred Garuda Mask may be retrieved from the seabed. The ocean will be drawn, allowing approximately 21 minutes and 15 seconds to enter the submerged city, retrieve the mask, and make an escape, before the ruins are destroyed forever by the full force of a tsunami.

As ever, I have attempted to pave the way with a little preparation, but much rests on your own skill, William.

The experience you have gained thus far should, I hope, stand you in good stead for this, the greatest challenge of all. There is one last piece of equipment I am sending you. Set the CODEX to the saddest date you know and follow the instructions.

HGF

One hundred and fifty-one

AT DAWN NEXT MORNING, Frank Pittzer left his shack armed with a machete. He strode off into the jungle. To anyone who might have seen him it would have appeared he was heading off for the call of nature. But tucked under his shirt was an Iridium satellite phone.

Ducking down behind a tree, he switched it on and waited for the unit to fire up. Eventually, the screen came alive, its yellowy-green display reflecting over Pittzer's face. Selecting a number from the contacts list, he flipped up the antenna and waited for the satellites to log on.

A minute later he was connected with a secretive agency in the Balkans, with an enduring preoccupation with the Alexander Mechanism and Hannibal Fogg.

'Code reference?' asked a female operator.

'Nine-two-four-Alpha-Delta-Foxtrot.'

'Confirm: Nine-two-four-Alpha-Delta-Foxtrot.'

'Code reference confirmed.'

'Setting code?'

'GARUDA: that's Golf-Alpha-Romeo-Uniform-Delta-Alpha.'

The operator repeated the code word.

'Setting code confirmed.'

'Thank you, Garuda, I shall connect you now…'

One hundred and fifty-two

WILL STOOD NEAR THE water, bare feet sinking into the wet sand. He had been there for an hour, eyes on the horizon.

'So do I just wait until the Red Sea parts?' he said brusquely when Emma came over.

'Frank's grilled some fish with Chaudhury. Come join us,' she said.

'But what if the water rolls back? I've got to be ready.'

Putting her arm around Will's shoulder, Emma twirled him one-eighty to face the trees.

'He'd have sent you a sign.'

'How can you be so sure?'

Emma did a double take.

'We're talking about Hannibal Fogg, are we not?'

Pittzer skewered a chunk of sea bream and dropped it

onto a banana leaf.

'It's called Ikan Panggang. Watch out for the bones, they're like needles.'

'Thanks.'

'How 'bout you…?'

'*Chaudhury.*'

'Don't you have a first name?'

'Everyone just calls him "Chaudhury",' said Will.

Pittzer grinned.

'Doesn't he have a tongue of his own?'

The manservant licked his upper lip timidly.

'My first name… it's Mihir.'

'Well, Mihir, it's time you lightened up, let your hair down.'

Chaudhury looked over at Will, then at Pittzer.

'I think that might be a little inappropriate,' he said stiffly.

'Tell me, Frank,' Will asked, 'have you ever heard of the Garuda Mask?'

Pittzer looked up.

'Sure I have. The tribe are obsessed with it.'

'What do they say?'

'That it's made from dark green jade, and that it was worn by the King of the Underworld.' He paused, took a bite of fish, and added: 'They believe it's conjured from what they call water magic.'

'Meaning?'

'Meaning it can bring the dead back to life.'

'Where is it?' asked Emma.

'Out there somewhere — under the waves.'

'In the ocean?'

Pittzer skewered another chunk of sea bream.

'In the city under the waves,' he said.

That evening, Will sat alone, away from the others, trying to make sense of all the loose ends. Above him, the stars were more dazzling than on any night he could remember, millions and millions of them, like salt sprinkled over a blackboard.

He thought about his great-aunts, and the way they quarrelled about nothing at all. And he thought about the woman he had seen mugged on Market Street. After that, he wondered how exactly the Alexander Mechanism might have worked.

But most of all, he pondered how his life had changed — stretched from a narrow line into full bandwidth. Gazing up at the Big Dipper, he thanked the universe, and said a prayer for his parents. Their death had been the most painful time of his life.

His saddest day.

How could Will have forgotten the last line of Hannibal's message?

Running over to the CODEX, he tapped in a date: 29th April 2005 — the day his parents had perished.

The gears began to turn, grinding in a way they had not moved before. The CODEX was growing warmer. Will could feel it, even through the leather case.

Squinting in the darkness, he read a set of instructions as they rolled into view, letter by letter.

Although apparently not in code, they still didn't make sense.

But then, as Will pondered it, in Hannibal's cloak and dagger world, very little made any sense at all.

One hundred and fifty-three

As LONDON'S BIG BEN chimed four, a tattered manila envelope was carried unceremoniously upstairs, in a grotesquely modern building half a mile from the Houses of Parliament. Following a series of curious alerts, the envelope had been dispatched from a secretive classified unit located in the vaults beneath the Home Office.

On the outside were stencilled the words 'TOP SECRET'.

Five minutes after reaching the department, the envelope was on the desk of the Home Secretary. She had just finished a long and painful meeting on anti-terrorism. Sipping a cup of Guatemalan blend, she cursed the day she had entered government.

'What's that?' the Home Secretary asked her secretary.

'It was sent up from Classified Storage A.'

A silver letter opener sliced the envelope down the side.

Inside was a single sheet of white paper. Folded three times, it appeared to be very old indeed.

Sipping her coffee without looking up, the Home Secretary read the typewritten text.

4th March 1912

To whom it may concern:

The government has a continuing duty to track the components of the Alexander Mechanism and, to that end, an appropriate apparatus has been long established. If this letter is brought to the attention of a departmental head, it most probably indicates that a descendant of Hannibal Fogg is working to reassemble the components.

Government is advised to strive to make certain that the Mechanism is not reconfigured. Should it be so, the political balance of the Empire will be de-stabilised in the most spectacular way.

I leave it to you to understand the importance of the situation at hand, and to act accordingly. Faithfully yours,

G. K. L.

One hundred and fifty-four

WILL WAS AWAKE LONG before dawn.

By the time the first rays of sunlight had broken through the jungle, he had made a series of fires down the beach, using kindling and driftwood. From ground level they looked quite random. There were more than a dozen of them, the damp wood spitting sparks up into the cool morning air.

'What are you doing?' Emma called, stumbling down onto the beach.

'Signalling.'

'Signalling *who*?'

Will glanced at his iPhone. Slipping it away confidently, he held his ear out to the sky.

'For that…'

'What?'

'Listen.'

Emma strained to concentrate. Her ears picked up the roar of the waves and the chatter of cockatoos in the high branches of the forest.

But there was another sound, too.

It was so faint it was almost inaudible, a hum… like the background noise a refrigerator makes, the kind you never quite hear because it's always there.

As she listened, the humming grew louder.

Every second it was twice as loud again, until it sounded like one of the hornets up at the temple.

Craning their necks back, they both scoured the sky.

'Don't see anything.'

'*There!*'

Will pointed at a dot way out over the horizon, where water became sky.

A minute later, the silver fuselage of an immense aircraft, a C-130 Hercules, had come into sight as it banked into the morning light.

'They've seen the signal,' said Will. 'Thank God for that.'

Emma clapped her hands.

'What's going on?!'

Will didn't reply. Instead, he ran forwards until his ankles were in the ocean, his face following the plane.

Another couple of minutes and the Hercules had made a full three-sixty. It was out over the sea again. The pilot eased the throttle back. The propellers slowed, and the cargo door at the rear dropped down.

No more than a speck, an object was falling through the clear air, plunging fast in the direction of the water.

'What the…?'

'Wait and see,' cried Will.

Halfway between the aircraft and the waves, a trio of parachutes deployed, blinding white canopies billowing outwards as they caught the wind.

Dangling below them, an enormous wooden crate was swinging to and fro.

'It's gonna land on the beach!' bawled Emma.

The crate descended rapidly, colliding into the sand fifty feet from where they were standing.

Will ran forwards, cut away the parachutes and gathered them up. Then he marched over to the crate, flipped up what looked like the cover to a fuse-box and punched in an eight-digit numerical code:

29-04-19-98.

In sequence, a dozen explosive bolts fired.

The front of the crate was blown clean away.

Following Will, Emma peered in.

Lost in shadows was a vehicle.

At the front was a raised silver radiator, crowned by the Spirit of Ecstasy figurine.

Beyond a giant-sized engine were dual yoke-style controls, a back row of seats and, after them, an extremely large sealed box made from oiled bridle leather.

As far as Will could make out, there were no wheels at all. Instead, the vehicle's underside was enveloped in a farrago of brass pipes, furling up over the bodywork and into the engine.

Emma's hand brushed over the Spirit of Ecstasy.

'Is it a Rolls-Royce?' she asked incredulously.

'Of course it is,' Will replied at once.

'I get the feeling Hannibal approved of nothing else.'

Will looked Emma in the eye.

'It's not any old Rolls,' he said. 'It's one of a kind.'

One hundred and fifty-five

THE HOME SECRETARY HAD forgotten about the letter brought up from Classified Storage A. Putting it down to colonial hysteria from another age, she had asked her secretary to 'take it along the hall', a euphemism for having it destroyed. By five o'clock on the day it was opened, the envelope and its contents had been shredded and then incinerated.

Three days passed.

The Home Secretary arrived early for work, Big Ben striking eight in the distance. So accustomed was she to the chimes, she didn't hear them at all.

Through the morning she worked on a speech due to be delivered on international terrorism in Brussels the next week. Writing had never been her strong point. She was sitting at her desk with an online thesaurus open, trying to find yet another synonym for the word 'evil', when there was a rap at the door.

'Come in.'

The door opened. Her secretary was standing there.

'What is it, Flo?'

'A car's arrived for you.'

'From where?'

'From the M.O.D.'

BY A QUARTER TO nine, the Home Secretary was sitting in the upstairs briefing room at 10 Downing Street. She

543

was wondering why an armoured vehicle had been sent to drive her the short distance, and why soldiers had been posted outside the Prime Minister's residence.

At five minutes to ten, four senior officers entered, along with the Prime Minister and a handful of her closest staff. There was none of the usual joviality, no laughter or smiles.

The Prime Minister took a seat at the head of the table. She looked drawn, as if she hadn't slept in days.

'This is an emergency COBRA meeting,' she announced in a cold voice. 'Let the record state who is present: Myself, Rear Admiral Phipps, General Sir John Whiteman, General Hackman-Jones, Group Leader Lambert, the Home Secretary, and the Ministers for Terrorism and Defence, in addition to my private security team.'

The Prime Minister took a sip of mineral water and cleared her throat.

'Thank you all for coming at such short notice,' she said. 'I would not have bothered you, believe me, but this is a matter of national security — one which affects us all. We are regarding it as "Critical". Now, I would be grateful if, Sir John, you might fill us in on the current situation.'

Rising to his feet, General Sir John Whiteman stiffened his back and thrust out his chest, allowing the rows of medal ribbons to catch the light.

'Thank you, Prime Minister,' he said in a stony voice.

'What I am about to tell you is classified at the highest level. Although scarcely believable, it's apparently completely true. About a century ago the British government learned that an ancient machine, known as the "Alexander Mechanism", had been created in antiquity for the purpose of unifying mankind with God.

'The machine was supposedly the reason Alexander the Great was able to conquer the known world without defeat. In the aftermath of his death, it was essentially defused, specific pieces having been removed and concealed. As we understand it, those who hid it hoped that sometime far in the future the various components would be reinstated when humanity was sufficiently ready.'

The general leaned back on his heels, taking in the politicians one by one. Hailing from a long line of soldiers, he despised civilians.

'That is where we come to Hannibal Fogg,' he said.

The Prime Minister winced.

'Hannibal *who*?'

'Hannibal Fogg. He was an explorer, an author, and a linguist too. At the turn of the last century, Fogg was understood to be searching for the components. He seemed to have believed that the business of reuniting the Alexander Mechanism was an ancestral duty. We did our best to discredit him, asserting he was a spy. We arrested him and purged his published work. Despite our best efforts, in the years since his disappearance, Fogg attracted an almost cult following.'

The general swallowed hard.

'There's even a Hannibal Fogg Society on the internet,' he said. 'As well as blogs devoted to his life and work. It's incredible, of course, because we have spent millions doing all we could to make Fogg out to be a fictional character and a hoax.'

'He sounds like a crackpot,' said the Minister of Defence.

'Perhaps. It's hard to be sure. What is certain though is that Fogg came very close to his goal.'

'To reconfiguring the machine... the Alexander Mechanism?'

'Precisely.'

'Forgive me, General,' the Home Secretary called out, 'but what matter is this Mechanism to us?'

The officer looked at her sternly.

'If the Mechanism is restarted,' he said, his eyes glaring, 'then the political balance of the world may well be destabilised in the most spectacular way.'

Remembering the letter she had received from the classified archives, the Home Secretary hoped no one would bring it up.

'What's the current situation?' the Prime Minister asked.

'It seems that Hannibal Fogg left information which would allow his descendant to locate the components and return them to the machine.'

'What descendant?'

General Sir John Whiteman glanced at the dossier open in front of him.

'Fogg's great-great-grandson,' he said. 'His name is William Fogg.'

One of the Prime Minister's advisers raised a hand.

'Is he British?'

'No,' said the general, 'I regret to say he's American.'

'Then why don't we let them deal with it in Washington?'

General Sir John wrung his hands together anxiously.

'I trust we are all in agreement that this is a rather British affair and ought to be handled by us.'

'So what to do?'

'Prime Minister,' said the general, 'I suggest sending in CRU, the Covert Reconnaissance Unit.'

'With what objective?'

'Either to capture or destroy the Mechanism.'

The Prime Minister frowned.

'Do we know where it is?'

'We shall find it.'

'How?'

'By following Mr Fogg Jr. We have been tracking him for weeks. He's been bouncing around like a rubber ball.'

'*So?*'

'As we understand it, he's about to get his hands on the last of the components.'

'What does that mean, General?'

'It means, Prime Minister, that it's only a matter

of time before Fogg has what he needs to restart the Mechanism.'

'How long?'

'We can't be certain.'

'How long do you need to mobilise the Covert Reconnaissance Unit?'

'Three hours at most.'

'Where are they?'

'At their base at Akrotiri.'

The Prime Minister stood up, her eyes trained on the desk blotter squared before her. Slowly, she looked up, scanned the room, pushed back her shoulders, and replied:

'Have them ready to deploy when Fogg appears to be nearing the Mechanism. Do you understand?'

General Sir John Whiteman nodded.

'Yes, Prime Minister.'

One hundred and fifty-six

THE ROLLS-ROYCE SLIPPED OUT onto the sand on its own hydraulic pallet. Set against the jungle backdrop, it looked like an invention from another world.

The vehicle was dominated by a V-12, 14-litre Falcon aviation engine, built at Rolls-Royce's fighter aircraft factory.

As he walked around the car, Will understood how

his great-great-grandfather had been lauded as a deity by the Garuda tribe. They must have been utterly amazed by him.

Having heard the C-130, Chaudhury came running out from the undergrowth, his arms up in the air, his head thrown back in laughter.

Pittzer shot out from the undergrowth, too, and tore across the beach. Not because of the Rolls but because of the tribe.

'They're not happy!' he cried. 'Not happy at all!'

'What's wrong?'

The anthropologist took in the vehicle and threw up his hands.

'There's disorder in their heaven!' he shouted. 'The sacred amulets have been defiled and they're mad as hell.'

'Are they coming down here to cut our throats?'

'Quite the opposite,' Pittzer replied, wide-eyed. 'They're running up to the hills.'

'Whatever for?' Emma asked.

'The shaman's telling them there's going to be a "wave-mountain".'

Will looked round.

'A tsunami?!'

'Yeah…'

'Chaudhury, help me get our luggage into this contraption.'

'But it doesn't even have wheels!' Pittzer bellowed.

'When did a boat need wheels?' said Emma.

Will cleared his throat.

'Almost right,' he said. 'Except this isn't a boat.'

Taking the right yoke in his hand, he pushed the ignition button. Instantly, the aviation engine groaned, but didn't turn over.

'Looks like your battery's dead.'

Pittzer hurried back across the beach, heading for the jungle.

'See you later. I've got to calm things down or else I'm screwed.'

The Indian manservant from Cooch Behar lifted the cowling and fell back at the sheer size of the machine. Searching the mass of intertwined pipes and vents for the carburettor, he adjusted it. His family had owned more Rolls-Royces than he cared to remember. The vehicles were favoured for tiger shoots because of their suspension and the size of their running boards.

Having tightened the carburettor's springs, Chaudhury furled the engine's cowling back down.

'Would you try the ignition again, sir?'

Will got in and pressed the starter button on the dash. Nothing happened at first. Then, after a delay, the Falcon engine turned over once, then again, and again, belching out clouds of dense oily smoke.

Steadily, the cushion inflated with air and the Rolls-Royce rose up off the sand.

'It's a hovercraft!' yelled Chaudhury triumphantly, his voice barely audible. 'It's a Rolls-Royce hovercraft!'

EMMA'S LINE OF SIGHT ranged beyond the car, down to the ocean.

'That's funny,' she shouted above the thunderous wall of noise.

'What is?'

'The tide's going out.'

'So what?'

'Well it's almost high tide. So it's supposed to be coming in.'

She walked down to the water. As she advanced, the ocean retreated.

Will looked round.

'What the…?'

'I believe it's called drawback, sir,' said Chaudhury. 'It precedes a…'

'A tsunami!'

Will sprinted down the beach.

'Quick! We have to get the stuff!'

A siren blasted loud and shrill above the noise of the Falcon engine. Will jerked round.

Chaudhury was racing the Rolls hover-car across the sand.

When he and the luggage were aboard, Will took the controls and steered the vehicle round one-eighty. Aiming at the horizon, they shot forwards across the beach and onto the flats where the ocean had so recently been.

Having walked far out into the wasteland, Emma was picking up shells, marvelling at the secret world that had been revealed. She heard the engine behind her and turned.

'Quick! Get in!' Will roared, struggling to apply the brakes.

The vehicle glided to a halt, its voluminous rubber air cushion deflating just long enough for Emma to get aboard. Will forced the accelerator down and the hovercraft surged forwards, the engine deafening beyond belief.

On the dash, a panel of gauges and dials rotated into place. The central instrument was the largest. Its digital display seemed to be winding backwards.

'What's that?'

'It appears to be a timer, sir,' said Chaudhury. 'It's set at twenty-one minutes.'

'It's counting down,' said Will.

As the hovercraft shot forwards towards the horizon at breakneck speed, the ocean retreated even more.

On the coral reef below, rainbow fish, crabs and other sea life floundered about in the mud.

As the water pulled back, the outline of a ruined city emerged.

'How the hell are we going to find a jade mask in all of that?' shouted Will above the noise of the engine.

'It's like searching for a needle in a haystack.'

'Think we may be in luck,' countered Emma.

Leaning in, she tapped a small dial on the dash.

'What's that?'

552

'I may be way wrong, but it looks like an FMMLU.'

'Huh?'

'A Ferro-Magnesium Magnetometer Location Unit.'

Will and Chaudhury looked at Emma in disbelief.

'And what good's that going to do us?'

'It'll locate a concentration of the isotope in nephrite, the appropriate form of jade,' she said.

Spotting a giant boulder straight ahead, Will jarred the yoke to the right. The vehicle banked sharply, missing the rock by inches.

Will thrust the pedal to the metal.

'I took enough chemistry to know you have to have some kind of index value for…'

'For the ferro-magnesium… the value of nephrite?'

'Yeah… something like that.'

Emma pinched a forefinger and thumb to the end of her nose.

'Its valence is eight.'

'How d'you know that?'

Emma jabbed a hand at a neat brass plaque fixed to the dash.

'Because it's written right there,' she said.

One hundred and fifty-seven

FOLLOWING THE SHAMAN, THE tribe had climbed up to the Temple of the Great Being.

Pittzer had remained down in the village, where he pulled out the satellite phone.

Once again, he underwent the security screening, before being patched through.

'Rogers here.'

'Rogers, this is Pittzer. Target Exposed! Repeat Target Exposed!'

There was silence at the other end.

'OK Pittzer, be advised to monitor Target. Report back on SGF. Channel 6 at 17.00 hours.'

CHAUDHURY SET THE FMMLU to digit eight on the atomic scale.

'Is it giving a reading?' Will asked.

'It appears to be in tracking mode, sir.'

'Tracking the jade concentration?'

'Yes, sir.'

Will glanced at the timer.

'Well it had better damn well hurry up. We've only got fifteen minutes until the tsunami hits.'

Thrusting the control yoke to the left, he skirted around the western edge of the city.

The main ruins were concentrated in a deep bowl between two hills. Clearly visible, the remnants were smothered under a grim mantle of slime.

On one side of the city there stood what looked like a ruined temple — great stone pillars tumbled by earthquakes in antiquity. Opposite was a collapsed palace — a homage to power and greed.

Will navigated up to a vantage point, from which the three of them peered down in awe.

'Are you getting a signal?'

'A faint one, sir.'

'Which direction?'

'South-south-west.'

Jerking the yoke to the left, Will jammed the accelerator down. Listing sharply, the hover-car surged forwards through the ruins.

'Getting stronger,' said Chaudhury.

Emma pointed straight up.

'Look at that!'

Towering above the vehicle was a cenotaph. It was topped by a magnificent bird, its wings outstretched, a human prey clutched in its talons.

'The Garuda!' cried Will.

'A touch to the west, sir.'

'Are we on track?'

Chaudhury nodded.

'Think so.'

As the Rolls-Royce hovercraft faltered over a pool of sea water, Chaudhury pressed his ear to the Location Unit, motioning for Will to slow down. The instrument was clicking like a Geiger counter picking up radiation.

The Rolls slip-slided to a halt.

'Must be in those ruins over there,' said Emma.

'The one with the staircase?'

'Yes.'

Will leapt down.

'Bring her around to the other side,' he shouted, scurrying over the blocks of stone.

As quickly as he could, he climbed up to the highest point.

Even if he had been able to dislodge the blocks, there was so much seaweed and mud that spotting the mask would be all but impossible.

Chaudhury took in the timer: 11 minutes 23 seconds.

He scanned the controls.

To the right of the yoke was a row of miniature brass levers. They were protected by a cover that prevented them from being accidentally knocked.

The personification of caution, Chaudhury would not normally have gambled. But he knew Hannibal would have planned meticulously, having realised full well the difficulty of the mission.

'There must be some way we can help Will,' Emma said.

It was the prompt Chaudhury needed.

Flipping up the protective cover, he jerked down the first lever.

A hydraulic lance shot out from the Rolls-Royce's left side. But the ruins were on the right. By gently manipulating the lever, Chaudhury found he could retract the lance and deploy it on the other side.

Calling out to Will, he urged him to make use of the hydraulic lance. Grabbing it, Will found the device was designed to lever away the blocks of stone — providing him entry into the building.

Chaudhury tugged down the second lever.

As soon as he did so, a stream of detergent blasted through the lance, transforming it into a high-pressure hose. Down below, Will used the fluid to wash away the mud.

He scanned right and left.

The chamber's stone walls were adorned with hieroglyphs featuring a great mythical bird. As Will searched desperately for the mask, Chaudhury nudged the third lever down.

The FMMLU clicked out of its holder.

Snatching it, Chaudhury scrambled out of the hover-car, up over the rocks and into the chamber where Will was searching.

The Location Unit clicked wildly.

'Quick! Over here!'

Chaudhury threw the unit to Will.

Guided by the sound, Will ran through into a passage, diving down into the sludge.

He was gone a full minute.

In an explosion of breathlessness, his head emerged.

Covered in seaweed and mud, an object was clutched in his hands:

The Garuda Mask.

By the time they were back at the vehicle, the timer read 5 minutes 31 seconds.

'There should be enough time,' said Will, pressing the ignition button.

The hover-car's cushion inflated, mud splashing out from under it. Will yanked the steering yoke round to the right. A second later the vehicle turned.

'All we have to do now is to get out of the...'

His words were cut short by the roar of another engine.

'Over there!' shouted Emma.

They all lurched round to look.

Heading straight for them from across the ruined city was a state-of-the-art military hovercraft.

'What the Devil?!' shouted Chaudhury.

'Must be the Magi,' responded Will, wrenching the yoke round and slamming his foot down. 'They were waiting till we got the last component.'

'Don't understand how they found us,' said Emma.

'Just like Hannibal said, they're everywhere. They never tried to get us while there were still components to find. They wanted all the work done for them.'

Gritting his teeth, Will heaved the yoke to the left. The rudder kicked in, fishtailing the vehicle round.

But, as it swerved in an arc, the engine went dead.

'Oh my God.'

'Hope this contraption's armoured!' grunted Will.

Chaudhury leapt out, unbuckled the cowling and loosened the carburettor springs.

'Try again now.'

'No joy.'

'What about now?'

'Nothing…'

Will looked straight ahead. The jet-black hovercraft was racing towards them at top speed. It was so close they could see the soldier piloting it, a reflective visor drawn down over his face.

As if the hovercraft were not danger enough, the Rolls shuddered.

'The tsunami… it's coming!' cried Will.

On the other side of the engine, Chaudhury was fumbling frantically with a dozen strands of multi-coloured wire.

'Shall I try it again?'

'Not quite, sir… a moment longer.'

'I hate to rush you, but even a moment's a luxury right now.'

'Three minutes,' said Emma. 'Make that two-fifty-eight.'

The jet-black hovercraft slalomed past the Garuda cenotaph and was seventy yards away. The pilot was firing an Uzi SMG mounted on the front.

'Try it now!' called Chaudhury.

Will jammed a hand on the ignition.

The engine came alive with smoke and noise, the hover-cushion ballooning out.

'Waoooo!'

Ripping ahead through a gap between the ruins, the Rolls narrowly missed the Uzi's spray.

'That way, sir!' snapped Chaudhury. 'We can lose him.'

'No time for a car chase,' said Will, swerving the yoke back to the left.

The black hovercraft was gaining on them.

Its air cushion sprayed with incoming fire, the Rolls automatically compensated, powering up all the more.

Will glanced at the last lever.

'I'm feeling lucky,' Will said, a touch of Clint Eastwood in his voice.

He flicked it down.

An RPG launched, twisted through the air above the ruined city, and made brutal and immediate contact with the enemy hovercraft.

'No time to gloat!' snapped Emma. 'Thirty seconds and we'll be washed away!'

Will thrust his foot down hard.

The tsunami's giant wave was thundering forwards.

They could feel the wind preceding it. Their ears were filled with the roar of water as it rolled towards the shore.

'We're not gonna make it!' said Emma, her voice cold.

'Fifteen seconds,' added Chaudhury.

'Ten... nine...'

They were out of the city, but there was still half a mile to go. And, in any case, the shoreline would provide no security.

Will scanned the controls.

Eight...

'C'mon Hannibal, you knew this was going to happen!'

Seven...

At that moment, a foghorn sounded and a mechanical hand telescoped out from the dash. Held between thumb and forefinger was a switch.

Six...

'What the hell?' spluttered Will.

'Push it!' shrieked Emma.

Five...

Will pushed the switch.

An explosion was triggered, like the noise of a cannon firing.

Four...

A colossal hot air balloon was deployed above the Rolls.

Helium pumped in from pressurised tanks stowed inside the hover cushion, the canopy billowing outwards.

Three...

Steel cords straining, the scarlet balloon tightened, its vast surface ornamented with the distinctive monogram of Hannibal Fogg.

Two...

With Herculean force the tsunami ripped through the ancient ruins.

One...

A second before the waters engulfed it, the Rolls-Royce hover-car lifted gently into the air.

Climbing onto the back seat, Will opened the helium valves fully.

But the gas wasn't filling the canopy fast enough.

The vehicle was descending.

Thinking fast, Will climbed over the windscreen and onto the bonnet. Jamming his feet into a pair of holes positioned perfectly, he opened up the cowling.

He knew next to nothing about vintage aircraft engines — but Will wasn't concerned with the engine itself.

As Chaudhury and Emma watched in alarm, and as the water came closer and closer, Will grabbed a lever on the right of the housing.

Wrenching it back, he braced himself.

In the nick of time, the Falcon engine fell away, like a spent booster rocket jettisoned in outer space.

Instantly, the Rolls-Royce rose into the clear blue sky, as the full force of the tsunami reached the lost city below.

Striking the shore, the water made landfall, surging up through the jungle.

High up on a plateau, the Garuda tribe were safe. Their awe at surviving the catastrophe was made more poignant by the sight of the scarlet helium balloon...

Emblazoned as it was with the symbol of the Great Being — Hannibal Fogg.

Part III

THE ALEXANDER MECHANISM

One hundred and fifty-eight

STEPPING OVER THE THRESHOLD of Dar Jnoun in Marrakesh, Will bent down and touched his lips to the terracotta floor.

'I've never been so utterly grateful to be home,' he said.

Emma tossed her daypack onto a sofa and slipped down beside it.

'Me neither.'

'Nor I,' said Chaudhury.

The three travellers exchanged an exhausted smile.

Once he had kicked off his shoes, Will took the manservant aside.

'I'm guessing my family have tended to be a little short on thanks,' he said. 'So I want to say for the record that you rock!'

The manservant tended to find praise awkward. Will leaned forward to hug him. As he did so, Chaudhury shied away, sloping away to unpack his case.

On the long journey westwards from Buru Island to Marrakesh, Will's mind had been on one subject and one subject alone: locating the Alexander Mechanism, and refitting the components.

But first things first.

Now that he had all seven components in his possession, Will realised the grave danger facing him. The Magi might arrive any minute. There was no doubt they knew the location of Hannibal's Marrakesh home.

Barricading the main door, Will pushed a solid oak table against it. Upstairs, he drew the shutters on the external windows and bolted the door to the roof.

When he was done, he reported the security measures to Chaudhury, who was again dressed in formal livery.

'From now on we trust no one,' he said. 'No one comes in here without being searched.'

The manservant confirmed the instructions.

'Would you like me to arm the property?' he asked.

Will didn't understand.

'Arm it?'

'Fortify it, sir.'

'However would you do that?'

Beckoning Will through into the kitchen, Chaudhury removed a blue-and-white willow dish hanging on the wall.

Behind it was a white ceramic handle and an enamelled plaque which read, 'Fortification'.

'What does it do?'

'I must admit that I am not exactly certain, sir.'

Taking a step forwards, Will grasped the handle and heaved it down with all his strength.

The effect was instantaneous and absolute.

Bullet-proof steel shutters descended over windows and doors. Up on the roof, a reinforced mesh grille glided out from stowage bays set in the walls, and a series of automatic grenade launchers swung into position.

In the second basement, a generator came to life — supplying a parallel electricity system. Once electrified by the supply, Dar Jnoun's external surfaces greased themselves with petroleum jelly.

Through the afternoon and late into the night, Will worked at the CODEX, in a desperate effort to coax out a clue. It was as though something was missing — the key part of the puzzle.

Emma asked how he was getting on.

'All I can think,' he replied, 'is that Hannibal's dug this one down deep. It's not going to be straightforward.'

'Like any of the others were straightforward,' Emma riposted with a smile.

'You know what I mean.'

Kissing her hand, Emma touched it to Will's head.

'I'm going up to bed,' she sighed.

Will placed the CODEX down on the coffee table. Unable to take his eyes off it, he was certain the mechanism housed the secret. It was just a matter of triggering it to release what it knew.

Thinking it over, Will came up with a hunch. Perhaps the day code had to be reset to a fresh numerical sequence — one somehow formulated from the components.

He stood up and made his way to Hannibal's roll-top desk in the north salon. It was there that he had hidden the flight case.

As he left the room, Dar Jnoun was shaken by an ear-splitting BANG!

Will rushed back into the east salon.

Where the machine had been moments before, lay a smouldering heap of twisted metal.

The CODEX had self-destructed.

Chaudhury and Emma came downstairs. They looked at Will, then down at the charred remnants.

Will shrugged.

'Guess the next clue wasn't in the CODEX after all,' he said.

Emma shrugged.

'Guess not.'

The manservant rolled up the sleeves of his pyjamas, the breast pocket of which bore the ancestral crest of Cooch Behar.

'I shall fetch a dustpan, sir.'

'It can wait until tomorrow.'

'Very good, sir.'

Will cracked his knuckles one by one.

'Tomorrow I'm going to scour this house from top to bottom,' he said. 'I'll go through every book, search behind every picture, and leave no stone unturned.'

One hundred and fifty-nine

1928

ON THE MORNING OF 4th November, Hannibal was working on the design for a golden pagoda he planned to erect in the gardens of his London home in memory of Alina.

During the night the first snow of the season had fallen, sending motor cars skidding down the Bayswater Road towards Notting Hill.

Hannibal sat in his study, a three-dimensional model on the desk bathed in silvery winter light. He was making some last calculations with a logarithm table, when there was a loud rap at the front door.

Craning his neck, he looked down to see who had come.

To his surprise it was a police inspector. He wasn't alone. A pair of sergeants were standing either side of him. Behind them were two dozen uniformed constables, their night-sticks drawn.

Chaudhury padded up the stairs.

'Forgive me, sir, but Inspector Newland sends his regards, and says he has come to arrest you.'

'*Me? Really?*' replied Hannibal, his interest piqued. 'Send him into the drawing-room at once.'

'Very good, sir.'

Ten minutes later, Hannibal Fogg had been formally charged with high treason.

Five minutes after that, he was being escorted from 10 Kensington Palace Gardens in chains.

Chaudhury found himself out on the street in the snow. The front door was locked and fastened with a wax seal from the court.

Exactly one week later, the Great Purge began.

On the authority of His Majesty's Britannic Empire, draconian legislation came into immediate effect.

Every book, letter, monograph or document found to bear the name 'Hannibal Fogg' was to be turned in to a special committee. Anyone neglecting to hand over offending material risked fines and even imprisonment.

Three weeks after the beginning of the Great Foggian Purge, as it became known, ordinary members of society, bookshops, and libraries — both public and private — had all obeyed.

A great bonfire of Fogg's work was assembled on the Victoria Embankment in the shadow of Cleopatra's Needle. On 2nd December, it was torched at the stroke of midnight, the flames visible down the road in Westminster.

As for Fogg himself, he was subjected to a special inquisition, headed by his arch-enemy since childhood, Lord Rothermere, known then as Harold Sidney Harmsworth.

The trial lasted twelve days.

During it, Hannibal was refused permission to call a single character witness. Manacled throughout and flanked by armed guards, he was subjected to an interminable diatribe of character assassination. At the end of the proceedings, he was ordered to listen to Rothermere's fabricated summary.

The Crown Inquisition found Fogg guilty of spying for Germany's Weimar Republic. Rothermere had pushed for hanging, but was overruled on grounds of clemency. Hannibal had donated generously to treat wounded British Tommies in the Great War, and the government feared a wave of public protest should he have ended up with a noose around his neck.

Having read the Treason Act of 1351, Lord Rothermere announced the Crown's ruling: life behind bars without any hope of parole, and the confiscation of all British titles and property — including the ancestral castle in Scotland.

Incarceration followed, in a solitary cell at the Tower of London.

Hannibal was permitted no visitation rights whatsoever. His son, Wilfred, petitioned the Prime Minister, Stanley Baldwin, and even King George V, but was refused even the shortest visit.

During the imprisonment, Hannibal left his cell in the White Tower only once — to be bathed in carbolic acid during a tuberculosis epidemic.

On the second anniversary of his arrival at the Tower, he was writing a memoir entitled '*The Cold Dawn of Seclusion*', when he heard the jailer, Herbert Peekes, limping down the corridor outside.

Quickly, Hannibal hid the manuscript in a niche he had carved specially between the floor and the wall. Then he waited for the inspection hatch to open.

Peekes's keys jangled longer than they usually did.

Sitting primly on his bed, Hannibal wondered why the jailer was visiting so soon after breakfast. He feared that the manuscript would be found and confiscated yet again. He had already begun it eight times and it was, at last, almost finished. Securing a supply of paper and ink had challenged all his skills of ingenuity.

The keys ceased jangling and the door creaked open.

Herbert Peekes's slender silhouette paused in the frame.

'Gawd-awful you look, Mr Fogg!' he exclaimed in a broad Cockney voice.

'Thank you Peekes,' he replied. 'Despite my good intentions, I find my lodgings at odds with hygiene.'

'Yeah, well, you'd better jump to it.'

'Jump to what, Mr Peekes?'

'Get ready.'

'Ready? For what?'

'Ready to go out.'

'*Out?*'

'Downstairs he is. Come to collect you himself he has.'

'Who has?'

'The bleedin' Sultan of bleedin' Morocco,' said Peekes.

One hundred and sixty

AFTER BREAKFAST WILL HURRIED into Hannibal's secret study, and started rooting through drawers and cabinets. Scrutinising the objects meticulously, he was searching for information and for clues.

As he reasoned it, almost anything in Dar Jnoun could hold the key to locating the Alexander Mechanism.

He examined the pickled organs in their bell jars and the postage stamps arranged in frames, the astrolabes and the amulets, the notebooks, the scientific apparatus, and even the trepanned heads.

Nothing was overlooked.

After the secret study, Will turned his attention to the reception rooms, and then made his way through the stores of expeditionary equipment. He didn't understand why the CODEX had blown up, and found it galling that there was no outright clue awaiting him.

As he progressed through the house, each object lifted the veil a little more into the peculiarities of Hannibal Fogg.

It wasn't as if there were no clues, because there were... dozens of them.

On his great search of the riad, Will discovered fragments of information he already knew: details about the Alexander Mechanism, and on locating individual components.

At dinner time he showed them to Emma.

'Don't understand why he would have left multiple clues for the same information,' Will said.

'A back-up,' Emma replied. 'If you didn't find one clue, you might have found another.'

'A failsafe mechanism?'

'Precisely.'

Emma touched a spoonful of soup to her lips. Her eyes widened.

'What's in this?' she whispered.

Chaudhury, whose ears nothing escaped, swept into the dining-room with the tureen.

'Walnut and chilli sauce, miss. A family recipe from Cooch Behar.'

'Delicious,' said Will.

Resting the soup spoon on the bowl, Emma touched a fingertip to her chin.

'If you had to pass on a clue while fearing it might fall into the wrong hands, how would you do it?' she asked.

'I'd use something wildly complicated,' said Will. 'An encryption that couldn't be broken by the wrong person.'

'Would you really?'

'Sure I would. Think back to the Enigma machine. It was unbreakable. Well, it was until Turing figured it out.'

Emma stared down into her soup.

'I'm not so sure that's right.'

'What d'you mean?'

'Well, if Hannibal wanted to pass on a key piece of information, he may have done it through something simpler.'

'Like?'

'I don't know.'

Will smiled.

'Then what do you know?'

Emma held up a finger.

'I know the safest place to hide the ultimate clue wouldn't be in a house.'

'So what would the safest place be?'

'The human mind,' said Emma.

'Huh?'

'Think back through your memories.'

'Think back to what?'

'For something that sticks out — something that's connected to your family.' Pausing, Emma looked at Will hard. 'What I'm saying is that the clue could already be inside you...'

Will closed his eyes. He thought back to his childhood, to the balmy days before his parents had died.

A series of memories emerged from the mist:

He was at a picnic in a clearing hidden in the Redwood Forest, his very favourite spot on earth. Spring sunshine was streaming through the trees, the scent of wild garlic heavy in the air.

Then a winter afternoon on the beach. Will and his father were flying a huge home-made kite, its long tail a

575

stream of multi-coloured bows.

Next, he watched as the twin coffins at his parents' funeral were being lowered into the ground.

A deep breath.

He smelled the scent of honeysuckle at his great-aunts' home. Aunt Edith was knitting in her favourite chair. Across from her, Aunt Helen was doing a crossword with a cheap ballpoint pen. However hard Will tried, he couldn't get that last image out of his head.

'I keep thinking of my great-aunts,' he said.

'What do you see?'

'They're just sitting there like they always do. Aunt Edith is knitting yet another itchy sweater, and Aunt Helen's doing the crossword. She's pretty good.'

'And where are you?'

'On the floor. I'm sitting cross-legged with my knitted toy dinosaur.'

'What can you smell?'

'A cherry flan cooling in the kitchen.'

'And what can you hear?'

Will smiled, his eyes still tightly closed.

'My own voice,' he said. 'I'm humming…'

'What are you humming?'

'I'm humming the *"Rhyme of Ernest Pie"*.'

Will opened his eyes.

'Oh my God,' he said.

'What?'

'Aunt Helen once told me the rhyme had been

passed down through a dozen generations of Foggs for a
reason — a reason we don't really understand. She said
it was part of us, like the secret recipe for her cherry flan.'

'How does it go?'

'It starts like this:

There was a man named Ernest Pie
Who loved to laugh and grin and lie,
He lived on mash and fish and moss
Wandering much but never lost…'

Chaudhury came in to clear the soup bowls.

When he was gone, Will reached out and touched
Emma's forearm with his hand.

'The Rhyme is the key,' he said.

AFTER DINNER, WILL WROTE out the entire *'Rhyme
of Ernest Pie'* on graph paper, and set about trying
to decipher it. The fact that the CODEX had self-
destructed surely meant another system of encryption
had been used.

For three days and nights he substituted letters for
numbers, and numbers for letters again. When it didn't
seem to work, he tried a hundred different things. But
he came up with nothing conclusive. At the end of it all,
Will presumed the rhyme was just that — a rhyme, and
nothing more.

Chaudhury shuffled into the salon bearing a tray of

cucumber sandwiches seasoned with sea salt, the crusts
trimmed off. Looking up from a sea of scribbled notes,
Will asked him to scour the library for anything on
encryption.

Forty minutes later, the manservant staggered into the
salon, his arms laden with heavy volumes — all of them
bound in uniform lizard-green leather. Laying them on
the table, he squared them so the spines were all lined up.

Will grabbed the first one. Entitled *Epistle on the
Secret Works of Art and of Nature and on the Invalidity
of Magic*, it was by Friar Roger Bacon. Written in the
thirteenth century, the work contained numerous
annotations in Fogg's own hand.

Finding nothing in it to help, Will moved on, through
centuries of scholarship. He skimmed the works of
Selenus, Al-Kindi, and Johannes Trithemius — whose
fifteenth-century publication on secret writing had been
banned by the Catholic Church.

Once again, Will began to feel as though he was on
yet another tangent leading nowhere. He selected a slim
volume entitled *Unbreakable Cryptography*. Printed
in 1902, it looked much like the other books. The
difference was that the author, Emile Myszkowski, had
inscribed it to Hannibal Fogg.

Thumbing through it, Will noticed that a
'cryptographic grille' had been slipped inside. Made
from simple cardboard, it had five rectangular slots
positioned at random points on its surface. On the top

right hand corner was a number — 43.

Turning to page forty-three, Will laid the grille over it. The tiny rectangular boxes lined up with specific words. Taking them vertically, he read: *Myszkowski transposition cipher conjunction pie.*

He leapt up.

'That's it!'

An hour later he had cracked the *'Rhyme of Ernest Pie'.*

In addition to a secret letter from Hannibal, the rhyme contained a central grid reference, and a start point — what Fogg had termed the 'Notification Quadrant'.

Checking both sets of coordinates on his iPhone, as well as against Hannibal's canvas-backed map, he got the answer he needed.

The Alexander Mechanism lay beneath the sands of the Empty Quarter, in the Great Arabian Desert.

Will's heart sank. He had hoped the Mechanism would be a little closer — like right there in Marrakesh. Calling Emma and Chaudhury in, he pointed to the location on his phone.

'We're coming with you!' they both said at once.

'He might as well have buried it on the moon,' groaned Will.

'We'll need camels,' Chaudhury said firmly.

Emma opened the canvas-backed map and traced a finger inland from the Arabian Sea.

'I'd say the best way to get in there would be through Oman.'

'This trip's going to call for some cutting-edge desert gear,' said Will. 'Any ideas on that front?'

Chaudhury straightened his tie.

'I do believe I could rustle something up, sir,' he said.

One hundred and sixty-one

A CARAVAN OF DROMEDARIES snaked its way northward across the border from Oman. On the back of each camel was a pair of wooden crates stencilled with Hannibal's monogram and with the word 'ARABIA'. Stretching out between the animals and the horizon lay a vast emptiness of honey-yellow sand.

From time to time towering dunes came and went, rising like mountains into the cobalt sky. Against such an awe-inspiring panorama, the slim cortège of beasts and men was nothing at all.

At the head an Arab named Khalil al-Khalil led a magnificent camel — her back laden with crates like all the rest. A great brute of a man, Khalil claimed to have crossed the Rub' al-Khali, the fearful Empty Quarter, twice before — the first time as a gunrunner, the second while spying for the Omani Secret Service.

Little more than a brigand, he was a liar, and frequently a thief. In reality, Khalil had never set foot anywhere near the Empty Quarter. Even now, he had only been coaxed to join the current expedition with the enticement of cold hard cash.

Thirty feet behind him, leading another dromedary, was a second man in Bedouin dress; most of his face was shielded by a turban. The only hint he was an outsider was the patch of skin around the eyes. Roasted red and raw, Will's face was so blistered that he had taken to sleeping with a damp towel wrapped over his face at night.

Behind him, some way after the camels and their crates, was Emma and, behind her, Chaudhury. Like Will, they were both dressed as Bedouins — coarse camel hair robes, turbans drenched black with sweat.

Khalil had promised a fabulous oasis another few miles to the north. He said they would camp there, refresh the animals, refill the water skins, and continue at dawn. Will and the others hoped this time their guide would come good on his promises.

Until then he had shown no skill at all in the ways of desert survival. The fact was that anyone who had really been in the Empty Quarter avoided it like the plague. They would not have returned for any sum of money. The hostile nature of the terrain made it the perfect place to hide an object for eternity.

Trudging, one foot after the next, the group moved listlessly in the direction of the distant horizon, like gassed soldiers retreating from the Front. In the two weeks since setting out from Salalah on the Omani coast, their bodies had been scorched, and ravaged day and night by fleas.

Technically speaking, they had crossed into Saudi Arabia, in what was just about the most desolate region on earth. Even the Bedouin steered well clear of the Empty Quarter if they could help it. As far as they were concerned, it was hell on earth.

The sun's heat reached its crescendo and, as it did so, Khalil thrust an arm above his head. Pointing at a far-off speck close to the horizon, he claimed it to be their salvation — the oasis.

Three hours later, the caravan reached a clump of desiccated date palms. Hidden among them were a jumble of parched animal bones and sun-baked water skins. There was dried mud too, cracked and brittle, but not a single drop of water.

Realising there was no hope, Khalil fell on the ground and thrashed his arms about as he wept. He begged forgiveness, beseeching God to provide sustenance in the form of a miracle.

Then, conjuring his last strength, he got up and ran impetuously into the desert. Will called to him to stop, but Khalil didn't listen. Shrinking against a grim backdrop, he vanished into the dunes.

'We're better off without him,' said Emma caustically.

'Means we can finally break into the gear,' added Will.

He trudged over to where a little pool of water had once stood, scooped up a handful of the dried mud and crumbled it between his fingers.

'Chaudhury, please bring box number five,' he said.

The manservant staggered down the line of dromedaries and urged the last one to sit. As it groaned and glowered, he untied the bindings and off-loaded a wooden crate.

Will jemmied off the side, revealing an early form of dehumidifying machine, designed by Hannibal Fogg back in 1912. Powered by electrolysis, it had an in-built hygrometer for measuring relative humidity. Sucking moisture from the air, it collected the precious liquid in a cylindrical reservoir.

The Empty Quarter was so dry that the device strained for an hour before it had gathered sufficient water to alleviate their thirst.

'The camels need to drink, too,' said Will, 'but this thing's never going to satisfy them.'

'How far d'you think it is to the Notification Quadrant?' asked Emma.

'Can't be more than another eighteen miles. Then about the same again before we reach the grid reference. If we push hard we should make it by dusk.'

Clambering up, they set off, with Will at the front.

For an hour they made headway, the dromedaries moving in a slow trot despite their burdens and their thirst.

Just as they thought they were making good progress, the sky went sienna-brown, the sun extinguished by a searing wind sweeping in from the west.

'Sandstorm!' screamed Emma.

'Get down!'

Throwing themselves onto the ground, they heaved the camels to kneel, nuzzling into their flea-infested underbellies, as Khalil had shown them to do.

A tornado ripped through.

It was so abrasive that it stripped the packing crates of their paint, tearing away the bindings.

The camels groaned as if the world were about to end.

Forcing himself into the folds of flesh, his back in line with the animal's shank, Will struggled to transport his mind far away.

He thought of the ordered corridors at Penshaw, Willis, Smink & Co. in London, where his journey had begun. Focussing hard, he pictured the details exactly — the long oil portraits of elderly men in legal robes, the chesterfield in the waiting-room, an Oriental rug laid over scuffed floorboards.

As he played the scene over and over, the sand-wind ripped past and disappeared. Half-wondering if he had gone deaf, Will unfurled a hand, cautiously sticking it out to his side.

The air was still, silent as a summer's day.

Lifting his head, he got out from the dune formed around him. The she-camel he had been riding had slipped into a catatonic state, a natural self-preservation system.

Will staggered over to check on Emma and

Chaudhury. Like him, they were shaken, but none the worse for wear.

As he turned to calm his dromedary, Will fell backwards in shock.

All around, for as far as they could see, were bones, both human and animal — an abominable caravan of death.

One hundred and sixty-two

WITH THE SUN FLAT on the horizon, its rays casting long shadows out over the dunes, Will checked the canvas-backed map for the thousandth time. He kicked himself for not bringing a solar charger — a uniquely appropriate piece of kit given the Empty Quarter's interminable sunshine. Without one, there was no way to charge his precious iPhone.

Without Apple high-tech, he resorted to another of Hannibal's inventions — his Patented Automatic Celestial Positioning Device.

A brass instrument with twin display dials and an in-built orrery, it was a mechanical model of the solar system. Hannibal had designed it in the weeks before his arrest for treason. Entrusting its construction to a master clockmaker on Fleet Street, he never had the opportunity to test it in the desert himself.

Rotating the bezel to the off position, Will closed the device and changed course six degrees to the east.

'Less than a mile now!' he yelled.

Coaxing his camel to move faster, he stood high in the stirrups and, squinting into the shadows, he called out:

'There it is! The Notification Quadrant!'

Three hundred yards ahead was a group of rocks. Scattered about, they seemed to be a marker of some kind.

On the leeward side stood the bleached bones of a camel and its rider.

'Looks like he hoped to find a well under there,' said Emma.

Riding past the stones, Will dismounted after another fifty feet. Moving his way down the caravan, he broke open one of the crates, took out a pair of shovels and passed one to Chaudhury.

'We'll take it in turns,' he said, driving the shovel into the desert's baked crust.

'What are you looking for?' asked Emma incredulously.

Will didn't answer at first. He was too occupied with the digging. Sweat poured down his face, drenching the turban.

After ten minutes he was down three feet. But, instead of being content with the progress, he tossed down the shovel.

'I must have made a mistake,' he said.

'The Celestial Positioning Device...' said Emma. 'Think it was calibrated wrong?'

'Wouldn't be like Hannibal to provide faulty equipment.'

'So what are we gonna do?'

Will fished out his ever-faithful iPhone.

'If only there was a way to charge this, we'd be up and running,' he said.

'If the all-seeing gaze of Hannibal Fogg saw us here,' Emma replied, 'surely he knew you needed to charge your phone.'

Will shrugged.

'Yeah, well I don't see a steampunk iPhone charger.'

Chaudhury stepped forward.

'What about this, sir,' he said. In his right hand was a retro-looking device concocted from glass, brass and polished mahogany. 'I believe it is a Telephonic Electricity Generator.'

'Where d'you get that?'

'Crate number nine, sir.'

By the time Will had set up the charger, night had fallen. Having kindled a fire with one of the packing crates, they chewed their way through a can of Hannibal Fogg's pemmican. Exhausted and thirsty beyond belief, they bivouacked in for the night, the stars above them a magnificent glimpse of heaven.

At dawn next morning, Will set up the Telephonic Electricity Generator.

As the sun's rays broke over the horizon, bringing a blush of pink to the desert dunes, Hannibal's portable charger turned light into power.

Within an hour Will's iPhone was fully charged. Right away it picked up a network — surprising considering how remote they were. Little did any of them realise that — as was so often the case — Hannibal was responsible for the success.

Within a few minutes they had isolated the exact point of the drop. This time it was Chaudhury who scooped away the cool sand.

Two feet down, the end of his shovel slammed into something hard — metal colliding with metal.

'What is it?' Emma asked.

Will slapped his hands together.

'A little treat from Hannibal!'

A dozen water barrels fashioned from solid silver had been buried along with a long steel trough. Arranged on a hydraulic rostrum so that they could be raised easily, they were tarnished from decades in the sand.

When the trough was full, Will turned to Chaudhury.

'Can you start watering the camels?'

'Very good, sir.'

Emma balked.

'How did you know where to dig?'

'Hannibal left us a clue.'

'What?'

'The Myszkowski transposition.'

'Don't get you.'

'It said the dividing line was fifty feet towards the sun.'

'What dividing line?'

'The dividing line between life and death.'

ONCE THE CAMELS WERE satisfied and the water skins filled to bursting, they pushed on towards the horizon. The heat was insufferable, and the mirages so frequent that all three of them questioned their sanity.

The next night they broke late in the afternoon and built another fire, the flames licking at the dark.

Will and Emma lay on their backs, gazing up at the canvas of stars.

'We're close now,' whispered Will. 'Can't be more than a day or two at the most.'

'What a journey,' sighed Emma.

'I'd never be here without you.'

'Or without Chaudhury,' she replied, turning to see if he was awake. The Indian manservant was fast asleep on the other side of the fire.

'He's incredible,' said Will. 'Make that way more than incredible.'

Emma squirmed to get comfortable.

'What are you going to do when this madcap adventure's over?' she asked.

'Don't know. Haven't given it any thought,' Will replied.

'What about you?'

Emma sat up. Her features tinged orange, she looked down into Will's eyes.

'I don't know,' she whispered. 'I really don't know.'

One hundred and sixty-three

SIX MINUTES AFTER THE command had come through the encoded ALPHA-NINE channel from London, the Covert Reconnaissance Unit — CRU for short — was standing to attention in the briefing room at the Akrotiri Field Base, Cyprus.

Dressed in the same uniform as their sister unit, the Special Air Service, only their lapel insignia were different — adorned with Excalibur.

The commander called his six-man team to attention.

'Listen up boys,' he said in a gravelly voice. 'Operation Desert Stealth. A night drop from 25,000 feet. A Special Op for the posh gits in Whitehall.'

'What's the target, sir?'

'Standard retrieval operation. A chunk of machinery as I understand it. Full details when we're airborne. This one goes all the way to the top. Orders from the PM herself. Fully classified, d'you understand?'

One by one the members of the elite strike force nodded.

'Chemlights are out of the question. Don't even pack them. We'll be using mono-wings. Can't risk alerting the

Saudis on this one. They gave a red light.'

'Weaponry, sir?'

'Going in fully loaded — C8s, M72s, and G60 stun grenades. We'll be deploying the Griffon, too. Understood?'

'Yes, sir!' the unit cried in unison.

'The ETD's in thirty minutes, so get cracking. Fall out!'

One hundred and sixty-four

WHILE EMMA AND CHAUDHURY slept, Will loaded up the dromedaries and prepared for the day ahead. The only certainty was that a great deal more hardship was on the cards.

As the first rays of sunlight broke over the horizon, he pulled out his iPhone. Thanks to Hannibal's Telephonic Electricity Generator, it was fully charged.

Will smiled, and then sighed.

Clicking a contact name, he was patched through to another world.

'Hello,' said the frail voice of a woman on the other end.

'Aunt Helen, it's me.'

'Hello? Who? Who's that?'

'William. It's me… William.'

A shriek of joy was followed by cries of jealousy and the sound of the phone being snatched away.

'*William*! Dearest William!' a second voice screeched. 'Where are you?'

'On an adventure. But don't worry, I'll be home soon.'

'Making sure to brush your teeth properly?'

Will grinned.

'Twice a day,' he lied. 'And three times on Sundays.'

'Hurry home as soon as you can, and I'll have a cherry flan waiting for you.'

Will kissed into the phone, and ended the call.

An hour later the caravan was on the move once again. In absolute silence it made its way around a colossal dune.

Chaudhury was wearing a pair of Hannibal's desert goggles. The lenses had polarising filters, the first of their kind, and the frames were trimmed with albino ostrich hide.

At exactly noon, Will raised his arm to halt the caravan. He jumped down, his canvas combat boots sinking into the loose sand.

Using one of the wooden crates as a makeshift table, he double-checked the location against the iPhone's GPS.

'We've arrived,' he said.

'Where do we dig?'

'I'd say, right about here. Shouldn't be so deep.'

Chaudhury unpacked a shovel. Taking it from him, Will struck it into the sand. Energised, he dug down fast. But despite his enthusiasm, he didn't find anything.

'Sure it's the right place?' asked Emma.

'Certain,' answered Will.

An hour later Chaudhury and he had dug a hole six feet deep.

'Think you're wasting your strength,' said Emma testily.

Will checked the coordinates.

'I don't understand it,' he said. 'The Mechanism's supposed to be buried right here.'

Emma counted the remaining water skins, and discovered half of them were leaking.

'I'd say we're good for a couple of days more at most,' she said. 'So if you're gonna use a joker, now's the time.'

Will wasn't listening. Squinting at the iPhone's display, he shook his head.

'It's supposed to be right here,' he repeated.

'Perhaps, sir, if we were to spread out a little, and dig randomly.'

Will looked up from the phone. Narrowing his eyes, he turned incredulously to face the manservant.

'Are you out of your mind?'

Chaudhury blushed — although in the dazzling light there was no way of telling.

'Forgive me, sir,' he said.

'What would Hannibal have done?' Will said. 'That's what we have to ask ourselves.'

'Turn around and head home?' Emma said.

Chaudhury trudged over to where the other two were

standing.

'If you would permit me to speak up, sir.'

'What is it, Chaudhury?'

'I do believe that we might profit from examining the luggage,' he said. 'After all, it was packed by Mr Fogg.'

'Good idea,' Will replied. 'Let's get all the crates down.'

A few minutes later all sixteen crates had been unloaded from the dromedaries, their contents strewn out on the sand. Will had been in such a hurry to get out into the desert, and so keen to conceal their mission from Khalil, he had paid little attention to the equipment itself.

As expected, Hannibal had packed a comprehensive manifest of gear for every eventuality. As well as campaign furniture and bedding, there was a wind generator, a self-inflating medical field tent, and a mechanical system for winching camels out of dry quicksand — all of it Hannibal's own design. There were dehydrated rations, too: self-heating cans of mock turtle soup, bouillon, and condensed coffee packed in tubes.

Rifling through the equipment and provisions, they picked out an assortment of wonders and delights. But nothing in particular stuck out.

Downcast at not having made any progress, Chaudhury wandered off to have a pee behind a huge sand dune. When he hadn't come back fifteen minutes later, Will signalled to Emma.

'Think I ought to go after him? It'll be getting dark soon.'

'He's probably got diarrhoea… again.'

'Maybe he's run out of paper.'

'You still use paper?' asked Emma with a smile.

Will frowned.

'What d'you use?'

'Sand of course.'

As Will screwed up his face, Chaudhury hurried out from behind the dune.

'You OK?'

'Rather more than merely OK, sir.'

'Stomach troubles over, then?'

The manservant motioned to the dune's leeward side.

'I suggest you have a look, sir,' he said.

'A look at what?'

'At the desert encampment.'

One hundred and sixty-five

THE C-130 LEVELLED OUT at 25,000 feet, its grey-green fuselage hardly visible in the night sky.

Inside, the Special Reconnaissance unit ran through their final checks. For the last half hour they had pre-breathed pure oxygen, standard practice to flush the nitrogen from their blood. Although veterans at covert insertion, it was the first time any of them had used carbon fibre mono-wings on a night jump.

At the commander's signal, the rear cargo bay door was lowered, blasting the hold with freezing wind.

Once the door was down, the Griffon was deployed. Equipped with a flying wing and drone technology, its automatic opening device was set at five thousand feet.

Advancing to the door, the CRU jumped in sequence — leaping in quick succession. Wearing heated aerodynamic suits, fitted with the carbon fibre wings, the Special Forces unit soared across the night sky.

One by one they deployed their chutes, landing in the drop zone.

One hundred and sixty-six

AS DARKNESS FELL, CHAUDHURY led the way round a towering sand dune. Will and Emma both assumed he was imagining things again.

As they circumnavigated the dune, they spotted a camp fire burning a short distance away — a blaze of orange and yellow, fanned by the wind.

'We should go back and arm ourselves,' said Will.

'They appear to be friendly, sir,' replied Chaudhury.

'How d'you know?'

'I have spoken to them, sir.'

'What?!'

'They were rather chatty as it happened, although they found my Moroccan dialect a little hard to grasp.'

Backtracking to where the camels were resting, Will opened one of the provision crates. Grabbing as many tin cans as he could carry, he led the way through the darkness to the flames. Beside him, Emma carried the flight case. Taking it along may have been asking for trouble, but leaving it behind was out of the question.

'*As salam wa alaikum!*' Will called loudly as he approached the encampment. A standard greeting used across the Islamic world, the phrase indicated peace. In such circumstances, to neglect it might have been perceived as a declaration of hostility.

'*Wa alaikum salam!*' came the immediate reply.

The silhouette of a figure moved from the camp fire, approaching them. Will stretched out his hand, felt the stranger's palm press against his own, and presented the canned food. Welcoming the visitors, the Bedouin gave thanks. He seemed unfazed to meet them out in the middle of nowhere.

Before they knew it, the three of them were seated beside the fire, drinking tea and eating dates. A sheep was slaughtered, roasted and served to the guests in an impromptu banquet.

'Think they're back at our camp stealing our stuff?' asked Will.

Chaudhury grunted a 'no'.

'If they were hostile they would have slit our throats by now,' he said. 'We have been welcomed as guests — and as such we are under their protection.'

'Can you ask what they're doing out here?'

Swallowing a mouthful of roasted mutton, the manservant translated the question into Arabic.

A reply shot back.

'They are guardians, sir.'

'Guardians of what?'

An exchange of chatter followed.

'Guardians of a tomb, sir?'

'Out here in the desert?'

Again, Chaudhury broke into Arabic, listened to the reply, and then nodded.

'A Sufi saint was once travelling through the Empty Quarter,' he said. 'But he fell ill and perished.'

'Where?'

'Right here at this spot. Since then the clan have regarded it as a sacred place.'

'How long have they guarded the tomb?'

Again, the manservant translated and, after some mumbling between themselves, one of the clansmen offered a reply.

'For longer than any of them know,' said Chaudhury.

'*Decades?*'

'Centuries.'

'What was the name of the saint?'

The Bedouin chief said an indistinct name. Chaudhury asked for him to repeat it.

'What was it?'

'*Al Fooq*. It means "The Family of the Regiment".'

Will tossed a lump of gristle into the fire.

'Sounds like *Fogg*,' said Emma.

Will signalled to Chaudhury.

'Can you ask if there's a tombstone — or something that bears the name?'

Having listened to the question, the chief closed his eyes, the fire's glow bathing his face in orange. After a full minute of silence, he grunted to his son, a child sitting on his right.

The boy went into the back of the black camel-hair tent and brought something out. Regarding it with great reverence, he touched his lips to it before passing it to his father.

'What's that?'

'The relic of the tribe,' said Chaudhury.

Examining the object, Will saw it was a sealed terracotta tube. Something was written in Arabic at one end.

The Bedouin chief pointed to it.

'*Al Fooq*,' he said.

Nodding respectfully, Will switched on his headlamp and examined the relic with care. Beside the Arabic lettering he noticed a symbol stamped into the base.

Will immediately knew what to do.

His back warming with adrenalin, he showed the symbol to Emma and Chaudhury.

'Have a feeling this won't be popular,' he said.

Closing his eyes he saw himself from above, the terracotta relic held lengthways between his hands.

Raising it above his head, he smashed it against a rock to the left of the fire.

Silence.

All together the clansmen jumped up and rushed forward.

'We may be in a spot of bother, sir,' said Chaudhury quickly.

Apologising in florid Arabic, he begged forgiveness.

The chief drew a silver dagger.

The Indian manservant from Cooch Behar held out his hands, petitioning for clemency in the most urgent tone.

The dagger's blade swept in an arc in front of Will's face.

But, instead of striking him, the weapon was placed squarely at his feet.

Pulling Will towards him, the Bedouin chief hugged him hard, kissing his cheeks over and over.

'What's going on?' he gasped from the corner of his mouth.

'Um, er,' Chaudhury stammered. 'Rather than being enraged, they appear to be rather delighted.'

'Why?' asked Emma.

The chief shouted jubilantly.

'Because they have waited for you for so long,' said Chaudhury.

One hundred and sixty-seven

ONCE AT THE DROP zone, the Covert Reconnaissance Unit unpacked the weaponry and equipment stowed in their mono-wings and loaded it onto their backs. Night-vision units built into their masks had activated automatically once they cleared two thousand feet.

All six members of the team had made the drop zone, as had the Griffon — expertly piloted by a drone coordinator back at Akrotiri.

The commander gave the order to make ready the Griffon and to fire up its fans.

Less than ten minutes after touching down, they were cruising full tilt across the sands on the stealth hovercraft.

Although they were all linked up by earpieces and throat microphones, only the commander communicated with Mission HQ, call-sign BRAVO-FOXTROT-FOUR.

'This is ALPHA-CHARLIE-SEVEN.'

'Go ahead ALPHA-CHARLIE-SEVEN.'

'Touch-down successful. Operation Desert Stealth initiated.'

'Roger that… Continue on heading TWO-SEVEN-SIX. Be advised that AWAC is guidance operational. ETA 05.14 GMT. Ninety-two minutes from now.'

'Roger BRAVO-FOXTROT-FOUR.'

'Good luck ALPHA-CHARLIE-SEVEN. Over and out.'

One hundred and sixty-eight

As SENIOR MEMBERS OF the clan gathered around pledging allegiance, Will thanked them, and fished through the shards of terracotta. He soon found what he was looking for — a curled parchment scroll. One entire surface was covered in writing. Although English, it was an ancient form.

'A message from Hannibal?' whispered Emma.

'Not this time. Looks much older.'

Chaudhury leaned into the light.

'Seems to be written in Middle English, sir,' he said.

'Can't make head nor tail of it,' added Will.

Emma held out her hand.

'Let me have a go,' she said. 'I took a course in Middle English at college.'

'Whatever for?'

'I was obsessed with *Beowulf*.'

'And I thought *I* was the nerd,' said Will.

Scanning the text, Emma sighed.

'Interesting,' she said.

'What is it?'

'A letter.'

'Who to?'

'To Guillaume, the son of Alec.'

'That's me,' said Will. 'My name in French, and my father was Alec... Alexander. What does the letter say?'

'"After twists and turns aplenty, the river is almost

at the sea. You stand in the shadow of your birthright. Take courage Guillaume and walk tall. You are among friends. God's fortune to you my son."' Emma broke off. 'It's signed "Friar Benedict of Faugg".'

'*Faugg*?'

'Your distant ancestor.'

The chief touched a hand to Will's shoulder and spoke in a low voice.

'What did he say, Chaudhury?'

'That the time has come.'

'The time for what?'

'The time to do your work.'

Will recoiled.

'Unless I missed something, there's no great magical mystery machine out here in the desert.'

'The chief is asking you to go with him, sir.'

'Where?'

'Down into the tomb.'

One hundred and sixty-nine

OUT NEAR THE HORIZON a black speck was moving fast across the desert's baked surface.

Even before they had heard a sound, the Bedouin looked round as though sensing it was there.

Will tugged out Hannibal's field binoculars and trained them on the object.

'It's a... a...'

'A what?'

'A hovercraft. Looks like a military one.'

The clan ushered their guests over to a low domed building. Fifteen feet square, it housed a simple marble grave, a headstone set into the back wall.

Wasting no time, the clansmen smashed away terracotta seals on either side of the tomb, then pushed away the sheet of marble.

A stone staircase was exposed.

Agitated, the chief signalled at the hole.

'He's telling us to follow him down,' said Chaudhury.

'What about the hovercraft? Looks like they're gonna attack!' cried Will.

Outside, one of the young clansmen roared at the top of his lungs — the Bedouin's ancestral battle cry.

Chaudhury listened to the chief's words.

'He says they'll defend the mausoleum to the last man.'

'But with what?'

Another of the young men cried out, hastening into the blinding light. When he was gone, the chief spoke, his voice even more agitated than before.

'Apparently they were given some weapons, sir.'

'Who by?'

'By the Americans.'

'When?'

'After Desert Storm.'

Will looked round incredulously.

'Did I hear you right?' he said.

WHILE MOST OF THE Bedouin stayed above ground to defend the tomb, the chieftain and two of his sons descended into the tunnel, burning torches in their hands. Chaudhury, Emma and Will followed them down.

The clansmen who stayed on the surface pulled the tarps away from a state-of-the-art attack system buried beneath desert sands.

Taking their positions, they waited until the Griffon was within range.

Then the firefight began.

Fifty feet below the surface, Will, Emma, Chaudhury and the three Bedouin scurried through a network of tunnels. Descending deeper and deeper, they could all hear the muffled sound of gunfire above.

The Covert Reconnaissance Unit had made a grave tactical error in bringing the Griffon so close. A single well-placed anti-tank missile, and five of the team were wiped out. The sixth, the commander, was taken down by a fragmentation grenade while running to the aid of his men.

Whooping like bandits after a raid, the Bedouin fired their rifles in the air. Calling the others to order, the second in command signalled to the horizon.

A second, far more fearful strike force was approaching.

The Magi.

One hundred and seventy

EIGHTY-SIX FEET BELOW THE desert, they reached a sheet of glazed terracotta. Impressed into it was the Seal of Zoroaster — a curiously symbolic insignia, dominated by what looked like a winter tree.

Without hesitating, Will thrust the end of his firebrand into the middle of the seal, shattering the wall.

'There's a door behind here,' he said, pushing his way in.

Holding him back, the chief shouted in Arabic.

'He says to allow his oldest son to go in first,' Chaudhury translated.

'Why?'

'Because your life is far too precious.'

'How can he risk his son's life before mine?!'

Clutching a hand to his heart, the Bedouin chief spat out a line in Arabic.

'He says it's his ancestral duty.'

Will looked at the chieftain, and then at the door.

'This is *my* duty as well,' he said.

Lowering the burning torch as he crawled through, he raised it up again once inside the space beyond.

But there was no need for illumination.

The vast chamber was lit by natural sunlight, which was somehow channelled in from ground level before being magnified by a complex system of lenses and mirrors.

At the centre of the chamber, raised on a stage, stood a colossal machine.

Pentagonal in shape, it was crafted from an array of dazzling metals — among them silver, gold, platinum and burnished brass. A multitude of dials and displays were linked to one another by dozens of conduits, each one running with mercury.

Circling it, Will got a view straight into the heart of the machine, through to the rows of interlinking cogs, the elliptical gears, and cantilevers. He marvelled at the complexity and the beauty of the device.

Having been preserved in the desiccated environment for centuries, the machine looked as it must have on the day the brethren of Zoroaster entombed it beneath the deserts of the infamous Empty Quarter.

Mindful that time was against him, Will opened the flight case and assessed the components.

'How do I know where to put them?'

Chaudhury had the answer:

'I believe I may be able to guide you, sir.'

'Huh?'

'Trust me, sir.'

Will shrugged.

'What am I missing here? How come you know so much about the Mechanism?' he asked accusingly.

Chaudhury swallowed nervously.

'Well, sir…' he faltered. 'Strictly speaking I'm a little more than a humble manservant.'

'I know — you're from the Princely State of Cooch Behar.'

'Indeed, sir. Although there is even a little more to it than that.'

Will shrugged again.

'*More…?*'

'Well, sir. To be frank with you, I am associated with an ancient and venerable Order.'

'Huh?'

'The Order of Zoroaster, sir.'

'Not quite with you,' said Will, frowning.

'The ancestral role of being service to the Foggs is, er, um…'

'Is what?'

'It's what might be termed as "subterfuge", sir… an ancestral one nonetheless.'

'Subterfuge?' questioned Emma. 'With what intention?'

'Protection and assistance, miss.'

'The Order of Zoroaster…?' said Will. 'You mean the guys who hid the Mechanism in the first place.'

'The very same, sir.'

Rolling his eyes, Will reached into the flight case and took out the double helix. As his hands grasped the silver object, he got a flash of the cliff-top monastery in Ethiopia.

'So assist me,' he said. 'Tell me where to put it.'

Crouching down low, Chaudhury pointed to a groove offset from the centre line.

'I believe it goes there, sir, turned on its side.'

'OK,' replied Will.

Inserting the double helix into position, he watched as, instantly, it seemed to melt into the machine — in the way droplets of mercury bond seamlessly together.

Chaudhury exhaled.

'The Hands of God next, sir.'

Again, he pointed out the intended position, below a golden counterbalance. His hands trembling, Will leaned and placed the symbol in its niche.

As with the Ladder, it was instantly absorbed.

Above ground, the Magi swiftly made mincemeat of the Bedouin. Armed with biological weaponry, they stormed forwards, slaughtering at will.

Dressed in reflective silver Level-A Hazmat Vapour suits, their faces were obscured with breathing apparatus. Having disposed of the ancestral guardians they descended into the tomb, storming through the tunnels.

It was unclear quite how many Magi there actually were, or where exactly they had come from. What was certain was that the weaponry at their disposal was utterly lethal.

Strapped onto each of their backs, between a pressurised oxygen cylinder and a survival unit, was a steel aerosol canister. Labelled 'N2G1-6', they were by coincidence filled with Leonard Polkovich's ultra-fast-acting bubonic bacteria.

Down in the chamber, Will had inserted the golden Tumi dagger of the Incas, and then took hold of the Orisha Stone in his right hand. Chaudhury signalled where to position the object.

The Bedouin chief turned sharply round, having heard enemy voices in the tunnel.

Lying under the machine, Will coaxed the Stone into one of the bearings.

'What's going on?!' he cried.

'Sounds like gunfire up there,' said Emma.

Chaudhury exchanged a rushed line with the chief.

'He says men in masks have broken in.'

'Where are they?'

'Fighting their way down here.'

Emma scurried over to get a better view. Her face drawn as though she had witnessed Death, she peered up into the tunnel.

Half his body under the Mechanism, Will sat up. Chaudhury threw him the Prayer Wheel.

'Where does it go?!'

'There, sir.'

'Where?!'

'Behind the third elliptical gear.'

'Left or right?'

'*Right.*'

Will thrust the Prayer Wheel of Kublai Khan into place. As with the other components, it was absorbed at once, as though it had never been parted from its intended home.

Seconds later, the blue diamond was also reunited.

Rushing over to the flight case for the Garuda Mask, Chaudhury heard what sounded like a body hitting the floor.

He pivoted round, the jade mask in his hands.

The chieftain was slumped in a heap, dead.

Emma was standing over him.

She had broken his neck.

Will stared at her, trying to make sense of the scene, as Emma's own eyes welled with tears.

'I'm so sorry,' she said.

'What…?!'

'This was never meant to happen.'

'Magi…' Will growled, after what seemed like an eternity.

Advancing until inches from her, he looked deep into her eyes.

'You're one of them, aren't you?'

Emma blinked, tears cascading down her cheeks.

'I had no choice,' she said in little more than a whisper. 'They took me as a kid and groomed me — all of it just for this moment. It's how they operate. Trust through friendship.'

'Who are they?' Will asked, his expression dazed.

Emma looked him in the eye.

'Descendants of Alexander's son,' she said.

'But why?'

'They vowed to regain the Mechanism, even if it were to take eternity.'

'And you believed in their cause?'

Cheeks damp with tears, Emma nodded.

'Yes.'

'Why didn't you kill me when you could?'

'Because I was sent to protect you, until...'

Will finished the sentence:

'Until I had all the components?'

Emma blinked again, more slowly.

'Yes.'

'But Hannibal would surely have known.'

'Of course he did. He was way ahead of you.'

'Guess he was.'

Emma managed a smile.

'Solving the clues with ease as you did,' she said, 'you believed you'd figured out how Hannibal thought.'

'But I had,' replied Will.

'No you hadn't,' Emma riposted. 'But rather Hannibal had worked out how *you* thought — and had done so decades before you were even born.'

'If he was running circles around us all, why didn't he stop you?'

'Because you needed me, and he knew it.'

Will caught a flash of all the times Emma had solved key problems, or saved his life. He was about to give voice to his thoughts when the Magi leader stormed into the chamber.

His face concealed by a bullet-proofed visor, he scanned the room. Seeing Emma so close to her target, he radioed to the rest of the unit to secure the tunnels.

Then he ordered Emma to terminate.

Standing motionless, staring into Will's eyes, she wept. In her hand was the rosary, the one Hannibal had left for her.

Touching it to her lips, she kissed it.

His speech unclear through the respiration system, the Magi officer voiced the order a second time. Pressing a button on his wrist, his visor rolled up.

'Terminate!' he commanded.

Still, Emma didn't move.

Raising his deployment gun to eye level, the officer released the trigger.

A tiny pellet of live bubonic bacteria shot across the chamber, striking Will in the side of the neck.

Instantly, he slammed onto the stone floor.

Leaning over him, Emma felt desperately for a pulse. There wasn't one.

Arcing round, the officer raised the barrel once again, aiming it at Emma.

In the fraction of a second before his finger executed

his brain's command, she pounced — strangling him with the rosary.

Distraught, her mind reeling in slow motion, she picked up the jade Garuda Mask, slipping it over Will's pustulated face.

Nothing happened.

'It was a myth,' she murmured, her words lost in grief.

Chaudhury shot forwards.

'We've lost him.'

They stood there, stock-still, looking down at Will's corrupted corpse.

'I have never loved so deeply,' Emma wept.

'And I have never felt so needed,' whispered the manservant from Cooch Behar.

Behind them came a roaring clatter of machinery.

Both turning at once, they took in the Mechanism.

Awakened by the components, it was glowing red and gold.

Will's diaphragm retracted slowly, filling his lungs with air.

Emma snatched the mask from his face, fell to her knees and kissed him.

'Forgive me! Forgive me!' she sobbed.

As the bubonic pustules melted away, Will struggled to push himself up. His memory replayed the sequence which had preceded his death. He was about to condemn Emma's treachery again, when he saw the jade mask in her hand. Working out what had taken place, he reached out to her.

Chaudhury ran over.

'I say, sir!' he shouted. 'Welcome back!'

'Hannibal might have warned me I was about to get shot dead!' growled Will.

'The mask had to be activated,' said Emma.

'Activated?'

'By restoring life, sir.'

'Always feel I'm the only one of us not in the know,' said Will, grabbing the Garuda Mask.

'Quickly, sir!' Chaudhury cried. 'Put it in there!'

'Where?'

'All the way in and to the left!'

'Huh?'

'Behind the ninth drive wheel. Do you see it… that silver slot — the one set on a bearing…?'

Before Chaudhury had finished, Will fell to his knees and manoeuvred into position, the mask clutched in his left hand. With all his strength he propelled it into a slot behind the drive wheel.

Instantly, the chamber filled with brilliant incandescent light — the brightness of a thousand suns, as the Garuda Mask completed the Alexander Mechanism.

Will, Chaudhury and Emma stood there, frozen, awed by an abyss projected within the light, and by a sense of the divine.

At the machine's own pace, a pathway was illuminated, bisecting the abyss.

As though seducing Will, calling to him, it urged him to approach.

Unsure whether it was solid or ethereal, he stepped onto it and seemed to glide ahead.

Standing at the far end, in a doorway bathed in platinum light, was the silhouette of a man.

As he neared him, Will made out the subtle features of his face.

A face he had come to know so well.

The face of Hannibal Fogg.

His arms stretched out, Will hugged the figure, who returned the embrace as though reunited with a long-lost son.

'Thank God you've come!' exclaimed Hannibal.

'What?'

Grasping him by the arm, the explorer pulled Will into the light.

'All hell's about to break loose!' he exclaimed. 'There's not a moment to waste!'

The Components of the Alexander Mechanism

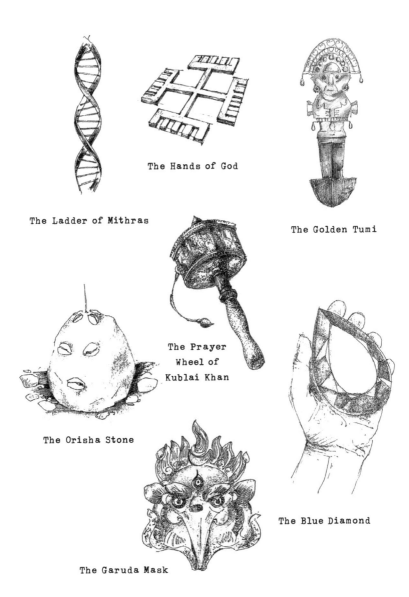

The Ladder of Mithras

The Hands of God

The Golden Tumi

The Prayer
Wheel of
Kublai Khan

The Orisha Stone

The Garuda Mask

The Blue Diamond

SECRET PLAN OF DAR JNOUN

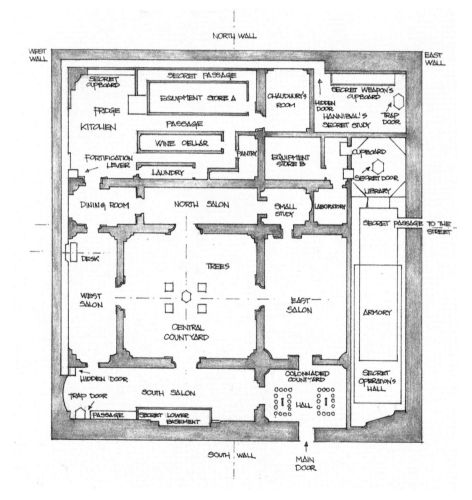

A Request

If you enjoyed this book, please review it on Amazon and Goodreads.

Reviews are an author's best friend.

To stay in touch with Tahir Shah, and to hear about his upcoming releases before anyone else, please sign up for his mailing list:

 http://tahirshah.com/newsletter

And to follow him on social media, please go to any of the following links:

 http://www.twitter.com/humanstew

 http://www.facebook.com/TahirShahAuthor

 http://www.youtube.com/user/tahirshah999

 http://www.pinterest.com/tahirshah

 http://tahirshah.com/goodreads

http://www.tahirshah.com

CPSIA information can be obtained
at www.ICGtesting.com
Printed in the USA
BVHW04s1402050618
518248BV00001B/47/P